# THE
# EDGE
# OF
# NEVER

# THE EDGE OF NEVER

## J. A. REDMERSKI

FOREVER

NEW YORK   BOSTON

Copyright © 2012 by J. A. Redmerski

Forever
Hachette Book Group
1290 Avenue of the Americas
New York, NY 10104

www.HachetteBookGroup.com

Printed in the United States of America

LSC-C

Originally published as an ebook

First Trade Edition: July 2013
20 19 18 17 16

Forever is an imprint of Grand Central Publishing.
The Forever name and logo are trademarks of Hachette Book Group, Inc.

The Hachette Speakers Bureau provides a wide range of authors for speaking events. To find out more, go to www.hachettespeakersbureau.com or call (866) 376-6591.

The publisher is not responsible for websites (or their content) that are not owned by the publisher.

ISBN: 978-1-4555-4898-9

LCCN: 2013930840

*To lovers and dreamers and anyone who hasn't truly experienced either.*

# THE EDGE OF NEVER

# ONE

*N*atalie has been twirling that same lock of hair for the past ten minutes and it's starting to drive me nuts. I shake my head and pull my iced latte toward me, placing my lips on the straw. Natalie sits across from me with her elbows propped on the little round table, chin in one hand.

"He's gorgeous," she says staring off toward the guy who just got in line. "Seriously, Cam, would you *look* at him?"

I roll my eyes and take another sip. "Nat," I say, placing my drink back on the table, "you have a boyfriend—do I need to constantly remind you?"

Natalie sneers playfully at me. "What are you, my mother?" But she can't keep her eyes on me for long, not while that walking wall of sexy is standing at the register ordering coffee and scones. "Besides, Damon doesn't care if I look—as long as I'm bending over for *him* every night, he's good with it."

I let out a spat of air, blushing.

"See! *Uh huh*," she says, smiling hugely. "I got a laugh out of you." She reaches over and thrusts her hand into her little purple purse. "I have to make note of that," and she pulls out her phone and opens her digital notebook. "Saturday. June 15th." She moves her finger across the screen. "1:54 p.m. – Camryn Bennett laughed at one of my sexual jokes." Then she shoves the phone back inside her purse and looks at me with that thoughtful sort of look she always has when she's about to go into therapy-mode. "Just look once," she says, all joking aside.

Just to appease her, I turn my chin carefully at an angle so that I can get a quick glimpse of the guy. He moves away from the register and toward the end of the counter where he slides his drink off the edge. Tall. Perfectly sculpted cheekbones. Mesmerizing model green eyes and spiked up brown hair.

"Yes," I admit, looking back at Natalie, "he's hot, but so what?"

Natalie has to watch him leave out the double glass doors and glide past the windows before she can look back at me to respond.

"Oh. My. God," she says eyes wide and full of disbelief.

"He's just a guy, Nat." I place my lips on the straw again. "You might as well put a sign that says 'obsessed' on your forehead. You're everything obsessed short of drooling."

"Are you *kidding* me?" Her expression has twisted into pure shock. "Camryn, you have a serious problem. You know that, right?" She presses her back against her chair. "You need to up your medication. Seriously."

"I stopped taking it in April."

"What? *Why?*"

"Because it's ridiculous," I say matter-of-factly. "I'm not suicidal, so there's no reason for me to be taking it."

She shakes her head at me and crosses her arms over her chest. "You think they prescribe that stuff just for suicidal people? No. They don't." She points a finger at me briefly and hides it back in the fold of her arm. "It's a chemical imbalance thing, or some shit like that."

I smirk at her. "Oh, really? Since when did you become so educated in mental health issues and the medications they use to treat the hundreds of diagnoses?" My brow rises a little, just enough to let her see how much I know she has no idea what she's talking about.

When she wrinkles her nose at me instead of answering, I say, "I'll heal on my own time and I don't need a pill to fix it for me." My explanation had started out kind, but unexpectedly turned bitter before I could get the last sentence out. That happens a lot.

Natalie sighs and the smile completely drops from her face.

"I'm sorry," I say, feeling bad for snapping at her. "Look, I know you're right. I can't deny that I have some messed up emotional issues and that I can be a bitch sometimes—"

"*Sometimes?*" she mumbles under her breath, but is grinning again and has already forgiven me.

That happens a lot, too.

I half-smile back at her. "I just want to find answers on my own, y'know?"

"Find *what* answers?" She's annoyed with me. "Cam," she says, cocking her head to one side to appear thoughtful. "I hate to say it, but shit really does happen. You just have to get over it. Beat the hell out of it by doing things that make you happy."

OK, so maybe she isn't so horrible at the therapy thing after all.

"I know, you're right," I say, "but..."

Natalie raises a brow, waiting. "What? Come on, out with it!"

I gaze toward the wall briefly, thinking about it. So often I sit around and think about life and wonder about every possible aspect of it. I wonder what the hell I'm doing here. Even right now. In this coffee shop with this girl I've known practically all my life. Yesterday I thought about why I felt the need to get up at exactly the same time as the day before and do everything like I did the day before. Why? What compels any of us to do the things we do when deep down a part of us just wants to break free from it all?

I look away from the wall and right at my best friend who I know won't understand what I'm about to say, but because of the need to get it out, I say it anyway.

"Have you ever wondered what it would be like to backpack across the world?"

Natalie's face goes slack. "Uh, not really," she says. "That might...suck."

"Well, think about it for a second," I say, leaning against the table and focusing all of my attention on her. "Just you and a backpack with a few necessities. No bills. No getting up at the same time every morning to go to a job you hate. Just you and the world out ahead of you. You never know what the next day is going to bring, who you'll meet, what you'll have for lunch or where you might sleep." I realize I've become so lost in the imagery that I might've seemed a little obsessed for a second, myself.

"You're starting to freak me out," Natalie says, eyeing me across the small table with a look of uncertainty. Her arched brow settles back even with the other one and then she says, "And there's also all the walking, the risk of getting raped, murdered and tossed on the side of a freeway somewhere. Oh, and then there's all the walking..."

Clearly, she thinks I'm borderline crazy.

"What brought this on, anyway?" she asks, taking a quick sip of her drink. "That sounds like some kind of mid-life-crisis stuff— you're only twenty." She points again as if to underline, "And you've hardly paid a bill in your life."

She takes another sip; an obnoxious slurping noise follows.

"Maybe not," I say thinking quietly to myself, "but I *will* be once I move in with you."

"So true," she says, tapping her fingertips on her cup. "Everything split down the middle—Wait, you're not backing out on me, are you?" She sort of freezes, looking warily across at me.

"No, I'm still on. Next week I'll be out of my mom's house and living with a slut."

"You bitch!" she laughs.

I half-smile and go back to my brooding, the stuff before that she wasn't relating to, but I expected as much. Even before Ian died, I always kind of thought out-of-the-box. Instead of sitting around dreaming up new sex positions, as Natalie often does about Damon, her boyfriend of five years, I dream about things that really matter. At least in my world, they matter. What the air in other countries feels like on my skin, how the ocean smells, why the sound of rain makes me gasp. *"You're one deep chick."* That's what Damon said to me on more than one occasion.

"Geez!" Natalie says. "You're a freakin' downer, you know that right?" She shakes her head with the straw between her lips.

"Come on," she says suddenly and stands up from the table. "I can't take this philosophical stuff anymore and quaint little places like this seem to make you worse—we're going to The Underground tonight."

"What?—No, I'm not going to that place."

"Yes. You. Are." She chucks her empty drink into the trash can a few feet away and grabs my wrist. "You're going with me this time because you're supposed to be my best friend and I won't take no *again* for an answer." Her close-lipped smile is spread across the entirety of her slightly tanned face.

I know she means business. She always means business when she has that look in her eyes: the one brimmed with excitement and determination. It'll probably be easiest just to go this once and get it over with, or else she'll never leave me alone about it. Such is a necessary evil when it comes to having a pushy best friend.

I get up and slip my purse strap over my shoulder.

"It's only two o'clock," I say.

I drink down the last of my latte and toss the empty cup away in the same trash can.

"Yeah, but first we've got to get you a new outfit."

"Uh, no," I say resolutely as she's walking me out the glass doors and into the breezy summer air. "Going to The Underground with you is more than good deed enough. I refuse to go shopping. I've got plenty of clothes."

Natalie slips her arm around mine as we walk down the sidewalk and past a long line of parking meters. She grins and glances over at me. "Fine. Then you'll at least let me dress you from something out of *my* closet."

"What's wrong with my own wardrobe?"

She purses her lips at me and draws her chin in as if to quietly argue why I even asked a question so ridiculous. "It's *The Underground*," she says, as if there is no answer more obvious than that.

OK, she has a point. Natalie and me may be best friends, but with us it's an opposites attract sort of thing. She's a rocker chick who's had a crush on Jared Leto since *Fight Club*. I'm more of a laid back kind of girl who rarely wears dark-colored clothes unless I'm attending a funeral. Not that Natalie wears all black and has some kind of emo hair thing going on, but she would never be caught dead in anything from *my* closet because she says it's all just too plain. I beg to differ. I know how to dress, and guys—when I used

to pay attention to the way they eyed my ass in my favorite jeans—
have never had a problem with the clothes I choose to wear.

But The Underground was made for people like Natalie and so
I guess I'll have to endure dressing like her for one night just to fit
in. I'm not a follower. I never have been. But I'll definitely become
someone I'm not for a few hours if it'll make me blend in rather
than make me a blatant eyesore and draw attention.

# TWO

*W*e make it to the Underground just as night falls, but not before driving around in Damon's souped-up truck to various houses. He would pull into the driveway, get out and stay inside no more than three or four minutes and never say a word when he came back out. At least, not about what he went inside for, or who he talked to—the usual stuff that would make these visits normal. But not much about Damon is usual or normal. I love him to death. I've known him almost as long as I've known Natalie, but I've never been able to accept his drug habits. He grows copious amounts of weed in his basement, but he's not a pothead. In fact, no one but me and a few of his close friends would ever suspect that a hot piece of ass like Damon Winters would be a grower, because most growers look like white trash and often have hairdos that are stuck somewhere between the 70's and 90's. Damon is far from looking like white trash—he could be Alex Pettyfer's younger brother. And Damon says weed just isn't his thing. No, Damon's drug of choice is cocaine and he only grows and sells weed to pay for his cocaine habit.

Natalie pretends that what Damon does is perfectly harmless. She knows that he doesn't smoke weed and says that weed really isn't that bad and if other people want to smoke it to chill out and relax, that she sees no harm in Damon helping with that.

She refuses to believe, however, that cocaine has seen more action from his face than any part of her body has.

"OK, you're going to have a good time, right?" Natalie bumps my backseat door shut with her butt after I get out and then she looks hopelessly at me. "Just don't fight it and *try* to enjoy yourself."

I roll my eyes. "Nat, I wouldn't deliberately *try* to hate it," I say. "I *do* want to enjoy myself."

Damon comes around to our side of the truck and slips his arms around both of our waists. "I get to go in with two hot chicks on my arms."

Natalie elbows him with a pretend resentful smirk. "Shut up, baby. You'll make me jealous." Already she's grinning impishly up at him.

Damon lets his hand drop from her waist and he grabs a handful of her butt cheek. She makes a sickening moaning sound and reaches up on her toes to kiss him. I want to tell them to get a room, but I'd be wasting my breath.

The Underground is the hottest spot just outside of downtown Raleigh, North Carolina, but you won't find it listed in the phone book. Only people like us know it exists. Some guy named Rob rented out an abandoned warehouse two years ago and spent about one million of his rich daddy's money to convert it into a secret nightclub. Two years and going strong; the place has since become a spot where local rock sex gods can live the rock n' roll dream with screaming fans and groupies. But it's not a trashy joint. From the outside it might look like an abandoned building in a partial ghost town, but the inside is like any upscale hard rock night club equipped with colorful strobe lights that shoot continuously across the space, slutty-looking waitresses and a stage big enough for two bands to play at the same time.

To keep The Underground private, everybody who goes has to park elsewhere in the city and walk to it because a street lined with vehicles outside an 'abandoned' warehouse is a dead giveaway.

We park in the back of a nearby Mickey D's and walk about ten minutes through spooky town.

Natalie moves from Damon's right side and gets in between us, but it's just so she can torture me before we go inside.

"OK," she says as if about to run down a list of do's and don't's for me, "If anybody asks, you're single, all right?" She waves her hand at me. "None of that stuff you pulled like with that guy who was hitting on you at Office Depot."

"What was she doing at Office Depot?" Damon says, laughing.

"Damon, this guy was *on her*," Natalie says, totally ignoring the fact that I'm right here, "I mean like all she had to do was bat her eyes once and he would've bought her a car—you know what she said to him?"

I roll my eyes and pull my arm out of hers. "Nat, you're so stupid. It wasn't like that."

"Yeah, babe," Damon says. "If the guy works at Office Depot he's not going to be buying anybody any cars."

Natalie smacks him across the shoulder playfully. "I didn't say he worked there—anyway, the guy looked like the lovechild of…Adam Levine and…" she twirls her fingers around above her head to let another famous example materialize on her tongue, "…Jensen Ackles, and Miss *Prudeness* here told him she was a lesbian when he asked for her number."

"Oh shut up, Nat!" I say, irritated at her serious over-exaggeration illness. "He did *not* look like either one of those guys. He was just a regular guy who didn't happen to be fugly."

She waves me away and turns back to Damon. "Whatever. The point is that she'll lie to keep them away. I don't doubt for a second that she'd go as far as to tell a guy she has Chlamydia and an out of control case of crabs."

Damon laughs.

I stop on the dark sidewalk and cross my arms over my chest, chewing on the inside of my bottom lip in agitation.

Natalie, realizing I'm not walking beside her anymore, runs back towards me. "OK! OK! Look, I just don't want you to ruin it for yourself, that's all. I'm just asking that if someone—who isn't a total hunchback—hits on you that you not immediately push him away. Nothing wrong with talking and getting to know one another. I'm not asking you to go home with him."

I'm already hating her for this. She swore!

Damon comes up behind her and wraps his hands around her waist, nuzzling his mouth into her squirming neck.

"Maybe you should just let her do what she wants, babe. Stop being so pushy."

"Thank you, Damon," I say with a quick nod.

He winks at me.

Natalie purses her lips and says, "You're right," and then puts up her hands, "I won't say anything else. I swear."

*Yeah, I have heard that before...*

"Good," I say and we all start walking again. Already these boots are killing my feet.

The ogre at the warehouse entrance inspects us at the door with his huge arms crossed in front.

He holds out his hand.

Natalie's face twists into an offended knot. "What? Is Rob charging now?"

Damon reaches into his back pocket and pulls out his wallet, fingering the bills inside.

"Twenty bucks a pop," the ogre says with a grunt.

"Twenty? Are you fucking kidding me?!" Natalie shrieks.

Damon gently pushes her aside and slaps three twenty dollar bills into the ogre's hand. The ogre shoves the money into his pocket and moves to let us pass. I go first and Damon puts his hand on Natalie's lower back to guide her in front of him.

She sneers at the ogre as she passes by. "Probably going to keep it for himself," she says. "I'm going to ask Rob about this."

"Come on," Damon says and we slip past the door and down one lengthy, dreary hallway with a single flickering fluorescent light until we make it to the industrial elevator at the end.

The metal jolts as the cage door closes and we're rather noisily riding to the basement floor many feet below. It's just one floor down, but the elevator rattles so much I feel like it's going to snap any second and send us plunging to our deaths. Loud, booming drums and the shouting of drunk college students and probably a lot of drop-outs funnels through the basement floor and into the cage elevator, louder every inch we descend into the bowels of The Underground. The elevator rumbles to a halt and another ogre opens the cage door to let us out.

Natalie stumbles into me from behind. "Hurry up!" she says, pushing me playfully in the back. "I think that's Four Collision playing!" Her voice rises over the music as we make our way into the main room.

Natalie takes Damon by the hand and then tries to grab mine, but I know what she has in store and I'm not going into a throng of bouncing, sweaty bodies wearing these stupid boots.

"Oh, come *on*!" she urges, practically begging. Then an aggravated line deepens around her snarling nose and she thrusts my hand into hers and pulls me towards her. "Stop being a baby! If anybody knocks you over, I'll personally kick their ass, all right?"

Damon is grinning at me from the side.

"Fine!" I say and head out with them, Natalie practically pulling my fingers out of the sockets.

We hit the dance floor and after a while of Natalie doing what any best friend would do by grinding against me to make me feel included, she eases her way into Damon's world only. She might as well be having sex with him right there in front of everybody, but no one notices. I only notice because I'm probably the only girl in the entire place without a date doing the same thing. I take advantage of the opportunity and slip my way off the dance floor and head to the bar.

"What can I get'cha?" the tall blond guy behind the bar says as I push myself up on my toes and take an empty barstool.

"Rum & Coke."

He goes to make my drink. "Hard stuff, huh?" he says, filling the glass with ice. "Going to show me your I.D.?" He grins.

I purse my lips at him. "Yeah, I'll show you my I.D. when you show me your liquor license." I grin right back at him and he smiles.

He finishes mixing the drink and slides it over to me.

"I don't really drink much anyway," I say, taking a little sip from the straw.

"Much?"

"Yeah, well, tonight I think I'll need a buzz." I set the glass down and finger the lime on the rim.

"Why's that?" he asks, wiping the bar top down with a paper towel.

"Wait a second," I hold up one finger, "before you get the wrong idea, I'm not here to spill my guts to you—bartender-customer therapy." Natalie is all the therapy I can handle.

He laughs and tosses the paper towel somewhere behind the bar.

"Well that's good to know because I'm not the advice type."

I take another small sip, leaning over this time instead of lifting the glass from the bar; my loose hair falls all around my face. I rise back up and tuck one side behind my ear. I really hate wearing my hair down; it's more trouble than it's worth.

"Well, if you must know," I say looking right at him, "I was dragged here by my relentless best friend who would probably do something embarrassing to me in my sleep and take a blackmail pic if I didn't come."

"Ah, one of those," he says, laying his arms across the bar top and folding his hands together. "I had a friend like that once. Six months after my fiancée skipped out on me, he dragged me to a nightclub just outside of Baltimore—I just wanted to sit at home and sulk in my misery, but turns out that night out was exactly what I needed."

Oh great, this guy thinks he knows me already, or, at least my 'situation'. But he doesn't know anything about my situation. Maybe he has the bad ex thing down—because we all have that eventually—but the rest of it, my parents' divorce, my older brother, Cole, going to jail, the death of the love of my life…I'm not about to tell this guy anything. The moment you tell someone else is the moment you become a whiner and the world's smallest violin starts to play. The truth is, we all have problems; we all go through hardships and pain, and my pain is paradise compared to a lot of people's and I really have no right to whine at all.

"I thought you weren't the advice type?" I smile sweetly.

He leans away from the bar and says, "I'm not, but if you're getting something out of my story then be grateful."

I smirk and take a fake sip this time. I don't really want a buzz and I definitely don't want to get drunk, especially since I have a feeling I'm going to be the one driving us home again.

Trying to take the spotlight off me, I prop one elbow on the bar and rest my chin on my knuckles and say, "So then what happened that night?"

The left side of his mouth lifts into a grin and he says, shaking his blond head, "I got laid for the first time since she left me and I remembered how good it felt to be unchained from one person."

I didn't expect that kind of answer. Most guys I know would've lied about their relationship phobia, especially if they were hitting on me. I kind of like this guy. Just as a guy, of course; I'm not about to, as Natalie might say, bend over for him.

"I see," I say, trying to hold in the true measure of my smile. "Well, at least you're honest."

"No other way to be," he says as he reaches for an empty glass and starts to make a Rum & Coke for himself. "I've found that most girls are as much afraid of commitment as guys are these days and if you're up front in the beginning, you're more likely to come out of the one-nighter unscathed."

I nod, fitting my fingertips around my straw. There's no way I'd openly admit it to him, but I completely agree with him and even find it refreshing. I've never really given it that much thought before, but as much as I don't want a relationship within one hundred feet of me, I am still human and I wouldn't mind a one-night stand.

Just not with him. Or anyone in this place. OK, so maybe

I'm too chicken for a one-night stand and this drink has already started going straight to my head. Truth is, I've never done anything like that before and even though the thought is kind of exciting, it still scares the shit out of me. I've only ever been with two guys: Ian Walsh, my first love who took my virginity and died in a car accident three months later, and then Christian Deering, my Ian rebound guy and the jerk who cheated on me with some red-haired slut.

I'm just glad I never said that poisonous three-word phrase that begins with 'I' and ends with 'you', back to him because I had a feeling, deep down, that when he said it to me, he didn't know what the hell he was talking about.

Then again, maybe he *did* and that's why after five months of dating, he hooked up with someone else: because I never said it back.

I look up at the bartender to notice he's smiling back at me, waiting patiently for me to say something. This guy's good; either that, or he really is just trying to be friendly. I admit, he's cute; can't be older than twenty-five and has soft brown eyes that smile before his lips do. I notice how toned his biceps and chest are underneath that tight-fitting t-shirt. And he's tanned; definitely a guy who has lived most of his life near an ocean somewhere.

I stop looking when I notice my mind wandering, thinking about how he looks in swim shorts and no shirt.

"I'm Blake," he says. "I'm Rob's brother."

*Rob? Oh yeah, the guy who owns The Underground.*

I reach out my hand and Blake gently shakes it.

"Camryn."

I hear Natalie's voice over the music before I even see her. She makes her way through a cluster of people standing around near the dance floor and pushes her way past to get to me. Immediately, she takes note of Blake and her eyes start glistening, lighting up with her huge, blatant smile. Damon, following behind her with her hand still clasped in his, notices, too, but he just locks emotionless eyes with me. I get the strangest feeling from it, but I brush it off as Natalie presses her shoulder into mine.

"What are you doing over here?" she asks with obvious accusation in her voice. She's grinning from ear to ear and glances between Blake and me several times before giving me all of her attention.

"Having a drink," I say. "Did you come over here to get one for yourself, or to check up on me?"

"Both!" she says, letting Damon's hand fall away from hers and she reaches up and taps hers fingers on the bar, smiling at Blake. "Anything with Vodka."

Blake nods and looks at Damon.

"I'll have Rum & Coke," Damon says.

Natalie presses her lips against the side of my head and I feel the heat of her breath on my ear when she whispers, "Holy shit, Cam! Do you know who that is?"

I notice Blake's mouth spread subtly into a smile, having heard her.

Feeling my face get hot with embarrassment, I whisper back, "Yeah, his name is Blake."

"That's Rob's *brother*!" she hisses; her gaze falls back on him.

I look up at Damon, hoping he'll get the hint and drag her off somewhere, but this time he pretends not to 'get it'. Where is the Damon I know, the one who used to have my back when it came to Natalie?

Uh oh, he must be pissed at her again. He only ever acts like this when Natalie has opened her big mouth, or done something that Damon just can't get past. We've only been here for about thirty minutes. What could she have done in such a short time? And then I realize: this is Natalie and if anyone can piss a boyfriend off in under an hour and without knowing it, it's her.

I slip off the barstool and take her by the arm, pulling her away from the bar. Damon, probably knowing what my plan is, stays behind with Blake.

The music seems to have gotten louder as the live band ends one song and starts the next.

"What did you do?" I demand, turning her around to face me.

"What do you mean what did I do?" She's hardly even paying attention to me; her body moves subtly with the music instead.

"Nat, I'm serious."

Finally, she stops and looks right at me, searching my face for answers.

"To piss Damon off?" I say. "He was fine when we came in here."

She looks across the space briefly at Damon standing by the bar, sipping his drink, and then back at me with a confused look on her face. "I didn't do anything...I don't think." She looks up as if in thought, trying to recall what she might have said or done.

She puts her hands on her hips. "What makes you think he's pissed?"

"He's got that look," I say, glancing back at him and Blake, "and I hate it when you two fight, especially when I'm stuck with you for the night and have to listen to you both go back and forth about stupid shit that happened a year ago."

Natalie's confused expression turns into a devious smile. "Well, I think you're paranoid and maybe trying to distract me from saying anything about you and Blake." She's getting that playful look now and I hate it.

I roll my eyes. "There is no 'me and Blake', we're just talking."

"Talking is the first step. Smiling at him—" (her grin deepens) "which I totally saw you doing when I walked up—is the next step." She crosses her arms and pops out her hip. "I bet you've already had a conversation with him without him having to pry the answers out of you—Hell, you already know his name."

"For someone who wants me to have a good time and meet a guy, you don't know how to shut up when things already appear to be going your way."

Natalie lets the music dictate her movement again, raising her hands up a little above her and moving her hips around seductively. I just stand here.

"Nothing's going to happen," I say sternly. "You got what you wanted and I'm talking to someone and have no intention of telling him I have Chlamydia, so please, don't make a scene."

She gives in with a long, deep sigh and stops dancing long enough to say, "I guess you're right. I'll leave you to him, but if he takes you up to Rob's floor, I want details." She points her finger at me firmly, one eye slanted and her lips pursed.

"Fine," I say, just to get her off my back, "but don't hold your breath because it's *not* gonna happen."

# THREE

*A*n hour and two drinks later, I'm on 'Rob's floor' of the building with Blake. I'm just a little buzzed, walking and seeing perfectly straight, so I know I'm not drunk. But I'm a little too happy and that bothers me a bit. When Blake suggested we 'get away from the noise for a while', my warning sirens were going off like crazy inside my head: *Don't you go off by yourself at a nightclub after a couple of drinks with this guy you don't know. Don't do it, Cam. You're not a stupid girl, so don't let the alcohol* make *you stupid.*

All of these things screamed at me. And I listened until at some point, Blake's infectious smile and the way he made me feel completely at ease calmed the voices and the sirens down so much that I couldn't hear them anymore.

"*This* is what they call Rob's Floor?" I ask, looking out over the cityscape from the roof of the warehouse. All of the buildings in the city are lit up brilliantly with glowing blue and white and green lights. The streets appear bathed in an orangish hue pouring down from the hundreds of street lamps.

"What did you expect?" he says, taking my hand and I inwardly flinch at the gesture but accept it. "A posh sex room with mirrors on the ceiling?"

Wait a second…that's exactly what I thought—well, in a

roundabout way—but then why in the hell did I come up here with him?

OK, *now* I'm panicking a little.

I think maybe I am slightly drunk after all, otherwise my judgment would not be this far off. And it freaks me out and almost completely sobers me up to think that I would ever be up for any kind of 'sex room' even in a drunken state. Is the alcohol really just making me stupid, or is it bringing out something inside of me that I don't want to believe is there?

I glance over at the metal door set in the brick wall and notice a light shining through it and the doorjamb. He left it open; that's a good sign.

He walks with me to a wooden picnic table and nervously I sit down next to him on the top of it. The wind brushes through my hair, pulling a few strands into my mouth. I reach up and tuck my finger behind them and pull the strands away.

"Good thing it was me," he says, looking out at the city with his hands draped between his knees; his feet are propped on the bench seat below.

I pull my legs up and sit Indian-style, folding my hands in my lap. I look over at him questioningly.

He smiles. "Good thing it was me who brought you up here," he clarifies. "A beautiful girl like you down there with all of those guys." He turns his head to look right at me; his brown eyes appear faintly luminescent in the dark. "If I had been someone else, you might've been the rape victim of your very own Lifetime movie."

I'm completely sober now. Just like that, in two seconds flat, it's as though I never drank a thing. My back shoots straight up rigidly and I suck in a deep, nervous breath.

*What the fuck was I thinking?!*

"It's all right," he says, smiling softly and putting up both hands, palms facing outward in front of him, "I would never do anything to a girl that she didn't want, or anything to one who's had a few drinks and just *thinks* it's what she wants."

I think I just dodged a very deadly bullet.

My shoulders relax somewhat and I feel like I can breathe again. I mean sure, he could just be filling my head full of more bullshit to make me trust him, but my instincts are telling me that he's perfectly harmless. Keep my guard up and be careful while I'm alone up here with him, but at least I can relax. I think if he intended to take advantage of me, he wouldn't have announced the danger of the possibility like that.

I laugh a little under my breath, thinking about something he said.

"What's so funny?" He looks across at me, smiling and waiting.

"Your Lifetime movie reference," I say, feeling my lips shape in a faint, embarrassed smile. "You watch that stuff?"

He looks away, sharing my embarrassment for him. "Nah," he says, "I think it's just common knowledge comparison."

"Really?" I taunt him. "I don't know; you're the first guy I've ever heard use 'Lifetime movie' in a sentence."

He's blushing now and I'm kicking myself for being so happy to see it.

"Well, just don't tell anybody, all right?" He gives me his best pouty face.

I smile back at him and then look out at the city lights, hoping to deter any hopeful expectations he might have developed over the course of our brief, playful exchange. I don't care how nice or charming or sexy he is, I'm not caving to him. I'm just not ready for anything other than what we're doing right now: having an innocent, friendly conversation with no sexual or relationship strings attached. It's so damn hard to have that with any guy because they always seem to think that a simple smile means something more than it is.

"So tell me," he says, "why are you here alone?"

"Oh, no…" I shake my smiling head and my finger at him, "…let's not go there."

"Come on, throw me a bone here. It's just conversation." He turns fully around at the waist to face me and rests one leg on the tabletop. "I genuinely want to know. It's not a tactic."

"A tactic?"

"Yeah, like digging around inside your problems to find something to pretend I care about just so I can get in your panties—if I wanted in your panties, I'd come out and tell you."

"Oh, so you don't want in my panties?" I look at him in a half-smiling sidelong glance.

A little defeated, but not deterred by it, he softens his face and says, "Eventually, yeah. I'd be fucking mental to not want to sleep with you, but if that's all I wanted from you and that's what I brought you up here for, I would've told you before you agreed to come up here."

I appreciate the honesty and definitely have more respect for him, but my smile sort of locked up when he said something about 'if that's all' he wanted from me. What *else* could he want from me? A date, which could lead to a relationship? Ummm, no.

"Look," I say, backing off a little and letting him know it, "I'm not looking for either, just so you know."

"Either of what?" And then he realizes 'what' a second later. He smiles and shakes his head. "It's all right. I'm with you on that one—I really did just bring you up here for the conversation, as hard as that may be to believe."

Something tells me that if I wanted either, sex or a date, or both, that Blake would give it to me, but he's smoothly backing off without making himself look rejected.

"To answer your question," I say, giving in to him for conversation's sake, "I'm single because I had a few bad experiences and right now I'm just not looking for any do-overs."

Blake nods. "I hear yah." He looks away from my eyes and the breeze catches his blond hair, pushing his semi-long bangs away from his forehead. "Do-overs generally suck, at least in the beginning. The learning process in itself is a nightmare." He looks back at me to elaborate. "When you're with someone for so long you get used to them, y'know? It's a comfort-zone thing. When we get settled in our comfort zone, trying to pull us out of it even if everything about it is hell and unhealthy, is like trying to pull a fat ass couch potato out of his living room long enough to get a life." Maybe realizing he was getting too deep with me too soon, Blake lightens the mood by adding, "Took me three months with Jen before I was comfortable taking a shit with her in the house."

I laugh out loud and when I'm brave enough to look back at him, I see that he's smiling.

I'm starting to get the feeling he's not over his ex-fiancée as much he's trying to make himself believe. So, I try to do him a favor by steering the hurtful topic to myself before he has that eureka moment and his world comes falling down around him all over again.

"My boyfriend died," I blurt out, mostly for his sake. "Car accident."

Blake's face falls and he looks right at me, his eyes full of remorse. "I'm sorry, I didn't mean—"

I put up my hand. "No, it's perfectly all right; you didn't do anything." After he nods subtly and waits for me to go on, I say, "It was a week before graduation." He places his hand on my knee, but I know it's not for anything other than to comfort me.

I start to tell him what happened when I hear a loud *smack!* and Blake falls off the tabletop and hits the roof floor. It happened so fast I never saw Damon rushing him from the side, or heard when he burst through the metal door several feet away.

"Damon!" I shriek as he tackles Blake before he can get up and starts pummeling his face with his fists. "STOP! DAMON! OH MY GOD!"

Another series of punches rain down on Blake before the shock wears off me and I run over and try pulling Damon off of him. I lunge on Damon's back, grabbing his flailing arms by the wrists, but he's so focused on beating the shit out of Blake that I feel like I'm on the back of one of those mechanical bulls. I'm thrown off and land hard on the concrete on my butt and hands.

Blake finally gets up after serving one good punch at the side of Damon's face.

"What the fuck is your problem, man?!" Blake says, stumbling to his feet. One hand never leaves his jaw where he continuously rubs it as if trying to pop it back into place. His nose is bleeding from both nostrils and his upper lip is busted and swollen. All of the blood looks black in the darkness.

"You *know* what the fuck!" Damon roars and goes to attack him again, but I rush over and do what I can to hold him back. I step around in front of him and shove the palms of my hands against his rock-hard chest.

"Just stop it, Damon! We were just talking! What the hell is wrong with you?" I'm yelling so loud already my voice feels strained.

I turn at the waist, keeping my hands firmly on Damon's chest and I look right at Blake. "I'm so sorry, Blake, I-I—"

"Don't worry about it," he says with a hard, rebuffed expression. "I'm outta here."

He turns and walks away through the metal door. A vociferous *bang!* resounds through the air as it slams behind him. I whirl back around at Damon with fire in my eyes and I push him as hard as I can in the chest. "You *asshole*! I can't *believe* you did that!" I'm literally screaming three inches from his face.

Damon's lip furrows and he's still breathing hard from the fight. His dark eyes are wide and unfettered and sort of feral. A part of me feels suspicious of him, but the part of me that has known him for twelve years cancels the suspicion out.

"What are you doing leaving with some guy you just fucking met? I thought you were smarter than that, Cam, even buzzed out of your mind!"

I step back from him and cross my arms angrily over my stomach. "Are you calling me stupid? We were just *talking*!" I shriek and my blonde hair falls down around my eyes. "I'm perfectly capable of recognizing the assholes from the nice guys and right about now I'm seeing a total fucking asshole!"

He appears to grit his teeth behind his tightly-closed lips. "Call me what you want, but I was just protecting you." He says it surprisingly calm.

"From *what*?" I shout. "Bad conversation? A guy who genuinely just wanted to talk?"

Damon smirks. "No guy just wants to talk," he says as if he's an expert. "No guy is going to lead a girl that looks like you out alone on the top of a goddamned warehouse building just to talk. Ten more minutes and he would've thrown your little ass on top of that table and had his way with you. No one can hear you scream out here, Cam."

I swallow down a lump in my throat, but another one forms in its place. Maybe Damon's right. Maybe I was so blinded by Blake's sincere and privately wounded personality that I completely fell for a tactic I never contemplated. Sure, I've envisioned these kinds of situations before and have seen the typical ones on television, but maybe Blake was trying something else on me . . . No, I don't believe it. He would've thrown me on the picnic table if I asked him to, but my heart tells me he wouldn't have otherwise.

I turn my back on Damon, not wanting him to see anything left in my face that might give away that for a second I actually believed him. I'm pissed as hell for the way he handled it, but I can't hate him forever because he really was just looking out for me. Overloaded on alpha male testosterone, no doubt, but looking out for me, nonetheless.

"Cam, look at me please."

I wait a few defiant seconds before turning around with my arms still crossed.

Damon peers in at me with a softer gaze than before. "I'm sorry, I just . . ." he sighs and looks off to the side now as though what he's about to say he can't while looking right at me, ". . . Camryn, I can't stand the thought of you with some other guy."

I feel like someone just punched me in the gut. I even let out a weird yelping sound from my throat and my eyes grow wide.

I glance nervously toward the metal door and then back at him. "Where's Natalie?" I have to drive this topic completely off this roof. What the hell did he just say? No, he can't mean what it sounded like. I must've heard him wrong. Yeah, my buzz is back and I'm not thinking straight.

He steps up closer to me and cups my elbows in his hands. Instantly, I feel the need to back away from him, but I'm frozen in the same spot, barely able to move anything other than my eyes.

"I mean it," he says, lowering his voice to a desperate whisper. "I've wanted you since seventh grade."

There's that punch to the gut again.

Finally, I manage to back away from him. "No. No." I shake my head back and forth, trying to make sense of this. "Are you drunk, Damon? Or strung out? Something's wrong with you." My arms come uncrossed and I put up my hands. "We need to go find Natalie. I won't say anything to her about what you said because you won't remember it in the morning, but we really do need to go. Now."

I start to walk toward the now closed metal door, but feel Damon's hand collapse around my bicep and he turns me around. My breath catches and that suspicious feeling I had about him earlier comes back full-force, completely reversing the years I've known him and have trusted him. He glares at me with eyes more feral than before, but manages to retain a sort of eerie softness in them, too.

"I'm not drunk and I haven't done any coke since last week."

The fact that he does coke at all is more than enough to make it impossible to ever be attracted to him, but he's always been one of my closest friends and so I've always overlooked his drug use. But he's telling the truth right now and being such a close friend for so long is what allows me to know this.

For the first time, I wish he *was* strung out because then we really could forget this ever happened.

I look down at his fingers clamped around my arm and finally notice how much pressure he's applying and it scares me.

"Let go of my arm, Damon, please."

Instead of loosening, I feel his fingers tighten and I try to pull away. He jerks me towards him and before I can react, he crushes his mouth over mine, his free hand wraps around the back of my neck forcing my head still. He tries to stick his tongue in my mouth, but I manage to rear my head back just enough to butt my forehead into his. It stuns him—and me—and instinctively he lets go of my body.

"Cam! Wait!" I hear him yelling out to me as I run away and throw open the metal door.

I hear his fierce footsteps moving after mine as he races down the loud metal stairs behind me, but I lose him once I make it back into the cage elevator, slam the fence gate closed and pound hard once on the MAIN button. The same ogre who let us in the club is standing at the door when I rush past him, having to partially shove him out of my way to get outside.

"Take it easy, babe!" he shouts as I run down the sidewalk and away from the warehouse.

I walk as far as the Shell station and call a cab to pick me up.

# FOUR

*M*y cell phone wakes me up the next morning. I hear it buzzing around on the nightstand beside my head. NATALIE reads in bold letters across the screen and her wide-eyed, toothy smiling face is staring back at me. Seeing her face wakes me the rest of the way up and I rise up stiffly from the bed and just hold the phone in my hand, letting it buzz against my palm for a few seconds more before finally getting the courage to hit the answer button.

"Where did you *go?*" her voice shrieks into my ear. "Oh my God, Cam, you just disappeared and I was freaking out and Damon was missing for a short while and then he showed back up and I saw Blake leaving at one point with blood all over his damn face and then I really started to see what you were talking about when you said that Damon was pissed—" She finally breathes. "And I kept asking him what I did or said or if it was because of last week at the restaurant, but he just ignored me and said it's time to go and I—"

"Natalie," I cut in, my head spinning with her run-on sentences, "just calm down for a second, all right?"

I toss the blanket off me and get out of the bed with the phone still pressed to my ear. I know that I have to do this, to tell her what Damon did. I have to. Not only would she never forgive me later when she found out, but I would never forgive myself. If the tables were turned I would want her to tell me.

But not over the phone. This is a mandatory face-to-face discussion.

"Can you meet me for coffee in an hour?"

Silence.

"Uhh, yeah, sure. Are you sure you're all right? I was so worried. I thought you got kidnapped or something."

"Natalie, yes, I'm..." *I'm totally* not *fine*, "yes, I'm fine, OK. Just meet me in an hour and please come alone."

"Damon's passed out at his house," she says and I detect the grin in her voice. "Girl, he did things to me last night I never knew he could do."

I shudder at her words. They're like screaming entities blaring at me on the other end of the phone but I have to pretend they're just words.

"I mean I couldn't even think about sex until I knew you were OK. You wouldn't answer your cell so I called your mom at like three and she said you were asleep in your bed. I was still so worried because you just left and—"

"One hour," I interrupt before she goes off on another tangent.

We hang up and the first thing I do is look at the missed calls on my phone. Six were from Natalie, but the other nine were from Damon. The only voice mails though were left by Natalie. I guess Damon didn't want to leave any incriminating evidence behind.

Not that I need evidence. Natalie and I have been best friends since the bitch stole my Corduroy Cool Barbie Doll at a sleepover.

———

I'm fidgeting by the time she shows up and have drunk down over half of my latte. She plops down on the empty chair. I wish she wasn't smiling so much; it's only making it that much harder.

"You look like hell, Cam."

"I know."

She blinks, stunned.

"What? No sarcastic 'thanks' followed by your famous rolling eyes?"

*Please stop smiling, Nat. Please, just take my strange UNsmiling behavior seriously for once and look at me with a serious face.*

Of course, she doesn't.

"Look, I'm just going to cut right to it, OK?"

There it is: finally the smile starts to fade.

I swallow and take a deep breath. God, I can't believe this happened! If it were some random guy she had been seeing during one of her and Damon's short breakups, this wouldn't be so difficult. But this is *Damon*, the guy she's been with for five years, who she always runs right back into the arms of after a breakup or a fight. He's the only guy she's ever truly been in love with.

"Cam, what's going on?" She senses the severe measure of what I'm about to tell her and I can see in her brown eyes how already she's trying to figure out if this is something she wants to hear, or not. I think she knows it has something to do with Damon.

I see the lump move down the center of her throat.

"Last night, I was out on the roof with Blake—"

Her worried face is suddenly assaulted by smiles. It's as if she's grabbing a hold of the opportunity to mask the inevitable news with something she can joke around about.

But I stop her before she has a chance to comment.

"Just listen to me for a minute, OK?"

Finally, I've reached her. The natural playful spirit that always exudes from her face drains right out of her.

I go on:

"Damon thought Blake took me out on the roof to have his way with me. He stormed out and blew up on Blake; beat the shit out of him. Blake left understandably pissed off and then it was just me and Damon. Alone."

Natalie's eyes are already giving away her fears. It's like she knows what I'm going to say and she's starting to quietly hate me for it.

"Damon forced himself on me, Nat."

Her eyes grow narrower.

"He kissed me and tried to tell me he's had a thing for me since seventh grade."

I can tell her heartbeat has sped up just by how heavy her short breaths have become.

"I wanted to tell you—"

"You're a lying bitch."

I feel punched in the gut again, except this time it completely knocks the breath out of me.

Natalie shoots up from the chair, shoulders her purse and glares down at me through ravenous dark eyes framed by equally dark hair.

I still can't move, stunned by what she said to me.

"You've wanted Damon since I started dating him," she hisses down at me. "You don't think I've seen it all these years, the way you look at him?" Her mouth stretches into a hard line. "Shit, Camryn, you're always taking up for him, bitchin' at me when I joke around about other guys." She starts motioning her hands out in front of her and imitating me in an exaggerated, nasally voice: "You've got a boyfriend, Nat—Don't forget about Damon, Nat—You should think about Damon." She slams her palms down on the table, causing the table to sway precariously side to side on its base before becoming still again. I don't even move to catch my drink, but it doesn't fall over. "Stay away from me and away from Damon." She points her finger in my face. "Or I swear to God, I will beat you senseless."

She walks away and right out the tall double glass doors, the ringing of the little bell at the top of the door echoes around the space.

Once I finally snap out of the shock, I notice about three customers watching me from their tables. Even the barista behind the counter looks away when my eyes fall on her. I just look down at the table, letting the patterns in the wood grain move around in my unfocused vision. I rest my head in my hands and sit there for the longest time.

Twice I go to call her, but force myself to stop and just set the phone back on the table.

How did this happen? Years of inseparable friendship— I cleaned up after the girl's stomach bug for Christ's sake!—and she tosses me out like moldy leftovers. *She's just hurting*, I try to tell myself. *She's just in denial right now and I need to give her time to let the truth sink in. She'll come around, she'll dump his ass and she'll apologize to me and drag me back to The Underground looking to find* both *of us new guys*. But I don't really believe anything I'm saying, or rather, the less rational, wounded part of me won't let me see past the angry red.

A customer walks by, tall older man in a wrinkled suit, and sneaks a glance at me before walking out. I'm totally humiliated. I look up again and catch the same pairs of eyes as before looking, only to look away. I feel like I'm being pitied. And I hate being pitied.

I grab my purse from the floor, stand up and throw the strap sloppily over my shoulder and storm out almost as indignantly as Natalie had.

———

It's been a week and I haven't heard a word from Natalie. I did eventually break down and try to call her—several times—but her voicemail always picked up. And the last time I called, she had changed her greeting to: *Hi, this is Nat. If you're a friend—a* real *friend—then leave me a message and I'll call you back, otherwise, don't bother.* I wanted to reach through the phone then and punch her in the face, but I settled with chucking it across the room. Thankfully, I bought that protection case when I bought this phone, otherwise I'm sure I'd be at the Apple store shelling out another couple hundred bucks for a new one.

I even broke down and tried to call Damon. He's the last person on this planet I want to talk to, but he's the one holding the key to mine and Natalie's friendship. Unfortunate, but apparently true. I don't know what I was thinking: That he would sell himself out and tell Natalie the truth? Yeah. Fat chance.

So, I stopped calling. I purposely avoided our favorite coffee shop and settled with the crap at the closest convenience store and I went two miles out of my way to go into my job interview at Dillard's, just so I didn't have to drive past Natalie's apartment.

I got the job. An assistant manager's position—my mom put in a good word for me; she's good friends with Mrs. Phillips, the lady who hired me—but I'm as excited about working at a department store as I am about drinking this craptastic coffee every morning.

And it hits me as I sit at the kitchen table and watch my bleach-blonde mom sift her way through the refrigerator: I'm no longer moving out on my own and in with my best friend. I'm going to either have to find an apartment and live by myself, or be stuck here for a while longer with my mother until Natalie comes to her senses. Which might be never. Or, it might take so long that I become unforgiving and tell her to screw off when she does.

The room feels like it's swaying.

"I'm going out with Roger tonight," my mom says behind the refrigerator door. She lifts up from leaning inside and looks across at me, wearing too much eye shadow. "You met Roger, didn't you?"

"Yes, I met Roger." Really I didn't, or maybe I did, but I'm getting his name mixed up with the last five guys she's gone out on a date with in the past month. She signed up to one of those weird speed-dating things. And she sure speeds right through these guys, so I guess the term is literal in her case.

"He's a nice guy. It's my third date with him."

I squeeze out a smile. I want my mom to be happy even if it means getting remarried, which is something that scares me to death. I love my dad—I'm Daddy's little girl—but what he did to my mom is unforgivable. Ever since the divorce four months ago, my mom has been this strange woman who I only know halfway anymore. It's like she reached inside a drawer that has been locked for thirty years and pulled out the personality she used to wear before she met my dad and had me and my brother, Cole. Except that it doesn't really fit anymore, but she tries her damnedest every day to wear it.

"He's already talking about taking me on a cruise." Her face lights up just thinking about it.

I close the lid on my laptop. "Don't you think three dates is a little soon for a cruise?"

She purses her lips and waves the notion away. "No baby, it's just right. He has plenty of money so to him it's as casual as taking me to dinner."

I just look away and nibble on the edge of the sandwich I made, though I'm not at all hungry.

Mom flits around the kitchen, pretending to clean. Usually, she has a housekeeper come in on Wednesdays, but when a man is stopping by, she thinks running a dish rag over the counter and spraying the house with air freshener is cleaning.

"Don't forget about Saturday," she says as she starts to load the dishwasher, which is a surprise.

"Yeah, I know, Mom." I sigh and shake my head. "Though I might take a rain check this time."

Her back straightens up and she looks right at me.

"Baby, you promised you'd go," she says desperately, tapping her nails nervously on the countertop. "You know I don't like going inside that jail by myself."

"It's prison, Mom." I casually pick off a few pieces of bread crust and drop them on the plate. "And they can't get to you; they're all locked up, just like Cole. And it's their own damn faults."

My mom lowers her eyes and a huge ball of burning hot guilt knots up in my stomach.

I sigh deeply. "I'm sorry. I didn't mean to say that."

I totally meant what I said, just not out loud and to her because it hurts her whenever I talk about my older brother, Cole, and his five-year sentence in prison for killing a man in a drunk-driving accident. This happened just six months after Ian died in the car accident.

I feel like I'm losing everybody...

I get up from the table and stand in front of the bar and she goes back to loading the dishwasher.

"I'll go with you, OK?"

She pushes out a smile still masked by a thin layer of hurt, and she nods. "Thanks, baby."

I feel sorry for her. It breaks my heart that my dad cheated on her after twenty-two years of marriage.

But we all saw it coming.

And to think, my parents tried to keep Ian and me away from each other when I confided in my mom at sixteen, telling her that we were in love.

Parents have this twisted belief that anyone under the age of about twenty simply can't know what love is, like the age to love is assessed in the same way the law assesses the legal age to drink. They think that the 'emotional growth' of a teenager's mind is too underdeveloped to understand love, to know if it's 'real' or not.

That's completely asinine.

The truth is that adults love in different ways, not the *only* way. I loved Ian in the now, the way he looked at me, how he made my stomach swim, how he held my hair when I was puking my guts up after eating a bad enchilada.

*That's* love.

I adore my parents, but long before their divorce the last time my mom was sick, the most my dad did for her was bring up the Pepto-Bismol and ask where the remote control was on his way out.

Whatever.

I guess my parents really screwed me up somewhere along the line because as good as they are to me, as much as they do for me and as much as I love them, I still managed to grow up terrified I would end up just like them. Unhappy and only pretending to live out this wonderful life with two kids, a dog and a white picket fence. But in reality, I knew they slept with their backs facing each other. I knew my mom often thought about what life would've been like if only she had given that boy in high school who she secretly 'loved' another chance (I read her old diary. I know all about him). I know that my dad—before he cheated on Mom with her—thought a lot about Rosanne Hartman, his prom date (and first love), who still lives over on Wiltshire.

If anyone's delusional about how love works, what real love feels like, it's the majority of the adult population.

Ian and I didn't have sex that night he took my virginity; we *made love* that night. I never thought I'd say those two words together: 'make love', because they always sounded corny, like it was an adult-only phrase. I winced when I heard someone else say it, or when that guy sang *Feel Like Makin' Love* from my dad's car stereo every morning on the classic rock station.

But I can say it because that's exactly what happened.

And it was magical and wonderful and awesome and nothing will ever compare to it. Ever.

———

I did go with my mom that Saturday to see Cole in prison. But I didn't say much, as usual, and Cole ignored me right back. He never does it to be hateful, but instead it's like he's afraid to say anything to me because he knows I'm still so pissed and hurt and disappointed by what he did. It wasn't like a one-time thing that can be filed away as a 'tragic accident'; Cole was an alcoholic before be turned eighteen. He's the black sheep of the family. He was a rotten little bastard growing up with stints in juvy and making my parents sick with worry when he'd disappear for weeks at a time while he was out doing whatever the hell he wanted. He's only ever really thought of himself.

I started my job as assistant manager the following Monday. I'm grateful to have a job because I don't want to live off my dad's money the rest of my life, but as I stood there dressed in a cute black pants suit and white button-up shirt and heels, I felt completely out of place. Not necessarily because of the clothes, but…I just don't belong there. I can't put my finger on it, but that Monday and the rest of that week when I woke up, got dressed and walked into that store, something was itching the back part of my consciousness. I couldn't hear the actual words, but it felt like: This is your life, Camryn Bennett. This is your life.

And I would look up at the customers walking by and all I could see was the negative: snooty noses in the air, carrying expensive purses, buying pointless products.

That was when I realized that everything I did from that point on produced the same results:

This is your life, Camryn Bennett. *This* is your life.

# FIVE

*T*he day when everything changed was yesterday.

That itch in my brain compelled me to get up. And so I did. It told me to put on my shoes, pack a small bag with a few necessities and grab my purse. And so I did.

There was no logic or any sense of purpose except that I knew I had to do *something* other than what I was doing, or I might not make it through this. Or, I might end up like my parents.

I always thought that depression was so overrated, the way people toss the word around (a lot like the L-word that I will *never* say to a guy again for as long as I live). When I was in high school, girls would often talk about how they were 'depressed' and how their moms took them to a shrink to get on medication and then they'd all gather around to see whose pills they wanted to try out. Depression to me meant three words: sadness, sadness and sadness. I saw those stupid commercials with the cartoonish figures moping around with black clouds constantly raining on their heads and thought to myself how people are really laying this depression stuff on thick. I feel bad for people. I always have. I never like to see someone hurting, but I admit whenever I heard someone play the depression card, I'd roll my eyes and go about my business.

Little did I know that depression is a serious disease.

Those girls at school had no idea what it really means to be depressed.

It's not only about sadness. In truth, sadness really has little to do with it. Depression is pain in its purest form and I would do *anything* to be able to feel an emotion again. Any emotion at all. Pain hurts, but pain that's so powerful that you can't feel *anything* anymore, that's when you start to feel like you're going crazy.

It bothers me immensely to realize that the last time I actually cried was that day at school when I found out that Ian was killed in that crash. It was in Damon's arms that I cried. *Damon*, of all people.

But that was the last time I ever shed a tear and that was a little over a year ago.

After that, I just couldn't anymore. Not over my parents' divorce, or when Cole got sentenced, or when Damon showed his true colors, or when Natalie stabbed me in the back. I keep thinking that any day now I'm going to break down and bawl my eyes out with my face buried in my pillow. I should be puking from crying so much.

But it never comes and I still *feel nothing*.

Except this sense of breaking free from it all. That itch, although vague and stingy, compels me to obey it. I don't know why, I can't explain it, but it's there and I can't stop myself from listening to it.

I spent most of the night at the bus station, sitting there waiting for that itch to tell me what to do.

And then I walked up to the counter.

"Can I help you?" the woman said blankly.

I thought about it for a second and said, "I'm going to see my sister in Idaho because she just had a baby."

She looked at me awkwardly, and I admit, it felt awkward. I don't have a sister and I've never been to Idaho, but it was the first lie that popped into my head. And she had been eating a baked potato. It was sitting behind the counter in a buttery bowl of foil and sour cream. So, naturally Idaho was the first state I thought of. It doesn't matter where I choose to go really, because I just don't care.

I thought, once I get to Idaho I'll just buy another ticket to somewhere else. Maybe I'll go to California. Or Washington. Or, maybe I'll just head south and see what Texas is like. I always imagined it a giant landscape of dirt and roadside bars and cowboy hats. And people in Texas are supposed to be some kind of badasses, or something. Maybe they'll stomp the crap out of me with their cowboy boots.

I won't feel it. I don't feel anything anymore, remember?

That was yesterday, when I decided to just get up and go, to break free from everything. I had always wanted to do it, to break free, but I never imagined it happening like this. Ian and I, before he died, planned our life in an unconventional way. We wanted to steer clear of anything predictable, anything that made us the same drones of society that get up at the same time every morning and duplicate yesterday. We wanted to backpack across the world—it's why I brought it up to Natalie that day in the coffee shop. Maybe a part of me hoped she'd share the passion for the idea that Ian and I had and *she'd* do it with me, but like everything else, it didn't exactly turn out like I hoped.

Tennessee slips by my window in a blur. Night falls and I eventually fall asleep, too. I don't have any dreams; haven't had a single dream since Ian died, but it's probably better that way. If I have dreams they might provoke emotion and I'm done with emotion. I'm starting to get used to this feeling of not caring about anything.

Aside from a few shady bus station dwellers, I'm really not afraid of anything anymore. I guess when you just don't care it kind of makes fear your bitch.

I never used to curse this much, either.

Everything looks the same. Between home and Missouri, it seems the only things that change are the license plates. In every state, there's always a car broken down on the side of the road. There's always a hitchhiker and a guy wearing a wife-beater carrying a gas can from his truck to the nearest exit where all the gas stations and fast food restaurants congregate. And there's always, *always* a single shoe on the shoulder somewhere. What is it with the shoes?

A bus ride is like being in another world.

Everybody knows that when they get on, they're gonna be here for a while. A *long* while. It's overcrowded. People are usually packed in so closely that you can smell every different sort of cologne and deodorant and the different kinds of detergent that people use. And unfortunately, you can also smell the people that don't wear cologne or deodorant at all and their clothes probably haven't been washed in several days.

The two hour delay drags by endlessly and when my next bus finally pulls into the station, I'm among the first small group of people to get up and stand in line. At least the seats on the bus have padding and I'll be able to get somewhat comfortable again.

The bus driver reaches out for my ticket and tears off his portion, handing the rest back to me. I tuck it safely down into my bag and board the bus, searching both rows of seats to find the one that feels like *the one*. I take a window seat near the back and instantly feel better once my body hits the comfort of the padding beneath me. I sigh and hold my bag close against my stomach, crossing my arms over it. It takes ten minutes or so for the bus driver to be satisfied that he has all of the passengers he's supposed to have for this round.

The driver goes to close the doors but then pulls back on the lever and they squeal open again. A guy gets on carrying a black duffle bag on his shoulder. Tall, stylish short brown hair and he's wearing a tight-fitting navy tee and a sort of crooked smile that could either be genuinely kind, or something more confident. "Thanks," he says to the driver in that laid-back way.

Even though there are plenty of empty seats for him to choose from, I still make it a point to slide my bag over onto the one next to me, just in case he decides it's *the one* for him. It's not likely, I know, but I'm a just-in-case kind of girl. The doors squeal shut again as the guy walks down the aisle toward me. I look down into the magazine that had been sitting inside the terminal and start reading an article about Brangelina.

I sigh with relief when he passes me up and takes the pair of empty seats behind me.

I doze off after staring out the window next to me for an hour.

Muffled headphone music blaring right behind me wakes me up sometime after dark.

At first, I just sit there, hoping maybe he'll notice the top of my now fully awake head bobbing over the seat and decide to turn the music down.

But he doesn't.

I lean up, reaching back to rub a crooked muscle in my neck from sleeping on my arm and then I turn around to look at him. Is he *asleep*? How can anyone actually sleep with music blasting in their ears like that? The bus is pitch dark except for a couple of dim reading lights shining down onto books and magazines from above the passengers' seats and the little green and blue lights at the front of the bus in the driver's dashboard. The guy sitting behind me is covered by darkness but I can see one side of his face lit up by the moonlight.

I contemplate it for a second and then push myself up with my knees on the seat and I lean over the back of it, reaching out and tapping him on the leg.

He doesn't move. I tap him harder. He stirs and slowly opens his eyes, looking up at me with my stomach hanging over the top of the seat.

He reaches up and pulls the earbuds from of his ears, letting the music funnel from the tiny speakers.

"Mind turning it down a little?"

"You could *hear* that?" he says.

I raise a brow and say, "Uhhh, yeah, it's pretty loud."

He shrugs and thumbs the MP3 player for the volume button and the music fades.

"Thanks," I say and slide back down in my seat.

I don't lie down across the seats in the fetal position this time, but lean against the bus and press my head back against the window. I cross my arms and close my eyes.

"Hey."

My eyes pop open, but I don't move my head.

"Are you asleep yet?"

I raise my head from the window and look up to see the guy hovering over me.

"I literally just closed my eyes," I say. "How can I already be asleep?"

"Well, I don't know," he whispers. "My granddad could fall asleep in two seconds flat after closing *his* eyes."

"Was your granddad narcoleptic?"

There's a pause. "Not that I know of."

*Wow, this is awkward.*

"What do you want?" I ask as quietly as he had.

"Nothing," he says grinning down at me. "Just wanted to know if you were asleep yet."

"Why?"

"So I can turn the music back up."

I think about it for a second, uncross my arms and lift the rest of the way from the seat, turning at the waist so that I can see him.

"You want to wait until I'm asleep to turn the music back up so that you can *wake me up again?*" I'm having a hard time getting this.

He smiles a crooked smile.

"You slept for three hours without it waking you up," he says. "So, I'm guessing it wasn't my music that did it, must've been something else."

My eyebrows draw together. "No, ummm, I'm pretty sure I know it was the music that did it."

"OK," he says, slipping away from the seat and out of sight.

I wait for a few seconds before closing my eyes in case this might get weirder and when it doesn't, I drift back into the Land of No Dreams.

# SIX

The sunlight beaming in through the bus windows wakes me the next morning. I lift up to get a better view, wondering if the scenery has changed any yet, but it hasn't. And then I notice the music blasting from the earbuds behind me. I creep up over the top of the seat, expecting to see him sound asleep, but he looks back at me with an I-told-you-so smile.

I roll my eyes and sink back down, pulling my bag onto my lap and sifting through it. I'm starting to wish I'd brought something to keep my mind busy. A book. A crossword puzzle. *Something.* I sigh heavily and literally start twiddling my thumbs. I wonder where we are in the United States, if I'm even still in Kansas and decide that we must be because every car that passes by the bus has Kansas license plates.

When I can't find anything interesting to look at, I pay more attention to the music behind me.

*Is that . . . ? You've got to be* kidding *me.*

*Feel Like Makin' Love* comes from the guy's earbuds; I can tell at first by the distinctive guitar riff in the solo that everyone knows even if Bad Company isn't their kind of music. I don't hate classic rock, but I much prefer newer stuff. Give me Muse, Pink or The Civil Wars and I'm happy.

The earbuds dangling over the back of the seat and practically on my shoulder scares the crap out of me. My body jerks up and a hand flies over as if to slap away a bug that at first I think just landed on me.

"What the hell?" I say, looking up at the guy as he hovers over me again.

"You look bored," he says. "You can borrow them if you want. Might not be your type of music, but hey, it'll grow on you. I promise."

I'm looking up at him with an awfully twisted face. Is this guy *serious*?

"Thanks, but no," I say and go to turn around again.

"Why not?"

"Well, for one," I say, "you've had those things stuck in your ears for the past several hours. Gross."

"And?"

"What do you mean, *and*?" I think my face is just getting more twisted. "That's not *enough*?"

He smiles that crooked smile again, which in the daylight I notice produces two tiny dimples near the corners of his lips.

"Well," he says, reeling the earbuds back in, "you said 'for one'; I just thought there might be another reason."

"Wow," I say, flabbergasted, "you are unbelievable."

"Thanks." He smiles and I can see all of his straight, white teeth.

I definitely didn't mean that as a compliment, but something tells me he knows as much.

I go back to digging in my bag already knowing I'm not going to find anything but clothes, but it's better than dealing with this weirdo.

He plops down on the empty seat next to me, just before another passenger walks past toward the restroom.

I just kind of freeze here, one hand buried inside my bag, unmoving. I may be looking right at him, but I have to let the shock wear off before I can actually figure out what kind of lecture I want to give him.

The guy reaches into his own bag and pulls out a little packet containing an antibacterial wipe, rips off the top half and unfolds the towelette. He wipes each earbud down thoroughly and then reaches over to me. "Like new," he says, waiting for me to take them.

Seeing as how it actually seems like he's trying to be nice, I let my defenses down just a little. "Really, I'm good. But thanks." It surprises me at how fast I got over the whole sit-next-to-me-with-out-asking thing.

"You're probably better off anyway," he says, putting the MP3 player in his bag. "I don't listen to Justin Bieber or that crazy meat-wearin' bitch, so I guess you'll just have to do without."

OK, defenses are back up. Bring it on.

I snarl over at him, crossing my arms. "First off, I don't *listen* to Justin Bieber. And second, Gaga isn't so bad. Playing the shock-value card a little too long, I admit, but I like some of her stuff."

"That's shit-music and you know it," he replies and shakes his head.

I blink twice, just because I'm at a loss and don't know what to say.

He puts his bag on the floor and leans back on the seat, propping one booted foot up on the back of the seat in front of him, but his legs are so long it looks uncomfortable to me. He's wearing those stylish work-boot-looking things. Dr. Martens, I think. Dammit. Ian always wore those. I look away, not really in any mood to further this very strange conversation with this very strange person.

He looks over at me, his head pressed comfortably against the itchy fabric behind him. "Classic Rock is where it's at," he says matter-of-factly and then gazes out ahead. "Zeppelin, the Stones, Journey, Foreigner." He lets his head fall to the side to look over at me again. "Any of that ringing any bells?"

I scoff and roll my eyes again. "I'm not *stupid*," I say, but then change my tune when I realize I can't think of many classic rock bands and I don't want to make myself look stupid after so eloquently saying that I'm not. "I like . . . Bad Company."

A little grin lifts one side of his mouth. "Name one song by Bad Company and I'll leave you alone about it."

I'm nervous as hell now, trying to think of any song by Bad Company other than the one he had been listening to. I'm not going to look this guy in the face and say the words: *I Feel Like Makin' Love.*

He waits patiently, that grin of his still intact.

"*Ready For Love*," I say because it's the only other one I can think of.

"*Are* you?" he asks.

"Huh?"

A smile etches deeper into his face. "Nothing," he says, looking away.

I blush. I don't know why and I don't want to know why.

"Look," I say, "do you mind? I was sort of using both seats."

He smiles, this time without the smirk hiding behind his eyes. "Sure," he says getting up. "But if you want to borrow my MP3 player, you know where it's at."

I smile slimly, relieved more than anything that he's going to move back to his seat without a fight. "Thanks," I say, appreciative, nonetheless.

Just before he makes it all the way back, he leans around the outside seat and says, "Where are you going, anyway?"

"Idaho."

His bright green eyes seem to light up when he smiles. "Well, I'm heading to Wyoming, so looks like we'll be sharing a few buses." And then his smiling face disappears somewhere behind me.

I won't deny that he's attractive. The short, tousled haircut, the toned arms and sculpted cheekbones, the dimples and how that stupid fucking grin of his makes me more willing to look at him even though I don't want to. But the reality is that it's not like I'm into him, or anything—he's a random stranger on a road-to-nowhere bus. No way in hell would I ever entertain something like that. And even if he wasn't, even if I knew him for six months, I wouldn't go there. Not ever. Not anymore.

———

The endless ride through Kansas seems to take longer than it should. I guess I never thought about how big states really are. You look at a map and it's just this piece of paper in front of you with oddly-shaped borders and veiny little lines. Even Texas seems pretty small when you're looking down at it like that, and always traveling everywhere by plane helps feed the delusion that the next state is just an hour away. Another hour and a half and my back and butt feel like stiff, hard pieces of meat. I'm constantly shifting on the seat, hoping to find some way to sit to relieve the tenderness, but I just end up making other parts of my body sore.

I'm only starting to regret this because the bus ride sucks.

I hear the bus intercom squeal once and then the driver's voice:

"We'll be stopping for a break in five minutes," he says. "You will have fifteen minutes to grab a bite to eat before we get back on the road. Fifteen minutes. I will not wait longer, so if you're not back in that time the bus will leave without you." The speaker goes dead.

The announcement causes everyone to stir in their seats and gather their purses and such—nothing like talk of getting to stretch your legs after hours on a bus to wake everyone up.

We pull into a spacious lot where several semis are parked, and in between a convenience store, a car wash and a fast food restaurant. Passengers are standing up in the center of the aisle before the bus even comes to a stop. I'm one of them. My back hurts so bad.

We file out of the bus one by one, and the second I step off I cherish the feel of concrete underfoot and the mild breeze on my face. I don't care that this area is hick-in-the-sticks remote, or that the convenience store gas pumps are so outdated that I know the restrooms will probably be scary; I'm just glad to be anywhere but cooped up inside that bus. I practically glide (like an ungraceful, wounded gazelle) across the blacktop parking lot and toward the restaurant. I take advantage of the restroom first and when I come back out there are several people in line in front of me. I stare up at the menu, trying to decide between a large fry or vanilla shake— never was a big eater of fast food. And finally when I walk out of the restaurant with a vanilla shake, I see the guy from the bus sitting on the grass that separates the parking lots. His knees are bent and he's eating a burger. I don't look at him when I start to walk past, but apparently it's not enough to keep him from bothering me.

"Eight more minutes before you have to crawl back into that tin can," he says. "You're *really* going to spend that precious time in there?"

I stop next to a little tree still being held up by a stick in the ground and tied with pink fabric.

"It's just eight minutes," I say. "Won't make that much of a difference."

He takes a huge bite of his burger, chews and swallows it down.

"Imagine if you were buried alive," he says and takes a drink of soda. "You wouldn't have much time before you suffocated to death. If only they'd gotten to you eight minutes earlier, hell, even one minute, you'd still be alive."

"OK, I get it," I say.

"I'm not contagious," he says and then takes another bite.

I guess I have been sort of a bitch. I mean, in a way he kind of deserved it, but he's really not being obnoxious or anything, so there's no reason to keep the defenses *all* the way up. I'd rather not make any enemies on this trip if I can help it.

"Whatever," I say and take a seat on the grass a couple of feet in front of him.

"So why Idaho?" he asks, though he looks at his food and all around him more than he looks directly at me.

"Going to see my sister," I lie. "She just had a baby."

He nods and swallows.

"Why Wyoming?" I ask, hoping to divert the topic from myself.

"Going to visit my dad," he says. "He's dying. Inoperable brain tumor." He takes another bite. It doesn't seem like what he just told me bothers him too much.

"Oh…"

"Don't worry about it," he says, looking right at me this time for a brief moment. "We all gotta go sometime. My old man isn't worried about it and told us not to be, either." He smiles and looks at me again. "Actually, he told us if we do any of that cryin' bullshit, that he'd write us out of his will."

I suck on my vanilla shake for a moment, only to be doing

something to keep my mouth from having to respond to the stuff he's saying. I'm not sure if I could anyway, really.

He takes another sip.

"What's your name?" he asks, setting his drink on the grass.

I wonder if I should give him my real name. "Cam," I say, settling on the short version.

"Short for what?"

I didn't expect that.

I hesitate, my eyes trailing. "Camryn," I admit. I figure with all the lies I'm going to have to keep track of, I might as well be truthful about my first name at least. It's one less-significant piece of information I don't have to remember to keep under wraps.

"I'm Andrew. Andrew Parrish."

I nod and smile slimly, not about to tell him my last name is Bennett. He'll have to make do with the first-name-basis only.

As he finishes the last of his burger and scarfs down a few fries, I secretly study him and notice the bottom of a tattoo poking out from underneath both sleeves of his t-shirt. He can't be older than mid-twenties, if even that.

"So, how old are you?" It still felt too personal of a question. I hope he doesn't read something in it that's not there.

"Twenty-five," he says. "What about you?"

"Twenty."

He glances at me ponderingly, pauses and then subtly purses his lips.

"Well, it's good to meet you, twenty-year-old Cam short for Camryn heading to Idaho to see her sister who just had a baby."

My lips smile, but my face doesn't. It'll take a while before any of my smiles directed at him can be genuine. Genuine smiles can sometimes give the wrong impression. At least this way, I can be civil and kind, but not the civil kind who after a few big smiles ends up in a trunk with their throat slit.

"So, are you from Wyoming?" I ask and take another sip of my shake.

He nods once. "Yeah, was born there, but parents divorced when I was six and we moved to Texas."

Texas. How funny. Maybe all of my crap-talk about their cowboy boots and reputation is finally catching up to me. And he doesn't *look* like he's from Texas, at least, not the stereotypical way that most people assume everyone from Texas looks like.

"That's where I'll be headin' back to after visiting my dad— what about you?"

OK, to lie or not to lie? Oh screw it. It's not like he's a private investigator sent by my dad to get information. As long as I steer clear of #1...my last name, and #2...any addresses or phone numbers that might lead him back to my house in the event that I ever go back home, and then end up in his trunk with my throat slit. I think telling mostly the truth will be a lot easier than trying to conjure up a fitting lie for just about every question that he asks me and then having to remember all of them later. This is going to be a long bus ride, after all, and just like he said, we've got several buses to share before we part ways.

"North Carolina," I say.

He looks me over. "Well, you don't look like you're from North Carolina."

*Huh? OK, that was really weird.*

"Well, what's a girl from North Carolina *supposed* to look like?"

"You're very literal," he says, grinning.

"And you're sort of confusing."

"Nah," he says with a harmless, humorous snarl, "just outspoken and sometimes people can't deal with that kind of shit. It's like, you ask that guy over there if your ass looks big in those jeans and he'll tell you, no. You ask me, and I'll tell you the truth—anything out of people's usual expectations throws them off track."

"Really?" I'm not any closer to understanding this guy's personality than I was before I knew his name. I just continue to look at him like he's sort of nuts and I'm sort of intrigued by it.

"Really," he answers matter-of-factly.

I wait for him to elaborate, but he doesn't.

"You are very strange," I say.

"Well, aren't you going to ask?"

"Ask what?"

He laughs. "If I think your ass looks big in those jeans."

I feel my face crinkle.

"I'd really rather not...I uhhh—" Screw this times two. If he's going to play games, I'm not going to sit back and let him win all the hands. I smirk at him and say, "I *know* my ass doesn't look big in these jeans, so I don't really need your opinion."

A devilishly handsome grin sneaks up at the corners of his mouth. He takes another drink from his soda and goes to his feet, offering his hand. "Looks like our eight minutes are up."

Maybe it's because I'm still completely confused by this entire exchange, but I accept his hand and he pulls me to my feet.

"See," he says looking over at me once and letting my hand go, "look how much we learned about each other in just eight minutes, Camryn."

I walk beside him, but still keep a little distance. I'm not sure yet if his crafty comebacks and that confident air about him annoys me, or if I'm finding it more refreshing than my brain wants to admit.

Everyone on the bus gets their usual seats. I had left the magazine

I took from the last terminal sitting on mine, hoping no one would come behind me and claim it. Andrew also got his usual pair of seats behind me. I'm glad he didn't take my willingness to actually hold a conversation with him as the O.K. to plop himself back on the seat next to me.

Hours pass and we don't talk. I think a lot about Natalie and Ian.

"Goodnight, Camryn," I hear Andrew say from his seat behind me. "Maybe tomorrow you'll tell me who Nat is."

I rise up quickly and lean over the top of the seat. "What are you talking about?"

"Calm down, girl," he says, lifting his head from his bag he pushed up against the bus to use as a pillow. "You talk in your sleep." He laughs quietly. "Heard you bitchin' at someone named Nat last night—something about Biosilk, or some shit like that." I notice his shoulders shrug even though he's lying down with his legs stretched across the empty seat, his arms crossed over his chest.

Great. I talk in my sleep. Just perfect. I wonder why my mom never told me.

Briefly, I think about what I could've been dreaming about and realize that maybe I have been dreaming after all, and I just don't remember anymore.

"Goodnight, Andrew," I say and slip back down into my own attempt at a comfortable position. I give a quick moment's thought to the way I just saw Andrew, who actually looked pretty comfortable, and I decide to try lying down the way he is. I thought about trying to sleep like that a few times, but I never wanted to be rude by letting my feet stick out into the aisle. No one's going to care, I guess, and so I ball my bag packed with clothes up and position it behind my head, laying my body out over both seats just like

Andrew. I'm already comfortable. I wish I'd have done this a long time ago.

————

The bus driver announcing that we'll be arriving in Garden City in ten minutes wakes me up the next morning.

"Be sure to gather all of your belongings," the driver says through his intercom, "and don't leave trash on the seats. Thank you for riding through the great state of Kansas and I hope to see you again sometime."

It sounded totally scripted and deadpan, but then I guess I probably would sound like that too, having to say the same thing to passengers every single day.

I lift up the rest of the way, pulling my bag from the seat and unzipping it to fish around for my bus ticket. I find it crumpled between a pair of jeans and my vintage-style Smurfs babydoll tee, unfold it and peer down into my next stop. Looks like Denver is about six and a half hours away, with two rest stops in between. Damn, why did I choose *Idaho*? Really. Of all the places on the map, I chose mine based on a baked potato. I'm riding all this way and don't even have anything to look forward to once I get there. Except more riding. Hell, I may just go ahead and use my credit card and buy a plane ticket home. No, I'm not ready for that yet. I don't know why, but I know I can't go back there yet.

I just can't.

Surprised that Andrew has been so quiet, I find myself trying to see if I can glimpse him through the tiny space between my seats, but I can't see anything at all.

"Are you up?" I ask, lifting my chin so maybe he'll hear me back there.

He doesn't answer and I lift up to see. Of course, he's plugged in at the moment. I'm a little shocked I can't hear the music funneling from the earbuds this time.

Andrew notices me and smiles, raising his hand and shaking his index finger as if to say good morning. I motion a finger too, toward the front of the bus to let him know there's been an announcement. He pulls the buds from his ears and looks up at me, waiting for me to put words to the gesture.

# Andrew

*A few days earlier…*

# SEVEN

*I* got a call from my brother in Wyoming today. He said our old man wasn't going to be around much longer. He'd already spent the last six months in and out of the hospital.

"If you're gonna see him," Aidan said on the other end of the phone, "you better come now."

I do hear Aidan. I do. But all I can really comprehend right about now is that my dad is about to fucking die. *"Don't you ever dare cry for me,"* he'd said to my brothers and me last year when they diagnosed him with a rare form of brain cancer. *"I'll cut you right out of my will, boy."*

I hated him for that, for telling me in so many words that if I cried for him, the one man in my life that I would die for, that I'd be a pussy for it. I don't care about the will. Whatever he leaves me I'll just let it sit. Maybe I'll give it to Mom.

Dad was always a hardass growing up. He drilled the shit outta me and my brothers, but I like to think we turned out decent (and that was probably the plan behind the drilling). Aidan, the oldest, owns a successful bar and restaurant in Chicago and is married to a pediatrician. Asher, the youngest, is in college and has his sights set on a career at Google.

Me? I'm embarrassed to say that I've secretly done a few model-ing gigs for several high profile agencies, but I only did it because I fell on hard times last year. Right after I found out about my dad. I couldn't cry, so I let it all out on my 1969 Chevy Camaro. Destroyed it with a baseball bat. Dad and I rebuilt that car from the ground up together. It was our 'father-son' project that began just before I graduated. I figured if he isn't going to be around, then neither should the car.

So yeah, modeling.

Hell no, I never went looking for a gig. I don't care about that kind of shit. I just happened to be at Aidan's bar when a couple of scouts found me getting shitfaced. I guess it didn't matter that I was... well, shitfaced, because they slipped me their card, offered me a generous sum of money just to show up at their building in New York and after three weeks of staring at that Camaro and regret-ting what I'd done to it, I decided, why not? That one check just for showing up could cover some of the body work. And I did show up. And despite the money I made from the few ads I shot being enough to fix the car, I turned down the fifty-thousand-dollar contract I'd been offered by LL Elite because, like I said, prancing around in my underwear for a living just isn't my thing. Hell, I felt dirty for accept-ing the few gigs I *did* accept. So, I did what any red meat-eating, beer-drinking guy would do and I tried to make myself look more man and less pansy by getting a few tattoos and a job as a mechanic.

Not the kind of future my old man wanted for me, but unlike my brothers, I learned a long time ago that it's my future and my life and I can't make myself live the way someone else wants me to live. I dropped out of college after I realized that I was studying some-thing I didn't give a shit about.

What is it with people and their willingness to follow?

Not me. I want one thing in life. It's not money or fame or a Photoshopped dick on a billboard in Times Square or a college education that may or may *not* benefit me later. I'm not sure what it is that I want, but I feel it deep in the pit of my stomach. It's there sitting dormant. I'll know it when I see it.

"A *bus?*" Aidan says, unbelieving.

"Yes," I say. "I'll take a bus there. I need to think."

"Andrew, Dad might not make it," he says and I can hear the restraint in his voice. "Seriously, bro."

"I'll be there when I get there."

I run my thumb over the end call button.

I think a small part of me hopes that he dies before I make it. Because I know I'll lose my shit if he dies while I'm there. This is my *father*, the man who raised me and who I look up to. And he tells me not to cry. I've always done everything he's ever told me and like the good son I've always tried to be, I know I'll force back the tears because he told me to. But I also know that by doing it, it'll create something in me more destructive.

I don't want to end up like my car.

A single duffle bag packed with a clean pair of clothes, toothbrush, cell phone and MP3 player with my favorite classic rock songs—another mark that Dad left on me: *"That new stuff kids listen to these days is shit music, son,"* he said at least once a year. *"Get the Led out, boy!"* I'll admit I didn't completely shun newer music just because my dad did. I have my own damn mind, remember? But I did grow up on a healthy dose of the classics and I'm very proud of that.

"Mom, I don't need those."

She's stuffing a Zip-lock bag with about a dozen little packets of hand-sanitizing wipes for me to take. She's always been a germaphobe.

I've lived back and forth between Texas and Wyoming since I was six years old. Ultimately, I realized that I fit better in Texas because I like the Gulf and the heat. I've had my own apartment in Galveston for four years now, but last night my mom insisted I stay at her place. She knows how I feel about my dad and she knows that sometimes I can be explosive when I'm hurting, or when I'm pissed off. Spent a night in jail last year for beating the fuck out of Darren Ebbs after he punched his girlfriend in front of me. And when I had to have my best friend, Maximus, put to sleep because of congestive heart failure, I busted my hands up pretty good taking my emotions out on the tree behind my apartment.

I'm not violent in general, only to douchebags and occasionally, myself.

"Those buses are nasty," she says, tucking the baggie down into my bag. "I rode on one back before I met your father and I was sick for a week afterwards."

I don't argue with her; it would be pointless.

"I still don't understand why you won't take a plane. You can get there in a fraction of the time."

"Mom," I say, kissing her cheek, "it's just something I need to do—like it was meant to be, or something." I don't really believe that second part, but I thought I'd humor her with something meaningful, even though she knows I'm full of shit. I walk over and open the kitchen cabinet, take two brown sugar and cinnamon Pop Tarts from the box and drop them in my bag. "Maybe the plane is supposed to crash."

"That's not funny, Andrew." She glances over at me sternly.

I smile and squeeze her. "I'll be all right, and I'll make it in time to see Dad before…" my voice trails.

Mom hugs me back tighter than I did her.

By the time I make it to Kansas, I'm starting to wonder if my mom was right. I thought I could use the long ride to think, to clear my head and maybe figure out what I'm doing and what I'm going to do after my dad dies. Because things will be different. Things always change when someone you love dies. You just can't prepare yourself for those changes no matter what you do in advance.

The only thing that's a certainty is always wondering who's going to be next.

I know I'll never be able to look at my mom the same again...

I think the bus ride has been more of a taunt than a time for meaningful contemplation. I should've known that time alone with my thoughts would be unhealthy. Already I've decided that my life has been pretty much wasted and I'm going through all the eye-opening emotions: What am I here for? What's the point in life? What the hell am I doing? I sure as hell haven't had any epiphanies, or stared out the bus window, lost in some dramatic movie-moment when suddenly life becomes clear to me. The only music playing in the background of *this* movie is Alice In Chains' *Would?*, and that's not exactly an epiphany-moment kind of song.

The driver is just about to close the doors on the bus when I step up and he notices me.

Thank God, a bus I might actually get to sleep on; plenty of empty seats.

I head toward the back, my sights set on two empty seats right behind the cute blonde who I'm pretty sure is jailbait. I always have my jailbait radar on, especially after almost hooking up with a girl I met at Dairy Queen. She said she was nineteen, but I found out later she was sixteen and her dad was on his way to the pool where we were to pummel me to death.

My dad said it right once: *"Can't tell twelve from twenty these days, son. It must be something the government has been puttin' in the water—be damn careful when you need to knock some boots."*

As I near the girl on the bus, I notice her move her bag over onto the aisle seat so that I won't sit there.

That's funny. I mean yeah, she's cute and all but there are about ten or so empty seats on this bus, which means I'm going to get two to myself so I can sprawl my ass out however I want and get some much-needed shuteye.

Things don't go as planned and several hours later, just after dark and I'm still wide awake, staring out the tall window beside me with music blasting in my ears. The girl in front of me has been passed out for about an hour and I got tired of hearing her talk in her sleep; though I could hardly make out anything she was saying, I didn't really want to know. Kind of feels like spying, hearing someone's thoughts when they have no idea what they're doing. I'd much rather hear my playlist.

After I finally fall asleep, my eyes crawl open when I feel something tapping against my leg. Wow, she's kind of beautiful even with her hair all smashed on one side of her face and the darkness covering the rest of her. Jailbait, Andrew. I don't have to remind myself that she's probably jailbait to keep myself from doing anything I know I shouldn't, no, I remind myself because I don't want to be disappointed when I find out that I'm right.

After a quick back-and-forth about the possibility of my music being what woke her up, I turn it down and she slips back down into her little bus-seat-cubicle.

When I lean up over the top of her seat to look down at her, I'm wondering to myself what possessed me to do it. But I've always been one for a challenge and her spunky attitude towards me in a conversation that lasted less than forty-five seconds was enough to shake her hand in this metaphorical bet.

I've always been a sucker for spunky attitudes.

And I never back down from a challenge.

The next morning, I offer to let her borrow my MP3 player, but apparently she's as much of a germaphobe as my mother.

A man, probably in his early forties, has been sitting on the other side of the bus, three seats up from the girl. I saw the way he was looking at her when I first got on. She had no clue he had been watching her and it's disturbing to think about how long he's been watching her since before I got on, or what he's been doing to himself sitting up there all alone in the dark.

I've been sort of keeping my eyes on him ever since. He's so enamored by her that I doubt he knows I've been watching.

His eyes keep glancing between her and down the center of the aisle towards the matchbox restroom. I can almost hear the gears churning in his head.

I wonder when he's going to try to make his move.

Just then, he gets up.

I slide out of my seat and into the one beside her. I just play it off like it's nothing. I can feel her eyes on me, looking at me wondering what the fuck I think I'm doing.

The man walks past, but I don't let him see my eyes because then that would give away that I'm onto him. Right now, he probably thinks I'm just playing my own game with the girl; that I'm making my own move and for now, he'll get over it and probably try again later.

And later is when I'll cave his face in with my fist.

I reach into my bag and fish for the baggie of antibacterial wipes my mom packed. Ripping one from the packet, I wipe the earbuds down and then reach over to her. "Like new," I say, waiting for her to take them, but I know she won't.

"Really, I'm good. But thanks."

"You're probably better off anyway," I say, putting the MP3 player in my bag. "I don't listen to Justin Bieber or that crazy meat-wearin' bitch, so I guess you'll just have to do without."

Judging by that irritated look on her face, I pissed her off. I laugh quietly to myself, turning my head at an angle so she doesn't catch me grinning.

"First off, I don't *listen* to Justin Bieber."

Thank God.

"And second, Gaga isn't so bad. Playing the shock-value card a little too long, I admit, but I like some of her stuff."

"That's shit-music and you know it," I quote my father, shaking my head.

I put my bag on the floor and lean back on the seat, propping up one foot on the seat in front of me. I wonder why she hasn't told me to leave yet. And this also worries me. Would she have been 'too nice' to tell that man to leave right away if he had made it here before me? There's no way someone like her would be into some-one like him, but face it, sometimes girls let that overly sympathetic gene get the best of them. And that few seconds is really all it takes.

I look over at her again, letting my head fall sideways against the seat. "Classic Rock is where it's at," I say. "Zeppelin, the Stones, Journey, Foreigner—any of that ringing any bells?"

She rolls her eyes at me. "I'm not stupid," she says and a grin lifts one side of my mouth because there's that spunky attitude again.

"Name one song by Bad Company and I'll leave you alone about it," I challenge her.

I can tell she's nervous, how she gently bites down on her bottom lip, and like talking in her sleep and being watched by bad men, she probably doesn't even know it.

I wait patiently, unable to peel the grin from my face because it's amusing watching her squirm, trying to sort through all of the times she was in the car with her folks listening to this stuff, searching for some memory that will help her in this critical moment.

"*Ready For Love*," she finally answers and I'm impressed.

"*Are* you?" I ask and something hits me in this moment. I don't know what the hell 'it' is, but it's there, waving at me from behind a wall, like when you know someone's watching you, yet you don't see anybody.

"Huh?" she says, as caught off-guard by my question as I was afterwards.

A smile creeps up on my face. "Nothing," I say, looking away.

The pervert from the restroom comes quietly back down the dark aisle and goes back to his seat, no doubt pissed off that I'm sitting where he wants to be sitting. I'm just glad she waited for him to pass by before finally asking me to move so she can have both of her seats back.

After I crawl back behind her, I lean around the edge of her seat and say, "Where are you going, anyway?"

She tells me Idaho, but I think there's more to her answer than that. I can't put my finger on it, but I get the feeling she's either lying, which is probably a good thing because I'm a total stranger, or she's hiding something else.

I let it go for now and tell her where I'm heading and then duck back in my seat behind her.

The man three seats up just looked at her again. I'm about ready to bash his fucking brains in right now, just for looking.

Hours later, the bus pulls into a rest stop and the driver gives us all fifteen minutes to get out, stretch our legs and get something to eat. I watch the girl head inside toward the restrooms and I'm the first in line to order food. I get my food and head back outside, taking a seat on the grass next to the parking lot. The pervert walks past me, stepping back inside the bus by himself.

I manage to talk her into sitting with me. She's hesitant at first, but apparently I'm charming enough. My mom always told me I was her charming middle-child. I guess she was right all along.

We talk for a minute or two about why I'm going to Wyoming and why she's going to Idaho. I'm still trying to figure her out, what it is about her that I can't quite place, but at the same time trying to force myself not to be attracted to her because it's like I just know she's jailbait, or she's going to lie about it.

But she looks close to my age, younger than me, but we can't be too far apart.

Goddammit! Why am I even considering an attraction to her? My dad is dying right now as I sit here on the grass next to her. I shouldn't be thinking about anything other than my dad and what I'm going to say to him if I do manage to get to Wyoming before he passes.

"What's your name?" I ask, setting my drink on the grass and trying to push thoughts of my dad's death somewhere else in my mind.

She thinks about it for a minute, probably wondering whether she should tell me the truth, or not. "Cam," she finally answers.

"Short for what?"

"Camryn."

"I'm Andrew. Andrew Parrish."

She seems a little shy.

"So, how old are you?" she asks and it completely surprises me. Maybe she's not jailbait, after all, because underage girls, when they want to lie about their age, usually steer clear of this topic at all costs.

I'm hopeful now that maybe she's legal. Yeah, I really want her to be...

"Twenty-five," I say. "What about you?" I can't breathe all of a sudden.

"Twenty," she says.

I think about her answer for a moment, pursing my lips. I'm still not sure if she's lying, but maybe after more time with her on this journey that seems to have brought us together, I will find out the truth eventually.

"Well, it's good to meet you, twenty-year-old Cam short for Camryn heading to Idaho to see her sister who just had a baby."

I smile. We talk for a few minutes more—eight minutes to be exact—about this and that and I screw with her head some more because that spunky mouth of hers deserves it.

Actually, I think she likes it, the way I treat her. I can tell there's an attraction. Though small, I sense it. And it can't really be because of the way I look—hell, my breath probably smells like ass right now and I haven't had a shower today—if it was because of looks, unlike most girls who are ever into me, *she* turned me down already. She didn't want me sitting next to her on that bus. She wasn't shy to tell me to turn my music down, with a snippy-ass attitude at that. She got pissed when I accused her of having Bieber Fever (it pisses *me* off that I even know what the fuck that means—I blame that on society) and I get the feeling that she would have no problem kicking me in the nuts if I touched her in an inappropriate way. Not that I would. Hell no. But it's good to know that she's the type.

Hell yeah, I like this girl.

We board the bus and I crawl back in my seat, letting my legs stretch out into the aisle and then I see her white tennis shoes poke out from her aisle seat and I smile at the thought that I'd been interesting enough for her to take ideas from. I check on her about twenty minutes later and just like I thought, she's passed out cold.

I turn the music back up and listen to it until I fall asleep, too, and wake up the next morning long before she does.

She pops her head over the top of her seat and I smile and wave a finger at her.

She's even prettier in the daylight.

# Camryn

# EIGHT

en minutes," I say, "and we're off this tin can."

Andrew grins and pulls his back away from the seat and goes to put his MP3 player away.

I'm not exactly sure why I felt the need to tell him.

"Did you sleep better?" he asks, zipping up his bag.

"Yeah, actually I did," I say, reaching around to feel the back of my neck where I don't feel any twisted muscles this time. "Thanks for the involuntary idea."

"You're very welcome," he says with a huge grin.

"Denver?" he asks, looking up at me.

I'm assuming he's asking if that's my next stop. "Yeah, almost seven hours away."

Andrew shakes his head, seeming as dissatisfied with that time-frame as I am.

Ten minutes later and the bus pulls into the Garden City station. There are three times as many people at this station than there were at the last one and this worries me. I make way my through the terminal and to the first empty seat I see because they are filling up quickly. Andrew slips around a corner underneath the vending area sign and comes back with a Mountain Dew and a bag of chips.

He sits down beside me and cracks the top on the soda can.

"*What?*" he asks looking over at me.

I didn't notice I had been watching him gulp that soda down with a disgusted look on my face.

"Nothing," I say, looking away, "I just think it's gross."

I hear him laugh under his breath beside me and then the chip bag rattles open.

"You seem to think a lot of stuff is gross."

I look over at him again, positioning my bag on my lap. "When was the last time you ate something less...heart-attack inducing?"

He crunches another chip and swallows. "I eat whatever I want to eat—what are you, one of those uppity vegetarian girls that complain about how fast food is making the country fat?"

"I'm not one of those," I say, "but I think the uppity vegetarian girls might be onto something."

He chomps down on a couple more chips and takes a swig of his soda, grinning over at me.

"Fast food doesn't make people fat," he says steadily chewing away. "People make their own choices. Fast food restaurants are just bankin' good on the stupidity of Americans who choose to eat their food."

"Are you calling yourself a stupid American?" I grin right back at him.

He shrugs. "I guess I am when my options are limited to vending machines and burger joints."

I roll my eyes. "Oh, like you'd actually choose to eat something better if you had the choice to make. I don't buy that."

I think I'm getting better at these comebacks.

He laughs out loud. "Hell yeah I'd choose something better. I'll take a fifty-dollar steak over a day-old burger any day, or a beer over a Mountain Dew."

I shake my head, but can't wipe the faint grin off my face.

"What do *you* normally eat, anyway?" he asks. "Salads and tofu?"

"Bleh," I say with a wrinkled face. "No way in hell would I ever eat tofu and salads are just weight-loss fads." I pause and grin over at him. "Honestly?"

"Well, yeah—spit it out," he says.

He's looking at me as though I'm something funny and cute that needs to be studied.

"I like SpaghettiO's with meatballs and sushi."

"What, like all mixed *together*?" Now he looks quietly disgusted.

It takes me a few seconds to catch on.

"Oh, no," I say, shaking my head back and forth, "that would be gross, too, by the way."

He smiles, looking relieved.

"I'm not big on steak," I go on, "but I'd eat one if offered to me, I guess."

"Oh, so you're asking me to ask you on a date?" His grin just got wider.

My eyes bulge and my mouth falls open. "No!" I say, practically blushing. "I was just saying that—"

Andrew laughs and takes another swig.

"I know, I know," he says, "don't worry. I'd never consider asking you on a date."

My eyes and mouth get even bigger and my face flushes hot.

He laughs even louder.

"Damn, girl," he says, still with laughter in his voice, "you don't catch on too quick, do you?"

I frown.

He frowns, too, but he's still sort of smiling at the same time.

"I'll tell you what," he says, looking a bit more serious, "if we happen to get lucky enough to find a steakhouse at one of our rest stops that can cook a steak in the fifteen minutes we have before the bus leaves us behind, then I'll buy you one and let you decide if while we eat our steaks together on the bus it's a date, or not."

"Well, I can tell you now that it won't be a date."

He smiles crookedly.

"Then it won't be," he says. "I can live with that."

I think he's done with the topic, but then suddenly he adds, "But then what would it be, if not a date?"

"What do you mean?" I say. "It would be a friendship thing, I guess. Y'know, two people who happen to be sharing a meal together."

"Oh," he says with a sparkle in his eyes, "so now we're friends?"

That catches me off-guard. He's good. I give it a moment's thought, pursing my lips in contemplation.

"Sure," I say. "I guess we are sort of friends at least until Wyoming."

He reaches over and offers his hand to me. Reluctantly, I shake it. His grip is gentle, but firm and his smile is genuine and kind.

"Friends until Wyoming it is then," he says, shaking my hand once and letting go.

I'm not sure what just happened, but I don't feel like I've done anything I'm going to regret later. I guess there's nothing wrong with having a traveling 'friend'. I can think of a hundred other kinds of people who Andrew could be and it could be worse. But he seems harmless and I admit he's interesting to talk to. He's not an old lady looking to tell me stories of when she was my age, or an older delusional man who still thinks he's as hot as he was when he was seventeen and that somehow he thinks I might be able to see him for what he used to look like. No, Andrew is right there in the goldilocks zone. Sure, it'd be better for many different reasons if he was a girl, but at least he's close to my age and he's not at all ugly. No, Andrew Parrish is far from being anywhere near the Ugly Tree.

Truthfully, he lives right next door to the Sexy Tree and I think that's the only thing that bothers me about this whole situation.

You know damn well that it doesn't really matter what's going on in your life, who you just lost, how much you hate the world, or how inappropriate it is to have an attraction to someone before that mending phase has reached the acceptable zone. You're still human and the moment you see someone attractive, you can't help but make note of it. It's human nature.

Acting on it is a whole other story and that's where I draw the line.

That's not gonna happen, no matter what.

But yeah, the fact that he's hot bothers me because it only means that I will have to try that much harder to make sure that nothing I say or do will give him the wrong impression. Hot guys *know* they're hot. They just do, even the ones who don't go around flaunting it. And it's also human nature for hot guys to automatically assume that an innocent smile, or a conversation that goes on for three minutes without awkward silence, are signs of an attraction.

So, this 'friendship' is going to take a lot of work on my part. I want to be nice, but not *too* nice. I want to smile when necessary, but I have to be careful and measure the level of the smile. I want to laugh if something he says is funny, but I don't want him to think it's an I'm-*so*-fucking-into-you kind of laugh.

Yeah, this is definitely going to take work. Maybe an old lady would've been better, after all...

Andrew and I wait in the terminal for nearly an hour before the next bus pulls into the station. And as expected, it doesn't look like we're going to have two seats to ourselves this time. The line waiting to board already looks like there might not be enough seats to hold everyone. Dilemma. Crap. Andrew and I are suddenly temporary friends, but I can't bring myself to ask him to sit with me. That might count as one of those things that gives the wrong impression. So, as the line inches forward and he follows close behind, I'm hoping he'll take it upon himself to sit next to me. I'd rather it be him than someone else who I haven't even spoken to.

I make my way toward the center of the bus and into two empty seats, passing up the one on the outside and taking the one by the window.

He sits next to me and I'm secretly relieved.

"Since you're a girl," he says, putting his bag on the floor between his feet, "I'll let you keep the window seat."

He smiles.

After the bus is full and I can already feel the extra body heat rising up all around us from so many people crammed inside the space, I hear the door squeal shut and the bus lurches into motion.

The drive doesn't seem so long and torturous anymore now that I have someone to talk to. It only takes about an hour of constant conversation about everything from what all of his favorite classic rock bands are, to why I like Pink and how much better her stuff is than Boston and Foreigner who sound the same to me. We argued about this for twenty minutes out of that hour—he's really stubborn, but then he said the same about me, so maybe we're both guilty. And I let him in on who 'Nat' is, though I don't go into the gruesome details of mine and Natalie's relationship.

By the time the night falls, I realize there hasn't been a single awkward moment of silence between us since we boarded the bus and he decided to sit next to me.

"How long are you staying in Idaho?"

"A few days."

"And then you're riding back on a bus?" Strangely, Andrew's face has lost all of its humor.

"Yeah," I say, not wanting to go too deeply into this topic because I don't already know my answers in advance.

I hear him sigh.

"It's none of my business," he says looking over at me and I feel the space between us closing in since he's sitting so close, "but you shouldn't be traveling around by yourself like this."

I don't look at him.

"Well, I kind of have to."

"Why?" he asks. "I'm not trying to hit on you or anything, but a young, devilishly gorgeous girl like you traveling by herself in the slums of the bus stations of America is dangerous."

I feel my face break into a smile, but I try futilely to hide it.

I look over at him. "You're not trying to hit on me," I say, "yet you call me 'devilishly gorgeous' and practically use that what's-a-girl-like-you-doing-in-a-place-like-this line all in the same sentence."

He seems gently offended.

"I'm serious, Camryn," he says and the playful smile on my face dissolves. "You could really get hurt."

In an attempt to shift the awkward moment, I grin and say, "Don't worry about me. I'm confident in my ability to scream really loud if I get attacked."

He shakes his head and takes a deep breath, slowly giving in to my attempts to lighten things up.

"So tell me about your dad," I say.

The almost-smile flees from his face and he looks away from me. It wasn't an accident, bringing it up like I did. I don't know, I just get this strange feeling that he's hiding something. When he briefly mentioned back in Kansas about his dad dying, on the outside it didn't seem to faze him. But he's going all this way, by bus at that, to see his dad before he dies, so he must love him. I'm sorry, but you're never unfazed when someone you love is dead, or dying.

Sounds strange coming from me, who can't cry anymore.

"He's a good man," Andrew says, still looking in front of him. I get the feeling he's picturing his dad right now, that he doesn't actually see anything in front of him except for his memories.

He looks over at me and is smiling now, but it's not a smile trying to cover up any pain, more so one washed with a good memory.

"Instead of taking me to a baseball game, my dad took me to a boxing match."

"Oh?" I feel my smile light up. "Do tell?"

He looks back out ahead, but the warmth in his face never leaves him in this moment. "Dad wanted us to be fighters—" He glances over. "Not boxers or *actual* fighters, though he probably wouldn't have minded that so much, either. But I mean fighters in general, you know, in life. Metaphorically."

I nod to let him know that I understand.

"I sat ringside, eight years old, mesmerized by these two men beating each other and the whole time I could hear my dad talking over the crowd next to me: *'They fear nothing, son,'* he said. *'And all of their moves are calculated. They move one way and it either works, or it doesn't, but they learn something from every move, every decision.'*

Andrew catches my eye briefly and his smile dissolves, leaving his expression standard. "He told me that a real fighter never cries, never lets the weight of any blow bring him down. Except that final blow, the inevitable one, but even then they always go out like men."

I'm no longer smiling, either. I can't tell exactly what's going on in Andrew's head right now, but we share the same sober mood. I want to ask him if he's OK, because it's obvious that he's not, but the timing doesn't feel right. It feels weird because I don't know him well enough to be digging around inside of his emotions.

I say nothing.

"You must think I'm a dick," he says.

I blink, surprised. "No," I answer. "Why do you say that?"

He backs off immediately and downplays the seriousness of his own question, letting that devastating smile slip back to the surface again.

"I'm going to see him before he kicks the bucket," he says, and his choice of words shocks me a little, "because that's what we do, right? It's a customary thing, kind of like saying 'bless you' when someone sneezes, or asking someone how their weekend was when really you don't give a shit."

*Damn, where is all of this coming from?*

"You have to live in the now," he says and I'm quietly stunned. "Don't you think so?" His head falls to the side and he's looking at me again.

It takes me a moment to get my head together, but even then I'm not sure about what to say.

"Living in the now," I say, quoting him, yet at the same time thinking of my own belief of *loving* in the now. "I guess you're right." But I still wonder exactly what his take on the belief is.

I straighten my back against the seat and raise my head a little to look over at him more closely. It's like suddenly I have this great desire to know all about his belief. To know everything about *him*.

"What is living in the now to you?" I ask.

I notice one of his eyebrows twitch for a second and his expression shifts, surprised at the seriousness of my question, or the level of my interest. Maybe both.

He straightens his back and raises his head, too.

"Just that dwelling and planning is bullshit," he says. "You dwell on the past, you can't move forward. Spend too much time planning for the future and you just push yourself backwards, or you stay stagnant in the same place all your life." His eyes lock on mine. "Live in the moment," he says as if making a serious point, "where everything is just right, take your time and limit your bad memories and you'll get wherever it is you're going a lot faster and with less bumps in the road along the way."

The silence between us is just two minds thinking about what he just said. I wonder if his thoughts are the same as mine. I also wonder, more than I want to admit, why so many of his thoughts already make me feel like I'm staring into a mirror when I look at him.

The bus glides heavily over the freeway, always loud and rarely soft. But after so long, it's easy to forget how unpleasant a bus ride is compared to the luxury of a car. And when you're thinking more about the positive aspects of a bus ride, instead of the negative, it's easy to forget that there's anything negative about it at all. There is a guy sitting next to me with beautiful green eyes and a beautiful sculpted face and a beautiful way of thinking. There's no such thing as a bad bus ride when you're in the company of something beautiful.

I shouldn't be here...

# Andrew

# NINE

*I* can't believe she brought up my dad. Not that I'm pissed about it, but I'm surprised that she seemed to really want to know. That she even remembered. She didn't dive into questions about what I do for a living to calculate how much money I might make, or giggle and blush and look all stupid while reaching out to touch my tattoos, using them as an excuse to touch *me*. Huge fucking turn-off. I mean yeah, it's a turn-on when you're just looking to get laid—makes it easier—but for some reason, I couldn't be happier that Camryn didn't do it.

Who the hell *is* this girl?

And why am I even thinking about this stuff?

She falls asleep before me with her head propped against the bus window. I resist the urge to watch her, noticing how soft and innocent she looks, which makes me that much more primal, more protective.

The pervert seems to have stopped watching her when he saw us sitting together inside the last terminal. In the eyes of men, he probably sees her as my 'territory' now, my property. And that's good thing because it means he'll leave her alone as long as I'm around. The truth is though, we'll only be together until Wyoming and this worries the fuck out of me. I hope the man changes buses before

Camryn and I have to part ways. Two more rest stops between here and Denver—I hope like hell Denver is his last stop and if not, I'll be watching him the rest of the way to Wyoming.

He's not going to Idaho. I'll kill the son of a bitch first.

I gaze through the dark and stillness of the bus. The man is asleep, his head pressed back against the aisle seat. A woman sits beside him next to the window, but she's way too old to catch this guy's eye. He likes them young, probably *really* young. It makes me fucking sick to think of what he may have already done to some other young girl.

Despite the bus generally being loud, the whistling of the wind pushing against the metal, the fast crushing sound of rubber moving swiftly over the road, the large engine progressively humming as it compels the heap of metal across the freeway, it's still quiet. It's almost peaceful. As peaceful as a bus ride can be.

I finger my earbuds in and turn on the power on my MP3 player, setting it to shuffle. What will it be? What will it be? I always let the first song set the mood. I have over three hundred songs on this thing. Three hundred different mood-setters. I think my MP3 player is biased though because the first song is almost always between Kansas' *Dust in the Wind*, Zeppelin's *Going to California* or something by The Eagles.

I wait for it, not looking down at the information on the playlist as if it's some kind of guessing game and I don't want to cheat. Ah, good choice. Aerosmith's *Dream On*. I lean my head back against the seat and shut my eyes, not realizing until after I'm in the middle of doing it that my finger is gently pressing the volume down. Because I don't want to wake Camryn up.

I open my eyes and look over at her, how she clutches that bag of hers so tightly that she must still be completely conscious of it even in a deep sleep. I wonder about what might be inside, if there's anything in it that could tell me more about her. If there's anything in it that can tell me the *truth* about her.

But it doesn't matter. I won't know her after Wyoming and she'll probably never even remember my name. But I know it's better that way. I have too much baggage and even as a friend, she doesn't need any of it in her lap. I wouldn't wish that on anyone.

The low, melodious droning of Steven Tyler's voice lulls me to partial-sleep. Except when he's screaming that high-pitched scream, where I wait for him to let it all out and then I drift off the rest of the way.

———

"Dude, seriously," I hear a voice say.

Something is pressing against my shoulder. I wake up to find Camryn pushing me off of her with her little arms. It's actually kind of funny, that awry look on her morning face and how no matter how hard she pushes, the weight of my body is too heavy to move me completely.

"Sorry," I say, still trying to wake up. I lift up disoriented and feel the back of my neck as stiff as wood. I really didn't mean to end up with my head pressed against her arm, but I'm not as mortified about it as she's pretending to be. At least I'm pretty sure she's pretending. She's trying really hard not to break a smile.

Let me help her a little with that.

I grin over at her.

"You think it's funny?" she says, her mouth partly hanging open and her eyebrows rumpled in her cute little forehead.

"Yeah, actually I do think it's funny." My grin gets bigger and finally that smile of hers breaks softly in her face. "But I am sorry. Really." And I mean it.

She narrows one eye and looks at me sideways, scrutinizing my sincerity, which is also kind of cute.

I look away and reach my arms above my head to stretch and that makes me need to yawn.

"Gross!" she says and that word doesn't surprise me at all. "Your breath smells like *ass*."

A single voluble laugh comes out through my words: "Damn, girl, how would you know what ass smells like anyway?"

That shuts her up. I laugh again and rummage through my bag after dropping my MP3 player inside of it. I pop the cap on my toothpaste and squirt a dab on the end of my tongue, move it around inside my mouth real good and then swallow. Of course, Camryn's watching me do all of this with a look of revulsion, but that's what I was shooting for.

The rest of the bus seems to have woken up before me. I'm surprised I slept this long and without waking up at least three times to find another comfortable position, which always manages to elude me.

My watch says that it's 9:02 a.m.

"Where are we anyway?" I ask, gazing out the large window next to Camryn, searching for any freeway signs.

"About four hours away from Denver," she answers. "Driver just announced another rest stop in ten minutes."

"Good," I say, stretching one leg out into the aisle, "I need to walk around. I'm stiff as hell."

I catch her grinning, but she turns to face the window. Stiff as hell. OK, so she also has a dirty mind. I just laugh thinking about it.

The next rest stop isn't too much different from the last several, with a series of gas stations on either side of the freeway and two fast food restaurants. I can't believe this girl has me actually debating whether or not to head inside one like I normally would without a thought otherwise. I just can't really tell if it's because I want to prove to her that I can choose to eat better stuff if given the choice, or because I know she's going to yell at me.

Wait a damn second. Who's the one in control of the situation here?

Clearly *she* is. Goddammit.

We file out of the bus, Camryn in front of me, and after walking around the front of the bus she stops and turns at the waist, crossing her arms and looking up at me, pursing her lips.

"Well, if you're so smart," I say, sounding sort of third grade and I admit it, "then see if you can find something healthy to eat— that doesn't taste like rubber dipped in shit—in one of *these* places."

A grin tugs one corner of her mouth.

"You're on," she accepts the challenge.

I follow her into the gigantic convenience store and she makes her way first to the drink coolers. Like that blonde chick on that game show (I don't know which because I don't watch game shows, but everybody knows about that blonde chick) Camryn waves her hands in front of the cooler doors, as if revealing the world of fruit juices and bottled water to me for the first time.

"We start off with a variety of juice, as you can see," she says in her proper showcase voice. "Any of this is better than soda. Take your pick."

"I hate juice."

"Don't be a baby. There's plenty to choose from. I'm sure you can find *something* you can stomach."

She moves back two steps to let me see the dozens of flavored bottled waters on display behind the next door.

"And there's water," she says, "but I just don't see someone like you sipping on a fancy bottle of water."

"No, that's too douchy." Really, I have no issue with drinking bottled water, but I like this game we're playing.

She smiles, but tries to keep a straight face.

I wrinkle my nose at her, purse my lips and look back and forth between her and the juice cooler.

I sigh heavily and step up closer, scanning over the different brands and flavors and mixed flavors and I wonder why there's so much with strawberry or kiwi, or strawberry *and* kiwi in it. I hate both.

Finally, I open one glass door and settle on plain OJ.

She sort of winces.

"*What?*" I ask, still holding the door open.

"Orange juice isn't so good to wash stuff down with."

I let out a spat of air and just look at her, unblinking.

"I pick something out and you tell me it's not good enough." I want to laugh, but I'm trying to lay a guilt trip on her here.

And I think it's working.

She frowns. "Well, it's just… well that's more of grab-n-go vitamin C boost, really. It just makes you thirstier."

She actually looks as though she's worried that she offended me and this strikes me in the strangest way. I let myself smile just to see her smile again.

She grins at me like the Devil.

Oh, she's *good* …

# Camryn

# TEN

*D*enver finally flies by and we're drawing closer to Andrew's final stop in Wyoming. I can't lie and say it doesn't bother me. Andrew was right in saying that it's dangerous for me to be traveling alone. I'm just trying to understand why that fact didn't faze me much *before* I met him. Maybe I just feel safer with him as my company because he does look like he can bust a few jaws without breaking a sweat. Damn, maybe I shouldn't have ever talked to him in the first place; definitely shouldn't have let him sit next to me because now I'm sort of used to him. Once we're in Wyoming and we go our separate ways, I'll be back to staring out the window watching the world fly by and not knowing where in it I'm going next.

"So, do you have a girlfriend?" I ask just to spark up conversation so I won't think about being alone again in a few hours.

Andrew's dimples appear. "Why do you want to know?"

I roll my eyes.

"Don't flatter yourself; just a question. If you don't—"

"No," he answers, "I'm happily single."

He just looks at me, smiling, waiting, and it takes me a second to understand what he's waiting for.

I point at myself nervously, wishing I had come up with a less personal topic. "Me? No, not anymore." Feeling more confident now, I add, "I'm happily single as well and want to *stay* that way. For about...forever." I should've just left it at 'happily single' instead of rambling my way right out of the confident zone and making myself look obvious.

Of course, Andrew notices right away. I get the feeling he's the type that never misses someone else's foot-in-your-mouth moment. He thrives on them.

"I'll keep that in mind," he says, grinning.

Thankfully he doesn't probe.

He rests his head back against the seat and absently taps his thumbs and pinky fingers against his jeans for a moment. Secretly, I glimpse his muscular, tanned arms and try to see once and for all what the tattoos are of on his arms, but as usual they're mostly hidden by the sleeves of his t-shirt. The one on the right side I saw a little more of earlier when he stretched down to tie his boot. I think it's a tree of some sort. The arm facing me now, I can't really tell but whatever it is, it has feathers. All of the tattoos I've seen so far are colorless.

"Curious?" he says and I flinch. I didn't think he saw me checking them out.

"I guess."

*Yes, I'm* very *curious, actually.*

Andrew lifts away from the seat and pulls the sleeve of his left arm over the tattoo, revealing a phoenix with a long, flowing beautiful feathered tail that ends a couple of inches past where his sleeve ends. But the rest of its feathered body is skeletal, giving it a more 'manly' appearance.

"That's pretty awesome."

"Thanks. I've had this one about a year," he says, pulling the sleeve back down. "And this one," he says, turning at the waist and pulling up the other sleeve (first, I notice the obvious outline of his abs underneath his shirt), "is my gnarly, Sleepy-Hollow-lookin' tree—I have a thing for wicked trees—and if you'll look real close..." I peer closer where his finger points within the tree trunk, "is my 1969 Chevy Camaro. My dad's car, really, but since he's dying I guess I have to keep it." He looks out in front of him.

There it is, that tiny glimmer of pain that he kept hidden before when talking about his father. He's hurting a lot more than he's letting on and it sort of breaks my heart. I can't imagine my mom or dad being on their deathbed and I'm sitting on Greyhound bus on my way to see them for the last time. My eyes scan his face from the side and I really want to say something to comfort him, but I don't think I can. I don't feel like it's my place for some reason; at least not to bring it up.

"I've got a couple of others," he goes on, looking back over at me with the back of his head lying against the seat again. "A small one here," he turns over his right wrist to show me a simple black star in the center right below the base of his hand; I'm surprised I didn't notice that one sooner. "And a larger one down the left side of my ribs."

"What is it, the one on your side? How big is it?"

His bright green eyes sparkle as he smiles warmly, tilting his head over to see me. "It's pretty damn big," I see his hands move as if he's going to lift his shirt to show me, but he decides against it. "It's just a woman. Nothing worth getting naked on a bus for."

Now I want to see what it looks like more than ever, just because he doesn't want me to see it.

"A woman you know?" I ask. I keep looking to and from his side, thinking maybe he'll change his mind and lift his shirt, but he never does.

He shakes his head. "Nah, it's nothing like that. It's of Eurydice." He waves his hand out in front of him as if to dismiss any further explanation.

The name sounds like something ancient, maybe Greek, and it's vaguely familiar, but I can't place it.

I nod. "Did it hurt?"

He smiles.

"A little. Well actually it hurts the most on the ribs, so yeah it hurt."

"Did you cry?" I grin.

He laughs lightly.

"No, I didn't cry, but hell, I might've if I decided to get it even a fraction bigger than it is. In total, it took about sixteen hours."

I blink back, stunned. "Wow, you sat there for sixteen hours?"

For such a detailed conversation about this tat, it makes me wonder why he won't actually show it. Maybe it doesn't look all that great and the tattoo artist screwed it up, or something.

"Not all at once," he says, "we did it over a few days' time—I'd ask if *you* have any tattoos, but something tells me that you don't." He smiles, knowingly.

"And you'd be right," I say, blushing a little. "Not that I've never thought about getting one." I hold up my wrist and wrap my thumb and middle finger around it. "Thought about getting something here, like script that says 'freedom' or something in Latin— obviously, I didn't think about it much." Smiling, I breathe out a little embarrassed spat of air. Me talking about tattoos with a guy who obviously knows more about them than I ever could is a bit intimidating.

When I go to set my wrist back down on the armrest, Andrew's fingers curl around it. It stuns me for a brief second, even sends a strange chill through my body, but it quickly fades when he starts talking so casually.

"A tattoo on the wrist for a girl can be very graceful and feminine." He traces the tip of his finger around the inside of my wrist to indicate where it should go. I shiver a tiny bit. "Something in Latin, very subtle, just about here would look nice." Then he lets go gently and I let my arm rest back on the armrest.

"I expected you to say 'no way' about ever getting one yourself," he laughs and brings up his leg, resting it at the ankle on his knee. He interlaces his fingers and slides back further against the seat to get more comfortable.

It's getting dark fast; the sun is barely peeking over the landscape now, leaving everything bathed in fading orange and pink and purple.

"Guess I'm not a predictable person." I smile over at him.

"No, I guess you're not," he says smiling back and then looking thoughtfully in front of him.

———

Andrew wakes me up the next day sometime after 2:00 p.m. at the bus station in Cheyenne, Wyoming. I feel his fingers poking me in the ribs. "We're here," he says and finally I open my eyes and lift my head from the window.

My breath I know smells God awful because it tastes dry and funky so I look away from him when I yawn.

The bus's brakes squeal to a stop at the terminal and like always, the passengers stir themselves out of their seats and start grabbing their carry-on bags from the overhead compartment. I just sit here, feeling a little panicked and I glance carefully over at Andrew. I literally feel like I'm going to have a mini-anxiety attack. I mean, I knew this time would come, that Andrew would leave and I would be alone again, but I didn't expect to feel like a scared little girl sent out in the world to fend for herself with no one to look after her.

*Shit! Shit! Shit!*

I can't even believe I let myself get comfortable with him and as a result I'm no longer able to make fear my bitch.

I fear being alone.

"Comin'?" he asks looking down at me from the center aisle and holding out his hand. He smiles at me gently, setting aside any smartass remarks or making jokes at my expense because, after all, it is the last time we will ever see each other. It's not like we're in love or something crazy like that, but something weird happens when you spend several days with a stranger on a bus, getting to know them and enjoying their company. And when they're not so different from you and you share that bond without actually telling one another why you're hurting, that just makes the inevitable departure more difficult.

But I can't let him know this. It's stupid. I put myself in this situation and I intend to go through with it. No matter where in the world it eventually leads me.

I smile back up at him and place my hand into his. And all the way down the aisle as he walks in front of me, he keeps my fingers clasped carefully within his hand from behind. And I find a sense of warmth in his touch, clinging onto it mentally for as long as I can so that maybe I can be more confident when I'm alone again.

"Well, Camryn…" he looks at me as if fishing for my last name.

"Bennett." I smile and cave to my own rule.

"Well, Camryn *Bennett*, it was a pleasure to meet you on the road to nowhere." He adjusts his bag strap on his shoulder and then slides his hands down inside the pockets of his jeans. The muscles in his arms harden. "I hope you find what you're looking for."

I try to smile and I do, but I know it looks like something in-between a smile and a frown.

I adjust the strap from my purse on one shoulder and my sling bag on the other and then just let my arms hang limply at my sides.

"It was nice meeting you, too, Andrew Parrish," I say, though I don't want to say it. I want him to ride with me just a little farther. "Do me a favor if you don't mind."

I've piqued his curiosity and he cocks his chin a little to one side. "All right. What kind of favor? Is it sexual?" His dimples deepen as his devilishly handsome lips start to curve.

I laugh a little and look down with a blush hot on my face, but then I let the moment fade because this really isn't a lighthearted kind of request. Instead, I soften my expression and look upon him with true sympathy.

"If your dad doesn't make it," I begin and his expression falls, "let yourself cry, OK? One of the worst feelings in the world is being unable to cry and eventually it . . . starts to make things darker."

He stares at me for a long, silent moment and then he nods, allowing a tiny thankful smile to appear only in the depths of his eyes. I reach out my hand to shake his goodbye and he does the same, but he holds it there for a second longer than normal and then pulls me into a hug. I hug him back tight, wishing I could just blurt out to him that I'm scared of him leaving me alone, but I know I can't.

*Suck it up, Camryn!*

He pulls away, nods at me one last time with that smile I grew so quickly to like and then he walks away and out of the terminal. I stand here for what feels like forever, unable to move my legs. I watch him get into a cab and I keep watching until the cab drives away and out of sight.

I'm alone again. Over a thousand miles away from home. No direction, no purpose, no goals other than to find myself on this journey I never imagined I could bring myself to begin. And I'm scared. But I have to do this. I have to because I need this time alone, away from everything back home which brought me here in the first place.

Finally, I take control again and walk away from the tall glass windows to find a seat. There's a four hour layover before I get on the next bus into Idaho, so I need to find something to make use of my time.

I hit the vending machines first.

Sliding my change into the slot I start to hit E4 to get the fiber bar—the closest thing to healthy in the whole machine—but then my finger makes a sharp U-turn to hit D4 instead and a fattening, disgusting, sugary chocolate candy bar falls from the spiral and into the bottom. Happily taking out my junk food, I move over to the soda machine, passing up the one before it which has bottles of water and juice, and I get a teeth-decaying, stomach bubbling, carbonated drink instead.

Andrew would be so proud.

*Dammit! Stop thinking about Andrew!*

I take my junk food and find an empty seat and wait out the day.

A four hour delay turns into a six hour delay. They announced it over the intercom, something about my particular bus being late due to mechanical failure. A chorus of disappointed moans rises throughout the terminal.

Great. Just great. I'm stuck in a bus station in the middle of nowhere and I could very well end up here all night, trying to sleep curled up in the fetal position on this hard plastic chair that's not even comfortable for sitting.

Or, I could just go ahead and buy another bus ticket somewhere else.

*That's it! Problem solved!*

I just wish I would've thought of this sooner and spared myself the six hours I've already wasted here. It's like I tricked my brain somehow into thinking I actually had to ride all the way to frickin' Idaho just because I already paid for the ticket.

I grab my bag and purse from the seat next to me and shoulder them as I march my way across the terminal, past a boatload of disgruntled passengers who clearly don't have the option that I do, and make my way to the ticket counter.

"We're closing the counter down ma'am," the employee says on the other side.

"Wait, *please*," I say, throwing my arms across the counter exasperatedly, "I just need to get another ticket somewhere else. Please, you'll be doing me a huge favor!"

The wiry-haired old woman wrinkles her nose at me and appears to chew on the inside of her cheek. She sighs and then taps a few keys on her computer keyboard.

"Oh thank you!" I say. "You're awesome! Thank you!"

She rolls her eyes.

I swing my purse around and toss it on the counter and search quickly through it to find my little zipper wallet.

"Where are you traveling?" she asks.

Oh great, there's that million dollar question again. I look around the counter for any other 'signs' like that baked potato back at the North Carolina terminal, but I don't see anything obvious.

The old lady is starting to get even more agitated with me and it makes me more anxious to hurry and figure this out.

"Miss?" she says with a heavy sigh. She glances at the clock on the wall. "I clocked out fifteen minutes ago. I'd really like to get home to my dinner."

"Yeah, I'm so sorry." I fumble my credit card out of my wallet and hand it to her. "Texas," I say first as a test, but then afterwards I realize it felt right on my tongue. "Yeah, anywhere in Texas would be great."

The old lady raises an ungroomed reddish brow. "You don't know where you're going?"

I nod furiously. "Uh, yeah, I just mean that I'll take any bus going to Texas that's next in line." I smile across at her hoping she's buying this load of crap and doesn't feel the need to have my driver's license checked out for anything suspicious. "I've already been here for six hours. I hope you understand."

She looks right at me for a long, unnerving moment and then takes my credit card from between my fingers and starts tapping her keyboard again.

"Next bus leaving for Texas is in an hour."

"Great! I'll take that one!" I say before she even has a chance to tell me whereabouts in Texas exactly.

It doesn't matter. And she's in such a hurry to get home that she's doesn't seem to think it matters, either. As long as I don't care, she surely doesn't.

I get my brand new bus ticket and shove it inside my purse next to the old one as the counter closes behind me at 9:05 p.m. and I feel a small sense of relief wash over me. Walking back towards my seat, I fish around in my purse for my phone, pulling it out to check to see if I missed any calls or text messages. My mom called twice and left a voicemail both times, but still no call back from Natalie.

"Baby, where are you?" my mom asks on the other end when I call her back. "I tried calling Natalie to see if you were staying with her but can't seem to catch her. Are you OK?"

"Yeah, Mom, I'm fine." I'm pacing in front of my chair with my phone pressed to my right ear. "I decided to take a trip up to see my friend Anna in Virginia. I'll be here for a little while hanging out with her, but I'm OK."

"But Camryn, what about your new job?" She sounds disappointed, especially since it was her friend who gave me the chance and hired me. "Maggie said you worked for a week and then didn't show up or call or anything."

"I know, Mom, and I'm really sorry, but it just wasn't for me."

"Well, the least you could've done was be courteous and tell her—give her a two-weeks-notice—*something*, Camryn."

I feel awful about how I handled that and normally would not have done something so inconsiderate, but the situation unfortunately warranted it.

"You're right," I say, "and when I get back I'll call Mrs. Phillips personally and apologize to her."

"But it's not like you," she says and I'm getting worried she's steering too close to the reasons why I really left and all that which I refuse to go into with her. "And to just up and leave to Virginia without calling me or leaving a note. Are you *sure* you're all right?"

"Yes, I'm fine. Stop worrying. Please. I'll call you again soon, but I gotta go now."

She doesn't want to and I can tell by how deeply she sighs on the phone, but she gives up.

"OK, well you be careful and I love you."

"I love you, too, Mom."

I check my phone one more time, hoping maybe Natalie sent

me a text message and I just didn't see it. I scroll back to several days, even though I know full well that if there were any unread text messages on my phone that there would be a little red circle on the icon indicating it.

I end up scrolling back down so far without realizing it that Ian's name pops up and my heart freezes inside my chest. I stop it right there and start to run my thumb over his name so that I can read the back-and-forth between us shortly before he died, but I can't.

I thrust the phone angrily back into my purse.

# ELEVEN

*N*ow I remember another reason I don't like soda: it makes me have to pee. The thought of being trapped on that bus with just a tiny matchbox restroom in the back forces me straight toward the facilities inside the terminal. I chuck the half-full soda in the trash on my way.

Passing up the first three stalls, because they're disgusting, I close myself up inside the fourth and hang my purse and bag on the hook mounted at the top of the blue door. I spread a good layer of toilet paper over the seat so I don't catch anything; do my business fast and now comes the strategic part. With one foot propped on the toilet seat to keep it from flushing on its own because of the sensor, I fumble the button on my jeans, reach out to get my bags from the hook and then open the door, all still with one foot propped awkwardly behind me.

And then I jump out fast right before the toilet flushes.

Blame it on Myth Busters; I was mortified for months after the episode on how the toilet really does spray invisible germs on you when it flushes.

The fluorescent lights in the restroom are duller than the ones in the waiting area. One flickers above me. There's two spiders burrowed behind webs tangled with dead bugs in the corner wall. It stinks in here. I step in front of a mirror and look for a dry spot on the counter to put my bags and then I wash my hands. Great, no paper towels. The only way I'm drying my hands is by that obnoxious blower hanging on the wall, which never really dries anything, but just spreads the water around. I start to wipe my hands on my jeans instead, but I hit the large silver button on the hand drier and it roars to life. I wince. I hate that sound.

As I'm pretending to dry my hands (because I know in the end, I'll be wiping them on my jeans anyway), a moving shadow behind me catches my eye in the mirrors. I turn around and at the same time the hand drier turns off, bathing the room in silence again.

A man is standing at the restroom entrance, looking at me.

My heart reacts and my throat goes dry. "This is the ladies restroom."

I glance at my bags on the counter. Do I have a weapon? Yeah, I did at least pack a knife, though little good it'll do me when it's several feet away inside a zipped-up bag.

"Sorry, I thought this was the men's room."

*Good, apology accepted, now please get the hell out of here.*

The man, wearing dirty, old running shoes and faded jeans with paint stains on the legs, just stands there. This isn't good. If it really was an accident that he came in here, surely he'd look more embarrassed and would've already turned tail and left.

I march over to my bags on the counter and I notice from the corner of my eye that he takes a few more steps toward me.

"I . . . didn't mean to scare you," he says.

I throw open my bag and dig around inside of it for my knife, while at the same time trying to keep my eyes on him.

"I've seen you on the bus," he says and he's still drawing closer. "My name is Robert."

I swing my head around to face him. "Look, you're not supposed to be in here. It's not exactly the place for conversation and I suggest you leave. Now." Finally, I feel the contours of the knife and grip it in my hand, keeping my hand hidden inside the bag. My finger presses down on the thin metal piece to set the blade free from the handle. I hear it click open and lock in place.

The man stops about six feet from me and smiles. His black hair is oily and slicked back. Yes, I remember him now; he's been on every bus change with me since Tennessee.

*Oh my God, has he been watching me all this time?*

I pull the knife out of the bag and hold it up clutched in my fist, ready to use it and letting him know that I will not hesitate.

He just smiles. That scares me, too.

My heart is banging against my ribs.

"Get the hell away from me," I say, gritting my teeth. "I swear to God I will fucking gut you like a pig."

"I'm not going to hurt you," he says, still smiling eerily. "I'll pay you—a lot—just if you suck my dick. It's all I want. You'll leave the bathroom about five hundred dollars richer and I'll get this image out of my head. We'll *both* get something out of it."

I start to scream at the top of my lungs when suddenly another dark shadow catches my eye. Andrew barrels into the man, hurling his body over a two foot space and onto the long counter. His back crashes into one of the mirrors. The glass shatters and shards rain down all over the place. I jump back and shriek, pressing my back against the hand drier, waking it up again. My knife fell from my hand at some point. I see it on the floor, but I'm too afraid to move right now to pick it up.

Blood drips off what's left of the mirror when Andrew pulls the man off the counter by the front of his shirt. He pulls back his other hand and buries his fist in the man's face. I hear a nauseating *crunch!* and blood pours from his nose. Again and again, Andrew rains blows down on his head, one bloody hit after another until the man can't hold his head up straight and it starts to bob and sway drunkenly on his shoulders. But Andrew goes in for more, digging both of his hands into the man's shoulders and lifting his feet from the floor, bashing his back twice against the tile wall.

He knocks him out cold.

Andrew lets go and the man's body falls against the floor. I hear his head thump against the tile. Andrew just stands there hovering over him, maybe waiting to see if he's going to get up, but there's something disturbingly untamed in his posture and his enraged expression as he stares down at the unconscious man.

I can hardly breathe but I manage to say, "Andrew? Are you all right?"

He snaps out of it and jerks his head around to face me. "*What?*" He shakes his head and his eyes narrow under lines of disbelief. He marches over. "Am *I* all right? What kind of question is that?" He fastens his hands around my upper arms and stares deeply into my eyes. "Are *you* all right?"

I try to look away because the intensity in his eyes is overpowering, but his head follows mine and he shakes me once to force me to look at him.

"Yeah . . . I'm fine," I finally say, "thanks to you."

Andrew pulls me into his rock hard chest and wraps his arms around my back, practically squeezing the life out of me.

"We should call the cops," he says, pulling away.

I nod and he takes me by the hand and pulls me with him out of the restroom and down the gloomy gray hallway.

By the time the cops get here, the man has disappeared.

Andrew and I agree that he probably slipped out right after we left. He must've gone out the back while Andrew was on the phone. Andrew and I give the cops a description of the man and our statements. The cops commend Andrew—sort of vacantly—for stepping in, but he really just seems to want to stop talking to them altogether.

My new bus to Texas left ten minutes ago and so once again I'm stuck in Wyoming.

"I thought you were going to Idaho?" Andrew says.

I had let it slip that my 'bus to Texas' just left without me.

I bite gently on the inside of my bottom lip and cross one leg over the other. We're sitting near the front doors inside the bus station, watching passengers come and go from the tall windows.

"Well, now I'm going to Texas," is all I say, even though I know I'm 'caught' and have a feeling I'll be spilling some of the truth very soon. "I thought you left in the cab?" I say, trying to divert the subject.

"I did," he says, "but don't turn this around on me, Camryn. Why aren't you going to Idaho anymore?"

I sigh. I know he won't stop asking until he gets it out of me so I throw in the towel.

"I don't really have a sister in Idaho," I admit. "I'm just traveling. Nothing more to it, really."

I hear him let out an irritated sigh next to me.

"There's always something more to it—are you a runaway?"

I look over at him finally. "No, I'm not a runaway, at least not in the underage illegal sense."

"Well then in what sense?"

I shrug.

"I just had to get away from home for a while."

"So, you ran away from home?"

I let out a sharp breath and look right into his intense green eyes staring right through me. "I didn't *run* away, I just had to *get* away."

"So you jumped on a bus alone?"

"Yes." I'm getting irritated at the drilling.

"You're gonna have to give me more than that," he says, relentless.

"Look, I'm more appreciative than you know for what you did. I *really* am. But I don't think you saving me gives you the right to know my business."

A small wave of insult subtly stuns his features.

I feel bad instantly, but it's the truth: I'm not obligated to tell him anything.

He gives up and looks out ahead, propping an ankle on the other knee.

"I saw that piece of shit eyeing you since I got on the bus in Kansas," he reveals and has all of my attention. "You didn't see it, but I did so I started watching *him*." He still hasn't looked over at me again, but I'm staring right at him from the side as he explains. "I saw him get into a cab and leave here before I did and only then did I feel it was OK to leave you here by yourself. But on the way to the hospital, I just had this bad feeling. I told the cab driver to drop me off at a restaurant instead, and I ate. Still couldn't get it out of my head though."

"Wait," I say, interrupting him, "you didn't go to the hospital?"

He looks at me.

"No, I knew if I went that…" he turns his eyes away again, "…I wouldn't be enough in my right mind to pay attention to the bad feeling I was having if I was staring down at my dying father."

I understand and I don't say anything else.

"So, I went to my dad's house and got his car, drove around for a while and when I couldn't take it anymore, I came back here. I parked across the street and waited for a while and sure enough, a cab pulled in and dropped the guy back off."

"Why didn't you come inside instead of waiting in the car?"

He looks down in thought.

"I just didn't want to freak you out."

"How would that freak me out?" I realize I'm smiling a little.

Andrew looks right at me and I see that playful, smartass look start to crawl back into his features again.

He holds his hands open, palms up. "Ummm, strange guy you met on the bus coming back hours later to sit next to you?" His eyebrows crinkle in his forehead. "That's almost as creepy as suck-my-dick-for-$500-guy, don't you think?"

I laugh. "No, I don't think it's *anything* like that."

He tries to bury his smile, but relents.

"What are you going to do, Camryn?" His face is serious again and my smile fades.

I shake my head. "I don't know; I guess I'm going to wait here until the next bus to Texas comes and then I'm on my way to Texas."

"Why Texas?"

"Why not?"

"Seriously?"

I slap my hands down against my thighs. "Because I'm not going home yet!"

He's unfazed by my shouting at him.

"Why don't you want to go home yet?" he asks calm and intently. "Might as well spill your fucking guts because I'm not leaving you alone in this bus station, especially not after what happened."

I cross my arms tight over my chest and stare out in front of me. "Well then I guess you'll be sitting here for a long time until I get on the bus."

"No. That *includes* not letting you get on another bus alone to go anywhere. Texas. Idafuckingho. Wherever. It's dangerous and I can tell you're an intelligent girl—so here's what we're going to do…"

I blink a few times, stunned by his sudden authoritarian arrogance. He goes on:

"I'll wait here with you until morning. That'll give you enough time to decide whether you're going to let me pay for your plane ticket back home, or if you want to call someone to fly here to get you. It's your choice."

I look at him like he's crazy.

His eyes say back at me: Yeah, I'm dead serious.

"I'm not going back to North Carolina."

Andrew shoots up from the chair and stands in front of me. "OK, then I'm going with you."

I blink, looking up at his intense eyes; his perfectly sculpted cheekbones seem more pronounced from this angle making his gaze even fiercer. A shiver moves through my stomach.

"That's insane," I laugh it off, but I know he's serious and then I say with more severity, "What about your dad?"

His teeth grind together and the intensity in his eyes becomes more forlorn.

He starts to look away but a thought pulls him back. "Then come with me."

*What? No way…*

He looks hopeful rather than determined now. He sits back down next to me on the plastic blue seat.

"We'll stay right here until morning," he goes on, "because surely you wouldn't leave with some strange guy from a bus station after dark? *Right?*"

He turns his chin away from me, looking at me in a questioning sidelong glance.

"No, I wouldn't," I say, even though I really do feel like I can trust him—he saved me from being raped, for God's sake! And nothing about him is giving me the same fears I had when Damon practically did the same thing. No, Damon had something darker in his eyes when he looked at me that night on the roof. All I see in Andrew's eyes is concern.

But I still won't leave with him like this.

"Good answer," he says, apparently glad I'm as 'intelligent' as he hoped I was.

"We'll wait until daylight and just to give you more peace of mind I'll have a cab drive us straight to the hospital instead of expecting you to get in my car."

I nod, glad he thought of that. I won't say that I hadn't exactly sorted that part out yet. I mean, I already trust him enough, but it's like he wants to be sure that I *don't*, like he's teaching me a lesson in a quiet, roundabout way.

I'm ashamed to admit that he has to 'teach me' any of this at all.

"And then from the hospital, we'll catch a cab back here and wherever you want to go, I'll go with you."

He holds out his hand to shake on it. "Deal?"

I think about it a moment, confused, yet at the same time utterly fascinated by him. I nod reluctantly at first and then again with more assurance.

"It's a deal," I say and place my hand into his.

Honestly, I'm not sure I agree with it entirely. Why would he even do that? Doesn't he have a life elsewhere? Surely he's not as miserable with home as I am.

*This is crazy! Who is this guy?*

We sit together for several hours right there in the station and talk about nothing important, yet I love every second of our conversations. About how I gave in and drank a soda and it was the soda's fault I ended up in the restroom with the man—he laughs it off and tells me I just have a weak bladder. We quietly gossip about the passengers that come and go; the weird-looking ones and those who look dead, as if they've been riding a bus for the past week and haven't been able to sleep. And we talk about classic rock some more, but the argument remains as much a stalemate as it was when we first discussed it on the bus.

He practically died when I said that I'd listen to Pink over The Rolling Stones, any day. I mean, I literally think I wounded him. He put his big hand over his heart and threw back his head in devastation and everything. It was very dramatic. And funny. I tried not to laugh, but it was hard not to when his hardened, over exaggerated face was practically smiling, too.

And just as we went to leave after the sun rose, I stopped to look at him for a moment. A slight breeze brushed through his stylish brown hair. He cocked his head to the side, smiling at me and waving me into the cab. "You're still coming, right?"

I smiled warmly back at him and nodded. "Of course." And I took his hand and slid into the backseat with him.

What I had been thinking about when I looked at him was that I realized I haven't smiled or laughed this much since before Ian died. Not even Natalie could get a genuine elated emotion out of me and she tried really hard. She went out of her way to help snap me out of my depression, but nothing she ever did came close to what Andrew has managed to do in such a short time and without even trying.

# Andrew

# TWELVE

*M*y throat closes up when we step foot inside the hospital, like a wall of blackness came out of nowhere and engulfed me. I stop for a second at the entrance and just stand here with my arms heavy at my sides. And then I feel Camryn's hand touch my wrist.

I look over at her. She's smiling so warmly that it melts me a little. Her blonde hair is pulled into a messy braid around to one side, lying freely over her right shoulder. A few strands that escaped the rubber band rest freely down the side of her face. I have this urge to reach up and brush them softly with my finger, but I don't. I can't be doing shit like that. I need to get rid of this attraction. But she's different from other girls and I think that's exactly why I'm having such a hard time with it. I don't need this right now.

"You'll be fine," she says.

Her hand falls away from my wrist when she sees that she has my attention. I smile faintly back at her.

We follow the hall to the elevator and ride up to the third floor. Every step of the way I feel like I should just turn around and leave this place. My father doesn't want me to show emotion when I go in there and right about now I'm about to explode with it.

Maybe I should go outside and punch a few trees and get it all out of my system before I go in there.

We stop at the waiting area where a few other people are all sitting around reading magazines.

"I'll wait here for you," Camryn says and I look right at her.

"Why don't you come with me?"

I really do want her to. I don't know why.

Camryn starts to shake her head no. "I-I can't go in there," she says, looking uncomfortable now. "Really, I . . . I just don't think it's appropriate."

I reach out and gently take her sling bag from her shoulder and put it on mine. It's light, but she's starting to look discomforted by it.

"It's fine," I say. "I *want* you to go with me."

*Why am I saying this?*

She looks down at the floor and then carefully gazes around at the rest of the room before her blue eyes fall on me again. "OK," she says with a subtle nod.

I feel my face break into a small smile and I instinctively take her by the hand. She doesn't pull away.

I'm comforted by her, needless to say, and I get the feeling she's happy to oblige. Surely she knows how hard something like this would be for anyone.

We walk hand in hand toward my father's room.

She squeezes once, looking over at me as if to give me more encouragement. And then I push open the hospital room door. A nurse looks up when we walk in.

"I'm Mr. Parrish's son."

She nods solemnly and goes back to adjusting the machines and tubes hooked up to my father. The room is a typical bland and sterile space with bright white walls and a tile floor so shiny the lights running along the ceiling panels blaze off of it. I hear a constant and steady beep coming from the heart rate monitor next to my father's bed.

I still haven't actually looked at my father. I realize I'm looking at everything in the room but him.

Camryn's fingers squeeze around mine.

"How is he doing?" I ask, but I know it's a stupid question. He's *dying*; *that's* how he's doing. I just can't get anything else out.

The nurse looks at me expressionless.

"He's in and out of consciousness, as you probably already know."

*No, I didn't know, actually.*

"And there hasn't been any change, good or bad." She adjusts an I.V. running from the top of his rugged hand.

Then she walks around the bed and picks up a clipboard from the side table and tucks it underneath her arm.

"Has anyone else been here?" I ask.

The nurse nods. "Family has been in and out for the past several days. Some left about an hour ago, but I expect they'll be back."

Probably Aidan, my older brother and his wife, Michelle. And my younger brother, Asher.

The nurse slips out of the room.

Camryn looks up at me, tightening her hand around mine. Her eyes smile carefully. "I'm going to sit over there and let you visit with your father, OK?"

I nod, though everything she said just kind of slipped through my head like a wispy memory. Her fingers slowly fall away from mine and she takes a seat against the wall on the empty vinyl chair. I suck in a deep breath and lick the dryness from my lips.

His face is swollen. Tubes are running from his nostrils, feeding him oxygen. I'm surprised he's not on life support yet, but this gives me a small sense of hope. Really small. I know he won't get better; that's pretty much already been established. What's left of his hair has been shaved off. They had talked about trying to perform surgery, but after my dad found out that it wasn't going to save him he, of course, complained:

"You're not cuttin' into my fuckin' head," he had said. "You want me to shell out thousands of dollars so you boys can have these cereal box doctors crack my damn skull open? *Dammit*, boy!" (He had been talking to Aidan specifically) "you are one nut shy of a man!"

My brothers and I were prepared to do whatever it took to save him, but he had gone behind our backs and signed some kind of 'stipulation' that when things got worse that no one would have the right to make these decisions for him.

My mom was who alerted the hospital of his wishes days before the surgery was to be performed and provided them with the legal papers. We were upset by it, but my mother is a smart and caring woman and none of us could ever be pissed at her for what she did.

I move closer and look the rest of him over. My hand sort of has a mind of its own and the next thing I know it's slithering up beside his and taking a hold of it. Even this feels odd. Like I shouldn't be doing it. If it were anyone else, I'd have no issue holding their hand. But this my dad and I feel like I'm doing something I shouldn't. I can just hear his voice inside my head: "You don't hold another man's hand, boy. What the hell is wrong with you?"

Suddenly, my dad's eyes crack open and instinctively I pull my hand away from his.

"That you, Andrew?"

I nod, gazing down at him.

"Where's Linda?"

"Who?"

"Linda," he says and his eyes can't decide if they want to stay open. "My wife, Linda. Where is she?"

I swallow hard and glance over at Camryn who is sitting so quietly, watching.

I turn back to my dad. "Dad, you and Linda divorced last year, remember?"

His pale green eyes are glazed over by moisture. Not tears. Just moisture. He looks dazed for a moment and smacks his lips together, moving his dry tongue around in his mouth.

"Do you want some water?" I ask and go to reach for the long lap table on wheels that had been moved away from the bed. A pale pink pitcher of water sits on it next to a thick plastic mug with a pop-on top with a straw poking up through the center.

My dad shakes his head no.

"Did'ja' fix Ms. Nina?" he asks.

I nod again. "Yeah, she looks great. New paint job and rims."

"Good, good," he says, nodding a little, too.

This feels awkward and I know it's written all over my face and my posture. I just don't know what to say or if I should try to force him to drink some water or if I should just sit down and wait for Aidan and Asher to get back. I'd rather them do this than me. I'm not good with this kind of thing.

"Who's that pretty thing?" he asks, looking toward the wall.

I wonder how he can even see Camryn all the way over there and then I notice he's looking at her through the tall mirror on the other side of him which reflects that portion of the room. Camryn freezes up a little, but that pretty smile of hers brightens her face. She raises her hand and waves at him through the mirror with her fingers.

Even through his swollen skin, I see a grin on my dad's lips. "Is that your Eurydice's?" he asks and my eyes freeze wide open. I hope Camryn didn't catch that, but I don't see how she couldn't. My dad weakly raises one hand and gestures toward Camryn.

She gets up and walks over to stand next to me. She smiles so warmly at him it even impresses me. She's a natural. I know she's nervous and probably feels more uncomfortable than she ever has standing in this room with this dying man who she doesn't even know, yet she doesn't break.

"Hi, Mr. Parrish," she says. "I'm Camryn Bennett, a friend of Andrew's."

His eyes move to me. I know that look; he's comparing her answer with the look on my face, trying to decipher her meaning of 'friend'.

And then suddenly my father does something I have never seen him do: he reaches out his hand . . . to me.

The gesture stuns me numb.

Only when I notice Camryn covertly glaring at me to acknowledge him, do I break free from the numbness and nervously take his hand. I hold it for a long, awkward moment and my father closes his eyes and drifts back to sleep. I move my hand from his when I feel his weak grip go completely slack.

The door opens and my brothers walk in, along with Aidan's wife, Michelle.

I step away from my father right on cue, taking Camryn with me and not realizing that I'm holding her hand again until Aidan's eyes move down to see our interlocked fingers.

"Glad you could make it," Aidan says, though with a bit of contempt in his voice, no doubt.

He's still pissed at me for not taking a plane and getting here sooner. He'll have to fucking get over it; we grieve in our own ways.

Regardless, he pulls me into a hug, gripping one hand between us and patting my back with the other.

"This is Camryn," I say, looking back at her.

She smiles up at them, having already found her way back to the empty chair against the wall.

"This is my older brother, Aidan and his wife, Michelle." I point gently at them. "And that's the runt, Asher."

"Dickhead," Asher says.

"I know," I say.

Aidan and Michelle take the other two seats next to a table and start distributing the burger and fries they just bought.

"The ol' man still hasn't come to," Aidan says, stuffing a few fries in his mouth. "I hate to say it, but I don't think he's going to."

Camryn looks right at me. We both spoke to my father just moments ago and I know she's waiting for me to give them the news.

"Probably not," I say and see Camryn's eyes wrinkle in confusion.

"How long are you staying?" Aidan asks.

"Not long."

"Why doesn't that surprise me?" He takes a bite of his burger.

"Don't start your shit with me, Aidan, I'm not in the mood for it and this isn't the fucking time or the place."

"Whatever," Aidan says, shaking his head and working his jaws around to chew his food. He dips a few fries in a mound of ketchup Michelle just made on a napkin in between them. "Do what you want, but be here for the funeral."

There is no emotion in his face. He just continues to eat.

My whole body goes rigid.

"Damn, Aidan," Asher says from behind me. "Can you please not do this right now? Seriously, bro, Andrew's right."

Asher has always been the mediator between Aidan and me.

And always the most level-headed. When it comes to me or Aidan, we think better with our fists. He always won the fights between us when we were kids, but little did he know that all that time he was beating the shit out of me, he was training me.

We're pretty even now. We avoid actual contact fighting with each other at all costs, but I'll be the first to admit that I don't hold my shit back as good as he does. And he knows it. It's why he's backing off now and using Michelle as a distraction. He reaches up and wipes ketchup from the side of her mouth. She giggles.

Camryn catches my eyes; she's probably been trying to get my attention for the past couple of minutes, and for a second, I think she's trying to indicate that she's ready to go, but then she shakes her head, telling me instead to calm down.

Instantly, I do.

"So," Asher chimes in to lessen the tension in the room, "how long have you two been going out?" He leans against the wall near the television, crossing his arms over his chest.

We look almost exactly alike with the same brown hair and crazy fucking dimples. Aidan is the oddball of the three of us; his hair is a lot darker and instead of dimples, he has a small birthmark on his left cheek.

"Oh, no we're just friends," I say.

I think Camryn just blushed, but I can't be sure.

"Must be a good friend to come all the way to Wyoming with you," Aidan says.

Thankfully he's not being a dick. If he decided to take his anger at me out on her, I'd have to break his face.

"Yeah," Camryn speaks up and instantly I'm absorbed by the sweetness of her voice, "I live near Galveston; thought someone should ride along with him since he was taking a bus."

I'm surprised she remembers what city I told her I lived in.

Aidan nods kindly at her, his cheeks moving as he chews.

"She's hot, bro," I hear Asher whisper at me from behind.

I turn around at the waist and glare at him to shut up. He smiles, but he does shut up.

The ol' man stirs almost unnoticeably and Asher moves over to the side of the bed. He thumps Dad on the nose playfully. "Wake up. We brought burgers."

Aidan holds his burger up as if our dad can actually see it. "They're good, too. Better wake up soon or they'll be gone."

Dad doesn't stir again.

He has all three of us trained. We would never think to stand around his bed and look all depressed and shit. And when he dies, Aidan and Asher will probably order a pizza and buy a case of beer and shoot the shit until the sun comes up the next morning.

I won't be here for that.

In fact, the longer I stand here the better the chances are that he will die before I can leave.

I talk with my brothers and Michelle for a few more minutes and then walk over to Camryn.

"Are you ready?"

She takes my hand and stands up with me.

"Already leaving?" Aidan says.

Camryn speaks up before I do and says with a smile, "He'll be back; we're just going to grab something to eat."

She's trying to defuse an argument before it starts. She looks at me and I, agreeing to go along with it, turn to Asher and say, "Call me if there's any change."

He nods but offers nothing else.

"Bye Andrew," Michelle says. "It was good to see you again."

"You too."

Asher walks with us out into the hall.

"You're not coming back, are you?" he says.

Camryn turns away from us and walks a little ways down the hall to give us a minute.

I shake my head. "I'm sorry, Ash, I just can't deal with this. I can't."

"I know bro." He shakes his head. "Dad wouldn't even care, you know that. He'd rather you be getting laid, or shitfaced, than hanging around his old ass in that bed."

He does speak the truth, strangely enough.

He also glances at Camryn once after having said that.

"Just friends? *Really?*" he whispers at me with a devious grin.

"Yes, we're just friends, so shut the fuck up."

He laughs in his chest and then pats the side of my arm. "I'll call you when I need to, all right?"

I nod, agreeing. When he 'needs to' call me, he means when Dad has died.

Asher raises his hand to wave at Camryn. "Nice to meet you."

She smiles and he disappears back inside the room.

"I really think you should stay here, Andrew. I really do."

I start to walk faster down the hall and she keeps up right alongside me. I slide my hands down in my pockets. I always do that when I'm nervous.

"I know you probably think I'm a selfish bastard for leaving, but you don't understand."

"Well, tell me," she says, grabbing me around the elbow and we just keep walking. "I don't think you're being selfish, I think you just don't know how to deal with this kind of pain."

She's trying to catch my gaze, but I can't look at her. I just want to get out of this death sentence built with red bricks.

We make it to the elevator and Camryn stops talking since there are two other people inside with us, but as soon as we stop on the ground floor and the silver metal doors slide open, she goes back to it.

"Andrew. Stop. *Please*!"

I stop at the sound of her voice and she turns me around. She gazes up at me with such a tormented look on her face that it sort of hurts my heart. That long, blonde braid still hangs over her right shoulder.

"Talk to me," she says more softly now that she has my attention. "It doesn't hurt to talk."

"Kind of like how it doesn't hurt to tell me why Texas?"

That stings her.

# Camryn

# THIRTEEN

*H*is words shut me up for about five full seconds. My hand drops from his elbow.

"I think your situation is a little more important than mine right now," I say.

"Really?" he says, "And you wanting to ride around alone on a bus, not knowing where the hell you're going and putting yourself in danger; *that* doesn't seem imminently as important to you?"

He seems angry. I can tell that he is, but most of it, if not every bit of it, is because his father is upstairs dying, and Andrew doesn't know how to let him go. I feel sorry for him, for being raised to believe that he can't show the kind of emotion needed in a situation like this, or else it will make him less of a man.

I can't show the emotion, either, but I wasn't raised that way, I was forced into it.

"Do you cry at all?" I ask. "About other things? Have you *ever* cried?"

He scoffs. "Of course. Everybody cries, even big tough guys like me."

"OK, name one time."

He answers easily: "A...movie made me cry once," but he suddenly appears embarrassed and might be regretting his answer.

"What movie?"

He can't look me in the eyes. I feel the mood lightening between us, despite what created it.

"What does it matter?" he says.

I smile and step up closer to him. "Oh come on, just tell me—what, you think I'm going to laugh at you and call you a pussy?"

He breaks a small grin underneath the embarrassed flush of his face.

"*The Notebook*," he says so low that I didn't quite catch it.

"Did you say *The Notebook*?"

"Yes! I cried watching *The Notebook*, all right?"

He turns his back on me and I'm using every shred of strength I have to hold back the laughter. I don't think it's at all funny that he cried watching *The Notebook*; what's funny is his humiliated reaction admitting it.

I laugh. I can't help it, it just comes out.

Andrew whirls around with eyes wider than plates and he glares at me for a second. I yelp when he grabs me and throws me over his shoulder, carrying me right out of the hospital.

I'm laughing so hard I have tears in my eyes. Fun tears, not the ones I stop shedding after Ian died.

"Put me down!" I beat my fists against his back.

"You said you wouldn't laugh!"

Him saying that only makes me laugh harder. I cackle and let out weird noises I never knew I could make.

"Please, Andrew! Put me down!" My fingers are digging into his back through the fabric of his shirt.

Finally, I feel my shoes touch the concrete. I look at him and I do stop laughing because I want him to talk to me. I can't let him leave his father.

But he speaks up first:

"I just can't cry around or for *him*, like I told you before."

I touch his arm gently. "Well then don't cry, but at least stay."

"I'm not going to stay, Camryn." He stares deeply into my eyes and I know just by the way he's looking at me that I'm not going to be able to change his mind. "I appreciate you trying to help, but this isn't something I can give in to."

Reluctantly, I nod.

"Maybe sometime during this road trip you agreed to, we'll be able to tell each other the things we don't want to tell," he says and my heart, for some reason, reacts to his voice.

There's a flutter inside my chest, just between my breasts behind my ribcage.

Andrew smiles brightly, his perfectly-shaped green eyes like the centerpiece of his sculpted face.

*He really is gorgeous…*

"So, what have you decided?" he asks, crossing his arms and looking all inquisitive. "Am I buying you a plane ticket home, or are you really set on the road to Nowhere, Texas?"

"You *really* want to go with me?" I just can't believe it and at the same time, I want more than anything for it to be true.

I hold my breath waiting for him to answer.

He smiles. "Yes, I really do."

The fluttering turns into hot mush and my face smiles so hugely that for a long moment, I can't seem to soften it.

"I just have one complaint about tagging along though," he says, holding up a finger.

"What?"

"Riding on that bus," he says. "I really fucking hate it."

I chuckle quietly and have to agree with him on that one.

"So how else are we supposed to go?"

One side of his mouth lifts into a knowing smile. "We can take the car," he says. "I'll drive."

I don't hesitate.

"OK."

"OK?" he says, pausing. "That's it? You're just going to hop in the car with a guy you barely know and trust him not to rape you on a deserted highway somewhere—I thought we already went over this?"

I tilt my head to one side, crossing my arms. "Is it any different than meeting you at the library and going out with you a night or two later, alone in your car?" I tilt my head to the other side. "Everybody starts out as strangers, Andrew, but not everybody meets a stranger who saves her from a rapist *and* takes her to meet his dying father practically in the same night—I'd say you passed the trustworthy test a little ways back."

The left side of his mouth lifts into a grin, disrupting the seriousness of my heartfelt words. "So this road trip is a date then?"

"What?" I laugh. "No! It was just an analogy."

I know he's aware of that, but I need to say something to help distract him from my reddening cheeks. "You know what I mean."

He smiles. "Yeah, I know, but you do owe me a 'friendly' dinner in the company of a steak." He quotes with his fingers when he says 'friendly'. The smile never leaves his face.

"I do, I admit it."

"Then it's settled," he says, looping his arm through mine and walking me toward the cab waiting near the parking lot. "We'll pick up my dad's car from the bus station, stop by his house and grab a few things and then we're on the road."

He opens the back door on the cab to let me get in first, shutting it behind him once he slides in next to me.

The cab pulls out of the lot.

"Oh, I should probably set a few ground rules before we do this."

"Oh?" I turn at the waist and look at him curiously. "What kind of ground rules?"

He smiles.

"Well, number one: *my* car, *my* stereo; I'm sure I don't need to elaborate on that."

I roll my eyes. "So, basically you're telling me I'm stuck with you in a car on a road trip and can only listen to classic rock?"

"Ah, it'll grow on ya."

"It never grew on me when I was growing up and had to endure my parents listening to it."

"Number two," he says holding up two fingers and dismissing my argument altogether. "You have to do whatever I say."

My head snaps back and my brows draw together harshly. "Huh? What the hell's that supposed to mean?"

His smile gets bigger, crafty even.

"You said you trusted me, so trust me on this."

"Well, you're going to have to give me more than that. Really, no joke."

He leans back against the seat and folds his hands between his long, splayed legs.

"I promise you I won't ask you to do anything harmful, degrading, dangerous or unacceptable."

"So basically, you won't be asking me to suck your dick for five hundred dollars, or anything like that?"

Andrew throws his head back and laughs out loud. The cab driver shifts in the front seat. I notice his eyes veer away from the rearview mirror when I look up.

"No, definitely nothing like that—I swear." He's still sort of laughing.

"OK, but what would you ask me to do then?"

I'm totally leery of this whole idea. I still trust him, I admit, but I'm also a little terrified now in a worried-I'll-wake-up-with-a-Sharpie-moustache sort of way.

He pats my thigh with his hand. "If it makes you feel better, you can tell me to screw off if you want to refuse anything, but I hope you won't because I really want to show you how to live."

Wow, that totally catches me off-guard. He's serious; nothing humorous about those words and once again I find myself fascinated by him.

"How to live?"

"You ask too many damn questions." He pats my thigh one more time and moves his hand back into his lap.

"Well, if you were on this side of the car, you'd be asking a lot of questions, too."

"Maybe."

My lips part halfway. "You are a very strange person, Andrew Parrish, but all right, I trust you."

His smile becomes more warming as he lays his head against the seat looking over at me.

"Any more ground rules?" I ask.

He looks up in thought and chews on the inside of his mouth for a moment.

"Nope." His head falls back to the side. "That's about it."

It's my turn.

"Well I have a few ground rules of my own."

He lifts his head with curiosity, but leaves his hands flat over his stomach with his strong fingers interlocked.

"All right, shoot," he says, grinning, prepared for anything I can throw at him, surely.

"Number one: under no circumstances will you be getting in my panties. Just because I'm friendly to you and am agreeing to— well, the craziest thing I've ever done—I'm giving you advance warning that I'm not going to be your next lay, or fall in love with you" (he's grinning from ear to ear right now and it's very distracting) "or anything like that. Is that understood?" I'm trying to be very serious about this. I really am. And I do mean what I said. But that stupid grin of his is sort of forcing me to smile and I hate him for it.

He crinkles his lips in thought. "Completely understood," he agrees, though I feel there is a hidden meaning behind his words.

I nod. "Good." I feel better that I made myself clear.

"What else?" he asks.

For a second I forgot about the other ground rule.

"Yeah so number two is: no Bad Company."

He looks mildly mortified.

"What the hell kind of rule is *that*?"

"It's just my rule," I say, smirking. "You have a problem with it? You have all the other classic rock you can listen to and I'm not allowed to listen to anything *I* want, so I see nothing wrong with my tiny stipulation." I hold my thumb and index finger a half inch apart to show how tiny.

"Well I don't like that rule," he grumbles. "Bad Company is a great band—why such a hater?"

He looks wounded. I find it cute.

I purse my lips. "Honestly?" I'm probably going to regret this.

"Well yeah, honestly," he says, crossing his arms. "Out with it."

"They sing too much about love. It's cheesy."

Andrew laughs out loud again and I'm starting to think the cab driver is really getting an earful with us in his car.

"Sounds like someone is *bit-ter*," Andrew says and a deep grin warms his lips.

Yep, I regret it.

I look away from him because I can't let him see anything in my face to confirm that he's right on target with his assessment of me. At least where my cheating ex, Christian, is concerned. With him, it's bitterness. With Ian, it's cruel, unadulterated pain.

"Well, we'll fix that, too," he says nonchalantly.

I look back over.

"Ummm, well thanks Dr. Phil, but I don't need help with that sort of thing."

*Wait a damn minute! Who ever said I needed to be 'fixed' at all?*

"Oh?" He tilts his chin, looking curious.

"Yeah," I say. "Besides, that would sort of break my ground rule number one."

He blinks and smiles. "Oh, you automatically assume I was going to offer myself up as the guinea pig?" His shoulders bounce with gentle laughter.

*Ouch!*

I try not to look offended. Not sure if it's working all that well, so I use a different tactic:

"Well, I would hope not," I say, batting my eyes. "You're not my type."

Oh yeah, ball's in my court again; I think he actually flinched!

"And just what's wrong with me?" he asks, but I'm totally not buying anymore that my comment really hurt him. People don't normally smile after they've been offended.

I turn around the whole way, pressing my back against the cab door and look him up and down. I'd be lying my ass off if I said I don't like what I see. I haven't found anything yet that doesn't make him my type. In fact, if it weren't for me not being into sex or dating or relationships or love, Andrew Parrish is the kind of guy that I would totally go for and who Natalie would openly drool over.

She would wear him across her boobs.

"There's nothing 'wrong' with you," I say. "I just tend to end up with the . . . tame types."

For the third time, Andrew's head falls back into laughter.

"Tame?" he says, still laughing. He nods a few times and adds, "Yeah, I guess you're right in saying I'm not exactly the tame type." He holds up his finger as if to make a point. "But what interests me more about what you said is that you 'end up' with them—what do you think that means?"

How did the ball even get back in his court? I never saw him coming.

I look to him for the answer, even though he's the one who asked the question. He's still smiling, but there's something much softer and perceptive in it this time, rather than the usual jest.

He doesn't say anything.

"I-I don't know," I say distantly and then look right at him. "Why does that have to mean anything anyway?"

He shakes his head subtly, but just looks out in front of him as the cab pulls into the parking lot near the bus station. Andrew's dad's 1969 Chevy Chevelle is the only car left in the lot. They must really be into that whole vintage car thing.

Andrew pays the driver and we get out.

"Have a good night, man," he says, waving as the driver pulls away.

I end up riding to Andrew's dad's house mostly in a contemplative quiet, thinking about what he said, but then I let it go when we pull into the driveway of his dad's immaculate house.

"Whoa," I say with parted lips as I step out of the car. "That's *a lot* of house."

His door shuts. "Yeah, my dad owns a successful construction and design company," he says nonchalantly. "Come on, I don't want to spend too much time here in case Aidan shows up."

I walk alongside him down the curved, landscaped walkway leading to the front door of the three-story house. It's such a rich, immaculate place I just can't see *his* particular father living in it. His father just seems more of a simple kind of man and not one to be as materialistic as my mother.

Mom would faint in something like this.

Andrew thumbs through his keys and pushes the right one into the door lock.

It clicks open.

"Not to be nosey, but why would your dad want to live in a house this big?"

The foyer smells like cinnamon potpourri.

"Nah, this was his ex-wife's doing, not his." I follow him straight to the white-carpeted staircase. "She was a nice woman— Linda, the woman he mentioned at the hospital—but she couldn't deal with Dad and I can't blame her."

"I thought you were going to tell me she married him for his money."

Andrew shakes his head as he leads me up the stairs.

"No, it was nothing like that—my dad is just a difficult man to live with." He slips his keys down into his front right jeans pocket.

I steal a quick glance at his butt in those jeans as he pads up the stairs in front of me. I bite my bottom lip and then mentally kick myself.

"This is my room." We enter the first bedroom on the left. It's fairly empty; looks more like a storage room with a few boxes piled neatly against one taupe-colored wall, some exercise equipment and a weird-looking Native American statue pushed into the far corner and partially wrapped in plastic. Andrew moves across the space to the walk-in closet and flips a light switch inside. I stay near the center of the room, arms crossed, looking around and trying to not to look like I'm snooping.

"You say 'is' your room?"

"Yeah," he says from inside the closet, "for when I visit, or if I ever want to live here."

I walk closer to the closet to see him sifting through clothes hanging much how I hang mine.

"You're OCD, too, I see."

He looks at me questioningly.

I point to the clothes hung by color and on matching black plastic hangers.

"Oh, no, definitely not," he clarifies. "Dad's housekeeper comes in here and does this shit. I could care less that my clothes are hung up at all, much less by color—that's too...wait—" He pulls away from the shirts and looks at me in a sidelong glance. "You do this to your clothes?" He points his finger horizontally at the shirts and moves it back and forth.

"Yeah," I say, but I feel weird admitting it to him, "I like my stuff neat and everything has to have a place."

Andrew laughs and goes back to sifting through the shirts. Without really looking at them much, he yanks a few shirts and pairs of jeans from the hangers and throws them over his arm.

"Isn't that stressful?" he asks.

"What? Hanging my clothes up neatly?"

He smiles and shoves the small mound of clothes into my arms. I look down at them awkwardly and back up at him.

"Never mind," he says and points behind me in the room. "Can you put those in that duffle bag hanging from the workout bench?"

"Sure," I say and carry them over.

First I set them down on the black vinyl bench and then grab the duffle bag hanging from the weights.

"So, where are we going to go first?" I ask, folding the shirt on top of the pile.

He's still rummaging through the closet.

"No, no," he says from inside; his voice is kind of muffled, "no outlines, Camryn. We're just going to get into the car and drive. No maps or plans or—" He's popped his head out of the closet and his voice is clearer. "What are you doing?"

I look up, the second shirt from the pile already in a half-fold.

"I'm folding them for you."

I hear a *thump-thump* as he drops a pair of black running shoes on the floor and emerges from the closet towards me. When he makes it over, he looks at me like I've done something wrong and takes the half-folded shirt from my hands.

"Don't be so perfect, babe; just shove them in the bag."

He does it for me as if to show me how easy it is.

I don't know which has my attention more: his lesson in disorganization, or why my stomach flip-flopped when he called me 'babe'.

I shrug and let him have his way with his clothes.

"What you wear really doesn't matter much," he says, walking back to the closet. "All that matters is where you're going and what you're doing while you're wearing it."

He tosses the black running shoes to me, one at a time, and I catch them. "Shove those in there, too, if you don't mind."

I do exactly what he says, literally shoving them inside the bag and I cringe while doing it. Good thing the bottoms of the shoes look like they've never been worn, otherwise I would've had to protest.

"You know what I find sexy in a girl?"

He's standing with one muscular arm raised high above his head as he searches through some boxes on the top shelf of the closet. I can see the very end of that tattoo he has down his left side, peeking just at the edge of his shirt.

"Ummm, I'm not sure," I say. "Girls who wear wrinkled clothes?" I scrunch up my nose.

"Girls who just get up and throw something on," he answers and takes down a shoe box.

He walks back out with it perched on the palm of his hand.

"That just-got-up-and-don't-give-a-shit look is sexy."

"I get it," I say. "You're one of those guys who despise makeup and perfume and all that stuff that makes girls, girls."

He hands me the shoebox and just like with the clothes, I look down at it with vague question.

Andrew smiles. "Nah, I don't hate it, I just think simple is sexy, is all."

"What do you want me to do with this?"

I pat the top of the shoe box with my finger.

"Open it."

I glance down at it, uncertain, and back up at him. He nods once to urge me.

I lift the red top off the box and stare down at a bunch of CD's in their original jewel cases.

"My dad was too lazy to put an MP3 player in his car," he begins, "and when traveling you can't always get the best radio reception—sometimes you can't find a decent station at all."

He takes the shoebox top from my hand.

"That'll be our official playlist." He smiles hugely, revealing all of his straight, white teeth.

Me, not so much. I grimace and scrunch up one side of my mouth sourly.

Everything is here, all of the bands he mentioned when I met him on the bus and several others I've never heard of. I'm pretty confident that I've heard ninety percent of the music I'm staring at at one time or another being around my parents. But if anyone were to ask me the name of this or that song, or what album it's from, or what band sings it, I probably wouldn't know.

"Great," I say sarcastically, frown-smiling at him with a wrinkled nose.

His smile just gets bigger. I think he loves torturing me.

# Andrew

# FOURTEEN

*S*he's cute when I'm torturing her. Because she enjoys it.

I don't know how I got myself into this, but I do know that as much as my conscience is ripping into my fucking ears, telling me to leave her alone, I can't. I don't want to.

We've already gone too far.

I know I should've left it at the bus station, bought her a First Class plane ticket home so she would feel obligated to use it since it cost so much, then call her a cab and had it drop her off at the airport.

I should never have let her leave with me, because now, I know that I won't be able to let her go. I have to show her first. It's mandatory now. I have to show her everything. She might get hurt in the end after all is said and done, but at least she'll be able to go back home to North Carolina with something more to look forward to in her life.

I take the shoebox from her hands and place the top back over it and set it on top of the opened duffle bag. She watches me as I throw open the top dresser drawer and fish out a few clean pairs of boxers and socks and then shove them down inside the bag, too. All of my basic hygiene necessities are in the bag out in the car that I brought on the bus with me.

I hoist the duffle bag strap over my shoulder and look at her.

"Are you ready?"

"I guess so," she says.

"Wait, you guess?" I ask, stepping up to her. "You either are, or you aren't."

She smiles up at me with those beautiful crystal blue eyes. "Yes, I'm definitely ready."

"Good, but why the hesitation?"

She shakes her head softly to say I'm wrong.

"Absolutely no hesitation," she says. "All of this is just...strange, you know? But in a good way."

She looks like she's trying to untangle something in her head. Obviously, she's got a lot on her mind.

"You're right," I say. "It *is* kind of strange—OK, it's *a lot* strange because it's not natural, stepping out of the box like this." I peer in at her, forcing her to catch my eyes. "But that's the whole point."

Her smile brightens as though my words rang a little bell inside her mind.

She nods and says with a fun and eager air, "Well, then what are we waiting for?"

We walk back out into the hall and just before we start to head down the stairs, I stop.

"Wait one second."

She waits there at the top of the stairs and I turn back, passing my bedroom and head toward Aidan's. His room is as pathetic as mine. I see his acoustic guitar sitting propped against the far wall and I walk over and grab it by the neck and carry it out.

"You play guitar?" Camryn asks as I lead her down the stairs.

"Yeah, I play some."

# Camryn

Andrew chucks his bag in the backseat with his smaller bag and mine and my purse. He's a little more careful with the guitar, though, laying it neatly across the seat. We hop inside the vintage black car (with two white racing stripes down the center of the hood) and shut our doors at the same time.

He looks over at me.

I look over at him.

He thrusts the key in the ignition and the Chevelle roars to life.

I can't believe I'm doing this. I'm not afraid or worried or feel like I should stop this right now and just go home. Everything about it feels right; for the first time in a very long time, I feel like my life is back on track again, except on a very different sort of road, one in which I have no idea where it's going. I can't explain it…except that, well, like I said: it feels *right*.

Andrew punches the gas once we hit the entrance ramp and get on 87 going south.

I kind of like watching him drive, how he's so casual even when he speeds past a few slow drivers. It doesn't look like he's trying to show off as he's weaving between cars; it just looks like second nature to him. I catch myself getting a glimpse every now and then of his muscled right arm as his hand grips the steering wheel. And as my eyes carefully scan the rest of him, I go right back to wondering about that tattoo hidden underneath that navy t-shirt which fits him so well.

We talk about whatever for a while; about that guitar being Aidan's and that Aidan will probably blow up if he finds out that Andrew took it. Andrew doesn't care. "He stole my socks once," Andrew said.

"Your *socks*?" I said back with a rather screwed-up expression. And he looked over at me with an expression that read: hey; socks, guitars, deodorant—a possession is a possession.

I just laughed, still finding it ridiculous, but easily letting him slide.

We also got into a really deep conversation about the mystery of the single shoes that lie on the side of the freeways all across the United States.

"Girlfriend got pissed and tossed her boyfriend's shit out the window," Andrew had said.

"Yeah, that's a possibility," I said, "but I think a lot of them belong to hitchhikers, because most of them are raggedy."

He glanced over at me awkwardly, as if waiting for the rest.

"Hitchhikers?"

I nodded, "Well yeah, they do a lot of walking so I imagine their shoes get worn out fast. They're walking along, their feet are hurting and they see a shoe—probably one of those tossed out by that angry girlfriend" (I point at him to include his theory) "—and seeing that it's in better shape than the ones on his feet, he trades one out."

"That's stupid," Andrew says.

My mouth parts with a spat of offended air. "It could happen!" I laugh and reach over and smack him on the arm. He just smiles at me.

And we went on and on about it, each of us coming up with an even stupider theory than the one before.

I can't remember the last time I laughed this much.

We finally make it back into Denver nearly two hours later. It's such a beautiful city with the vast mountains in the background that look like white clouds at their peaks, sprawled across the bright blue horizon. It's still pretty early in the day and the sun is shining full-force.

When we make it into the heart of the city, Andrew slows the car to a forty mile per hour crawl.

"You have to tell me which way," he says as we coast toward another entrance ramp.

He looks in three directions and then over at me.

Caught off-guard, my eyes dart around at each route and the closer we get to having to make a decision on which way to turn, the slower he drives.

Thirty-five miles per hour.

"What's it gonna be?" he asks with sparkling bright green eyes flecked by a little bit of taunt.

I'm so nervous! I feel like I'm being asked to choose which wire to cut to defuse a bomb.

"I don't know!" I shout, but my lips are smiling wide and nervously.

Twenty miles per hour. People are honking at us and one guy in a red car zooms past and flips us off.

Fifteen miles per hour.

Ahhh! I can't stand the anticipation! I feel like I want to burst out laughing, but it's being held captive in my throat.

*Honk! Honk! Fuck you! Move out of the way asshole!*

It all just rolls off Andrew's back and he never stops smiling.

"That way!" I finally yell, throwing my hand up and pointing to the east ramp. I squeal out laughter and slide my back down further against the seat so that no one else can see me, I'm so embarrassed.

Andrew flips his left blinker on and slides over into the left lane with ease, in between two other cars. We make it through the yellow light just before it turns red and in seconds we're on another freeway and Andrew is pressing on the gas. I have no idea which direction we're traveling, only that we're going east, but where it leads exactly is still up in the air.

"Now that wasn't so hard, was it?" he says, glancing over at me with a grin.

"Kind of exhilarating," I say and then let out a sharp laugh. "You really pissed those people off."

He brushes it off with a shrug. "Everybody's in too much of a hurry. God forbid you drive the speed limit or you might get lynched."

"So true," I say and look out ahead through the windshield. "Though I have to come clean—I'm usually one of *them*." I wince admitting it.

"Yeah, me too sometimes."

Everything gets quiet all of a sudden and it becomes the first quiet moment that the both of us notice. I wonder if he's thinking the same thing, wondering about me and wanting to ask, just as I'm curious about so much when it comes to him. It's one of those moments that are inevitable and almost always open the door to the stage where two people *really* start to get to know each other.

It's very different from when we were on the bus together. We thought that our time was limited then and if we were never going to see each other again, there was no reason to get all personal.

But things have changed and personal is all that's left.

"Tell me more about your best friend, Natalie."

I keep my eyes on the road for several long seconds and I'm slow to answer because I'm not sure which part of her I should tell.

"If she's even still your best friend," he adds, sensing the animosity somehow.

I look over.

"Not anymore. She's sort of whipped, for lack of a better explanation."

"I'm sure you have a better explanation," he says, putting his eyes back on the road. "Maybe you just don't want to explain it."

I make a decision.

"No, I *do* want to explain it, actually."

He looks pleased, but keeps it at a respectful level.

"I've known her since second grade," I begin, "and I didn't think anything could break up our friendship, but I was *so* wrong about that." I shake my head, disgusted just thinking about it.

"Well, what happened?"

"She chose her boyfriend over me."

I think he expected more of an explanation and I intended to give him more, but it just came out the way it did.

"Did you make her choose?" he asks with a subtly raised brow.

I turn around to look at him. "No, it wasn't like that at all." I sigh long and heavily. "Damon—her boyfriend—got me alone one night and tried to kiss me and tell me he wanted me. Next thing I know, Natalie is calling me a lying bitch and says she never wants to see me again."

Andrew nods one of those long, hard nods that show he completely understands now.

"An insecure girl," he says. "She's probably been with him for a long time, huh?"

"Yeah, about five years."

"You know, this best friend of yours, she believes you, right?"

I gaze over at him confusedly.

He nods. "She does; think about it, she's known you practically all her life. Do you really think she'd just toss away a friendship like that because she *didn't* believe you?"

I'm still confused.

"But she did," I say simply. "It's *exactly* what she did."

"Nah," he says, "it's just a reaction, Camryn. She doesn't *want* to believe it, but not so very far down, she knows it's true. She just needs time to think on it and to see it for what it is. She'll come around."

"Well, by the time she does, I might not want her."

"Maybe so," he says and flips on his right blinker and switches lanes, "but I don't take you for the type."

"Unforgiving?" I say.

He nods.

We speed past a crawling semi and move around in front of it.

"I don't know," I say, unsure myself anymore, "I'm not like I used to be."

"How did you used to be?"

I'm not even sure about that, either. It takes me a second to find a way around mentioning Ian. "I used to be fun and outgoing and I…" I laugh suddenly as the memory tickles my mind, "…and I used to run naked into a freezing lake every winter."

Andrew's whole beautiful face twists into a curious, energized smile. "Wow," he says, "I can just picture it…"

I smack him on the arm again. Always smiling. He pretends it stings, but I know better.

"It was a fundraiser for the hospital in my town," I say, "and they put it on every year."

"*Naked?*" He looks thoroughly confused aside from grinning thinking about it.

"Well, not *fully* naked," I say, "but in a tank top and shorts in freezing water, you might as well be naked."

"Shit, I should sign up for hospital fundraisers when I get home," he says, hitting the steering wheel once. "Didn't know what I was missing out on."

He tames the smile a little and looks back at me. "So why is that something you *used* to do?"

*Because Ian was the one who talked me into it and who I did it with for two years.*

"I just stopped about a year ago—just one of those things you fall out of."

I get the feeling he doesn't believe there's not more to it than that, so I jump onto something else to distract from it.

"What about you?" I ask, turning around at the waist to give him my full attention. "What's something crazy that you've done?"

Andrew purses his lips in thought, looking out at the road. We pass another semi and get around in front of it. The traffic is thinning out the farther away from the city we drive.

"I hood-surfed once—not so much crazy as it was stupid, though."

"Yeah, that's pretty stupid."

He reaches his left hand up and puts the underside of his wrist into view. "I fell off the damn thing and sliced my wrist open on no telling what." I peer in at the two-inch scar running along the skin from the bottom of the thumb bone and onto his arm. "I rolled across the road. Cracked my head open." He points to the back right side of his head. "Got nine stitches there in addition to the sixteen on my wrist. I'll never do that again."

"Well, I would hope not," I say sternly, still trying to see the scar through his brown hair.

He switches hands on the steering wheel and takes a hold of my wrist, sliding his index finger over the length of the top of mine so he can use his as a guide.

I pull closer, letting his hand guide mine.

"Right about...there," he says when he finds it. "Do you feel it?"

His hand falls away from mine, but I watch it for a moment.

Coming back to the issue of his head, I look up and run the tip of my finger along an obvious uneven smooth strip of skin on his scalp and then I part his short hair away with my fingers. The scar is about an inch long. I run my finger over it one more time and reluctantly pull away.

"I imagine you have a lot of scars," I say.

He smiles. "Not too many; got one on my back from when Aidan clipped me with a bicycle chain, swingin' it around like a whip (I wince, gritting my teeth). And when I was twelve, had Asher riding on the handlebars of my bike. Hit a rock. Bike flipped forward and sent us both skidding across the concrete." He points to his nose. "Broke my nose, but Asher broke an arm and had fourteen stitches on his elbow. Mom thought we'd been in a car wreck and were just lying about it to cover our asses."

I'm still looking at his perfectly shaped nose; don't see any evidence that it had ever been broken before.

"Got a weird L-shaped scar on my inner thigh," he goes on and points to the general area. "Not gonna show you that one though." He grins and puts both hands on the wheel.

I blush, because it really took me all of two seconds to start envisioning him dropping his pants to show me.

"That's a good thing," I laugh and then lean up toward the dashboard so I can pull my babydoll Smurfette shirt up just over my hip. I catch his eyes on me and it does something to my stomach, but I ignore that. "Camping one year," I say, "jumped off these bluffs into the water and hit a rock—I almost drowned."

Andrew frowns and reaches over, tracing the edges of the small scar on my hipbone. A shiver runs up my spine and through the back of my neck like something freezing racing through my blood.

I ignore that too, as much as I can.

I let my shirt fall back over my hip and I lean back against the seat.

"Well, I'm glad you didn't drown." His eyes warm up with his face.

I smile back at him. "Yeah, that would've sucked."

"Definitely."

# FIFTEEN

*I* wake up after dark when Andrew slows down through a toll. I don't know how long I slept, but I feel like I got a full night in, despite being curled up in the corner of the passenger's seat with my head against the door. I should be trying to rub out a couple of stiff muscles like when I rode on the bus, but I feel good.

"Where are we?" I ask, cupping my hand over my mouth to cover the yawn.

"Middle of nowhere Wellington, Kansas," he says. "You slept a long time."

I rise up the rest of the way and let my eyes and body adjust to being awake again. Andrew pulls onto another road.

"I guess I did, better than I slept on the bus the entire trip from North Carolina to Wyoming."

I look at the glowing blue letters on the car stereo: 10:14 p.m. A song is funneling low from the speakers. It makes me think of when I met him back on the bus. I smile to myself feeling like he made sure to keep it at a low level in the car while I slept.

"What about you?" I ask, turning around to see him, the darkness casting his face in partial shadow. "I feel weird offering because it's your dad's car, but I'm good to drive if you need me to."

"Nah, you shouldn't feel weird," he says. "It's just a car. A precious antique that my dad would string your ass up from a ceiling fan for if he ever knew you were behind the wheel, but I would totally let you drive it." Even in the shadow, I see the right side of his mouth pull into a devious grin.

"Well, I'm not so sure I want to anymore."

"He's dying, remember? What's he gonna do?"

"That's not funny, Andrew."

He knows it's not. I'm fully aware of the game he's playing with himself, always looking for anything to help him cope with what's going on but coming up short. I just wonder how much longer he'll be able to keep this up. The misplaced jokes will eventually run dry and he's not going to know what to do with himself.

"We'll stop at the next motel," he says, turning onto another road. "I'll get some shut-eye there."

Then he glances over at me. "Separate rooms, of course."

I'm glad he had that part sorted out so fast. I may be driving awkwardly across the U.S. alone with him, but I don't think I can share a room with him, too.

"Great," I say, stretching my arms out in front of me with my fingers locked. "I need a shower and to brush my teeth for about an hour."

"No arguments there," he jokes.

"Hey, your breath isn't all that great, either."

"I know it," he says, cupping one hand over his mouth and breathing sharply into it. "It smells like I ate that horrid shit casserole my aunt makes for Thanksgiving every year."

I laugh out loud.

"Bad choice of words," I say. "Shit casserole? Really?" I mentally gag.

Andrew laughs, too.

"Hell, it might as well be—I love my Aunt Deana, but the woman was *not* blessed with the ability to cook."

"Sounds like my mom."

"That must suck," he says, glancing over. "Growing up on Ramen noodles and Hot Pockets."

I shake my head. "No, I taught myself how to cook—I don't eat unhealthy food, remember?"

Andrew's smiling face is lit up by a soft gray light pouring from the light posts along the street.

"Oh, that's right," he says, "no bloody burgers or greasy fries for little Miss Rice Cakes."

I make a *bleh!* face, disputing his rice cake theory.

Minutes later we're pulling into a small two-floor motel parking lot; the kind with rooms that open up outside instead of an inside hallway. We get out and stretch our legs—Andrew stretches legs, arms, his neck, pretty much everything—and we grab our bags from the backseat. He leaves the guitar.

"Lock the door," he says, pointing.

We enter the lobby to the smell of dusty vacuum cleaner bags and coffee.

"Two singles side by side if you've got them," Andrew says, whipping out his wallet from his back pocket.

I swing my purse around in front of me and reach in for my little zipper wallet. "I can pay for my room."

"No, I got it."

"No, seriously, let me pay."

"I said, no, all right, so just put your money away."

I do, reluctantly.

The middle-aged woman with graying blond hair pulled into

a sloppy bun at the back of her head looks at us blankly. She goes back to tapping on her keyboard to see what rooms are available.

"Smoking or non-smoking?" she asks, looking at Andrew.

I notice her eyes slip down the length of his muscled arms as he fishes for his credit card.

"Non-smoking."

*Tap, tap, tap. Click, click, click.* Back and forth between the keyboard and the mouse.

"The only singles I have right next to each other are one smoking and one non-smoking."

"We'll take them," he says, handing her a card.

She pulls it from between his fingers and all the while she watches every little move his hand makes until it falls away from her eyes down behind the counter.

*Slut.*

After we pay and get our room keys, we head back outside and to the car where Andrew grabs the guitar from the back seat.

"I should've asked before we got here," he says as I follow alongside him, "but if you're hungry I can run up the street and get you something if you want."

"No, I'm good. Thanks."

"Are you sure?" He looks over at me.

"Yeah, I'm not hungry at all, but if I do get hungry I can just get something from the vending machine."

He slides the keycard into the first door and a green light appears. He clicks open the door afterwards.

"But there's nothing but sugar and fat in those things," he says, recalling our earlier conversations about junk food.

We walk into the fairly dull-looking room with a single bed pressed against a wood headboard mounted behind it on the wall.

The bedspread is brown and ugly and scares the crap out of me. The room itself smells clean and looks decent enough, but I have never slept in any motel without stripping the bed of the bedspread first. There's no telling what's living on them, or when the last time was they were washed.

Andrew inhales deeply, getting a good whiff of the room.

"This is the non-smoking room," he says, looking around as if inspecting it first. "This one's yours." He sets the guitar down against the wall and walks into the small bathroom, flips on the light, tests out the fan and then goes over to the window on the other side of the bed and tests the air conditioner—it is the middle of July, after all. Then he goes to the bed and carefully pulls back the comforter and examines the sheets and pillows.

"What are you lookin' for?"

He says without looking at me, "Making sure it's clean; I don't want you sleeping in any funky shit."

I blush hard and turn away before he can see it.

"Kind of early for bed," he says, stepping away from the bed and taking up the guitar again, "but the drive did take a lot out of me."

"Well, technically you haven't slept since before we got off the bus back in Cheyenne."

I drop my purse and bag down on the foot of the bed.

"True," he says. "So that means I've been up for about eighteen hours. Damn, I didn't realize."

"Exhaustion will do that to you."

He walks to the door and places his hand on the silver lever, clicking it open again. I just stand here at the foot of the bed. It's an awkward moment, but it doesn't last.

"Well, I'll see you in the morning," he says from the doorway.

"I'm right next to you in 110, so just call or knock or bang on the wall if you need me." There's only kindness and sincerity in his face.

I nod, smiling in answer.

"Well, goodnight," he says.

"Night."

And he slips out, shutting the door softly behind him.

After absently thinking about him for a second, I snap out of it and rummage around inside my bag. This will be the first shower I've had in couple of long days. I'm drooling just thinking about it. I yank out a clean pair of panties and my favorite white cotton shorts and varsity babydoll tee with pink and blue stripes around the quarter-sleeves. Then I find my toothbrush, toothpaste and Listerine and head to the bathroom carrying it all with me. I strip down naked, happily pulling all of the days-old dirty clothes off and tossing them in a pile on the floor. I stare at myself in the mirror. Oh my God, I'm hideous! My make-up has completely worn off; I barely even have any mascara on anymore. More wandering strands of blond hair have fallen from my braid and are smashed against one side of my head in a rat's nest.

I can't believe I'm been driving around with Andrew looking like this.

I reach up and pull the hairband from the braid to release the rest of the hair and then run my fingers through it to break it all apart. I brush my teeth first and leave my mouth full of mint Listerine long until after the burning has already stopped.

The shower is like heaven. I stay in it forever, letting the semi-scalding hot water beat on me until I can't take it anymore and the heat starts to lull me to sleep standing up. I clean everything. Twice. Just because I can and because it's been so damn long. Lastly I shave, glad to get rid of that gross wig I was starting to grow on my legs. And finally, I turn off the squeaky faucets and go for the white motel towel folded OCD-like on a rack over the back of the toilet.

I hear the shower running in Andrew's room next door and I catch myself just listening to it. I picture him in there, just showering, nothing sexual or perverted even though something like that wouldn't be hard to do at all. I just think about him in general, about what we're doing and why. I think about his dad and it breaks my heart all over again knowing how much Andrew is hurting and how I feel helpless to do anything for him. Finally, I force myself back into me and into my life and my issues, which really have nothing on Andrew's.

I hope it never comes down to me being forced to tell him my problems and all of the things that led me on that road-to-nowhere bus trip, because I will feel so stupid and selfish. My problems are nothing compared to his.

I get into bed with wet hair, combing it out with my fingers. I turn on the TV—not tired at all since I just slept most of the way from Denver—and flip through the channels, eventually leaving it on some random movie with Jet Li. But it's more for background noise than anything.

Mom called four times and left four messages.

Still nothing from Natalie.

"How are you doing in Virginia?" my mom says into my ear. "Having loads of fun, I hope."

"Yeah, it's been great. How are you?"

My mom giggles on the other end of the phone and instinctively it repels me. There's a man with her. Oh gross, I hope she's not talking to me in bed, naked, with some guy licking her neck.

"I've been good, baby," she says. "Still seeing Roger—going on that cruise next weekend."

"That's great, Mom."

She giggles again.

I scrunch up my nose.

"Well, baby, I need to go (Stop it, Roger)." She giggles again. I'm going to throw up in my mouth. "I just wanted to know how you were doing. Please call me tomorrow sometime and give me an update, all right?"

"OK, Mom, I will. Love you."

We hang up and I let the phone fall on the bed in front of me. Then I fall back against my pillows, instantly thinking about Andrew being in the room next door. He may be leaning his head against the same wall. I flip through the channels some more until I've been through every one of them at least five times and then just give up.

I slump down further and look at the room.

The sound of Andrew playing the guitar pulls me out of myself and I lift my back slowly from the pillows so I can hear it more clearly. It's a soft tune, kind of something in between searching and lamenting. And then when the chorus comes around, the speed picks up just a fraction only to lament again for the next verse. It's absolutely beautiful.

I listen to him play for the next fifteen minutes and then it goes silent. I had turned the TV off when I first heard him and now all that I can hear is a constant drip coming from the bathroom sink and the occasional car driving through the motel parking lot.

I drift off to sleep and the dream comes back:

*That morning, I didn't get my usual string of text messages from Ian before I got out of bed. I tried calling his phone, but it rang and rang and the voicemail never picked up. And Ian wasn't at school when I got there.*

*Everybody was staring at me as I walked through the halls. Some couldn't look me in the eye. Jennifer Parsons burst into tears when I walked past her at her locker, while another group of girls, cheerleaders, turned their noses up at me and eyed me as though I was something contagious. I didn't know what was going on, but I felt like I had walked into some freaky alternate reality. No one would say a word to me, but it was so damn obvious that everybody in that school knew something that I didn't. And it was bad. I never really had any enemies, except sometimes a few of the cheerleaders showed jealousy towards me because Ian loved me and wouldn't give them the time of day. What can I say? Ian Walsh was hotter than the star quarterback and it didn't matter to anyone, not even Emily Derting, the richest girl in Millbrook High School, that Ian didn't have much and that his parents still drove him to school.*

*She still wanted him.*

*Everybody did.*

*I went on to my locker, hoping to see Natalie soon so maybe she could tell me what was going on. I lingered around my locker longer than usual waiting for any sign of her. It was Damon who found me and told me what happened. He pulled me off to the side, in between the alcove that housed the water fountains. My heart was hammering inside my chest. I knew something was wrong when I got up that morning, even before I realized there were no text messages from Ian. I felt…off. It was like I knew…*

*"Camryn," Damon said and I knew right then the seriousness of what he was about to tell me because he and Natalie always call me 'Cam'. "Ian was in a car accident last night..."*

*I felt my breath catch and both of my hands flew to my mouth. Tears were burning my throat and streaming from my eyes.*

*"He died early this morning at the hospital." Damon was trying so hard to tell me this, but the pain in his face was unmistakable.*

*I just stared at Damon for what felt like an eternity before I couldn't stand up on my own anymore and I collapsed into his arms. I cried and cried until I made myself sick and finally Natalie found us and they both helped me into the nurse's office.*

I wake up from the nightmare sweating, my heart racing like mad. I throw the sheet off of me and sit in the center of the bed with my knees drawn up, running my hands across my head, and I let out a long sigh. The dream had stopped a long time ago. In fact, it was the last dream I remember having. Why is it back?

———

A loud banging on my room door jolts me up.

"RISE AND SHINE BUTTERCUP!" Andrew says harmoniously from the other side.

I don't even remember when I fell back asleep after the dream. The sun is shining through a sliver parted between the curtains, pooling on the tan carpet just below the window. I rise up from the bed and push back the sloppy hair away from my face and go to open the door before he wakes up the whole motel.

He's gawking at me when I open the door.

"Damn girl," he says, looking me over, "what the hell are you trying to do to me?"

I look down at myself, still trying to wake up the rest of the way and realize I'm in those tiny cotton white shorts and varsity tee with no bra on underneath. Oh my God, my nipples are like beacons shining through my shirt! I cross my arms over my chest and try not to look him in the eyes when he helps himself the rest of the way inside.

"I was going to tell you to get dressed," he goes on, grinning as he walks into the room carrying his bags and the guitar, "but really, you can go just like that if you want."

I shake my head, hiding the smile creeping up on my face.

He plops down on the chair by the window and sets his stuff on the floor. He's wearing a pair of tan cargo shorts that drop just past his knees, a plain dark gray t-shirt and those low black running shoes with no-show socks, or no socks at all. I glimpse the tattoo on his ankle; looks like some kind of circular-shaped Celtic design positioned right over his ankle bone. And he definitely has runner's legs; his calves are bulging with tight muscles.

"Wait there and I'll get ready," I say, going toward my bag sitting on the elongated dresser where the TV sits on the opposite end.

"How long will this take?" he asks and I detect a hint of interrogation in his voice.

Remembering what he said back at his dad's house, I think about my answer first and weigh my options: my usual thirty-minute prep time, or cave to a throw-it-on-and-go?

He helps me out with the dilemma:

"You have two minutes."

"*Two minutes?*" I argue.

He nods, grinning. "You heard me. Two minutes." He holds up two wriggling fingers. "You agreed to do whatever I said, remember?"

"Yeah, but I thought it was going to be crazy stuff like mooning someone from a moving car or eating bugs."

One of his brows rises and he draws back his chin as if I just slapped two ideas into his lap. "In time you will moon someone from a moving car and eat a bug—we'll get to that."

*What the hell just I just do?*

My head rolls backward in dispute and mortification and my hands fly to my hips. "Uh, there is no way—" I notice his grin has changed into something more 'crafty school boy' and I look down, realizing my arms are no longer covering my nipples poking so proudly through the thin fabric of my shirt. I let out a spat of air and my mouth falls open. "*Andrew!*"

He lowers his head with false shame, but it just makes him appear more devious the way he looks back up under hooded eyes at me.

*He is so fucking hot...*

"Hey, you're the one who'd rather complain about the ground rules than protect your girls from my eyes—I should warn you they have a mind of their own."

"Yeah, I bet they aren't the only things on you with a mind of their own." I smirk and grab my bag, shuffling my way barefooted into the bathroom and shutting the door.

I'm smiling like one of those 1980's cheesy portrait studio photos when I look at myself in the mirror.

OK, two minutes. I literally dive into my bra and tight jeans, jumping up and down to get them to slide over my butt. Zip. Button. Brush teeth thoroughly. A quick shot of Listerine. Swish. Gargle. Spit. Comb out raggedy hair and twist it into a sloppy braid over my right shoulder. A little bit of foundation and a light layer of powder. Black mascara, because mascara is the most important piece of makeup in the arsenal. Lipsti—

*BAM! BAM! BAM!*

"Your two minutes are up!"

I smooth the lipstick on anyway and blot with a square of toilet paper.

I can tell he's smiling on the other side of the bathroom door and when I open it a second later, I see that I was right. He stands with both arms raised above his head, propped on the doorjamb. His hard six-pack is partially visible with his shirt raised up high with his arms. A little happy trail moves from just below his bellybutton and down beneath the waist of his shorts.

"See? Look at you?" He whistles while blocking the door, but I'm definitely not the one of us I'm looking at. "Simple is sexy."

I push my way past him, finding the perfect opportunity to press my palms against his chest and he lets me pass.

"Didn't know I was trying to be sexy for you," I say with my back turned, throwing the clothes I slept in inside my bag.

"Wow, look at that," he goes on, "simple, sexy *and* disorganized—I'm proud!"

I didn't even realize it. I just shoved my clothes into the bag without even thinking of trying to be neat about it. I'm not 'clinically' OCD; I'm just one of those people who claim the acronym because of a few methodical habits. Still, folding my clothes and trying to be neat is something I've always done since I was like eleven.

# Andrew

# SIXTEEN

*T*alk about early morning sexual frustration. All right, I'm going to have to take it down a notch with her or she'll start to think that's really what I'm hanging around for. Any other time, with some other random girl, I would've already gotten out of bed to toss the condom in the toilet, but with Camryn, it's different. It's hard (pun intended), but I'm going to have to try laying off the flirting. This is an important trip, for both of us. I only have one shot to get this right and I'll be damned if I fuck it up.

"So what's next on our spontaneous trip?" she asks.

"Breakfast first," I say, grabbing my bags from the floor, "but I guess it wouldn't be spontaneous if I had a plan in place."

She grabs her cell phone from the table beside the bed, checks it for new text messages and phone calls and then tosses it in her purse.

We head out.

Enter stubborn, whiney Camryn:

"Please, Andrew; I can't eat at those places," she says from the passenger's seat.

The town is small and most of the food joints are fast food or not open this early.

"I'm *serious*," she says with a cute pouty face I just want to cup in my hands and lick so she shrieks and pretends it's the grossest thing ever. "Unless you want an annoying road trip companion, holding her nauseous stomach and moaning for the next hour, you won't make me eat that stuff, especially this early in the morning."

I draw my head back and press my lips together looking over at her. "Come on, you're exaggerating."

I'm starting to think she's not.

She shakes her head and props her elbow on the car door and then rests her thumb between her front teeth.

"No, I'm serious; every time I eat fast food I get sick. I'm not trying to be difficult, believe me, it creates a problem whenever I go anywhere with my mom or Natalie. They have to go out of their way to find a place to eat that won't make me miserable."

OK, so she's telling the truth.

"All right, well I definitely don't want to make you sick," I laugh lightly, "so we'll drive a little farther and find something else along the way. More places will be open in a couple of hours."

"Thank you." She smiles sweetly.

*You're very welcome...*

Two and a half hours later, we're in Owasso, Oklahoma.

Camryn looks up at the big yellow and black restaurant logo and I think she's debating whether she wants to eat here, or not.

"There's really only one place to eat breakfast," I say, pulling into a parking space, "especially across the South—kind of like Starbucks, there's a Waffle House on every corner."

She nods. "I think I can handle this—do they have salad?"

"Now look, I agreed not to make you eat the fast grease," I tilt my head to one side and turn at the waist on the seat, "but I draw the line with salads."

She puckers her lips and chews on the inside of her mouth and then says, nodding, "All right, I won't eat a salad, even though salads can come with chicken and all sorts of good stuff that someone like you probably never thought of."

"No. So just give it up," I say resolutely and then gently jerk my head back in gesture. "Come on, I've waited long enough to eat. I'm *starving*. And I get grumpy when I'm hungry."

"You're *already* grumpy," she mumbles.

I grab her arm and pull her next to me. She tries to hide her blushing face.

I love the smell of Waffle House; it's the smell of freedom, being on the open road and knowing that ninety percent of the people eating around you are also on that road. Truck drivers, road-trippers, hangovers—those who don't live that monotonous life of society slavery.

The restaurant is nearly full. Camryn and I get a booth close to the grill farthest away from any of the tall windows. A mandatory jukebox—symbolic of Waffle House culture—sits against one of those windows.

The waitress greets us with a smile, standing with a notepad resting in one hand, and a pen ready to write with the tip poking the paper in the other. "Can I get you some coffee?"

I look up at Camryn, who's already scanning over the menu on the table in front of her.

"I'll have a glass of sweet tea," she says.

The waitress jots that down and looks back at me.

"Coffee."

She nods and goes to make our drinks.

"Some of this stuff looks good," Camryn says peering down at the menu with one cheek propped on the top of her folded hand. Her index finger slides over the plastic and lands on the tiny salad section. "See, look," she glances up at me, "they have Grilled Chicken Salad and Chicken Apple Pecan Salad."

I can't resist that hopeful look in her wide blue eyes.

I cave. Totally fucking cave.

"Order whatever you want," I say with a warm expression. "Really, I won't hold it against you."

She blinks twice, mildly stunned I gave in so easily and then her eyes seem to smile back at me. She closes the menu and places it back on the menu holder above the table as the waitress returns with our drinks.

"Ready to order?" the waitress asks after placing our drinks in front of us. The tip of her pen, as if it never really leaves that spot, is still pressed against the notepad waiting to be put to work.

"I'll have the Fiesta Omelet," Camryn says and I catch a small grin in her face as her eyes skirt mine.

"Toast or biscuit?" the waitress asks.

"Biscuit."

"Grits, hash browns or tomatoes?"

"Hash browns."

The waitress jots the last of Camryn's order down and turns to me.

I pause for a second and then say, "I'll have the Chicken Apple Pecan Salad."

Camryn's grin shuts down immediately and her face just freezes like that. I wink at her and slide the menu behind hers.

"Livin' on the edge, huh?" the waitress says.

She rips off the top ticket.

"For today," I tell her and she shakes her head and walks away.

"What the *hell*?" Camryn says holding her hands out, palms

up. She can't decide whether to smile or look at me awkwardly, so she ends up doing a little of both.

"I figure if you're willing to eat something for my sake, then I can do the same for you."

"Yeah, well I just don't see that salad doing it for you."

"You're probably right," I say, "but fair is fair."

She scoffs lightly and leans her back against the booth seat. "It won't be so fair if I'm listening to you complain about being hungry when we get back on the road—you said yourself that you're grumpy when you're hungry."

I couldn't *really* be grumpy towards her, but she's right: the salad's *not* going to do it for me. And lettuce gives me gas—she'll definitely hate riding in the car with me if I eat this shit. But I can do this. I just hope I can eat the whole thing without letting any one of a hundred complaints about it, which are already tap-dancing on the tip of my tongue, give me away.

This should be interesting.

Several minutes later, the waitress is bringing Camryn her food and setting my plate of blasphemy down in front of me. She refills our drinks, asks if we need anything else and then goes back to her other customers.

Camryn is already scrutinizing me.

She looks down at her plate, arranges the biscuit on the other side of the hash browns and then twists the plate around by its edges to put the omelet in reach. I pick up my fork and poke the salad around a few times, pretending, just like Camryn, to prepare it.

We look up at each other and pause as if waiting for the other to say something. She purses her lips. I purse mine.

"Wanna trade?" she asks.

"Yeah," I say without hesitation and we're sliding the food across the table to one another.

Relief washes over both of our faces.

It's not something I would've ordered on my own, but it beats lettuce.

Halfway through the meal—well, halfway for her; I'm done with mine—I'm ordering a slice of chocolate pie and getting another coffee refill. And we go on and on about her ex best friend, Natalie, and how Natalie is some over-the-top bi-sexual with huge boobs. At least that's what I've been getting out of Camryn's descriptions of her.

"So what happened after the restroom incident?" I ask, taking a bite of my pie.

"I never went in a public restroom with her again after that," she says. "The girl has no shame."

"She sounds fun," I say.

Camryn looks thoughtful. "She was."

I study her quietly. She's lost in some memory, poking her fork at the last piece of chicken in her salad. My fork clinks against the plate as I make a decision and set it down. I wipe my face with my napkin and slide out of the booth.

"Where are you going?" She looks up at me.

I just grin and walk away toward the jukebox by the window. I slip the money in and scan the titles, finally choosing one song and pressing the buttons. *Raisins In My Toast* starts to play as I make my way back.

All three of the waitresses and the cook eyeball me with glaring, unforgiving looks. I just smile.

Camryn's whole body has locked up on the seat. Her back is rigid, the whites of her eyes blaring at me and then when I start mouthing the words to the fifties-sounding song, she slinks *way* down onto the seat, her face redder than I have ever seen it.

I slide back into my seat, moving my hips all the way down.

"Oh God, Andrew, please don't *sing* it!"

I'm trying my damndest not to laugh, but I just sing along to the lyrics with a giant grin plastered all over my face. She buries her face in her hands, her little shoulders, covered by a thin white shirt bounce up and down as she suppresses her laughter. I snap my fingers in tune with the music as if my hair is greased back and when the high-pitched voice comes on, I mimic it, my face all scrunched up with exaggerated emotion. And I hit the deeper notes, too, dropping my chin toward my chest and looking all serious. I never stop snapping my fingers. The further into the song I go, I start to put a little more emotion into it. And by the middle, Camryn can't contain herself any longer. She laughs so hard under her breath that her eyes water up.

She's let herself fall so far down onto the seat by now that her chin is almost level with the table's edge.

When the song ends—to the relief of the employees—I get one pair of hands clapping for me from the old lady sitting in the booth behind Camryn. Nobody else cares, but by the look on Camryn's face, you'd think everyone in the restaurant was watching and laughing at us. Hilarious. And she's so cute when she's embarrassed.

I prop my elbows on the table and lay my arms across it, folding my hands together.

"Ah, it wasn't *that* bad was it?" I smirk.

She slides the edge of her finger underneath each of her eyes to wipe off that tiny streak of black that she instinctively knows is there. A few more laughs still rattle through her calming chest.

"You have no shame, either," she says, laughing one more time.

———

"It was embarrassing, but I think I needed that." Camryn kicks off her shoes and pulls her bare feet onto the front seat in the car.

We're back on the road again, and taking direction only from Camryn's pointing finger. Heading east on 44; looks like we're going to be passing through the bottom half of Missouri.

"Glad I could oblige."

I reach out and press the power on the CD player.

"Oh no," she teases, "I wonder how far back into the seventies we'll go *this* time."

I tilt my head over and smirk at her.

"This is a good song," I say, reaching out to turn the volume up a little and then tapping my thumbs on the steering wheel.

"Yeah, I've heard it before," she says, laying her head against the seat. "*Wayward Son*."

"Close," I say, "*Carry On Wayward Son*."

"Yeah, close enough you didn't need to correct me." She pretends to be offended, but isn't doing a very good job.

"And what band is it?" I test her.

She makes a face at me. "I don't *know*!"

"Kansas," I say with an intellectually raised brow. "One of my favorites."

"You say that about all of them." She purses her lips and flutters her eyes.

"Maybe I do," I relent, "but really, Kansas songs have a lot of emotion. *Dust in the Wind*, for example; can't think of a more fitting piece of music for death. It has a way of stripping your fear of it."

"Stripping your fear of *death*?" she says, not convinced.

"Well yeah, I guess so. It's like Steve Walsh is the reaper and he's just telling you that there's nothing to be afraid of. Shit, if I could choose a song to die to, that one would be at the top of my playlist."

She looks discouraged.

"That's a little too morbid for my blood."

"If you look at it that way, I guess so."

She's fully facing me now with both legs pulled onto the seat, knees drawn up, and her shoulder and head lying on the back of the seat. That golden braid of hers which makes her look that much softer always draped over her right shoulder.

"*Hotel California*," she says. "The Eagles."

I look at her. I'm impressed.

"That's one classic song that I like."

That makes me smile. "Really? That's a great one; very chilling—kind of makes me feel like I'm in one of those old black and white horror films—Good choice."

I'm actually *really* impressed.

I tap my thumbs some more on the steering wheel to *Carry On Wayward Son* and then I hear a loud *pop!* and a constant *flap-flap-flap-flap-flunk-flap-flunk* until I veer slowly off the side of the freeway and pull onto the shoulder.

Camryn has already dropped her bare feet back onto the floorboard and is looking all around the car trying to figure out the direction of the noise.

"Do we have a flat?" she asks, though it's more like: "Oh great, we have a flat!"

"Yep," I say putting the car in park and turning the engine off. "Good thing I have a spare in the trunk."

"Is it one of those ugly mini tires?"

I laugh.

"No, I have a life-sized tire in there with a rim and everything and I promise it'll match the other three."

She looks slightly relieved, until she realizes I was making fun of her and she sticks her tongue out at me and crosses her eyes. Not sure why that made me want to do her in the backseat, but to each his own, I guess.

I put my hand on the door handle and she pulls her legs back onto the seat.

"What are you getting all comfortable for?"

She blinks. "What do you mean?"

"Get your shoes on," I say, nodding to them on the floorboard, "and get your ass out with me and help."

Her eyes get wider and she just sits there as though waiting for me to laugh and tell her I'm only kidding.

"I-I don't know how to change a tire," she says when she realizes I'm not.

"You *know* how to change a tire," I correct her and it stuns her even more. "You've seen it done hundreds of times in real life and in movies—trust me, you know how; *everybody* knows how."

"I've never changed a tire in my life." She all but sticks out her bottom lip.

"Well you're going to today," I say grinning, opening my door just a few inches so the semi coming toward us doesn't knock it off.

A few more seconds of disbelief and Camryn is slipping her feet down into her running shoes and shutting the car door behind her.

"Come over here." I motion to her and she walks to the backside of the car with me. I point to the flat one, back passenger's side. "If it had been one of those two on the side with the traffic, you might've gotten out of it."

"You're seriously gonna make me change a tire?"

I thought we already established this.

"Yes, babe, I'm *seriously* going to make you change a tire."

"But in the car you said help you, not actually do all the work."

I nod. "Well you *are* going to help technically, but—just come here."

She walks around to the trunk and I lift the spare out and set in on the road. "Now get the jack and the tire iron out of the trunk and bring them over."

She does what I say, grumbling under her breath something about getting 'black gook' on her hands. I restrain my very passionate desire to laugh at her as I roll the tire over near to the flat one and lay it on its side. Another semi zooms by; the wind rocks the car gently side to side.

"This is dangerous," she says, dropping the jack and the tire iron on the ground at my feet. "What if a vehicle veers off the road and hits us? Don't you watch World's Dumbest?"

*Holy shit! She watches that show, too?*

"As a matter of fact I do," I say, "now get over here and let's get this done. If you're the one squatting down, hidden from the traffic by the car then we're less likely to get run over by anyone."

"How does that make it less likely?" Her eyebrows are knotted in her forehead.

"Well, if you're standing out here in the open lookin' all sexy and shit, I'd probably veer off the road looking at you, too."

She rolls her eyes so hard and bends over to pick up the tire iron.

"Ugh!" she grunts, trying to get the lug nuts loosened. "They're too damn tight!"

I loosen them for her but let her twist them off the rest of the way, all the while keeping my eyes on the oncoming traffic without letting her know that it's making me nervous. If I'm watching, I've got a better chance of grabbing her in time and getting us both out of the way than if it were the other way around.

Next is the jack; I help her with it, showing her how to loosen it so it expands and I guide her about the best spot to place it, though she seemed to know where without my help. She fumbles at first with the jack handle, but quickly gets the hang of it and she hoists the car up a little. I check her butt out because I'd be an idiot, or gay, not to.

And then out of nowhere, not even a hint of thunder or lightning beforehand, rain literally starts pouring from the sky in buckets.

Camryn starts yelling about getting soaked and it starts to distract her from the tire completely. She shoots up from the ground and starts to run toward the car door, but stops once she realizes she probably shouldn't try to get in with the car being held up by the jack.

"Andrew!" She's completely drenched, holding her hands over her head as though it's actually going to do something to help shield her from the rain.

I laugh my ass off.

"*Andrew!*"

She's laughably furious.

I take her shoulders into my hands and say with rain pounding on my face, "I'll finish the tire." It's hard to keep a straight face. And I don't.

In a few minutes, the new tire has been tightened and I chuck the flat one along with the jack and the tire iron back into the trunk.

"Wait!" I say as Camryn starts to get inside the car now that it's safe.

She stops. She's shivering in the rain and every part of her is drenched. I slam the trunk closed and step up to her, feeling the water squishing around inside my shoes because I'm not wearing socks and I smile at her, hoping to make her smile, too.

"It's just rain."

She relents a little, searching for more playful encouragement from me, no doubt.

"Come here." I hold out my hand and she clasps hers around it.

"What?" she asks coyly.

Her braid is heavy with water; the few loose strands that always lie softly about her face are stuck to her forehead and on one side of her neck. I walk her around to the trunk and hop onto it. She just stands there as the rain continually washes over her. I reach out my hand again and hesitantly she takes it and I hoist her onto the back of the car. She climbs to the roof with me, all the while looking at me like I'm some crazy person that she can't resist.

"Lay down," I say over the loud, pounding rain as I lay my back against the roof and let my feet dangle over the end and on the windshield.

Without question or objection—although both are kind of written all over her face—she lies down next to me.

"This is crazy," she shouts. "*You* are crazy."

She must like crazy because I'm getting the feeling she wants to be up here with me.

Tossing that earlier plan of mine out the window, the one where I needed to control myself around her, I let my left arm lie straight out at my side and instinctively she lays her head on it.

I swallow hard. I really didn't expect that. But I'm glad she did it.

"Now just open your eyes and look up," I say, already looking up myself.

A smaller truck zooms past, followed by a few cars, but neither of us notices. Another semi flies by and the wind knocks the car a little, but we don't care about that, either.

She winces at first as the rain gets in her eyes, but she does it, every now and then squinting and trying to curl her face into my side to shield it from the rain and the whole time, laughing gently. She forces herself to look straight up, but this time closes her eyes and lets her mouth part halfway. I watch her lips, how the rain moves over them in rivulets and how she smiles and flinches when the drops hit her in the back of the throat. How her shoulders push up when she tries to bury her face, smiling and laughing and soaking wet.

I watch her so much that I forget it's raining at all.

# Camryn

# SEVENTEEN

When I could hold my eyes open long enough, I did stare up at the rain pelting down on me. I've never looked at it like that, straight up into the sky, and while I flinched more than I could actually see, when I *could* see it was absolutely beautiful. Like each drop rocketing towards me was separate from the thousands of others and for a suspended moment in time, I could glimpse it and see its delicate facets. I saw the gray clouds churning above me and felt the car shake when the wind from the traffic pushed against it. I shivered even though it's warm enough to swim. But nothing I saw or felt or heard was as warm and fascinating as Andrew's closeness.

I scream and laugh as we race to get back inside the car minutes later.

The door slams shut and then his does after mine.

"I'm *freezing*!" I shudder out a laugh, pressing my uplifted arms between my breasts with my fingers tightly interlocked and my chin pressed against them.

Andrew, smiling so hugely that it stretches his entire face, shivers once and flips on the heat.

Instinctively, I try to forget that I had lain against his arm, or that he put it out there for me to begin with. I think he tries to forget, too, or at least not to make it obvious.

He rubs his hands together, trying to get warm as the heat blasts from the vents. My teeth are chattering.

"Wearing wet clothes sucks," I say with shivering jaws.

"Yeah, I'm with you on that one," he says, stretching his seatbelt around and clicking it in place.

I do the same, though like always, after being in the car so long I'll end up slipping out of it so that I can find another comfortable seating position.

"My toes feel slimy," he says, looking toward his feet.

My whole face crumples. He laughs and then reaches down and pulls his shoes off, tossing them in the back floorboard.

I decide to do the same because even though I won't say it, my feet feel slimy, too.

"We need to find a place to change," I say.

He puts the car in drive and looks at me. "There's a backseat," he says, grinning. "I won't look, I swear." He puts his hands up for assurance and then grips the steering wheel again, pulling back onto the freeway when he has an opening between traffic.

I scoff. "Nah, I think I'll wait until we find a place."

"Suit yourself."

I know he would totally look. And, well, it wouldn't bother me much…

The windshield wipers are swishing back and forth full blast and it's raining so hard that it's still difficult to see the road out ahead. Andrew leaves the heat on until it starts to feel like a sauna and he turns it down after checking first to see if I'm good with it.

"So, *Hotel California*, huh?" he asks, grinning over at me with deep dimples. He reaches out and presses the button to choose another CD and then keeps pressing until he finds the song. "Let's see how much you know."

His hand drops back on the wheel.

The song begins like I always remembered with that eerie guitar, slow and haunting. We look at each other back and forth, letting the music move through and between us, waiting for the lyrics to begin. Then at the same time, we raise our hands as if knocking on the air *one, two, three* with the beat and we start to sing with Don Henley.

We get fully into it, line after line and sometimes we switch off, him letting me sing a line and then he sings one. And when the first chorus comes, we sing together at the top of our lungs, practically shouting the lyrics at the windshield. We squint our eyes and bob our heads and I pretend I'm not mortified by my singing. Then the second verse comes and our taking-turns starts to get a little tangled, but we totally have fun with it and only trip up a couple of times. And we say *1969!* loudly together. Then we lose a little of the passion to sing and just let the music funnel through the car instead. But when the iconic second chorus comes around and the song slows and becomes more haunting, we get serious again and sing every single word together, looking right at each other. Andrew hits *'alibis!'* so flawlessly that it sends shivers up my arms. And we both 'stabbed the beast' together, pumping our fists at our sides and getting into it.

And that was how the drive was to wherever for the next several hours.

I sang so much with him that my throat became sore.

Of course, all of it was classic rock with the occasional early nineties: Alice in Chains and Aerosmith mostly, and none of it bothered me one bit. I actually loved it all and the memory it was creating in my mind. A memory with Andrew.

We find a rest stop off the freeway in Jackson, Tennessee, and take full advantage of it. We slip inside the restrooms to change out of our wet clothes, which we've been in for longer than either of us realized. I guess our fun together in the car with my less-than-stellar singing and him pretending he loves it distracted us from everything else.

He's dressed before me and already waiting inside the car when I stroll out wearing the only thing I had left in my bag that was clean: the white cotton shorts and varsity tee I like to sleep in. I only brought one bra and I happened to be wearing it when I was being rained on so it's completely wet still. But I'm wearing it anyway because there's no way I'm getting in that car with him bra-less.

"I am *not* wearing these shorts for *your* benefit," I say, pointing sternly at him as I crawl back inside the car. "For the record."

The corner of his mouth lifts into a grin.

"Note taken," he says, jotting it down on a pretend tablet.

I lift my butt from the seat and grasp the end of my shorts, pulling them just a little so they aren't crawling up my crotch and to cover a little more skin on my thighs. I start to kick my black flip-flops onto the floorboard until I see how saturated the floor mat is and decide to leave them on. It's a good thing the seats are leather.

"I'm gonna have to find some more clothes," I say.

Andrew's wearing jeans again and his black Doc Marten boots, and another plain gray t-shirt, lighter in color than the last one. Like anything, it looks good on him, but I kind of miss his tanned muscled calves and the black and gray Celtic tattoo on the ball of his ankle.

"Why is that all you brought?" he asks, keeping his eyes on the road. "Not that I'm complaining, of course."

I smirk over at him. "I guess since I didn't know where I was going I didn't want to lug a bunch of crap around."

"Makes sense."

The sun is shining in Tennessee and we're heading south now. The other side of the freeway is grid-locked because of road construction and we both express how glad we are that we're not on *that* side of the road'. Eventually, the daylight fades behind the landscape and dusk bathes the rice and cotton fields in a purplish haze; there's always *some* kind of massive field on either side of the freeway, stretching far off in the distance.

We make it to Birmingham, Alabama a little after 7:00p.m.

"Where do you wanna stop for clothes?" he asks, creeping along a city street lined by stop lights and gas stations.

I rise up from the seat and look around, trying to glimpse the lighted signs for someplace suitable.

Andrew points out ahead. "There's a Walmart."

"I guess it's as good any," I say and he makes a left at the stoplight and we pull into the parking lot.

We get out and the first thing I do is pull my panties out of the crack of my butt.

"Need some help?"

"No!" I laugh.

We walk together through the sea of cars in the parking lot, my flip-flops snapping against my heels. Instantly, I recoil into myself, knowing I look like hell with a dirty, matted braid over my shoulder and dressed in these skimpy shorts that keep crawling up my ass. No makeup anymore, since my becoming-one-with-the-rain washed it all off. I keep my eyes on the bright white floor as we walk through the store and avoid eye contact with anyone.

We head to the women's clothes first and I grab a few simple things: two more pairs of cotton shorts that are still short but not up-my-crotch short like the ones I'm wearing, and a couple of cute v-neck graphic tees with random stuff on them. I hold out on my desire to visit the panties and bras section. I think for now I'll make do with what I have.

Then I follow Andrew over to the area by the pharmacy where all of the vitamins and cold medicines and toothpaste and stuff are.

We go straight into the aisle with the razors and shaving cream.

"I haven't shaved in a week," he says, rubbing the stubble that has been growing on his face for the past few days.

I think it's sexy, but with or without it, it's still sexy so I don't complain.

Why would I anyway?

I grab a pack of razors, too, as well as some Olay shaving cream in a gold can. Then in the next aisle, I pick up a small bottle of mouthwash because one can never have enough mouthwash. I adjust my purse on the opposite shoulder as the items start to fill up in the other arm. We go into the next aisle and I pluck a set of shampoo and conditioner from the shelf, trying to balance them in my hands with the other stuff, but Andrew takes it from me and carries it instead. He takes the mouthwash, too.

We head over to the medicines and there's a middle-aged couple standing in front of the cough syrup, reading the labels.

Andrew says casually, without lowering his voice, "Babe, did you find that yeast infection stuff?"

My eyes spring open and I freeze in front of the Tylenol.

He removes a small box of Advil from the shelf.

The couple pretends not to have heard what he said, but I know they heard him.

"I mean are you even sure that's what's causing the itch?" he goes on and I feel like I'm melting from the heat in my face.

The couple does glance over this time, covertly.

Andrew is grinning his ass off at me from the side, pretending to be reading labels.

I want to smack him, but instead, I play him at his own game.

"Yeah, baby I found it," I say as casually as he had. "What about you? Did you see if they have extra-small sized condoms?"

The woman turns her head and looks right at him, up and down, and then she eyes me before going back to reading labels.

Andrew doesn't break; somehow I knew he wouldn't. He just smiles over at me, enjoying every second of this.

"One size fits all, baby," he says. "I told you they fill out better when you can actually make it hard."

A spitting noise bursts from between my lips followed by laughter.

The couple leaves the aisle.

"You are so bad!" I hiss at him, still laughing. The can of shaving cream clanks against the floor after it falls from my arm and I bend over to pick it up.

"You're not so innocent yourself."

Andrew grabs a tube of antibiotic ointment and holds it in the same hand with the Advil and we head to the register. He tosses two packages of beef jerky on the moving belt and a pack of Tic Tacs. I get a travel-sized bottle of hand sanitizer, a tube of Chap-Stick and a package of beef jerky for myself.

"Gettin' brave aren't yah?" he says about the beef jerky.

I smirk at him and put the plastic gray item divider in between his stuff and mine. "Nope," I say. "I love jerky. If it contained radio-active material I'd still eat it."

He just smiles, but then tries to tell the cashier that his and my stuff is 'together' as he pulls his credit card from his wallet.

"No, not this time," I argue, laying my arm on the belt next to the item divider. I look right at the cashier and shake my head, daring her to ring my stuff up with his. "I'll pay for mine." She looks between me and Andrew briefly, as if waiting for his turn.

When he starts to argue back I turn my chin at a stern angle and say, "I'm paying for my stuff and that's that. Deal with it."

He sort of rolls his eyes and gives in, sliding his card through the machine.

When we get back in the car, Andrew rips the top strip off one of his beef jerky bags and pops a jagged piece into his mouth.

"Are you sure you don't want me to drive some?" I ask.

He shakes his head, his jaws working hard on that stiff piece of jerky.

"We'll get another motel and crash for the night."

He swallows and pops another piece in his mouth and puts the car in drive and we pull away.

We find a motel a few miles out and grab everything and take it up to our side-by-side king rooms. Green checkered carpet in this one with matching dark green, heavy curtains and a dark green flowery bedspread. I turn the television on immediately, just to give some light and animation to the dark and gloomy atmosphere.

He paid for the rooms again, using how I 'got my way' with paying for the stuff at Walmart as his excuse to get away with it.

Andrew checks the room out first, just like the last time, and then plops down on the recliner by the window.

I drop my stuff on the floor and rip the bedspread from the bed and toss it in the corner next to the wall.

"Is there something on it?" he asks, leaning back into the recliner and letting his legs splay below.

He looks exhausted.

"No, they just scare me." I sit on the end of the bed and kick off my flip-flops, drawing my legs onto the bed Indian-style. I place my hands within my lap because still wearing the white cotton short shorts, I feel a little exposed to him with my knees open like this.

"You said: since you didn't know where you were going," Andrew says.

I look up and it takes me a second to understand what he's referring to: back in the car when I mentioned my reason for not bringing more clothes. He knits his fingers together, laying his hands flat over his stomach.

It takes me a moment to answer, although the answer I give him his vague:

"Yeah, I didn't know."

Andrew lifts his back straight up from the chair and leans over forward, resting his arms on his thighs, his hands draped together below his knees. He cocks his head to one side looking across at me. I know we're about to have one of those conversations where I can't foresee if I'll accept or dodge his questions. It'll depend on how good he is at drawing the answers out of me.

"I'm no expert on this stuff," he says, "but I don't see you setting out alone like you did on a *bus*, of all things, with a purse, a small bag and absolutely no idea where you're going just because your best friend stabbed you in the back."

He's right. I didn't leave because of Natalie and Damon; they were just part of the pattern.

"No, it wasn't because of her."

"Then what was it?"

I don't want to talk about it; at least, I don't *think* I do. A part of me feels like I can tell him anything and I sort of *want* to, but the other part is telling me to be careful. I haven't forgotten that his issues outweigh mine and I would feel stupid and whiney and self-ish telling him anything at all.

I look at the TV instead of him and pretend to be halfway interested in it.

He stands up.

"It must've been pretty bad," he says walking over to me, "and I want you to tell me."

Pretty bad? Oh great, he just made it worse; even if I did tell him, at least before I wouldn't have had it in my head that he expected something really horrible. Now that I know he does, I feel like I should make something up.

I don't, of course.

I feel the bed move when he sits down next to me. I can't look at him yet; my eyes stay focused on the TV. My stomach swims with guilt and also something tingly when I think about how close he is. But mostly guilt.

"I've let you get away with not telling me anything for a long time," he says. He rests his elbows on his thighs again and sits the way he had been sitting on the recliner, with his hands folded and hanging between his legs. "You have to tell me sometime."

I look over and say, "It's nothing compared to what you're going through," and leave it at that, facing the TV again.

*Please stop prying, Andrew. I want more than anything to tell you because somehow I know you can make some sense of it all, you can make it all better—what am I saying?—Please just stop prying?*

"You're comparing it?" he says, piquing my curiosity. "So, you think that because my dad is dying that whatever made you do what you did somehow doesn't live up?" He says this as if the very thought of it is absurd.

"Yes," I say, "that's exactly what I think."

His eyebrows draw inward and he looks at the TV briefly before turning back to me.

"Well that's complete bullshit," he says matter-of-factly.

My head snaps back around.

He goes on:

"Y'know, I've always hated that expression: *Others have it worse than you do*; I guess if you want to look at it in a competitive way, sure, give me welfare over blindness any day, but it's not a fucking competition. *Right?*"

Is he asking me because he wants to know how I feel, or was that his way of telling me how it is and hoping I get it?

I just nod.

"Pain is pain, babe." Every time he calls me 'babe' I notice it more than anything else he says. "Just because one person's problem is less traumatic than another's doesn't mean they're required to hurt less."

I guess he makes a valid point, but I still feel selfish.

He touches my wrist and I look down at it, the way his masculine fingers drape over the bone along the side of my hand. I want to kiss him; the urge inside of me just climbed its way to the surface, but I swallow and force it back down into the pit of my stomach which has been trembling for the past few seconds all on its own.

I pull my hand away from his and get up from the bed.

"Camryn, look, I didn't mean anything by that. I was just trying to—"

"I know," I say softly, crossing my arms and turning my back on him. It's definitely one of those it's-not-you-it's-me moments, but I'm not about to lay *that* on him.

I sense him stand up and then I turn carefully at the waist to see him grab his bags and his guitar from against the wall.

He walks to the door.

I want to stop him, but I can't.

"I'll let you get some sleep," he says gently.

I nod but don't say anything because I'm afraid that if I do, my mind will betray my mouth and I'll just dig myself deeper into this dangerous situation with Andrew that I'm finding more conspicuous every day that I spend with him.

# EIGHTEEN

*I* hate myself for letting him walk out that door, but it had to be done. I can't *do* this. I can't let myself fall into the world that is Andrew Parrish even though everything in my heart and in my desires is telling me to. It's not just about being afraid of getting hurt again; everybody goes through that phase and maybe I'm not out of it completely yet, but it's about so much more.

I don't *know* myself.

I don't know what I want or how I feel or how I *should* feel and I don't think I ever really have. I would be a selfish bitch to let Andrew into my life. What if he falls in love or wants something from me that I can't give him? What if I add a broken heart on top of his dad's death? I don't want his pain hanging over my head.

I turn abruptly and look at the door again, picturing the way he looked right before he walked through it.

Maybe that's not even an issue. How conceited of me to even entertain the thought of him ever falling in love with me. Maybe he just wants a friend with benefits, or a one-time thing.

My head is swimming with a chaotic swarm of thoughts, none of which I feel are right and all of which I know are possible. I walk over to the mirror and stare at myself in it, looking into the eyes of some girl that I feel like I've met, but never really got acquainted with. I really do feel detached from myself, from everything.

*Fuck this!*

I grit my teeth and smack the palms of my hands against the TV stand. Then I grab a new pair of black cotton shorts, my new white tee with *je t'aime* written in script across it, wrapped around the Eiffel Tower, and I head for the shower. I spend forever letting the water beat on me not because I feel dirty but because I feel like shit. All I can think about is Andrew. And Ian. And why suddenly I feel this strange, provoking need to think about them both in the same thought at all.

After my skin feels stripped of its top layer by the hot water, I get out and dry off, soaking up the water from my hair into the towel. I blow-dry it naked in front of the mirror and then go back into the room to get dressed because I didn't bring a clean pair of panties in with me. Finally, I comb out my halfway dried hair and leave it down to air-dry the rest of the way, pushing it back behind both ears and out of my face.

I hear Andrew playing the guitar through the wall again. The TV is still yapping and it pisses me off so I stomp over and turn it off so I can hear Andrew more clearly.

I just stand here for a few seconds, taking in the notes funneling through the wall and painfully into my ears. It's not a sad kind of tune, but for some reason it's still painful for me to hear.

Finally, I grab my room key, slip my feet into my flop-flops and leave the room.

Nervously licking the dryness from my lips, I take a deep breath, swallow and raise my hand to knock lightly on his door.

The sound of the guitar ceases and a few seconds later, the door clicks open.

He has showered, too. His brown hair is still wet; pieces of it a little messy in the front above his forehead. He stares at me, shirtless and wearing nothing else but a pair of black cargo shorts. I try not to look at his lightly-tanned six-pack abs or the veins running along the length of his arms that somehow appear more pronounced with the rest of his skin in plain view.

*Oh…my God. Maybe I should just go back…*

No, I came over here to talk to him and that's what I'm going to do.

For the first time, I see the tattoo down his left side and I want to ask about it, but I'll save that for later.

He smiles gently at me.

"It started about a year and a half ago," I just come out with it, "a week before graduation—my boyfriend was killed in a car accident."

His gentle smile fades and he softens his eyes, letting me see just enough remorse to show that he feels bad for me without it seeming fake or exaggerated.

He pushes the door open the rest of the way and I walk inside. The first thing he does before I even sit down on the end of the bed is pull a shirt over his chest. Maybe he doesn't want me to feel like he's trying to be distracting or flirty, especially when I came here to tell him something obviously painful. I respect him even more for that. That small, seemingly insignificant gesture speaks volumes, and although it might be unfortunate that he hid that body away, I'm OK with it. That's not what I came here for.

I think…

There's a sort of genuine sadness in his green eyes, mixed with something thoughtful. He turns the TV off and sits down next to me, the same way he did on my bed and he looks over, waiting patiently for me to go on.

"We fell in love at sixteen," I begin and look out ahead of me, "but he waited for me for two years—*two years*—" I glance over once in emphasis, "before I slept with him. I don't know any teen-age guy who would wait that long to get in a girl's panties."

Andrew makes a slight you-have-a-point face.

"I had had a couple of short-term boyfriends before Ian, but they were so..." I look up in thought searching for the word, "...mundane. To tell you the truth, I started seeing *a lot* of people as mundane by the time I was twelve."

Andrew looks reflective, his brows gently creasing inward.

"But Ian was different. The first thing he said to me after we met and had our first real conversation was: *'I wonder if the ocean smells different on the other side of the world.'* I laughed at first because I thought it was a weird thing say, but then I realized that simple sentence set him apart from everyone I knew. Ian was a guy standing on the outside of the glass, looking in at the rest of us shuffling back and forth, doing the same thing every day, taking the same paths, like ants in an ant farm.

"Now, I had always known that I wanted something more in life, something different, but it was when I met Ian that things started to become clear to me."

Andrew smiles gently and says, "Established and matured before twenty—that's a rare trait."

"Yeah, I guess so," I say, smiling back at him and then I let out a small laugh. "You wouldn't believe how often Damon or Natalie or even my mom and my brother, Cole, messed with me about how 'deep' I was." I quote 'deep' with my fingers and roll my eyes.

"Deep is good," he says and I glance over coyly because I detect the attraction even though he's taming it very well for the sake of the conversation. But then his smile fades and his voice drops a little. "So when you lost Ian, you lost your partner in crime."

My smile fades, too, and I prop my hands on the edge of the bed and let my body slump between my shoulders. "Yes. We were going to backpack across the world after graduation, or maybe just Europe, but we were determined; had *that* much planned out at least." I look straight at Andrew now. "We knew we didn't want to do the college thing and end up working the same job for forty years—we wanted to work *everywhere*, try *everything* while on the road!"

Andrew laughs. "That's actually a pretty cool idea," he says. "One week you're waitressing at a bar and bankin' on tips and the next week, in a different city or town, you're belly-dancing on a street corner and tourists are tossing money in a jar as they walk by."

My slumped shoulders bounce softly with laughter and I blush, looking over at him. "Waitressing, sure, but belly-dancing?" I shake my head. "Not so much."

He grins and says, "Ah, you could pull it off."

Still with a hot, blushing face I look out ahead of me again and let the blush fade.

"Six months after Ian died," I go on, "my brother, Cole, killed a man in a drunk-driving accident and now he's in prison. And after that, my dad cheated on my mom and they got divorced. My new boyfriend, Christian, cheated on *me*. And then, of course, you already know about what happened with Natalie."

That's all of it. I told him everything that, combined, made me want to get away. But I can't look at him because I feel like I shouldn't be done, like he's thinking to himself: OK, where's the rest of it?

"That's a lot of shit to dump on a person's lap," he says and I look back up when I feel him adjusting on the bed beside me. I smell his minty breath now that he has turned fully at the waist to face me from the side. "You have every right to be hurt, Camryn."

I don't say anything, but I thank him with my eyes.

"I guess I can see now why you weren't hard to convince to go on this road-trip with me," he says.

His face is unreadable. I hope he doesn't think I'm using him to mimic that part of my life I had planned with Ian. The whole road-trip situation seems similar, even to me now that I think about it, but it couldn't be further from the reason I left with Andrew. I'm with him now because I want to be.

It's in this moment that I realize I haven't been thinking of Ian and Andrew so much because I'm trying to find Ian *in* Andrew... I think it's guilt... maybe I'm trying to replace Ian completely.

I stand up from the bed and shake those thoughts from my mind.

"So what are you going to do?" Andrew asks from behind. "After this road-trip is over, what do you plan to do with your life?"

My heart hardens in my chest. Not once during this trip with Andrew, or even before I met him after I left North Carolina, have I thought beyond the present. It wasn't ever that I tried not to think about what lies ahead, I simply just didn't think about it at all. Andrew's question wakes me up and now I feel panicked inside. I never wanted a dose of that reality; I was content with my illusion.

I turn around, my arms crossed over my chest. Andrew's beautiful eyes are gazing intensely at me.

"I... don't really know."

He looks mildly surprised, his gaze becoming more contemplative and his eyes stray.

"You can still go to college," he says, offering ideas to help me feel better, I guess, "and it doesn't mean you have to get a job afterwards and work there until you die—hell, you can still backpack across Europe if you want."

He stands up with me. I can tell the thinking gears are churning in his head as he paces the dark green carpet a few times.

"You're gorgeous," he says and my heart flutters, "you're intelligent and obviously have more determination than the average girl; I think you could do just about anything you wanted—shit, I know that all sounds commonplace, but it couldn't be truer in your case."

I shrug. "I guess so," I say, "but I don't have the slightest idea about what I want to do except that I don't want to go home to figure it out. I think I'm afraid that if I go back there, I'll be drowned in the same crap I pulled myself out of when I got on that bus that day."

"Tell me something," Andrew says suddenly and my eyes lock on him, "what part of being around everyone else frustrates you the most?"

*Frustrates me?*

I think on it for a second, my gaze fixated on the brass lamp mounted on the wall beside the bed.

"I-I'm ... not sure."

He steps up to me and places two fingers at the bend of my arm, guiding me to sit back down with him and I do.

"Just think about it," he goes on, "based on what you've told me already, what is different between you and them?"

I hate it that it's taking me longer to figure something out that he seems to already have an idea about. I stare down at my hands within my lap and think about it long and hard until I come up with the only answer I feel *might* be right, but I'm still unsure of myself:

"Expectations?"

"Is that a question, or your answer?"

I give up.

"I really don't know—I mean I feel...*restricted* around every-one, with the exception of Ian, of course."

He nods and listens, letting me go on without interruption while the answer is hanging on the tip of my brain.

And then out of nowhere, the answers just come:

"No one wants to do what I want to do," I say and my explana-tion begins to unfold more quickly now that I feel more confident in the answer. "Just like with living free and not taking the ordinary route, y'know? No one wants to step out of their comfort zone to do that with me because it's not something most people do. I was afraid to tell my parents I didn't want to go to college because that's what they *expected* me to do. I accepted a job at a department store because my mom *expected* it to fulfill me in some way. I went with my mom every Saturday to visit my brother in prison because she *expected* me to go, because he's my brother and I should *want* to see him even though I didn't. Natalie relentlessly tried to hook me up with guys because she thought it was abnormal that I be single.

"I think I've been afraid most of my life to be myself."

My head whirls around to face him. "In a way, that was even true with Ian."

I look away quickly because that last part was not something I really expected to say out loud. It just came out while the realization was taking shape in my mind so fast.

Andrew looks inquisitive, but at the same time, unsure if he should probe.

I'm not sure if I should elaborate.

He nods.

Apparently, he decides it's not his place to further this particular subject.

He twists the inside of his cheek in between his teeth. I watch him for a moment, always trying to force down the obvious attraction I have for him, but it's becoming harder to do. I glimpse his lips and wonder what they taste like. And then I force my eyes away— I'm doing it again. Right now. I'm afraid to tell him what I want. Or, at least what I *think* I want.

"Andrew," I say and his face quietly reacts to my voice saying his name.

*Think about this, Cam,* I say to myself. *Are you sure this is what you want?*

"What is it?" he asks.

"Have you ever had a one-night stand?"

It feels like I just let the biggest secret I've ever been told slip while standing in front of a microphone in a room full of people. But it's out of the bag now. I'm still not entirely sure if it's even what I want, but it's there in my mind and has been for a while. I remember vaguely thinking about it while up on that roof with Blake.

Andrew's face loses all emotion and he can't seem to find words to say. Instantly, my heart freezes and I feel sick to my stomach. I knew I shouldn't have said that! He's going to think I'm a slut or something.

I jump up from the bed.

"I'm sorry—God, you must think I'm—"

He reaches out and takes my wrist. "Sit back down."

Reluctantly, I do, but I can't look at him. I'm completely fucking mortified.

"What's *wrong* with you?" he asks.

"Huh?"

I look back at him.

"You're doing it *right now*." He motions his hands to emphasize 'right now'; his eyebrows are knotted.

"Doing what?"

He licks his lips, sighs as if disappointed and finally says, "Cam-ryn, you started to tell me something that maybe you've contem-plated a time or two and just when you got the courage to speak your mind, you did a one-eighty and regretted it." He looks deep into my eyes, his full of intensity and knowledge and something else I can't yet place. "Ask me the question again and this time, wait for me to answer."

I pause, searching that tense look on his face, unsure of it. Or, maybe it's just me that I'm unsure of.

I swallow and say, "Have you ever had a one-night stand?"

His expression doesn't shift or fall. "Yes, I've had a few here and there."

He's waiting for *me* now, even though I'm not sure yet how to make myself feel comfortable in this awkwardly-developing conver-sation. It's like he knows I'm squirming inside, but to teach me a lesson he's going to make me do the talking instead of being my shrink like he's been since I came into his room.

His eyebrows arch a little as if to say: *Well?*

"Well, I was just wondering...because I've never done some-thing like that."

"Why not?" he says so casually.

I look down and then back up at him so he doesn't scold me for it.

"Well, it's just kind of slutty, I guess."

Andrew laughs and it surprises me.

Finally, he relieves me somewhat of my torture.

"If a girl did that *a lot*," he draws out that word with a squeamish smile, "then it would be slutty, sure. Once or twice, I don't know…" he motions his hands at level with his shoulders as if shaking the numbers around in his mind indecisively, "there's nothing wrong with that."

Why isn't he taking full advantage of this right now? I start freaking out a little inside, wondering why he's still all shrink-mode rather than amping up the flirting and getting down to business.

"All right, so…"

I can't say it. It's just not me, to be able to casually talk about my sexual *anything*. I can only vaguely do that with Natalie.

Andrew sighs and his shoulders slouch over. "Are you wanting to sleep with me, to have a one-night stand with *me*?" He knew I wasn't going to come out and say it, so he gave in and did it for me.

The question, although obvious for both of us, stops my breath. It embarrasses and mortifies me with him saying it as much, maybe more, than if I would have.

"Maybe…"

He stands up and looks down at me and says, "I'm sorry, but I'm not into you in that way."

The biggest fist in existence just slammed into my stomach. My hands go rigid, gripping the edge of the mattress, making my arms all the way up to the top of my shoulders, completely unmovable. All I want to do right now is run out that door and lock myself inside my room and never look at Andrew again. Not because I don't want to see him, but because I don't want him to see *me*.

I've never been so embarrassed in my entire life.

And *this* is what speaking my mind got me!

I don't know whether to accept it as a lesson learned, or to hate *him* for making me do it.

# NINETEEN

*I*n a split-second, I leap off the bed and walk as fast as I can to the door.

"Camryn, stop."

I just keep moving, even faster when I feel him coming up behind me, and I grab the lever and swing the door open and then I run out into the hall.

"Please, just wait a damn minute!" he says, following me and I can hear the aggravation elevating in his voice.

I ignore him and reach into the little pocket on the back of my shorts and yank out my card key, thrusting it in my door. I push my way inside the room and go to close the door, but Andrew is already through it behind me.

The door shuts after him.

"Will you just *listen* to me?" He tries once more, exasperated.

I don't want to look at him, but I do anyway.

His eyes are wide and fierce and sincere when finally I turn around.

He steps up to me and grips my upper arms carefully in his hands. And then he leans in and presses his lips softly against mine. I wilt, but I'm still too confused to react properly to it. Confused and stunned and my heart is racing.

He pulls away and looks in at me, his face every bit of sincere and he tilts his head to one side...*smiling*.

"Why is that funny?" I ask sharply and go to push away from him.

He holds me still by my arms and forces my humiliated gaze, which is beginning to reflect resentment.

"I say that I'm not into you like that, Camryn, because..." he pauses, searching my face, looking at my lips for a moment as if deciding whether or not he should kiss them again, "...because you're not the girl I could only sleep with once."

His words snap the thoughts out of me and my racing heart flickers behind my ribs. I can't make myself understand what he just said and instead of trying to figure out exactly what he means, I pull my head together the best I can and try to gain back some of the composure I lost when I stormed out of his room.

"Look," he says, moving to my side and slipping his hand around the back of my waist. Just feeling his fingers graze my skin causes shivers along that side of my body. What the hell is happening to me? I *do* want him...I mean, right now I feel like there's no going back, that I would force myself to be a slut just for tonight just to keep him in the room. But what I don't understand is why I feel like I want more from him than sex...

"Camryn?" His voice snaps me back into whatever it was he was trying to say moments ago. He guides me to sit down on the bed and then crouches down in front of me on the floor. He gazes up into my eyes. "I *won't* have a one-night stand with you, but I *will* make you come, if you let me."

A tiny jolt of electricity just shot through my belly and down in between my legs.

"...What?" I can't say anything else, really.

He smiles gently, deepening those dimples just a little, and he rests his arms across the length of my naked thighs, clasping his hands to my sides.

"No strings attached," he says. "I'll get you off and tomorrow morning when you wake up, I'll be in my room next door getting ready to head out with you to our next location. Nothing will change between us—I won't even bring up what happened joking around or otherwise. It'll be like it never happened at all."

I can hardly *breathe.* He just made the sweet spot between my legs swell with just a few direct words.

"But...what about *you?*" I manage to get out.

"What *about* me?"

He presses his fingertips into my sides a little more. I pretend not to notice.

"That doesn't...seem fair."

I really have no idea what I'm saying. I'm still shocked that this is happening at all.

Andrew just smiles up at me, unfazed by my observation, and then suddenly he lifts up from being crouched on the floor and moves in between my legs, causing me to slide backward a little on the bed. He sits in front of me and pulls me onto his lap, one leg over each side of him. I'm wide-eyed and practically biting into my bottom lip. He's being so casual about this that it alone, the mere unexpectedness of it, makes me wetter.

He wraps his firm arms around my back and leans in, brushing the edge of my chin with his mouth. Chills attack me from head to toe. Then he pulls me closer toward his body and whispers near my mouth, "It's fair. I *want* to make you come, and trust me; I'll *definitely* be getting something out of it." I hear the grin in his voice and

I look down into his eyes and I can't resist them. If Andrew told me right now to bend over and get on my hands and knees for him, I would without hesitation.

He brushes the other side of my jaw with his lips.

"Then why won't you just sleep with me?" I ask quietly, but then try to re-word it, "I mean, if you wanted to do...something else to me—"

He leans back from my jaw and puts his three middle fingers over my lips to hush me.

"I'm going to say this just once," he begins and his eyes are so bottomless, churning with intensity, "but I don't want you to comment when I say it, all right?"

I nod nervously.

He pauses, moistening his lips with his tongue and then says, "If you were to let me fuck you, you would have to let me *own* you."

A wave of unrestricted pleasure shudders through my entire body. His words shock me into submission. My heart is telling me to say one thing. My mind is telling me to say another. But I can't hear what the fuck either one of them are saying because of this feeling between my legs that just keeps getting more and more impossible to ignore.

I swallow hard, searching desperately for saliva. It feels like every part of me that normally produces its own moisture has stopped working because all of the moisture has localized that to one spot in the center of my body.

I still can't breathe.

Oh my God, he hasn't even *touched* me yet and I *already* feel this way?

Am I dreaming?

"But what if I give you a hand-job, or something?"

I admit it; the idea of this is making me feel guilty.

He cocks his head to one side, smirking, and it makes me want to kiss him hungrily. "I told you not to comment."

"I-I well, I didn't comment on what you said, exactly, I just—" He slips his fingers underneath the thin fabric of my panties and touches me. I gasp, forgetting about what I had started to say.

"Be quiet," he demands gently, though he completely means it. My lips snap shut and I gasp again when he slips two fingers inside of me and just holds them there, his thumb pressing on the outside against my pelvic bone. "Are you going to be quiet, Camryn?"

I shudder out the word, y-yes, and bite my bottom lip.

Then his fingers slide out of me. I want to beg him not to move them away, but he told me to be quiet in such a way that makes me utterly mad for him and equally submissive, so I say nothing. My eyes open carefully when he moves his wet fingers across my lips and instinctively I lick them, just a little, until he pulls them toward his own lips and takes in the rest of me on his tongue. I lean toward him, touching his mouth to my own, shutting my eyes softly just wanting to taste him and myself on him. His tongue snakes out to touch mine, but then he pushes me carefully back on the bed, instead of giving in to the ravenous kiss I so desperately want.

He slips both hands on the fabric around my waist and slides my shorts and panties over my hips and down my legs, dropping them somewhere on the floor.

Then he crawls up and lies next to me, draping one arm over my body and slipping his hand up the front of my shirt. I never did put a bra on earlier. He gently pinches one nipple, then the other and kisses me along the jaw again. Every tiny hair along the back of my neck rises when his tongue traces the curvature of my ear. "Do you want me to touch it?" His breath is warm against the side of my face.

"*Yes*," I gasp.

He pins my earlobe between his teeth and his hand starts to slide down my belly, but it stops near my bellybutton.

"*Tell me* that you want me to touch it," he breathes into my ear.

I can hardly open my eyes.

"I *want* you to touch it..."

He slides his hand down further and my heart starts pounding fiercely in my chest, but when I think he's going to touch me, his hand moves to my inner thigh instead. "Spread them for me." I let my legs fall gently apart, but he moves them apart further with his hand, the edges of his fingers pushing against my flesh until I'm completely exposed.

He lifts up from my side and leans over my body, pushing my shirt up to expose my breasts and then pins my nipples between his teeth, one after the other. Then he flicks the tip of his wet tongue over them and places his mouth around them, kissing each one of them hungrily. I wind my fingers through the top of his hair, wanting to grip it and pull it, but I don't. Andrew makes his way down my chest and to my ribs, tracing each one with his tongue before my bellybutton.

He looks up at me with dominant, hooded eyes and says with his lips gently pressed against my stomach, "You have to *tell* me what you want, Camryn." He licks my belly once so slowly that my skin ripples with shivers. "You won't get it unless you tell me and make me believe you."

I breathe in an unsteady breath that literally rattles my chest. "Please, please touch it..."

"I don't believe you," he says tauntingly and licks my clit once. Just once. He stops and looks at me across the landscape of my body, waiting for me.

Because I'm afraid to say the word, I whisper so softly, "Please...I want you to lick my pussy," that he pretends he didn't hear me.

"What was that?" he says and licks my clit again, this time taking a little longer and a wave of shivers runs through me below. "I didn't quite catch that."

I say it again, raising my voice just a little, still too embarrassed to say that forbidden word, the one I've always found dirty and wrong and belonging only in a porno movie.

Andrew slides his hand between my legs and parts my lips with two fingers. He licks me once. Only once. My thighs are starting to tremble heavier.

I don't know how much longer I can wait.

"A woman who knows what she wants sexually," he licks me again, his hooded eyes always watching me, "and isn't afraid to express it is *so* fucking hot, Camryn—Tell. Me. What. You. Want. Or, I won't give it to you." He licks me again and I can't take it anymore.

I reach my hands down and grab fistfuls of his hair, pushing his face further between my legs, as much as he'll allow me, and I say looking right into his eyes, "Lick my pussy, Andrew; *goddammit*, lick my fucking pussy!"

I catch the darkest grin I've ever seen on his face just before my eyelids slam shut and my head arches back when he starts to lick me and this time doesn't stop. He sucks hard on my clit and works his fingers in and out of me at the same time and I think I want to faint. I can't open my eyes; they feel drunk with pleasure. I buck my hips toward him and pull the shit out of his hair, but he never misses a beat. He licks me hard and fast and every now and then he'll slow down to suck on me and roll the pad of his thumb over my swollen clit, before diving right back in. And when I start to feel like I can't take it anymore and try to slide myself away from his face, he grasps my thighs and forces me to stay put until I come hard, my legs trembling uncontrollably, my hands gripping his head with all my strength. A moan shudders from my lips and both of my hands come up behind my head, clutching the headboard with my fingertips, trying to use it as leverage to pull away from Andrew's lashing tongue. But he grips me harder, his hands curled under my thighs and over my hips; he puts so much pressure on me that it hurts, digging his fingertips into my skin, but I like it.

And as my shuddering body begins to calm and my labored breathing starts to slow, although unevenly, Andrew also starts to lick me more gently. When my body stops moving, he kisses the inside of both of my thighs and then right below my bellybutton before crawling upward towards my mouth, bracing his tight, muscled arms against the mattress on each side of me. His soft, wet lips fall on my neck and both sides of my jawline first and then my forehead. Lastly, he looks down into my eyes for a long moment and then leans in and pecks my lips softly.

And then he gets up from the bed.

I can't move.

I want to reach out and grab him and pull him down on top of me, but I can't move. Not only am I still reeling from the orgasm he just gave me, but my mind is still reeling from the entire experience.

I just look at him, barely raising my head from the pillow as he goes toward the door. He looks at me once just after he places his hand on the door lever.

But I'm the one who speaks first:

"Where are you going?"

I know where he's going, but it was the only thing I could think to say to delay him from leaving my room.

He smiles gently. "To my room," he says as if I should already know.

The door opens and light from the hallway floods into the space around him, illuminating his features over there in the shadow. I want to say something, but I'm not sure what. I raise my back from the bed and sit up straight; my fingers restlessly fidget with the sheet near my lap.

"Well, I'll see you in the morning," he says and he gives me one last meaningful grin just before he closes the door behind him and the light from the hall snaps out. But it's still fairly bright in my room; I had left the lamp on by the bed. I look over, thinking about the lamp. It was on the whole time. I had always been kind of shy in bed and even with Ian the most light I ever had sex with him in was from a television, but never bright light. I didn't even think about it this time.

And the words that came out of my mouth...I have never said something like that before. Not the P-word. I can't even say it right now. Sure, I often told Ian to 'please fuck me' or 'fuck me harder', but that was the extent of my pornographic vocabulary.

What is Andrew Parrish doing to me?

Whatever it is...I don't think I want it to stop.

I get up from the bed and dive back into my panties and shorts and go to the door, intent on marching right back over there and...I don't know what.

I stop at the door before opening it and just look down at my bare feet against the green carpet. I don't know what I'd say if I went over there because I don't even know what I want or what I *don't* want. Then I let my arms fall loosely at my sides and a deep sigh bursts through my lips.

"Like it never happened at all," I mock him dryly. "Yeah, you're not good enough to pull that *one* off."

# Andrew

# TWENTY

*I*'ve been awake since 8:00a.m. I got a call from my brother, Asher, and was afraid to answer because I thought it would be the 'news' of my father. He was just calling to let me know that Aidan is pissed off about me taking his guitar. I don't give a shit; what's he gonna do, drive down to Birmingham and fight me for it? I know it really has nothing to do with the guitar; Aidan is just pissed that I left Wyoming while our dad is still alive.

And Asher wanted to check up on me.

"Are you doin' all right, bro?" he said.

"Yeah, I'm perfect, actually."

"Is that sarcasm?"

"No," I said into the phone, "I'm being straight with you, Ash, I'm having the time of my life right now."

"It's that girl, isn't it? Camryn? Was that her name?"

"Yeah, that's her name and yeah, it's the girl."

I grinned inwardly, distracted by the very vivid image in my mind of what happened last night, but then I just smiled, thinking about Camryn in general.

"Well, you know where I'm at if you need me," Asher said and I heard the quiet message in his voice that he wanted to convey but knows better than to speak of it more openly. I told him before never to bring it up again, or I'd have to beat the shit out of him.

"Yeah, I know, thanks, bro—hey, how's Dad doin'?"

"He's the same as he was before you left."

"That's better than worse, I guess."

"Yeah."

We hung up and I called my mom to let her know I was all right. A day longer and she would've had the police looking for me.

I get up and shove my stuff into my duffle bag. As I walk past the television, I pound on the wall with the bottom of my palm next to where Camryn's head is probably lying against her pillow on the other side. If she wasn't already awake, that might've done the trick. Well, OK maybe not, since she is such a deep sleeper—except when it comes to music, apparently. I take a quick shower and brush my teeth and I think about her being in my mouth last night and it's kind of a shame I have to brush my teeth at all. Oh well, maybe I'll do it again later. If she wants me to, of course. Shit, I have absolutely no issues with it whatsoever, except that afterwards I have to take care of myself, but that's all right, too. I'd rather do it than risk letting her touch me. I know that when she does, it'll all be over. For me anyway. I fucking want her, but I'll only take her if the street goes both ways. And right now, I can tell she doesn't know *what* she wants.

I get dressed and slip my bare feet down into my black running shoes, glad they're dry now after being soaked by the rain. I shoulder both of my bags and take Aidan's guitar by the neck and head out into the hallway and next door to Camryn's room.

I hear the TV on inside, so I know she must be up.

I wonder how long it'll take her to crack.

# Camryn

I hear Andrew knock on the door. I suck in a sharp breath, hold it there for a long, tense minute and then let it out in a spat of air, blowing a tassel of hair outward that hangs freely from my braid—preparation to keep me from cracking.

Like it never happened, *my ass*.

Finally, I open the door and when I see him standing there so casually—and *so* edible—I crack. Well, it's more like a really red blush, so hot that my face literally feels like it's on fire. I look down at the floor because if I look at his smiling eyes a second longer my head might melt.

I manage to look back up at him seconds later.

His close-lipped smile is bigger now and much more telling.

*Hey! I think an expression like that is the same as talking about it!*

He looks me up and down, seeing that I'm already dressed and ready to go and then jerks his head back a little and says with a huge grin, "Come on."

I grab my purse and my bag and head out with him.

We hop inside the car and I do what I can to distract myself from the best oral sex I've ever had in my life by finding something random to talk about. He smells extra good today: natural skin with a hint of soap and some kind of shampoo. That's not helping me, either.

"So, are we just going to drive to random motels and not stop anywhere except Waffle Houses?"

Not that that bothers me one bit, but I'm struggling to find 'random' here.

He clicks his seatbelt on and starts the engine.

"No, I actually have something in mind." He glances over.

"Oh?" I ask, my curiosity piqued. "You're breaking from the spontaneous rule of our trip and actually have a plan?"

"Hey, technically it wasn't ever a rule," he says, underlining the fact.

We back out of the parking lot and the vintage Chevelle purrs onto the road.

He's wearing the same black cargo shorts he wore yesterday and I get a quick glimpse of his rock-hard calves, one foot pressing gently on the gas pedal. A dark navy t-shirt fits his chest and arms just right, the fabric tighter around his biceps.

"Well, what's the plan, then?"

"New Orleans," he says, smiling over at me. "It's only about five and a half hours from here."

My face lights up. "I've actually never been to New Orleans before."

He smiles inwardly, as if excited about being the one who gets to take me there my first time. I'm as excited about it as he is. But really, I don't care where we go, even if it's the mosquito swarms of Mississippi, as long as Andrew is with me.

Two hours later, after we've exhausted the random topics which have only been a distraction from talking about what happened last night, I decide to be the one to break it. I reach out and push the down button on the volume. Andrew looks over at me curiously.

"Stuff like that has never come out of my mouth before, just so you know," I get it off my chest.

Andrew grins and moves his hand down on the steering wheel, letting his fingers casually steer instead. He appears more relaxed, his left arm lying across the door on the other side of him, left knee bent upward while the right foot stays on the gas pedal.

"But you liked it," he says, "saying it, I mean."

*Ummm, there wasn't anything about last night that I didn't like.*

My face is only a little red.

"Yeah, I did, actually," I admit.

"Don't tell me you've never thought about saying something like that during sex before," he says.

I hesitate. "Actually, I have." I look over sharply. "Not that I sit around and dream about it though, I've just thought about it."

"Why didn't you ever do it before then, if you had the urge?" He's asking me these questions, but I'm pretty sure he already knows the answers.

I shrug. "I guess I was just chicken shit."

He laughs lightly and moves his fingers back up the steering wheel, holding it more securely as we go around a curvy section of highway.

"I guess I've just always thought of it as something Dominique Starla or Cinnamon Dreams would say in *Legally Boned* or *Friday Night Dykes*."

"You've *seen* those flicks?"

My head jerks around and I gasp. "*No!* I...I didn't know they were *real*, I was just making up—"

Andrew's smile becomes playful.

"I don't know if they're real, either," he says, giving in before I die of mortification, "but I wouldn't doubt it, really. And I get what you mean."

My face relaxes.

"Well, it's hot," he says, "for the record."

I blush some more. Might as well just leave the blush on all the time because I find myself doing it around him a lot more every day.

"So, you think porn stars are hot?" I cringe inwardly, hoping he says no.

Andrew gently purses his lips and says, "Not really, well it's hot in a different way when they do it."

My brows draw together. "Different as in how?"

"Well, when…Dominique Starla," he picks the name from the air, "does it, it's just to some random guy lookin' to get off behind a keyboard." His green eyes fall on me. "That guy's not dreaming about anything with her except her face in his lap." Then he looks back out at the road. "But when someone…*I dunno*…like a sweet, sexy, completely *un*-slutty girl does it, the guy is thinking about a lot more than her face in his lap. He's probably not even thinking about that at all, at least on a deeper level."

I definitely caught the secret meaning behind his words and he probably knows as much.

"It drove me mad," he says, glancing at me long enough to lock eyes with me, "just so you know." But then he turns away completely and pretends to be concentrating more on the road. Maybe he doesn't want me to accuse him of 'talking about it', even though I'm the one that started this conversation. I take full blame and I don't regret it.

"What about you?" I ask, stirring the brief silence. "Were you ever afraid to try something sexually you had the urge to try?"

He thinks about it a moment and says, "Yeah, when I was

younger, like around seventeen, but I was only afraid to try things with girls because I knew they were…"

"They were what?"

He smiles softly, pressing his lips together and I get the feeling there's about to be some kind of comparison.

"Younger girls, at least the ones I hung out with, were 'grossed out' by anything unconventional. They were probably like you in a way, secretly turned on by something different than the missionary position, but too shy to admit it. And at that age it was risky to say: 'Hey let me do you in the ass,' because chances are she'd be freaked out by it and think you're some sexually disturbed pervert."

A laugh pushes through my lips.

"Yeah, I think you're right," I say. "When I was a teenager, I was grossed out when Natalie would tell me things she let Damon do to her. I didn't start actually finding them hot until I lost my virginity at eighteen, but…" my voice starts to trail thinking about Ian, "…but even then, I was still too nervous. I wanted to…umm…"

I'm nervous admitting it *now*.

"Go on, just say it," he says, but not with any measure of playfulness. "You should know by now you can't run me off."

That takes me aback (and makes my heart flutter). Is the truth written all over my face, that I'm afraid of giving him any bad impressions of me? He smiles gently as if to give me that much more assurance that nothing I can say to him will give him a bad impression.

"OK, if I tell you, do you promise not to think it's an invitation?" Perhaps it is, even though I'm not sure about that myself yet, but I definitely don't want him to think that. Not right now, maybe never. I don't know…

"I swear," he says, his eyes serious and not at all offended, "I won't think that at all."

I take a deep breath.

Ugh! I can't believe I'm about to tell him this. I've never told anyone; well, except for Natalie, in a roundabout way.

"Aggression." I pause, still feeling embarrassed to go on. "Most of the time when I daydream about sex, I'm..."

His eyes are grinning! When I said 'aggression' something triggered in his features. It almost seems as if...no, surely that can't be right.

He softens his eyes once he notices.

"Go ahead," he says, smiling gently again.

And I do, because for some reason I'm less afraid to finish than I was seconds ago:

"I'm usually dreaming about being...manhandled."

"Rough sex turns you on," he says evenly.

I nod. "The *thought* of it does, but I've never really experienced it, not in the way I think about it, anyway."

He seems faintly surprised, or, is that contented?

"I think it's what I meant when I told you I always end up with tame guys."

Something just clicked in my head: Andrew knew before me what I really meant back in Wyoming when I said I 'end up with' tame guys. Without realizing it, I basically expressed that ending up with them was unfortunate, something I didn't prefer. He may not have known my definition of 'tame' until now, but he knew before I did that it wasn't something I wanted.

But I loved Ian, and right now I feel awful for thinking this way. Ian was tame sexually, and the thought of having any bad thoughts of him at all makes me feel guilty.

"So, you like hair-pulling and…" he starts to say inquiringly, but his voice trails when he notices my eristic expression.

"Yeah, but *more* aggressive," I say suggestively, trying to get him to say it so I don't have to. I'm getting nervous again.

He shifts his chin sideways, his eyebrows rise a little. "What, like… wait, *how* aggressive?"

I swallow and look away from his eyes. "Force, I guess. Not like flat-out rape or anything extreme like that, but I have a very sexually submissive personality, I think."

Andrew can't look at me now, either.

I turn enough to see that his eyes are slightly wider than seconds ago, and full of shrouded intensity. His Adam's Apple moves gently as he swallows. Both of his hands are on the steering wheel now.

I change the subject:

"You never did technically tell me what *you* were afraid to ask a girl to do." I smile, hoping to bring the playful atmosphere back from before.

He relaxes and grins looking back over at me. "Yeah, I did," he says and adds after an odd pause, "anal sex."

Something tells me that's not what he was really afraid of. I can't put my finger on it, but that whole mention of anal sex I think is just a smokescreen. But why would Andrew, out of the two of us, be the one afraid to admit the truth? He's the one pretty much helping me to be more comfortable with myself sexually. He's the one who I thought wasn't afraid to admit anything, but now I'm not so sure.

I wish I could read his mind.

"Well, believe it or not," I say, glancing at him, "Ian and I did try that once, but it hurt like hell and needless to say, I mean 'once' in the most literal way possible."

Andrew laughs lightly.

Then he looks up at the road signs and seems to be making a quick route decision in his head. We ease off the highway and onto another one. More fields are sprawled out on both sides of the road. Cotton and rice and corn and no telling what else; I really don't know the difference in most crops except the obvious: cotton is white and corn is tall. We drive for hours and hours until the sun starts to set and Andrew pulls off the side of the road. The tires grind to a stop onto the gravel.

"Are we lost?" I ask.

He leans across the seat towards me and reaches for the glove box. His elbow and the under part of his lower arm grazes my leg as he pops the glove box and pulls out a rather worn road map. It's folded awkwardly as if after it had been opened it was never folded back into the same creases. He unfolds the map and lays it against the steering wheel, examining it closely and running his finger along it. He twists the right side of his mouth in his teeth and makes an inquisitive clicking noise with his lips.

"We're lost, aren't we?" I want to laugh, not at him, just at the situation.

"It's your fault," he says, trying to be serious, but failing miserably seeing as how his eyes are smiling.

I let out a spat of air. "And how is it *my* fault?" I argue. "*You're* the one driving."

"Well, if you weren't being so 'distracting', talkin' about sex and secret desires and pornography and that slut, Dominique Starla, I would've noticed I was taking 20 instead of staying on 59 like I should have." He flicks the center of the map with the snap of his finger and shakes his head. "We drove two hours in the wrong direction."

"*Two hours?*" I laugh this time and slap the dashboard. "And you're just *now* realizing this?"

I hope I'm not bruising his ego. Besides, it's not like I'm mad or disappointed; we can drive ten hours in the wrong direction and I wouldn't care.

He looks wounded. I'm pretty sure he's faking it, but I grab a hold of this opportunity and take a chance at doing something I've wanted to do since our time together in the rain on the roof in Tennessee. Reaching over my waist, I unlock my seatbelt and slide across the seat and sit next to him. He seems quietly surprised, but inviting as he lifts his arm so that I can curl myself underneath it. "I'm just messing with you about being lost," I say, laying my head against his shoulder. I feel a little bit of reluctance before his arm comes down around me.

It feels so right to be here like this. *Too* right…

I pretend not to notice how comfortable both of us feel right now and be as nonchalant as before. I look up into the map with him, running my finger along a new route.

"We can just go this way," I say, running my finger south, "and hit 55 straight into New Orleans. Right?" I tilt my head over to see his eyes and my heart jumps when I notice how close his face is to mine now. But I just smile, waiting for him to answer.

He smiles back, but I get the feeling he really didn't hear much I said. "Yeah, we'll just hit 55." His eyes search my face and briefly skim my lips.

I reach out and start to fold the map back together and then I turn the volume back up. Andrew moves his arm from around me to put the car in gear.

When we pull away, he rests his hand on my thigh pressed next to his and we ride like that for a long time; the only time he moves his hand is to take better control of a sharp curve or to adjust the music, but he always puts it right back.

And I always want him to.

# TWENTY-ONE

*A*re you sure we're still on 55?" I ask much later after dark and haven't seen any headlights coming or going in either direction in forever, it seems.

All I see are fields and trees and the occasional cow.

"Yes, babe, we're still on 55; I've made sure of that."

Just as he says that, we pass another highway sign that actually reads: 55.

I lift away from Andrew's arm, which my head has been pressed against for the past hour, and start to stretch my arms and legs and back. I lean over and massage my calf muscles afterwards; I think every muscle in my body has fused like cement around my bones.

"You need to get out and stretch your legs for a while?" Andrew says.

I look over to see his face in shadow; a light blue hue is washed over his skin. His sculpted jawline looks more pronounced in the dark.

"Yeah," I say and lean up toward the dashboard to get a better look out the windshield at what the landscape looks like. Of course. Fields and trees and—there goes another cow—I should've known. But then I notice the sky. I press myself up further against the dash and look upward at the stars wrapped in the infinite blackness, noticing how easy they are to see and how many of them there are without any light pollution for miles.

"Do you want to get out and walk around?" he asks, still waiting for the rest of my answer.

Getting an idea of my own, I smile brightly at him and nod. "Yes, I think that's a great idea—is there a blanket in the trunk?"

He looks at me curiously for a moment. "Actually, yes, I keep one in that box back there with the rest of my emergency roadside supplies—why?"

"I know it might be cliché," I begin, "but it's something I've always wanted to do—have you ever slept under the stars?" I feel a little silly asking, I guess because it *is* kind of cliché and nothing about Andrew thus far has come anywhere near cliché.

His face spreads into a warm smile. "As a matter of fact, no, I have never slept under the stars—are you gettin' all romantic on me, Camryn Bennett?" He looks at me with a playful sideward stare.

"No!" I laugh. "Come on, I'm serious; I just think it's the perfect opportunity." I motion my hands toward the windshield. "Look at all of the fields out there."

"Yeah, but we can't lay a blanket out in a cotton or corn field," he says, "and most of the time those fields are saturated with ankle-deep water."

"Not the ones covered with grass and cow bombs," I say.

"You want to sleep in a field where cows shit?" he says casually, but equally humored.

I snicker. "No, just the grass. Come on…" then I glare at him teasingly. "What, are you afraid of a little cow shit?"

"Haha!" He shakes his head. "Camryn, there's nothing little about a pile of cow shit."

I scoot back over next to him and lay my head right dead-center on his lap, looking up at him with a pouty face. *"Please?"* I bat my eyes.

And I try hopelessly to ignore what my head is actually lying on.

# Andrew

I absolutely fucking melt when she looks up at me like that. How would I ever say no to her? Whether it was about sleeping next to a pile of cow shit or under a bridge overpass next to a homeless drunk—I would sleep *anywhere* with her.

But that's the problem.

I think this became a problem the second she decided to sit next to me in the car. Because that's when she changed, when I think she started to believe she wants more from me than oral sex. I may have done that for her back in Birmingham, but I can't let her want more than that. I can't let her touch me and I can't sleep with her.

I *do* want her, I want her in every way imaginable, but I can't bear to break her heart—that little body of hers, that's another story; I could bear to break that. But if she ever lets me have her, breaking her heart (and mine) is what will happen in the end.

It's harder since she told me about her ex...

"Please," she says one more time.

Despite just giving myself the third-degree, I reach down and brush my fingertip along the side of her face and say very gently, "All right."

I never was one to listen to reason when it came to something that I wanted, but with Camryn, I'm finding myself telling reason to fuck off a lot more than usual.

Another ten minutes of driving and I find a field that looks like a flat, endless sea of grass and I park the car on the side of the road. We are literally in the middle of nowhere. We get out and lock the doors, leaving everything inside the car. I pop the trunk and rummage that roadside box for the rolled-up blanket, which smells like old car and somewhat like gasoline.

"It stinks," I say, taking a whiff.

Camryn leans in and sniffs, wrinkling her nose at it. "Oh, well, I don't care."

I don't, either. I'm sure she'll make it smell better.

Without even thinking about it, I grab her hand and we walk down a small slope through a ditch and up the other side to the low-lining fence separating the field from us. I start looking for the easiest way for her to get over it. Next thing I know, her fingers are falling away from mine and she's climbing over the damn thing.

"Hurry!" she says as she lands on the other side in a crouched position.

I can't wipe the grin off my face.

I leap over the fence and land beside her and we take off running into the wide open; her like a graceful gazelle, me like the lion chasing after her. I hear her flip-flops slapping against her feet as she runs and see the way wisps of stray blond strands of hair appear illuminated around her head as the breeze stirs it. I've got the blanket in one hand as I run behind her, letting her stay a few steps ahead of me so if she happens to fall I'll be there to laugh at her first and then help her up afterwards. It's so dark with only the light from the moon bathing the landscape. But there's enough light that we can see where we're stepping and not fall into a chasm or trip over a tree on our way.

And I don't see any cows, which means this might be a shit-free field and that's a plus.

We get so far away from the car that the only part of it I can see anymore is the reflective glint from the silver rims.

"I think this is good enough," Camryn says coming to a winded stop.

The nearest trees are thirty or forty yards out in every direction.

She raises her arms high above her head and tilts her chin back, letting the breeze rush over her. She's smiling so hugely, her eyes closed, that I'm afraid to say anything and disturb her moment with nature.

I unroll the blanket and lay it on the ground.

"Tell me the truth," she says, curling her fingers around my wrist and guiding me to sit down on the blanket with her, "you've never spent the night under the stars with a girl before?"

I shake my head. "It's the truth."

She seems to like that. I watch her smile at me as a light wind moves between us and brushes loose hair across her face. She reaches up and moves a few pieces from in between her lips, slipping her finger behind them carefully.

"I'm not really the rose petals-on-the-bed kind of guy."

"No?" she asks, a bit surprised. "I think you're probably a really romantic guy, actually."

I shrug. Is she fishing? I think she's fishing.

"I guess it depends on your definition of romantic," I say. "If a girl expects a candlelit dinner and Michael Bolton playing in the background, she's definitely got the wrong guy."

Camryn giggles.

"Well, that's a little *too* romantic," she says, "but I bet you've had your share of romantic gestures though."

"I guess," I say, honestly not really coming up with any at the moment.

She looks at me with her head cocked to one side.

"You're one of those," she says.

"One of what?"

"Guys that don't like to talk about their exes."

"You want to know about my exes?"

"Sure."

She lies down on her back, leaving her bare knees drawn up and she pats the blanket beside her.

I lie next to her in the same position.

"Tell me about your first love," she says and already I feel like this isn't a conversation we should be having but if it's what she wants to talk about, I'll do my best to tell her what she wants to know.

I guess it's only fair since she told me about hers.

"Well," I say, looking up at the star-filled sky, "her name was Danielle."

"And you loved her?" Camryn looks over at me, letting her head fall to the side.

I keep looking at the stars.

"Yeah, I loved her, but it wasn't meant to be."

"How long were you together?"

I'm wondering why she wants to know this; most girls I know snap into that jealousy-fueled mood-swing stuff that makes me want to cover my nuts when it comes to talking about exes.

"Two years," I answer. "The break-up was mutual; we started

checking out other people and I guess realized we didn't love each other as much as we thought we did."

"Or, you just fell out of love."

"No, we were never in love to begin with."

I look over at her this time.

"How did you know the difference?" she asks.

I think about it for a moment, searching her eyes just about a foot from mine. I can smell the cinnamon toothpaste she brushed with this morning when she breathes.

"I don't think you ever really fall *out* of love with someone," I say and see a flicker of thought move through her eyes. "I think when you fall in love, like true love, it's love for life. All the rest is just experience and delusions."

"I didn't know you were so philosophical." She grins. "I should tell you, that counts as romantic."

Usually, it's her doing the blushing, but she got me this time. I try not to look at her, but that's not so easy to pull off.

"So, who were you ever *in* love with, then?" she asks.

I straighten my legs out in front of me, crossing my ankles and locking my fingers together over my stomach. I look up at the sky and from the corner of my eye see Camryn do the same.

"Honestly?"

"Well yeah," she says, "I'm just curious."

I stare at a bright cluster of stars and say, "Well, no one."

A tiny burst of air escapes her lips. "Oh please, Andrew; thought you were going to be honest?"

"I am," I say, glancing over, "a few times I thought I was in love, but—why are we talking about this anyway?"

Camryn lets her head fall sideways again and she isn't smiling anymore. She looks sort of sad.

"I guess I was using you as my shrink again."

My eyes draw inward. "What do you mean?"

She looks away; her pretty blond braid falls away from her shoulder and onto the blanket. "Because I'm starting to think maybe I wasn't... No, I shouldn't say something like that." She's not the happy, smiling Camryn anymore that I ran out here with.

I raise my back from the blanket and prop myself up on my elbows. I look over at her curiously. "You should say whatever you feel whenever you need to. Maybe saying it is exactly what you need."

She doesn't look at me.

"But I feel guilty even *thinking* it."

"Well, guilt is a bitch, but don't you think if you're thinking it in the first place that it just might be true?"

Her head falls to the side.

"Just say it. If after you say it, it doesn't feel right, then deal with that, but if you hold that shit in, the uncertainty will be a bigger bitch than the guilt will be."

She stares up at the stars again. I do, too, just to give her some time to think about it.

"Maybe I wasn't ever in love with Ian," she says. "I did love him, a lot, but if I was *in* love with him... I think maybe I'd still be."

"That's a good observation," I say and smile slimly, hoping she might again, too. I really hate to see her frown.

Her face is blank, contemplative.

"Well, what makes you believe that you were never in love with him?"

She looks right at me, searching my face and then says, "Because when I'm with you, I don't think about him much anymore."

I immediately lie back down and fix my gaze on the black sky. I could probably count all of those stars if I tried, just as a distraction, but there's a much bigger distraction lying next to me than all the stars in the Universe could be.

I have to stop this, and soon.

"Well, I'm very good company," I say with a grin lacing my voice. "And I had your little ass crawling across that bed the other night, so yeah I can see how you might be more inclined to think of my head between your legs than anything else." I'm just trying to shift her mood back to playful, even if it means she'll smack me for it and accuse me of breaking my like-it-never-happened promise.

And she does smack me, right after lifting up and propping herself on her elbows like I had.

She laughs. "Asshole!"

I laugh louder; I'd throw my head back if it wasn't pressed against the ground.

Then she moves closer to my side, propped up on one elbow as she looks down at me. I can feel the softness of her hair brushing against my arm.

"Why wouldn't you kiss me?" she asks and it surprises me. "When you went down on me last night, you never kissed me. Why?"

"I *did* kiss you."

"You didn't *kiss-kiss* me," she says and she's so close to my lips that I want to kiss her *now*, but I don't. "I don't know how to feel about that—I don't *like* how I feel about it, but I'm not sure how I *should* feel."

"Well, you shouldn't feel bad, that much I do know," I say, being as vague as I can.

"But why?" she probes and her expression is beginning to harden.

I give in and say, "Because kissing is very intimate."

She cocks her head. "So, you won't kiss me for the same reason you won't fuck me?"

I'm instantly hard. I hope like hell she doesn't notice.

"Yes," I say and before I have a chance to say anything else, she's crawling on top of my lap. Shit, if she didn't know I was as hard a rock then, she definitely knows now. Her bare knees are pressed against the blanket on each side of me and she leans over, her arms holding up her weight and I fucking die when she brushes her lips across mine.

She looks right into my eyes and says, "I won't try to make you sleep with me, but I want you to kiss me. Just a kiss."

"Why?" I ask.

She really needs to move off my lap. Oh shit…it's not helping that my dick is pressed between her ass cheeks right about now. *If she moves just an inch backward—*

"Because I want to know what it feels like," she whispers onto my mouth.

My hands move up her legs and then her waist where I grip my fingers around her form. She smells so damn good. She feels amazing and all she's doing is sitting on me. I can't even begin to understand what she would feel like inside; the thought makes me crazy.

Then I feel her pressing herself against me through our clothes, her little hips moving gently, just once to persuade me, and then she stops and holds herself there. I'm throbbing painfully. Her eyes search my face and my lips and all I want to do is rip off her clothes and bury my cock inside of her.

She leans in and places her lips over mine, slipping her warm tongue into my reluctant mouth. My tongue moves against hers slowly, tasting it first, feeling the warm wetness of it as it begins to tangle with mine. We breathe deeply into each other's mouths and, unable to resist her or deny her this one kiss, I grab each side of her face and press her forcefully against me, locking my lips around hers with ravenous intent. She moans into my mouth and I kiss her harder, wrapping one arm around her back and pulling the rest of her body closer.

And then the kiss breaks. Our lips linger on one another for a long moment until she lifts away and looks down at me with an enigmatic expression I've never seen before, one that does something to my heart that I've never felt before.

And then her face falls and the expression withers into the darkness, replaced by something confused and wounded, but she tries to hide it by smiling down at me.

"With a kiss like that," she says, grinning playfully as if to mask something deeper, "you'd probably never have to sleep with me."

I can't help but laugh; it is kind of ridiculous, but I'll let her believe what she wants.

She crawls off my lap and lies beside me again, resting the back of her head in the cradle of her hands.

"They're beautiful, aren't they?"

I look up at the stars with her, but I don't see them really; she's all I can think about and about that kiss.

"Yeah, they are beautiful."

*And so are you...*

"Andrew?"

"Yeah?"

We keep our eyes on the sky.

"I wanted to say thank you."

"For what?"

She answers after a pause: "For everything: for making me

shove your clothes into that bag instead of folding them and for turning the music down in the car so it wouldn't wake me up and for singing about raisins." Her head falls to the side and so does mine. She looks me in the eyes and says, "And for making me feel alive."

A smile warms my face and I glance away and say, "Well, everybody needs help feeling alive again every once in a while."

"No," she says seriously, and my gaze falls back on hers, "I didn't say *again*, Andrew; for making me feel alive for the *first time*."

My heart reacts to her words and I can't respond. But I can't look away from her, either. Reason is screaming at me again, telling me to stop this before it's too late, but I can't. I'm too selfish.

Camryn smiles gently and I return it and then we both gaze up at the stars again. The hot July night is just right with a light breeze blowing through the wide open space and not a cloud in the sky. There are thousands of crickets and frogs and a few whippoorwills singing into the night. I always did like to listen to those birds.

The quiet is shattered suddenly by Camryn's shrieking voice and she's jumping up from the blanket faster than a cat from a bathtub.

"A snake!" She's pointing with one hand and the other is clasped over her mouth. "Andrew! It's right there! Kill it!"

I jump up when I see something black slithering over the foot of the blanket. I jump back quickly to keep my distance and then I go to stomp on it.

"No-no-no-no!" she screams, waving her hands in front of her. "Don't *kill* it!"

I blink back, confused. "But you just said to kill it."

"Well, I didn't mean it literally!"

She's still freaking out, her back slightly hunched over as if shielding the rest of her body from the snake, which is hilarious.

I raise my hands out, palms-up. "What, you want me to *pretend* to kill it?" I laugh, shaking my head at how funny she is.

"No just—there's no way I can sleep out here now." She grabs my arm. "Let's just go." She's literally shaking and trying not to laugh and cry at the same time.

"All right," I say and lean over to snatch the blanket off the grass now that the snake has moved off it. I shake it out with one hand since Camryn's holding on for life to the other. Then I take her hand and we start to head back toward the car.

"I hate snakes, Andrew!"

"I can see that, babe."

I'm trying so hard not to laugh.

As we're walking across the field, she starts to pull me along a little, picking up the pace. She yelps when her almost-bare foot steps on a harmless soft mound of soil and I see we might not make it back to the car before she faints.

"Come here," I say, stopping her in mid-sprint. I pull her around behind me and help her onto my back, holding her straddled around my waist with her thighs in my arms.

# TWENTY-TWO

*C*amryn wakes me up the next morning adjusting her head on my lap in the front seat of the car.

"Where are we?" she asks, rising up; the sun beams in through the car windows and pools against the inside of her door.

"About half an hour from New Orleans," I say, reaching behind me and rubbing a muscle loose in my back.

We got back on the road last night after leaving the field and intended to just drive on to New Orleans, but I was so damn tired I almost fell asleep at the wheel. She had fallen asleep first. So, I pulled off the side of the road, leaned my head back and passed out. I could've slept more comfortably in the backseat alone, but I would rather be stiff in the morning if it meant I was next to her when I woke up.

Speaking of stiff…

I wipe the blur from my eyes and move around some to work out a few muscles. And to make sure my shorts are loose enough in the front that my obvious hard-on isn't a blatant conversation piece.

Camryn stretches and yawns and then pulls her legs up and props her bare feet on the dashboard, causing her shorts to ride up far past her thighs.

*Not* a good idea first thing in the morning.

"You must've been really tired," she says, pulling her fingers through her hair to break apart the braid.

"Yeah, if I tried to drive any longer we might've ended up wrapped around a tree."

"You're gonna start letting me drive some, Andrew, or—"

"Or *what*?" I smirk at her. "You'll whine and lay your head on my lap and say *please*?"

"It worked last night, didn't it?"

She has a point.

"Look, I don't mind if you drive." I glance over at her and then start the engine. "I promise, after New Orleans, wherever we go, I'll let you take the wheel for a while, OK?"

A sweet forgiving smile lights up her face.

I pull back onto the highway after an SUV speeds past and Camryn goes back to working her fingers through her hair. Then she starts winding the hair back into a neater braid so fast and without having to look that I can't wrap my head around how something like that is done.

My eyes keep trailing back to her naked legs though.

I really need to stop doing that.

I turn away and glance out the window beside me, back and forth between it and the windshield.

"We need to find a laundromat soon, too," she says, snapping the rubber band in place around the end of her hair. "I've run out of clean clothes."

I've been waiting for an opportunity to 'adjust myself' and when she starts looking down into her purse, I take it.

"Is it true?" she asks, looking over at me with one hand in her purse.

I move my hand away from my lap, thinking I'm getting away

with it appearing to be nothing more than making my shorts more comfortable when she says, "That all guys get massive hard-ons in the mornings?"

My eyes grow bigger in my face. I just watch out the windshield.

"Not *every* morning," I say, still trying not to look at her.

"What, just like Tuesdays and Fridays or something?"

I know she's smiling, but I refuse to confirm it.

"Is *this* a Tuesday or Friday?" she adds, taunting me.

Finally, I glance over at her.

"It's Friday," I say simply.

She lets out an aggravated breath.

"I'm not a slut, or anything," she says, dropping her legs from the dashboard, "and I'm sure you don't think that since *you* are the one who has sort of pushed me to be more open with my sexuality and what I want…" Her voice trails. It's as if she's waiting for me to confirm what she just said, like she's still worried of what I might think of her.

I look right into her eyes. "No, I would never think you were a slut unless you went around screwing a bunch of guys, for which then I would be in jail because I would have to beat the fuck out of all of them—but no, why are you saying this?"

She blushes and I swear her shoulders almost come up around her cheeks.

"Well, I was just thinking…" she's still not sure if she wants to say it, whatever it is.

"What did I tell you, babe? Say what's on your mind."

She tilts her chin and looks at me gently. "Well, since you did something for me, I thought maybe I could do something for you." She changes her tune fast afterwards, as if still worried what I might think. "I mean, no strings attached, of course. It'll be like it never happened."

Ah, shit! Why didn't I see *that* coming?

"No," I say instantly.

She flinches.

I soften my face and my voice. "I can't let you do anything like that for me, all right?"

"Why the hell not?"

"I just can't—God, I want to, you have no idea, but I just can't."

"That's stupid."

She's getting seriously aggravated.

"Wait..." she looks at me inquiringly and turns her face at an angle, "you got some kind of 'issue' down there?"

My mouth falls open. "Ummm, no?" I say with wide eyes. "Shit, I'll pull over and show you."

She throws her head back and laughs and then gets serious again:

"Well you won't have sex with me, you won't let me get you off and I had to force you to kiss me."

"You didn't force me."

"You're right," she snaps, "I seduced it out of you."

"I kissed you because I wanted to," I say. "I want to do *every-thing* with you, Camryn. Trust me! In just a few days I've imagined more positions with you than there are in the Kama Sutra. I've wanted to—" I notice I'm white-knuckling the steering wheel.

She looks wounded, but this time I don't break.

"I told you," I say carefully, "I can't do anything like that with you or—"

"Or I'll have to let you own me," she finishes my sentence angrily, "yeah, I remember what you said, but what does that mean exactly: let you *own* me?"

I think Camryn knows exactly what it means, but she wants to be sure of it herself.

Wait a second . . . she's playing games with me; either that or she still doesn't know what she wants, sexually or otherwise and she's just as confused and reluctant as I am.

# Camryn

He passed my test. I'd be a liar if I said I *didn't* want to have sex with him, or pleasure him in other ways like he did for me—I totally want to do all of those things with him. But really I wanted to see if he would take the bait. He didn't.

And now I'm terrified of him.

I'm terrified because of how I feel about him. I shouldn't feel this way and I hate myself for it.

I said I would never do it. I promised myself I wouldn't...

Trying to gain some sense of lighthearted normalcy back in our conversation, I smile gently at him. All I want to do is take back the offer and go back to how we were before I brought it up, except with the knowledge I have now: Andrew Parrish respects me and wants me in ways that I don't think I can give him.

I bring my knees toward me, propping my feet on the leather seat. I don't want him to answer my last question: what does it mean to let him own me? I hope he forgets that I asked at all. I already know what it means, or at least I think I do: to own me is to be with him, the way I was with Ian. Except with Andrew I believe in my heart that I could fall in love with him, *true* love. So easily I could. Already I can't stand the thought of being away from him. Already all of the faces in my daydreams have been replaced with Andrew's face. And already, I dread the day our road trip ends, when he has to go back to Galveston or to Wyoming and to leave me behind.

Why does it scare me? And where did this sick feeling in the pit of my stomach come from all of a sudden?

"I'm sorry, babe, I really am. I didn't mean to hurt you. Not in any way."

I look up and over at him and then I shake my head hard. "You haven't hurt me. Please don't think you hurt me."

I go on:

"Andrew, the truth is…" I take a very deep breath. He's having a hard time keeping his eyes on the road now. "…the truth is that I—well, first off, I won't lie and say that pleasuring you isn't something that I wouldn't do—I *would* do it. But I want you to know that I'm glad you refused me."

I think he understands. I can see it in his face.

He smiles gently and reaches out his hand to me. I take it and scoot over next to him and he wraps his arm around my shoulder. I tilt my chin upward to see him and drape my fingers over his thigh.

He is so beautiful to me…

"You scare me," I finally say.

My admission sparks a faint reaction in his eyes.

"I said I would never do this; you have to understand. I promised myself that I would never get close to anyone again."

I feel his arm harden around my arm and the beating of his heart has picked up speed; it thumps rapidly against the side of my throat.

Then a grin slides across his mouth and he says, "Are you in love with me, Camryn Bennett?"

I blush super-hard and twist my lips into a hard line, pressing my face deeper against his hard pec.

"Not yet," I say with a smile in my voice, "but I'm gettin' there."

"You're so full of shit," he says, squeezing my arm a little tighter. He kisses the top of my hair.

"Yeah, I know," I say with the same amount of jest in my voice as was in his and then my voice trails, "I know…"

———

I get my very first glimpse of New Orleans from afar: Lake Pontchartrain and eventually the sprawling landscape of cottages and townhouses and bungalows. I'm in awe of it: from the Superdome, which I'll always be able to recognize after seeing it all over the news during Katrina, to the giant, expansive oak trees that are creepy and beautiful and old, and to the people shuffling along the streets of the French Quarter, though I think most of them are tourists.

And as we drive along, I'm mesmerized by the familiar balconies, which wrap around the entire length of many of the buildings. They look just like they do on TV, except that Mardi Gras isn't going on and no one's flashing their boobs or throwing beads from the balconies.

Andrew smiles over at me, seeing how excited I am to be here.

"I love it already," I say, curling back up next to him after practically pressing my face against the window looking out at everything for the past several minutes.

"It's a great city." He beams, proudly; I wonder just how intimate he is with this place.

"I try to come every year," he says, "usually Mardi Gras, but anytime of the year is good, I think."

"Oh, so you usually come when there are boobs." I wink at him.

"Guilty!" he says, moving both hands from the steering wheel and holding them up in surrender.

We get two rooms at the Holiday Inn in walking distance of the famous Bourbon Street. I almost told him to just get a single room with two beds this time, but I stopped myself. *No, Camryn, you're just feeding the desire. Don't move into a room with him. Stop this while you can.*

And for a moment as we stood side by side at the counter when the clerk asked how he could 'help us', Andrew had paused and I got the strangest feeling from it. But we ended up with side-by-side king rooms, like always.

I head toward mine and he strolls over to his. We look at each other in the hallway with our keycards in our hands.

"I'm gonna hop in the shower," he says, holding the guitar in one hand, "but whenever you're ready, just come on over and let me know."

I nod and we smile at each other before we disappear inside our rooms.

Not five minutes in and I hear my phone buzzing around inside my purse. Pretty sure it's my mom, I pull it out and am prepared to answer and tell her that I'm still alive and I'm having a good time, but I see that it's not her.

It's Natalie.

My hand just freezes around the phone as I stare down at the glowing screen. Should I answer it, or not? Well, I better figure it out quick.

"Hello?"

"Cam?" Natalie says in a careful voice on the other end.

I can't get any words out yet. I'm not sure if enough time has passed that I should be pretend-unforgiving, or if I should be nice.

"Are you there?" she asks when I don't say anything else.

"Yeah, Nat, I'm here."

She sighs and makes that weird whiney, moaning sound she always does when she's nervous about saying or doing something.

"I'm a total fucking bitch," she says. "I know that and I'm a horrible best friend and I should be groveling at your feet right now for forgiveness, but I...well, that was the plan, but your mom said you were in...*Virginia?* What the hell are you doing in Virginia?"

I plop down on the bed and kick my flip-flops off.

"I'm not in Virginia," I say, "but don't tell my mom or anyone else."

"Well then where are you? And where could you be for over a week?"

Wow, has it only been a week? It feels like I've been on the road with Andrew for a month at least.

"I'm in New Orleans, but it's a long story."

"Ummm, well, *hell-o?*" she says sarcastically, "I've got plenty of time."

Getting irritated with her quickly, I sigh and say, "Natalie, you're the one who called me. And if I remember correctly, you're the one who called me a lying bitch and didn't believe me when I told you what Damon did. I'm sorry, but I don't think jumping right back into being best friends and acting like nothing happened, is the best thing right now."

"I know, you're right and I'm sorry." She pauses to gather her thoughts and I can hear the tab on a can of soda crack open in the background. She takes a small sip. "It wasn't that I didn't believe you, Cam, I was just really hurt. Damon is a bastard. I dumped him."

"Why, because you caught him cheating in the act as opposed to believing your best friend since second grade when she tells you he's a pig?"

"I deserved that," she says, "but no, I didn't catch him cheating. I just realized I missed my best friend and that I committed the worst crime against the Code of Best Friends. I finally confronted him about it and of course he lied, but I just kept nagging at him about it because I wanted him to admit it to me. Not because I needed the validation from him, but I just…Cam, I just wanted him to tell me the truth. I wanted it to come from him."

I hear the pain in her voice. I know she means what she's saying and I intend to fully forgive her, but I'm not ready to let her know I forgive her enough to tell her about Andrew. I don't know what it is, but it's like the only person that exists in my world right now is Andrew. I love Natalie with all my heart, but I'm not ready for her to know yet. I'm not ready to share him with her. She has a way of…cheapening an experience, if that's fair to say.

"Look, Nat," I say, "I don't hate you and I want to forgive you, but it's going to take some time; you really hurt me."

"I understand," she says, but I detect the disappointment in her voice, too. Natalie has always been an impatient, instant-gratification kind of girl.

"Well, are you all right?" she asks. "I can't imagine why you'd run off to New Orleans of all places—is this hurricane season?"

I hear the shower running in Andrew's room.

"Yeah, I'm doing great," I say, thinking about Andrew. "To tell you the truth, Nat, I've never felt so alive and as happy as I have been this past week."

"Oh my God…it's a guy! You're with a guy, aren't you? Camryn Marybeth Bennett, you fucking bitch you better not keep these things from me!"

That's exactly what I mean by cheapening the experience.

"What's his name?" She gasps loudly as though the answer to the world's mysteries just fell into her lap. "You got laid! Is he hot?"

"Natalie, *please*," I shut my eyes and pretend she's a mature twenty-year-old and not still stuck on the high school campus. "I'm not gonna talk about this with you right now, all right? Just give me a few days and I'll call you and let you know how things are going, but please—"

"I'll take it!" she says, agreeing, but not at all getting the hint that she needs to tone her enthusiasm down a notch. "As long as you're OK and you don't still hate me, I'll take it."

"Thank you."

Finally, she comes down from her horny gossip cloud:

"I really am sorry, Cam. I can't say it enough."

"I know. I believe you. And when I call you later, you can also tell me what happened with Damon. If you want to."

"All right," she says, "sounds good."

"I'll talk to you later . . . and Nat?"

"Yeah?"

"I'm really glad you called. I've missed you a lot."

"Me too."

We hang up and I just stare at the phone for a minute until my thoughts of Natalie fade into my thoughts of Andrew. Just like I said: all of the faces in my daydreams have become Andrew's face.

I take a shower and put on a pair of jeans which still haven't been washed, but they don't stink so I guess it's OK for now. But if I don't get my clothes washed soon I'm going to be hitting another department store for something new. I'm just glad I packed twelve pairs of clean panties in that duffle bag of mine.

I start to put on makeup and do the usual, but then I let my fingers rest on the bathroom sink and I look at myself in the mirror, trying to see what Andrew sees. He's almost seen me at my absolute worst: no makeup, circles under my eyes after being awake on the road for so long, nasty breath, wild, grungy hair—I smile thinking about it and then picture him standing behind me, right now, in the mirror. I see his mouth buried in the curve of my neck and his hard arms wrapped around my body from behind, his fingers pressing against my ribs.

There's a knock on my room door, snapping me out of my daydream.

"Are you ready?" Andrew asks when I open the door for him.

He comes the rest of the way into the room.

"Where are we going, anyway?" I ask walking back into the bathroom where my makeup is. "And I need some clean clothes. Seriously."

He walks up behind me and it shocks me a little because it almost feels like that daydream I was having moments ago. I start to put on mascara, leaning over the sink toward the mirror. I squint the left eye while applying mascara to the right eye while Andrew checks out my butt. He's not being secret about it at all. He *wants* me to see him being bad. I roll my eyes at him and go back to my mascara, switching to the other eye.

"There's a laundry facility on the twelfth floor," he says.

He locks his hands around my hips and looks at me in the mirror with a devilish grin and his bottom lip pinned between his teeth.

I swing around.

"Then that's the first place we're going," I say.

"*What?*" He looks disappointed. "No, I want to go *out*, walk around the town, have a few beers, see a few bands play. I don't want to do laundry."

"Oh, quit whining," I say and turn around back to the mirror whipping my lipstick out of my bag. "It's not even two o'clock in the afternoon—you're not one of those beer-for-breakfast guys, are you?"

He flinches and presses his palm against his heart, pretending to be wounded. "Absolutely not! I wait at least until lunch."

I shake my head and push him out of the bathroom; toothy, dimpled smile and all, and then shut the door with him on the other side.

"What was *that* for?" he says through the door.

"I have to pee!"

"Well, I wouldn't have looked!"

"Go get your dirty clothes from your room, Andrew!"

"But—"

"Now, Andrew! Or, we're not going out later!"

I can picture his bottom lip puckered out, though of course that's totally *not* what he's doing. He's grinning a hole through that damn door.

"Fine!" he says and then I hear the room door open and then shut behind him.

When I'm done in the bathroom, I gather up all of my dirty laundry and stuff it into my sling bag and I slip on my flip-flops.

# TWENTY-THREE

*W*e do laundry first and while we're there I *do* fold everything after I take it out of the dryer, rather than shoving it all back into the bags. He tries to protest, but I get my way this time. Afterwards, we hit the town and he takes me everywhere, even to the St. Louis cemetery where the tombs are above ground and I've never seen anything like that before. We walk together all the way down Canal Street toward the World Trade Center New Orleans, and soon after we find a much-needed Starbucks. We talk forever over coffee and I tell him that I got a call from Natalie last night. And we go on and on about her and Damon, who Andrew has grown quickly to detest.

Later we pass up a steak house which Andrew tries to get me to stop with him at by throwing that deal I made with him back on the bus in my face. But I'm not the slightest bit hungry and try to explain to a whimpering steak-deprived Andrew that I have to be ready for a big meal if he wants me to enjoy a steak.

And we find a mall: The Shops at Canal Place, where I am actually excited to go after being stuck wearing the same boring clothes for the past week.

"But we just did laundry," Andrew protests as we head inside. "What do you need new clothes for?"

I hoist my purse strap on the opposite shoulder and grab him by the elbow.

"If we're going out tonight," I say, dragging him along, "then I want to find something cute that looks halfway decent."

"But what you're wearing now is cute as hell," he argues.

"I just want a new pair of jeans and a top," I say then stop and look at him. "You can help me pick it out."

That got his attention.

"All right," he says, smiling.

I pull him along again. "But don't get your hopes up," I say, jerking his arm in emphasis, "I said you can *help*, not *choose*."

"You sure are getting your way a lot today," he says. "You should know, babe, I'll only let you get away with so much before I start playing my cards."

"What cards do you think you have to play exactly?" I question with confidence because I think he's bluffing.

He purses his lips when I glance over and my confidence is starting to drain.

"If you recall," he says all sophisticatedly, "you're still on whatever-I-say duty."

Confidence lost.

He grins and jerks my arm towards him this time.

"And since you already let me go down on you once," he adds and my eyes widen, "I think I could tell you to lie back and spread your legs and you'd have to listen, right?"

I can barely move my eyes around to see if anyone walking by had heard him. Andrew didn't exactly say that in a whisper, but I wouldn't expect as much.

Then he slows our pace and leans in toward my ear and says quietly, "If you don't let me have my way with something simpler soon, I might have to torture you again with my tongue between your legs." His breath on my ear, combined with his wetness-inducing words, sends shivers up the side of my neck. "Ball's in your court, babe."

He pulls away and I want to slap that grin off his face, but he'd probably like it.

Dilemma? Let him have his way with something simple, or keep getting my way and him 'torture' me later? Hmmm. I guess I'm more of a masochist than I thought.

———

The night falls and I'm ready for our night out. I'm wearing a new pair of tight jeans, a sexy black strapless top that hugs my waist and the cutest black heels I've ever found in any mall.

Andrew gawks at me in the doorway.

"I should play my card right now," he says coming into the room.

I've braided my hair into two loose braids this time, one resting over each shoulder, stopping just above my breasts. And I always leave a few strands of blond hair to fall freely about my face because I always thought it was cute on other girls, so why not me?

Andrew seems to like it. He reaches up and slides each one within his fingers.

I blush inwardly.

"Babe, no fucking joke, you are *smokin'*."

"Thanks..." *Oh my God, did I just...* giggle.

I look him up and down, too, and although he's back to jeans and a simple t-shirt and his black Doc Martens, he's the sexiest thing I've ever seen no matter *what* he's wearing.

We head out and I turn a few old guys' heads in the elevator and down the hall. Andrew is eating the hell out of that, I can tell. He's beaming walking next to me and it just makes my face beet red.

We hang out at d.b.a first and watch a band play for about an hour. But when I get carded and it looks like I'm not going to get to drink here, Andrew takes me farther down the street to another bar.

"It's a hit or miss," he says as we approach the bar, hand in hand. "Most of them will card you, but every now and then you get lucky and they don't bother if you look twenty-one enough."

"Well, I'll be twenty-one in five months," I say, gripping his hand as we cross a busy intersection.

"I was worried you were seventeen when I met you on the bus."

"*Seventeen?!*" I hope like hell I don't actually look *that* young.

"Hey," he says glancing over once, "I've seen *fifteen-year-olds* that look twenty—hard to tell anymore."

"So you think I look seventeen?"

"No, you look about twenty," he admits, "I'm just sayin'."

That's a relief.

This bar is slightly smaller than the last and the people in it are a mixture of fresh-out-of-college and early thirty-somethings. A few pool tables are set side by side near the back and the lighting is dim in the place, mostly localized over the pool tables and in the hallway to my right, leading into the restrooms. The cigarette smoke is thick unlike the last place where it was non-existent, but it doesn't bother me much. I'm not fond of cigarettes, but there's something natural about cigarette smoke in a bar. It would almost seem naked without it.

Some kind of familiar rock music is playing from the speakers in the ceiling. There's a small stage to the left where bands usually play, but no one's playing tonight. That doesn't diminish the party-like mood in the atmosphere though, because I can barely hear Andrew talking to me over the music and the shouting voices all around me.

"Can you play pool?" he leans in, shouting near my ear.

I shout back, "I have a few times! But I suck at it!"

He tugs my hand and we walk toward the pool tables and the brighter light, pushing our way carefully through people standing around in just about every available walkable space.

"Sit here," he says, able to lower his voice a little with the speakers in front of us. "This'll be our table."

I sit down at a small round table pressed against a wall where just over my head and to my left there is a staircase leading up to a second floor on the other side of me. I nudge the cigarette-laden ashtray across the table and away from me with the tip of my finger as a waitress walks up.

Andrew is talking to a guy a few feet away next to the pool tables, probably about joining a game.

"Sorry about that," the waitress says, taking the ashtray and replacing it with a clean one, setting it upside-down upon the table. She washes the top of the table off afterwards with a wet rag, lifting the ashtray to get the spot under it.

I smile up at her. She's a pretty black-haired girl, probably just turned twenty-one herself and she's holding a serving tray on one hand.

"Can I get yah anything?"

I only have one chance to act like I'm asked that question a lot without being carded, so I say almost immediately, "I'll have a Heineken."

"Make that two," Andrew says stepping back up with a pool stick in his hand.

The waitress does a double-take when she notices him, and like Andrew in the elevator with me, I'm eating the hell out of it. She nods and glances back down at me with that you-are-one-lucky-bitch look before walking away.

"That guy's got one more game and then we've got the table," he says, sitting down on the empty chair.

The waitress comes back with two Heinekens and sets them in front of us.

"Just wave if yah need anything," she says before leaving again.

"She didn't card you," he says, leaning across the table so no one will hear.

"No, but that doesn't mean I won't eventually get carded—that happened once in a bar in Charlotte; Natalie and me were almost drunk by the time we were carded and sent packing."

"Well, then just enjoy it while you can." He smiles, bringing his beer to his lips and taking a quick drink.

I do the same.

I'm starting to wish I hadn't brought my purse so I wouldn't have to keep up with it, but when it's our turn to play a game of pool, I set it on the floor under our table. We're kind of off in a cubby-hole so I'm not too worried about it.

Andrew takes me over to the stick rack.

"What's your pleasure?" he asks, waving his hands across the space in front of the rack. "You have to pick one that feels right."

Oh, this is going to be fun; he actually thinks he's teaching me something.

I play coy and clueless, scanning the pool sticks like one might books on a shelf and then take one down. I run my hands along the length of it and hold it out like I would to hit a ball, as if to get the feel of it. I know I look totally dumb-blonde right about now, but that's exactly how I want to look.

"This one's as good as any," I say with a shrug.

Andrew racks the balls in the triangular rack, switching solid for stripe all around until he gets the sequence right and then slides them across the table and into position. Carefully, he removes the rack and shoves it in a slot underneath the table.

He nods. "Want to break em'?"

"Nah, you can."

I just want to see him lookin' all sexy, concentrating and leaning over the table.

"All right," he says and positions the cue ball. He spends a few seconds twisting the head of his stick into a square of chalk and then sets the chalk on the side of the table.

"If you've played before," he says, moving back around in position with the cue ball, "then I'm sure you know the basics." He points the end of the stick at the cue ball. "Obviously, you only hit the white ball."

This is funny, but he's got this one comin'.

I nod.

"If you're stripes, the only balls you want to sink in any pockets are the striped balls—hit one of the solids and you're only helping me beat you."

"What about that black ball?" I point at the 8 ball near the center.

"If you sink that one before all of your stripes," he says with a grim face, "you lose. And if you sink the white ball, you lose your turn."

"Is that all?" I ask, twisting the head of my stick in a square of chalk now.

"For now, yeah," he says; I guess he's letting me slide about the few other basic rules.

Andrew takes a couple steps back and leans over the table, arching his fingers on the blue felt and resting the stick strategically within the curl of his index finger. He slides the stick back and forth a couple of times to steady his aim before pausing and then slamming the head of it into the cue ball, scattering the others all over the table.

*Good break, baby,* I say to myself.

He sinks two—one stripe, one solid.

"What'll it be?" he asks.

"What'll *what* be?" I continue to play dumb.

"Solids or stripes? I'll let you choose."

"Oh," I say as if I'm just getting it, "doesn't matter; I'll take the ones with stripes, I guess."

We're straying a little from the proper way to play 8 Ball, but I'm pretty sure he's doing it for my benefit.

My turn comes and I walk around the table searching for that perfect shot. "Are we calling them, or what?"

Andrew looks at me curiously—maybe I should've said it more like: Do I hit any of my balls that I want? Surely, he's not onto me already.

"Just pick any striped ball you think you can sink and go for it."

OK, looks like I'm still hustling his clueless butt.

"Wait, aren't we going to bet something?" I ask.

He looks surprised, but then surprise turns to devious.

"Sure, what do you want to bet?"

"My freedom back."

Andrew frowns. But then his delicious lips turn upward again once he realizes that I apparently don't know how to play pool.

"Well, I'm a little hurt you would want it back," he says, switching the stick back and forth between his hands with one end of it standing against the floor, "but sure, I'll take that bet."

Just when I think the agreement has been made he adds, putting up one finger: "However, if *I* win, I get to take that do-whatever-I-say to a whole new level."

It's my turn to raise a brow.

"A whole new level how?" I ask in a leery, sidelong glance.

Andrew rests his stick against the table and props his hands on the edge, leaning into view of the light. His deep-set grin, just the sheer intent behind it, sends a shiver up my back.

"Is it a bet, or not?" he asks.

I'm pretty sure I can beat him, but now he kind of has me scared shitless. What if he's better than me and I lose this bet and end up eating those bugs or hanging my bare ass out of the moving car? Those were the types of things I wanted to keep him from eventually trying to force me to do—I never did forget that he said: *we'll get to that.* Sure, I could refuse anything he told me; he assured me of that before we left Wyoming, but not having to go through all that in the first place is all I wanted.

Or ... wait ... what if it's sexual in nature?

Oh, it's on now ... I almost hope that he *does* win.

"It's a deal."

He smiles wickedly and pulls away from the table, taking his stick with him.

A small group of guys and two girls just finished their game at the table next to ours and a few of them have started watching us.

I lean over the table, position my stick much the same way Andrew had, slide it back and forth through my fingers a few times and smack the cue ball dead-center. 11 smacks into 15 and 15 smacks into 10, sinking both of them into a corner pocket.

Andrew just looks at me, his pool stick resting vertically between his fingers in front of him.

He raises a brow. "Was that beginner's luck, or am I being hustled?"

I grin and walk around to the other side of the table to gauge my next shot. I don't answer. I just smile faintly and keep my eyes on the table. Purposely taking the shot closest to Andrew, I bend over the table in front of him (covertly glancing down to make sure my boobs aren't in full view of the guys watching directly across from me) and measure my shot before hitting the 9 hard into the side pocket.

"I'm being hustled," Andrew says behind me, "*and* teased."

I rise up and skim my grinning eyes across his as I make my way to the end of the table.

I miss this shot on purpose. The table is set almost perfectly and I might actually be able to pull off an easy win, but I don't want it to be easy.

"Ah, hell no, babe," he says stepping up, "none of that pity-shot bullshit—you could've sunk the 13 easily."

"My finger slipped." I look at him coyly.

He shakes his beautiful head at me and narrows his eyes, knowing full well I'm lying.

Finally, we just go at it: he sinks three balls flawlessly, one turn after the next, before missing the 7. I sink another one. Then he sinks one. And we do this back and forth, taking our time with each shot, but both of us missing every now and then to keep the game going.

Now it's down to business. It's my turn and the only balls left on the table are his 4, the cue and the 8. The 8 is six inches too far from a perfect corner shot in either direction, but I know I can bank it on one side of the table and let it come back to this side and sink it in the left.

Two more guys have started watching, no doubt because of the way I'm dressed (I've been listening to their quiet comments about my 't-n-a' the whole time, especially when I bend over to take a shot), but I don't let them distract me. Though, I've noticed Andrew's eyes on them a lot and it excites me that he's at all jealous.

I point my stick at the table and call it, "Left pocket."

I move around to the side and crouch down at eye-level with the table to see if my lining is off. I stand back up and check the lining of the cue and the 8 again from another perspective and then lean over the table. One. Two. Three. On the forth slide-back, I smack the cue gently and it hits the 8 at just the right angle, sending it against the right side of the table where it bounces back a few inches over and sinks flawlessly into the left pocket.

The few guys watching on the other side of me make various noises of tamed excitement as if I can't hear them.

Andrew is on the other side of the table grinning wide at me.

"You're good, babe," he says racking the balls again. "I guess you're free now."

I can't help but notice that he seems a little sad about that fact. His face may be smiling, but he can't hide the disappointment in his eyes.

"Nah," I say, "I don't want that freedom unless it comes to eating bugs or hanging my ass out the car window—I kind of like you being in control of the rest."

Andrew smiles.

# TWENTY-FOUR

*W*e play another game, which he wins fairly, and afterwards I decide to sit back down at our table before these new shoes start rubbing blisters on my feet. I'm on my second Heineken and still am only feeling it in my toes and the bottom of my stomach. It'll take another one to get me a good buzz.

"Want a game, man?" a guy asks stepping up to Andrew just as he starts to sit down with me.

Andrew looks over and I wave him on.

"Go on, I'm fine—gonna check my messages and rest my feet for a while."

"All right, babe," he says, "just let me know if you're ready to go before I'm done and we'll go."

"I'm good," I say, urging him, "go on and play."

He smiles in at me and walks back over to the table not more than fifteen feet away. I get my purse from underneath the table and set it in front of me, rummaging inside in search of my phone.

Just as I suspected: Natalie has blown my phone up with text messages, sixteen in all, but at least she hasn't tried to call. My mom hasn't called, either, but I remember she was going on that cruise with her new boyfriend this weekend. I hope she's having a great time. I hope she's having as great of a time as I am.

A new song starts funneling through the speakers in the ceiling and I notice the number of people inside the bar has tripled since we got here. Even though Andrew isn't that far away, I can only see his lips moving when he says anything to the guy he's shooting pool with. The waitress comes back and I ask for another beer and she goes off to get it, leaving me to the Text Message Queen. Natalie and I go back and forth a few times about what she did today and where she's going tonight, but I know it's all just filler-conversation, taking place of what she's dying to know more about: me in New Orleans with this 'mystery guy', who he looks like (not 'what' because she always compares guys to famous people) and if I've 'bent over for him' yet. I keep everything vague just to torture her. She still deserves it, after all. Besides, I'm still not ready to go into Andrew with her. Not with anyone, really. It's like if I talk about him at all, even just to confirm he exists and that I'm with him, that this whole experience will go up in a puff of smoke. I'll jinx it. Or, I'll wake up and realize that Blake slipped something in one of the drinks he served me that night before I went out onto the roof with him and I've just been hallucinating this entire road trip with Andrew.

"I'm Mitchell," a voice says above me, accompanied by a strong waft of whiskey and cheap men's cologne.

The guy is of average build, the buff-but-not-*too*-buff kind. His eyes are bloodshot like the blond-haired guy standing next to him.

I smile back squeamishly and glance at Andrew who is already walking this way.

"I'm with someone," I say gently.

The buff guy looks at the other chair and then back at me as if to make note of how empty it is.

"Camryn?" Andrew says standing behind them. "Are you all right?"

"Yeah, I'm fine," I say.

The buff guy turns at the waist to see Andrew.

"She said she's fine," he says and I hear the challenge in his voice.

I didn't mean 'I'm fine, leave me alone, Andrew' and Andrew knows as much, but these guys apparently do not.

"She's with me," Andrew says, trying to remain calm, though probably only for my sake—he already has that unmistakable look of aggression in his eyes.

The blond guy laughs.

The buff guy looks at me again, a bottle of Budweiser in one hand. "Is he your boyfriend or something?"

"No, but we're—"

The buff guy smiles tauntingly and looks back at Andrew, cutting me off. "You're not her boyfriend, so back off, man."

Aggression just shifted into murderous rampage. Andrew isn't going to be able to hold back much longer.

I stand up.

"Maybe she wants to talk to us," the buff guy says and takes another swig of his beer. He doesn't look drunk, just buzzed.

Andrew steps up closer and cocks his head to one side, staring the guy down. Then he looks at me:

"Camryn, do you want to talk them?"

He knows that I don't, but this is his way of adding vinegar to the wound he's about to give this guy.

"No, I don't."

Andrew rounds his chin and I can see his nostrils flare as he gets in the buff guy's face and says, "Back the fuck off or you're eatin' your teeth."

The small crowd from around the pool tables is gathering at a distance.

The blond guy, the smarter one of the two, puts his hand on his shoulder. "Come on, man, let's head back over." He nods toward wherever they must've been sitting before.

The buff guy pushes his hand off him and steps up in Andrew's face further.

That's all it took.

Andrew rears back with the pool stick and bashes it across the guy's chest, knocking him from his feet and the breath from his lungs. The guy stumbles backward, narrowly missing my table but reaches out to grab the edge of it to keep him on his feet. I yelp and yank my purse from the top of it just before it goes crashing onto the floor with him. My beer shatters against the floor. Before the guy can get up, Andrew is on top of him, standing over him raining his fists down on his face.

I push myself farther away and closer to the end of the staircase, but other people are rushing in to see now and they create a barrier behind me.

The blond guy jumps on Andrew from behind, grabbing him around the neck to pull him off his friend. Then I jump on *him*, beating the side of his face with my flimsy little fist, my purse wrapped tightly around my shoulder hindering my blows as it flops around behind me. But Andrew gets out of the blond guy's hold easily, swings around behind him and kicks him square in the back, sending him onto the floor face-first.

Andrew grabs my wrist.

"Move out of the way, baby!" He shoves me back toward the crowd behind me and turns back to the two guys in a split second.

The buff guy has finally gotten back to his feet, but not for long when Andrew comes around with two fast punches to both sides of his jaw and then one blood-splattering uppercut to the underside. I see a bloody tooth fall onto the floor. I cringe. The guy falls backward into another small table, knocking it from its metal base, too. And when the blond guy comes at Andrew again, the guy Andrew had been playing pool with jumps in and takes him on, leaving Andrew to the buff guy.

By the time the bouncers get through the crowd to break up the fight, Andrew has already blackened both the buff guy's eyes and blood is draining from his nostrils. The buff guy stumbles, holding his hand over his nose as the bouncer pulls him by the shoulder toward the crowd.

Andrew pushes away the other bouncer's hand that comes after him. "I got it," he threatens, putting up one hand telling the bouncer to back off, and wiping a trickle of blood from his nose with the other. "I'm out of here, no need to help me see the door."

I run over to him and he takes my hand.

"Camryn, are you OK? Did you get hit?" He's looking me over everywhere, his eyes fierce and uncontrolled.

"No, I'm fine. Let's just go."

He tightens his hand around mine and pulls me beside him, pushing our way through the parting crowd.

When we make it outside into the night air, the funneling music from the bar shuts off once the door closes. The two idiot guys from the fight are already outside walking down the street, the buff guy still with his hand pressed over his bloodied face. I'm convinced Andrew broke his nose.

Andrew stops me on the sidewalk and takes my upper arms into his hands. "Don't lie to me, baby, did you get hurt anywhere? I swear to fucking God if you did I'm going after them."

He's melting my heart, calling me 'baby'. And that concerned, fierce look in his eyes...I just want to kiss him.

"I mean it," I say, "I'm fine. I actually hit that one guy a few times myself when he jumped you from behind."

He moves his hands from my arms and cups my face in his palms, looking me all over as if he still doesn't believe me.

"I'm not hurt," I say one last time.

He presses his lips hard against my forehead.

Then he grabs my hand. "We're going back to the hotel."

"No," I argue, "we were having a good time and dammit I lost my buzz because of that."

He tilts his head to one side and softens his gaze.

"Where do you want to go then?"

"Let's go to another club," I suggest. "I don't know, maybe a more laid back one?"

Andrew sighs heavily and squeezes my hand. Then he looks me up and down again: first my feet where my painted toenails are peeking through the front of my heels and then up my body straight to my tight strapless black top that could use a little adjusting.

I pull my hand from his and grasp the fabric above my boobs and pull the top up a little so that it feels better in place.

"I love you in that," he says, "but you have to admit, it's a distraction for douchebags."

"Well, I don't want to walk all the way back to the hotel just to change my top."

"No, you don't have to do that," he says, reaching for my hand again. "But if you want to go to another club, you're gonna have to do something for me, all right?"

"What?"

"Just *pretend* you're my girlfriend," he says and a little smile spreads across my lips. "At least that way no one will fuck with you, or they're less likely to try, anyway."

He pauses and looks at me and says, "Unless you *want* guys to hit on you?"

It takes no time at all for my head to start shaking. "No. I do *not* want any guys to hit on me. Innocent flirting, fine—it does wonders for my confidence—but not douchebags."

"Good, then it's settled. You're my sexy girlfriend for the night, which means I get to take you back to the room later and make you squeal a little." There's that boyish grin of his again that I love so much.

I'm tingling between the legs now. I swallow hard and play it off by playfully narrowing my eyes at him.

I'm just glad to see his dimples again, as opposed to that wrathful—although incredibly sexy—expression that consumed his features moments ago.

"As much as I like it—well, 'like' is really putting it lightly— I'm not going to let you do that anymore."

He looks hurt and a little shocked. "Why not?"

"Because, Andrew, I...well, I just won't let you—now come here." I cup my hands around the sides of his neck and pull him toward me.

And then I kiss him softly, letting my lips linger on his afterwards.

"What are you doing?" he asks, staring down into my eyes.

I smile sweetly up at him. "I'm getting into character."

A grin tugs the corners of his lips. He turns me around and locks his arm around my waist as we head toward Bourbon Street.

# Andrew

# TWENTY-FIVE

*M*aybe I *can* do this with Camryn. Why do I have to torture myself and deny myself what I want most when it should be the time when I've earned the right to have anything I want? Maybe things will turn out differently and she won't get hurt. I could go back to Marsters. What if I do let her go and I never see her again and then afterwards, Marsters realizes his fuck-up?

*Goddammit!* Excuses.

Camryn and I hit two more bars in the French Quarter and she managed to pass for twenty-one in both of them. Only one asked to see her I.D. and I guess since her birthday is in December the waitress decided to let her slide.

But now she's drunk and I'm not sure if she'll be able to walk back to the hotel.

"I'll call a cab," I say, holding her up beside me on the sidewalk.

Couples and groups of people come and go from the bar behind us, some stumbling from the doorway.

I've got my arm tight around Camryn's waist. She reaches up a hand and drapes it over my shoulder from the front; she can hardly hold her head up straight.

"I think a cab is a good idea," she says with heavy eyes.

She's either going to pass out or throw up soon. I just hope she waits until we get back to the hotel.

The cab drops us off at the front of the hotel and I help her out of the backseat, finally just lifting her in my arms because she can barely walk on her own anymore. I carry her to the elevator with her legs dangling over one arm and her head lying against my chest. People are staring.

"Fun night?" a man in the elevator asks.

"Yeah," I nod, "some of us can hold our liquor better than others."

The elevator dings and the man walks out after the doors slide open. Two more floors up and I carry her out and toward our rooms.

"Where's your key babe?"

"In my purse," she says weakly.

At least she's coherent.

Without putting her down, I pull her purse around from her arm and unzip it. Normally, I would crack some joke about what the hell she carries in this thing and if anything in it is going to bite me, but I know she's not in the joking mood. She's miserable.

This is going to be a long night.

The door shuts behind us and I carry her right over to the bed and lay her down.

"I feel like shit," she moans.

"I know, babe. You'll just have to sleep it off."

I take off her shoes and set them on the floor.

"I think I'm going to be—" She throws her head over the side of the bed and starts puking.

I reach over to grab the trash can pressed against the nightstand and catch most of it, but it looks like the housekeeper is going to be pissed in the morning. She throws up everything in her stomach, which surprises me because she didn't really eat much today. She stops and falls back against the pillow. Tears, caused by the vomiting, stream from the corners of her eyes. She tries to look at me, but I know she's too dizzy to focus.

"It's so hot in here," she says.

"All right," I say and get up to turn the AC on full blast.

Then I go into the bathroom and run a wash cloth under the cold water and then wring it out. I go back in the room and sit beside her on the bed, swabbing her face with the cloth.

"I'm so sorry," she mumbles. "I should've stopped after the vodka shot. Now you're cleaning up my puke."

I wipe her cheeks and forehead some more, pushing away the loose strands of hair stuck to her face, and then I swipe the cold rag over her mouth.

"No apologies," I say, "you had a good time and that's all that matters." I add, grinning, "Besides, I can take complete advantage of you now."

She tries to smile and reach up and hit me on the arm, but she's too weak even for that. Her almost-smile turns into something anguished and sweat instantly beads on her forehead.

"Oh no..." She raises herself from the bed. "I need the bathroom," she says, holding onto me trying to get up and so I help her.

I walk her to the bathroom where she practically throws herself over the toilet, both hands gripping the sides of the porcelain. Her back arches and falls as she starts to dry-heave and cry harder.

"You should've had that steak with me, babe." I stand over her from behind, making sure her braids don't get hit in the crossfire and I keep the cold rag pressed to the back of her neck. I hurt for her, just watching her body heave violently like that, but hardly anything being produced from it. I know her throat and chest and insides are going to hurt after this.

When she's done, she lies against the cool tile floor.

I try to help her up, but she protests softly:

"No, please... I want to lay here; the floor is cooler on my skin."

Her breathing is shallow and her lightly-tanned skin is as sickly pale as a pneumonia patient. I get a clean rag, soak it and keep wiping down her face and neck and bare shoulders. Then I unbutton her pants and carefully pull them off, relieving her stomach and legs from the pressure of how tight they were.

"Don't worry, I won't molest you," I say, jokingly, but she doesn't answer this time.

She's passed out on her side with her face pressed against the floor.

I know if I move her right now she'll probably wake up and start dry-heaving again, but I don't want to leave her like this lying next to the toilet. So, I lie down beside her and I swab her forehead and arms and shoulders with the cloth for hours until eventually I fall asleep with her.

Never thought I'd intentionally sleep on a bathroom floor next to a toilet while sober, but I meant it when I said I would sleep anywhere with her.

# Camryn

The door to my room opens. Bright sunlight is shining in through a slim opening in the curtain on the other side of me. I flinch like a vampire at it, squinting long enough to turn away. It takes me a second to realize that I'm lying on my bed in the strapless top I wore last night and my purple bikini panties. The bed has been stripped of everything but the sheet I'm lying on and a top sheet that smells and feels like it had recently been washed. I guess I puked on the other one; Andrew must've gotten this one from housekeeping.

"Feeling any better?" Andrew asks coming into the room with an ice bucket in one hand and a stack of plastic cups and a bottle of Sprite in the other.

He sits down beside me and places the stuff on the nightstand, breaking the seal on the Sprite.

My head is pounding and I still feel like I could throw up again at any moment. I hate hangovers. I would rather fall down shitfaced drunk and bust my nose or something than deal with a hangover of this magnitude. I've had one like this before; it's so bad that it's not much different from alcohol poisoning. At least, according to Natalie, who actually had alcohol poisoning once and described it as 'being shit on by Satan himself the next morning'.

"Not at all," I finally answer and my own words send pain

shooting through the back of my head and around behind my ears. I close my eyes tight when the room starts to double.

"You've got it bad, babe," Andrew says and then I feel a cool cloth dab the side of my neck.

"Can you close that curtain? Please?"

He gets up immediately and I hear him walk over and then the sound of the thick fabric being moved until he gets it into place. I draw my bare legs up toward my chest, taking the sheet with me to keep myself partially covered and I lie in the fetal position against the softness of the pillow.

Andrew removes a plastic cup from its wrapping and I hear the ice shuffling into it afterwards. He pours the Sprite over the ice and then I hear a bottle of pills moving around in his hand.

"Take these," he says and I feel the bed move as he sits back down and rests his arm over my leg.

My eyes crack open slowly. There's already a straw poking from the top of the plastic cup so I won't have to try lifting from the bed too much to get a sip. I reach out and take three Advil from the palm of his hand and pop them in my mouth, afterwards sipping enough of the Sprite just to wash them down with.

"Please tell me I didn't do or say anything completely humiliating at the bars last night."

I can only look at him through slit eyelids.

I sense him smiling. "Yeah, actually you did," he says and my heart sinks. "You told this one guy that you were happily married to me and that we were gonna have like four kids—or maybe you said five, I don't remember—and then this chick came over later and was hitting on me and you shot up from the chair and got in her face all white-trash-like—it was hilarious."

I think I'm going to throw up now for sure.

"Andrew you better be lying—how embarrassing!"

My head hurts worse. I didn't think it could get any worse.

I hear him laugh lightly and I open my eyes a little more so I can see his face more clearly.

"Yeah, I'm lying, babe." He reaches up and moves the cool rag over my forehead. "Actually, you handled yourself very well, even all the way up here with me." I notice him look my body over. "Sorry, I had to strip you down—well I enjoyed the opportunity personally, but it was in the line of duty. It had to be done, you see." He looks all pretend-serious now and I can't help but smile.

I shut my eyes and sleep another couple of hours until the housekeeper knocks on the door.

I wonder if Andrew has left my side much.

"Yeah, come on in and let me take her next door to my room so you can clean."

An older lady with a bad red dye-job on her hair enters the room wearing her housekeeping uniform. Andrew walks over to me on the bed.

"Come on, babe," he says, lifting me into his arms with the sheet still wrapped around my lower half, "let's let the lady clean."

I could probably walk over there on my own, but I'm not about to protest. I rather like being right where I am.

As we walk past my purse on the TV stand I reach out for it and Andrew stops, picking it up for me and carrying it out with me. I lay my head against his chest and drape my arms around his neck.

He stops in the doorway and looks back at the housekeeper.

"Sorry about the mess beside the bed." He nods in that direction with a grimace. "There'll be a good tip in it for you."

He walks out with me and takes me over to his room.

First thing he does is close the curtains after he lays me against his pillow.

"I hope you're better before tonight," he says walking about the room as if he's looking for something.

"What's tonight?"

"Another bar," he says.

He finds his MP3 player beside the recliner cushion by the window and sets it on the TV stand beside his bag.

I moan in protest. "Oh no, Andrew, I refuse to go to another bar tonight. I will never drink again for as long as I live."

I catch him flash me a grin from across the room.

"Everybody says that," he declares. "And I wouldn't let you drink tonight if you decided you wanted to. You need at least one night in between hangovers or you might as well get your AA card stamped early."

"Well, I hope I feel good enough to do *something* besides hang around in bed all day—but the prospect isn't lookin' too good right now."

"Well, you have to eat, that's mandatory. As much as the thought of food right now probably makes you sick, if you don't eat something you'll feel like shit all day for sure."

"You're right," I say, feeling nauseous, "It *does* make me sick just thinking about it."

"Toast and eggs," he says, walking back over to me, "something light—you know the drill."

"Yeah, I know the drill," I say blankly, wishing I could just snap my fingers and be better already.

# TWENTY-SIX

*B*y late afternoon, I do feel better; not one hundred percent, but good enough to ride around New Orleans with Andrew in a streetcar to a few places we didn't get to see yesterday. After I managed to get down some eggs and two pieces of toast we took the Riverfront Streetcar to the Audubon Aquarium of the Americas and walked through a thirty-foot long tunnel with water and fish all around us. And we hand-fed parakeets and worked our way through rain forest exhibits. We fed stingrays and took pictures together with our cell phones, the stupid-looking kind with our arms out in front holding the phone. I later looked closer at the pictures we took, how our cheeks were pressed together and the way we smiled into the camera as if we were any other couple having the time of our lives.

Any other couple...but we're not a couple and I realize I just had to remind myself of that.

Reality is a bitch.

But then again, so is not knowing what you want. No, the truth is that I *do* know what I want. I can't force myself to doubt it anymore, but I'm still afraid of it. I'm afraid of Andrew and what kind of pain he could inflict if he ever hurt me, because I get the feeling it wouldn't be any kind that I could bear. Already it's unbearable and he hasn't even hurt me yet.

I sure got myself knee-deep in a mess, no doubt.

By the time the night falls over New Orleans again and the party-people have come out of their dwellings, Andrew has me crossing the Mississippi by ferry and walking to a place called Old Point Bar. I'm glad I decided to wear my black flip-flops again, rather than the new heels. Andrew sort of insisted, especially since we would be walking.

"I never leave New Orleans until I've come here first," he says, walking alongside me with my hand clasped within his.

"What, so you're a regular?"

"Yeah, I guess you can say that; a once or twice a year regular, anyway. I've played there a couple of times."

"The guitar?" I assume, looking over at him curiously.

A group of four people walk past from the opposite direction and I move closer to Andrew to give them space on the sidewalk.

He moves his hand from mine and slips it around my waist from behind.

"I've been playing the guitar since I was six." He smiles over at me. "I wasn't very good at six, but you have to start somewhere— didn't play anything worth listening to until I was about ten."

I let out an impressed spat of air. "Young *enough* to be musically talented, I'd say."

"I guess so; I was the 'music boy' when we were growing up and Aidan was the 'architect boy'" (he glances at me) "because he used to build things—built a massive tree house in the woods once. And Asher, he was the 'hockey boy'. My dad loved hockey, almost more than he did boxing" (he glances at me again), "but only almost. Asher gave up hockey after the first year—he was only thirteen" (he laughs lightly); "Dad wanted it more than Asher did. All Asher ever really wanted to do was mess with electronics—tried to communicate with aliens on a contraption he built out of random stuff lying around the house after he saw the movie *Contact*."

We laugh gently together.

"What about your brother?" he asks. "I know you told me he's in prison, but what was your relationship like with him before that?"

My face sours delicately.

"Cole was an awesome big brother until he went into eighth grade and started hanging out with the neighborhood trash—Braxton Hixley; I always hated that guy. Anyway, Cole and Braxton started doing drugs and all kinds of crazy stuff. My dad tried putting him away in a home for troubled youths to get him some help, but Cole ran away and just got into even more trouble. It got worse from there." I look back out ahead as more people come shuffling toward us along the sidewalk. "And now he's where he deserves to be."

"Maybe he'll be more like the big brother you remember once he gets out."

"Maybe." I shrug, highly doubting it.

We make our way to the end of the sidewalk and onto the corner where Patterson runs into Olivier and there's Old Point Bar that from the outside looks more like a historic two-story house with an add-on apartment on the side. We pass under the elongated old sign where next to the building there are a couple of plastic tables and chairs with several people smoking and talking really loud.

I can hear a band playing inside.

Andrew holds the door open after a couple comes out and he takes my hand. It's not a huge place, but it's cozy. I look up at the tall ceilings, noticing the many photographs and license plates and beer lights and colored banners and old signs hanging around on every inch of space. Several ceiling fans hang low from the wooden ceiling. And to my right is the bar that, like just about any bar, has a TV on the back wall. Even through a mild throng of people a woman working behind the bar raises her hand and it appears she's waving at Andrew.

Andrew smiles at her and waves back with two fingers as if to say 'talk to you in a few'.

It looks like all of the tables are taken and there are people dancing on the floor. The band playing along the back wall is really good; some kind of blues rock, or something. I like it. There's a black man strumming a silver guitar sitting on a stool and a white man singing with an acoustic secured to his front by the guitar strap. A heavyset man is on drums and there's a keyboard on the stage, though it's unoccupied.

I do a double-take when my gaze skims the floor and I see a scruffy black dog looking up at me and wagging its tail. I reach over and scratch it behind the ears. Satisfied, it waddles over next to its owner sitting at the table next to me and lies at his feet.

After waiting a few minutes, Andrew notices three people get up from a table not far from where the band is playing and pulling me along, we walk over and get it.

I still feel off from the hangover and my head isn't completely free of pain, but surprisingly enough, as loud as it is in here, it's not making my headache worse.

"She's not drinking," Andrew points at me and says kindly to the woman who had been standing behind the bar.

She had weaved her way through the people and over to our table by the time I sat down.

The woman, with soft brown hair pulled behind her ears, looks to be in her early forties and she's smiling so hugely as she takes Andrew into a bear hug that I'm starting to wonder if she's his aunt or a cousin.

"It's been ten months, Parrish," she says, patting his back with both hands. "Where the hell have you been?"

She smiles down at me.

"And who is this?" She looks at Andrew playfully, but I detect something else in her smile: assumption, perhaps.

Andrew takes my hand and I stand up to be properly introduced. "This is Camryn," he says. "Camryn, this is Carla; she's been working here for at least six of my atrocious performances."

Carla pushes him on the chest, laughing, and she looks back at me. "Don't let him lie to you," she points at him and raises both brows, "this boy can sing." She winks at me and then shakes my hand. "Good to meet you."

I smile at her likewise.

*Sing?* I thought he played guitar here; I didn't know he sang, too. I guess it doesn't surprise me. He already sort of proved to me that he can sing back in Birmingham when he hit that 'alibis' note in *Hotel California*. And every now and then while we were riding in the car he would forget I was there—or not care—and let his vocals loose on any number of classic rock songs funneling from the speakers.

But I never expected that he has actually performed somewhere. Too bad he didn't bring his guitar; I'd love to see him perform tonight.

"Well, it's good to see you again," Carla says and then points to the black man on the stage. "Eddie will be glad to know you're here."

Andrew nods and smiles as Carla makes her way back through the small crowd and to the bar.

"Do you want a soda or anything?"

I wave my hand at him. "No, I'm good."

He remains standing and when the band stops playing, I realize why. The black man with the silver guitar notices Andrew and smiles as he sets the guitar against the chair and comes over. They hug much in the same way he and Carla had and I stand up again to be introduced, shaking 'Eddie's' hand.

"Parrish! Been gone a long time," Eddie says in his thick Cajun accent. "What it been, a'yea?"

Carla had sounded somewhat Cajun, too, but not as much as Eddie.

"Almost," Andrew says, beaming.

Andrew seems really happy to be here, like these people are some long-lost family members and he's never been at odds with any of them. Even his smile is warmer and more inviting than I've ever seen it before. In fact, when he introduced me to both Carla and Eddie, his smile lit up the room. I felt like I was the one girl he finally decided to bring home to meet the family and by the looks in their eyes when he introduced me, they felt like that, too.

"Gon' play t'night?"

I take my seat again and look up at Andrew, as curious about his answer as Eddie seems to be. Eddie has that won't-take-no-for-an-answer look on his smiling face, the wrinkles around his eyes and mouth deepening.

"Well, I didn't bring my guitar this time."

"Oh," Eddie shakes his head; "you know betta—play me a cooyon?" He points at the stage. "Got plent' guita'."

"I want to hear you play," I say from behind.

Andrew looks down at me, unsure.

"I'm serious. I'm asking you." I tilt my head gently to one side, smiling up at him.

"Uh huh, dat girl got dem eyes, she does." Eddie grins at Andrew from the side.

Andrew gives in.

"All right, but only one song."

"Onl' one, no?" Eddie tightens his wrinkly chin and says, "Gon' be *one* it gon' be *my* pick." He points to himself, just above his white button-up shirt. A pack of cigarettes are poking from the top left pocket on his chest.

Andrew nods, agreeing. "OK, you pick then."

Eddie's grin deepens and he looks down at me with a suspicious sidelong glance. "One ta woo da' ladies wit like you did las'time."

"Rolling Stones?" Andrew asks.

"Uh huh," Eddie says. "Dat da one, boy."

"*Which* one?" I ask, propping my chin on top of my knuckles.

"*Laugh, I Nearly Died*," Andrew answers. "You've probably never heard that one before."

And he's right. I shake my head gently. "No, can't say that I have."

Eddie nods to Andrew for him to follow him towards the stage. Andrew leans down and surprises me with a soft peck on the lips and then leaves the table.

I sit nervous, but excited on the chair with my elbows propped on the table. There are so many conversations going on all around me that it all sounds like a consistent hum of noise floating on the air in the room. Every now and then I hear a glass or a beer bottle clink against another, or against a table. The whole space is rather dark, lit only by the filtering lights from the numerous beer signs and the tall sections of glass windows that allow in the moonlight and light from the street to wash through them. Every now and then a burst of yellow light shines from behind the stage on the right side when people come and go from what I'm assuming are the restrooms.

Andrew and Eddie make it to the stage and start setting up: Andrew takes another barstool from somewhere behind the drum set and places it center stage right in front of the standing micro-phone. Eddie says a few words to the drummer—probably telling him what song to play—and the drummer nods. Another man emerges from a shadow behind the stage with another guitar, or maybe that one's a bass; I've never really paid attention to the dif-ference. Eddie gives Andrew a black guitar, already plugged into a nearby amp and they exchange words that I can't hear. And then Andrew takes a seat on the stool, propping one booted foot on the lower spindle. Eddie sits on his afterwards.

They start adjusting this and tuning that and the drummer hits his cymbals a few erratic times. I hear a *pop-squeal* as another amp is either turned on or just turned up and then a *thump-thump-thump* when Andrew taps his thumb on the microphone a few times.

My stomach is already fluttering, nervous as though I'm the one up there about to sing in front of a bunch of strangers. But mostly, my stomach flutters because it's Andrew. He glances at me from the stage, locking eyes with me once and then the drummer starts to play, just barely hitting the cymbals a few times in tune. And then Eddie starts to play the guitar; a slow, catchy tune that easily makes most of the people all standing around turn and take notice of a new song beginning—obviously one that they've all heard before and never get tired of. Andrew plays a few chords along with Eddie and already I feel my upper body gently swaying with the music.

When Andrew starts to sing it feels like there's a spring in my neck. I stop swaying and jerk my head back, not believing what I'm hearing; so bluesy and captivating. He keeps his eyes closed as he sings on, his head moving in time with the sultry, soulful beat of the music.

And when the chorus starts Andrew takes my breath away...

I feel my back gently pressing into the chair behind me and my eyes growing wider as the music picks up and Andrew's soul comes out with every word. His expression shifts with each intense note and calms when the notes calm. No one is talking in the bar anymore. I can't look away from Andrew to see, but I can tell that the atmosphere changed in that second when Andrew started that powerful chorus, that sexy bluesy timbre coming out of him that I never could've imagined he possessed.

By the second verse when the beat slows again, he's already got the complete attention of every person in the room. People are dancing and swaying all around me, couples getting close with their hips and lips because there's no other way to do it to this song. But me...I just stare breathless across the space, letting Andrew's voice course through every loft and bone in my body. It's like irresistible poison: I'm mesmerized by the way it's making me feel though it has the potential to crush my soul and I drink it down anyway.

Still, he keeps his eyes closed as if needing to shut out the light around him to feel the music. And when the second chorus comes, he gets even more into it, almost enough to raise himself from the stool, but he stays put, his neck stretched out toward the microphone and every passionate emotion etched on his face as he sings and plays the guitar on his lap.

Eddie, the drummer and the bass player start to sing two lines with Andrew, and the audience joins in faintly.

By the third verse, I want to cry but I can't. It's like it's there, sitting dormant in the pit of my stomach, but it wants to torture me.

*Laugh, I Nearly Died...*

Andrew sings on and on, so passionately that *I* nearly die, my heart beating faster and faster. And then the band starts singing again and the music slows to drums only; a deep, rough rapping of the bass drum that I feel underneath my feet within the floor. And the audience stomps against the floor in time with the bass drum and they start singing along to the repetitive chorus. They clap once at the same time sending a sheer ripple through the air as their palms smack together. One more time. And Andrew sings: "*Yeah-Yeah!*" and the music ends abruptly.

There are shouts and high-pitched whistles and plenty of 'yeah's' and a few 'holy shit's'. Chills are running up my spine and spreading through the rest of my body.

*Laugh, I Nearly Died...* I will never forget that song for as long as I live.

*How can he be* real?

I'm waiting for the jinx to go into effect any moment, or for me to wake up in the back of Damon's car with Natalie hovering over me saying something about how Blake roofied me at The Underground.

Andrew sets the borrowed guitar down against the stool and walks over to shake Eddie's hand and then the drummer and lastly the bass player. Eddie walks with him halfway toward me, but stops and winks at me before going back to the stage. I really like Eddie. There's something honest and good and soulful about that man.

Andrew doesn't get all of the way back to our table without a few people from the audience stopping to shake his hand and probably to tell him how much they liked his performance. He thanks them and slowly but surely makes his way back to me.

I see a few women watching him with a little more than appreciation.

"Who *are* you?" I ask, halfway just messing with him.

Andrew sort of blushes and moves an empty chair around so that he can sit in front of me.

"You're *amazing*, Andrew. I had no idea."

"Thanks, babe."

He's very modest. I sort of halfway expected him to joke around by calling me his groupie and asking me to go behind the building with him or something. But he really doesn't seem up for talking about his talent at all, as if he's uncomfortable with it. Or perhaps uncomfortable with real praise?

"I'm serious," I say, "I wish I could sing like that."

That gets a reaction out of him, although slight.

"Sure you could," he says.

I draw my head back and shake it heavily. "No-no-no-no," I stop him before he gets any ideas. "I can't sing very well. I don't think I suck, but I'm not stage material, that's for sure."

"Why not?" Carla brings him over a beer, smiles at me and goes back to her customers. "Stage fright?"

He places the bottle to his lips and tips his head back.

"Well, I've never given it any thought past singing in the car to a stereo, Andrew." I lean back against my chair. "I've never gone far enough with the idea to be personal with something like stage fright."

Andrew shrugs and takes another sip before setting his beer on the table. "Well, for the record, I think you have a pretty voice. I heard you in the car."

I roll my eyes and cross my arms over my chest. "Thanks, but it's easy to sound like you can sing when you're singing along to someone else's voice. Get me alone without music and you'll probably cringe."

I lean forward toward him and add:

"How did this get turned around on me, anyway?" I narrow one eye playfully at him. "You're the one we should be talking about—where did that come from?"

"Influence, I guess," he says. "But no one can sing it like Jagger."

"Oh, I beg to differ," I say, drawing my chin back. "What, is Jagger your musical idol or something?" I ask half-joking and he smiles warmly.

"He's up there with my influences, but no, my musical idol is a little older than him."

There's something secret and deep hiding behind his eyes.

"Who?" I ask, completely immersed.

Without warning, Andrew leans forward and grabs me around the waist, lifting me onto his lap facing him. I'm a little shocked, but not at all rejecting of the gesture. He peers up into my eyes as I sit straddled on his lap.

"Camryn?"

I smile at him, only able to wonder what brought this on. "What?" I tilt my head to one side gently; my hands are resting on his chest.

A flicker of thought moves across his face and he doesn't respond.

"What is it?" I ask, more curious now.

I feel his hands lock around my waist and then he leans up and brushes his lips across mine. My eyes shut softly, taking in his touch. I feel like I could kiss him, but I'm not sure really if I should.

My eyes come open when he pulls his lips away.

"What's wrong, Andrew?"

He smiles and it literally warms my insides.

"Nothing," he says, slapping my thighs gently with the palms of his hands and so quickly back to being playful, not-so-serious Andrew. "I just wanted you on my lap." He grins wickedly.

I go to wiggle my way away—not really—and he wraps his arms around my waist and just holds me there. The only time he lets me up from his lap the rest of the night is when I need to use the restroom and he stood outside the door and waited for me. We stayed at Old Point watching Eddie and the band play blues and blues rock and even a few old jazz songs before we left to go back to the hotel after eleven.

# TWENTY-SEVEN

$\mathcal{B}$ack at the hotel, Andrew stays with me over in my room long enough to watch a movie. We talked for a long time and I could feel the reluctance between both of us: he wanted to say something to me as much as I wanted to say things to him.

I guess we're too much alike and so neither of us stepped over that line.

What's stopping us? Maybe it's me; maybe whatever this is between us can't go any further until he senses that I know it's what I want. Or, it could just be that he's not sure of anything, either.

But how can two people who are undeniably *more* than just attracted to one another not give in? We've been on the road together for almost two weeks. We've shared intimate secrets and we've *been* intimate in some ways. We've slept next to each other and touched one another, yet still here we are, standing on opposite sides of a thick glass wall. We reach up and touch our fingers to the glass, we look into each other's eyes and we know what we want but that glass *won't fucking budge*. This is either inviolable discipline or pure, unadulterated self-torture.

"Not that I'm in any hurry to leave," I say as Andrew gets ready to head back to his room, "but how long will we be staying in New Orleans?"

He picks his cell phone up from the nightstand and checks the screen briefly before wrapping it in the palm of his hand.

"We're paid up until Thursday," he says, "but it's up to you; we can leave tomorrow, or stay longer if you want."

I purse my lips, smiling, pretending to be deeply contemplating the decision, tapping my index finger on my cheek.

"I don't know," I say standing up from the bed. "I kind of like it here, but we still have to go to Texas eventually."

Andrew looks at me curiously. "Oh? So, you're still set on Texas, huh?"

I nod slowly, contemplating it for real this time. "Yeah," I answer distantly, "I think I am—it started out as Texas..." and then the words: *maybe it'll end in Texas*, enter my mind and my face suddenly falls.

Andrew kisses my forehead and smiles.

"I'll see you in the morning."

And I let him go because that glass wall is too thick and intimidating for me to reach out and stop him.

Hours later, well into the dark early morning when most are asleep, I wake up swiftly and sit up in the center of the bed. I'm not sure what woke me, but it feels like it might've been a loud noise. As my mind comes together, I gaze around the pitch-dark room, letting my eyes adjust to the darkness and look to see if anything had fallen. I get up and walk around, opening the curtains just a sliver to let in more light. I look toward the bathroom and then the TV and lastly the wall. Andrew. It's coming to me now: I think what I heard was something from *his* room, right behind my head.

I slip my white cotton shorts on over my panties and take my card key and the extra one he gave me to his room and I walk barefooted out into the brightly-lit hallway.

I raise my knuckles and knock lightly at first.

"Andrew?"

No answer.

I knock again a little harder and call out his name, but still get no response. After a pause, I slide his key in the door and open it quietly in case he's still asleep.

Andrew is sitting on the edge of his bed with his elbows on his knees and his hands folded together draped between his legs. His back is slumped over forward in an arch where his head has fallen to where he can only be looking at the carpeted floor.

I glance to my right and see his cell phone on the floor with a shattered glass front. I know immediately that he must've thrown it at the wall.

"Andrew? What's wrong?" I ask, approaching him slowly, not because I'm afraid of him, but because I'm afraid *for* him.

The curtains have been pulled wide open, letting the moonlight in and bathing the entire room and Andrew's half-naked body in a grayish-blue haze. He's wearing only a pair of boxers. I step up to him and slide my hands from his arms down to his hands, taking them gently into my fingers. "You can tell me," I say, but I already know what it's about.

He doesn't look up at me, but he takes my fingers into his and cradles them.

My heart is breaking...

I move closer, standing in between his legs, and he doesn't hesitate to wrap his arms tightly around my body. Feeling my chest begin to shudder as I take on his pain, I wrap my arms around his head and pull him toward my stomach.

"I'm so sorry, baby," I shudder out the words, tears are streaming from my face, but I try my best to hold my composure. I grip his head gently and he presses his forehead deeper into my belly. "I'm here, Andrew," I say carefully.

And he cries quietly into my stomach. He never makes a sound, but I can feel his body trembling gently against my own. His father has died and he's allowing himself to grieve the way he should. He holds me here for the longest time, his arms constricting around me when the worst waves of pain move through him and I hold him tighter, my hands locked within his hair.

Finally, he raises his eyes and looks up at me. All I want to do is take away that pain in his face. Right now, it's all that I care about in this world. I just want to take away his pain.

Andrew pulls me by the waist over onto the bed with him and just holds me there, gripped within the hardness of his arms with the entire length of the back of my body pressed against the front of his. Another hour passes and I watch the moon move from one point to another in the sky. Andrew never says a word and I don't try to prompt him because I know he needs this moment and if neither of us ever speaks again, I can live with that as long as we stay just like this.

Two people unable to cry finally cry together and if the world ended today, we would be fulfilled.

The early morning sun begins to wash away the moonlight, and for a time, both of them are hidden in the same vast expanse of sky so that neither dominates the other. The atmosphere is bathed in dark purple and gray with splashes of pink, until the sun finally prevails and wakes up our side of the world.

I roll over onto my other side, facing Andrew. He's still awake, too. I smile at him softly and he welcomes me when I lean in to kiss him softly on the lips. He reaches his hand out and brushes the back of his finger across my cheek and then touches my mouth, the pad of his thumb barely skimming the center of my bottom lip before falling away. I move closer and he grips my hand within his, both of them resting between our pressed bodies. His beautiful green eyes smile gently at me and then he lets go of my hand and wraps that arm around my waist, pulling me so close that I can feel the warmth of his breath on my chin as he breathes in and out.

I know he doesn't want to talk about his father and to bring it up might ruin this moment, so I don't. As much as I want to and as much as I believe he needs to talk about it to help him grieve, I will wait. He needs time.

I bring up my free hand and trace the outline of the tattoo on his right upper arm. And then my fingers make a delicate trail to his ribs.

"Can I see it?" I whisper softly.

He knows I'm talking about the tattoo of Eurydice down his left side, which is still pressed into the bed beneath him.

Andrew gazes at me, but his face is unreadable. His eyes stray for a long moment before he rises up from the bed and crawls over onto the other side so that the tattoo is visible. He lies on his side just like before and pulls me a little closer, afterwards moving his arm away from his ribs. I lift up to get a better look and run my fingers along the intricate artwork that is so beautiful and lifelike. The head of the woman begins about two inches from underneath his arm and extends to her bare feet to the middle of his sculpted hip and a few inches onto his stomach. She's wearing a long, flowing see-through white gown which presses against her body as if a strong wind is pushing against her. Wisps of long fabric blow behind and all around her within the invisible wind.

She's standing on a ledge, looking downward with one arm drifting delicately behind her.

But then it gets weird.

Eurydice is reaching out with the other arm, but the ink stops at her elbow. Another arm has been added in on the other side, but it's not hers; it appears to come from someone else and it looks more masculine. Streams of fabric also appear out of place within the image; it's blowing in the wind like hers. And just below it, propped upon the same ledge is a foot on the end of a muscular calf where the ink cuts off just below the knee.

I run my fingers along every inch of the tattoo, mesmerized by the beauty of it, but at the same time trying to understand the complexity and why the missing pieces.

I look up at Andrew and he says, "You asked who my musical idol was last night and the answer is Orpheus—kind of weird, I know, but I've always loved the story of Orpheus and Eurydice—especially the one told by Apollonius of Rhodes and it just kind of stuck with me."

I smile softly and gaze at the tattoo again; my fingers still resting on his ribs. "I know of Orpheus, but not so much Eurydice." I feel a little ashamed that I don't know their story, especially since it seems to mean so much to Andrew.

He begins to explain:

"Orpheus' musical ability was unrivaled being the son of a Muse, and when he played his lyre or sang, every living thing listened. There was no musician greater than him, but his love for Eurydice was even more powerful than his talent; he would do anything for her. They married, but soon after the wedding Eurydice was bitten by a Viper and died. Stricken with grief, Orpheus went into the Underworld, determined to bring her back."

As Andrew tells this story, I can't help but be selfish and picture me in Eurydice's place. Andrew in place of Orpheus. I even compare the silly moment in the field that night with Andrew when the snake slithered across our blanket. So selfish and stupid of me to think this way, but I can't help it...

"In the Underworld, Orpheus played his lyre and sang and everyone there was enchanted by him, brought to their knees with emotion. And so they let Eurydice go into Orpheus' care, but only under one condition: Orpheus could not look back at Eurydice even for a moment on their way back to the Upper World." Andrew pauses. "But on the way up, he couldn't fight that desire, that need to turn around to make sure that Eurydice was still there."

"He looked back," I say.

Andrew nods sadly.

"Yeah, he did just a moment too soon and he saw Eurydice in the dim light from the top of the cave. They reached their hands out to each other and just before their fingers touched, she faded into the darkness of the Underworld and he never saw her again."

I swallow down my emotions and just stare longingly into Andrew's face. He isn't looking at me, but seems lost in thought, staring past me instead.

Then he snaps out of it.

"People get deep, meaningful tattoos all the time," he says, looking at me again. "This one happens to be mine."

I glance down at it again and then up into his eyes, recalling something I remembered his father say that night in Wyoming.

"Andrew, what did your father mean when he said that in the hospital?"

His eyes soften and he briefly looks away. Then he moves his arm back down and takes my hand into his, running his thumb along the side of my fingers.

"You caught that?" he asks, smiling gently.

"Yeah, I sort of did."

Andrew kisses my fingers and then releases my hand.

"He used to mess with me about it," he says. "I got the tattoo and told Aidan what it meant and why it wasn't technically complete and then he told our father." Andrew rolls his eyes. "I never lived it down, that's for damn sure. For the last two years, my father has cracked my ass about it, but I know he was just being Dad: tough guy that doesn't cry and doesn't believe in emotions. But he told me once when Aidan and Asher weren't around, that as 'pussified' as the meaning behind my tattoo was, that he understood—he said to me:" (Andrew twirls his fingers in the air harmoniously) "'Son, I hope you find your Eurydice one day—as long as she doesn't turn you into a pussy, I hope you find her.'"

I try to push the little smile off my lips, but he sees it and smiles, too.

"But why is it unfinished?" I ask, looking at it again and moving his arm away from the top of it. "And what exactly is the meaning behind it?"

Andrew sighs, though he knew all along that I would get to those questions. I get the sense that he might have been hoping that I would just let it go.

Not a chance.

Suddenly, Andrew raises himself from the bed and guides me to sit up with him. He curls his fingers at the bottom of my tank-top and starts to lift it off my body. Without question, I raise my arms above me as he slips my shirt off and I sit naked from the waist up in front of him. Only a small part of me feels self-conscious and instinctively my shoulder moves inward as if to cover my nakedness with its shadow.

Andrew guides me back down upon the bed and he pulls

me so close to him that my bare breasts are crushed between our bodies. Guiding my arms around his arms the same way his are around mine, he pulls me tighter against him, tangling our naked legs below. Our ribs are touching, my body fitting into his like two smooth-edged puzzle pieces.

And suddenly, I'm starting to understand...

"My Eurydice is only half of the tattoo," he says and his eyes trail downward to where the tattoo is in relation to my body next to it. "I thought that one day, if I ever got married, my girl would get the other half and reunite them."

My heart is in my throat. I try to swallow it down, but it's wedged there swollen and warm.

"But it's crazy, I know," he says and I feel his arms around me begin to loosen.

I grip him a little tighter, holding him in place.

"It's not crazy," I say, my voice low and intent. "And it's not pussified; Andrew it's *beautiful. You're* beautiful..."

A solitary emotion that I can't place flits across his face.

Then he gets up and reluctantly, I let him.

He plucks his dark brown cargo shorts from the floor next to the bed and slips them on over his boxers.

Still a little stunned about how quickly he got up and why, it takes me a moment longer before I slip my tank-top back on.

"Yeah, well, I think maybe my dad was right all along," he says standing in front of the window, looking out at the city of New Orleans below. "He was onto something and using that whole real-men-don't-cry bullshit to cover it up."

"To cover what up?"

I step up behind him, but this time I don't touch him. He's unreachable in the sense that I'm getting the feeling he doesn't want me here. It's not disinterest or a faded attraction, but it's something else . . .

He answers without turning around, "That nothing lasts forever." He hesitates, still looking out the window with his arms crossed over his chest. "It's better to shun emotion than to fall for it and let it make you its bitch—and since nothing lasts forever, in the end everything that was once good, always hurts like hell."

His words slice right through me.

Any part of me that had been changed during my time with Andrew, all of the walls that I let down for him, just shot right back up around me.

Because he's right and I fucking *know* he's right.

That logic is what kept me from jumping fully into his world all this time. And in a matter of seconds the truth in his words made me submissive to that logic once again.

I decide to drop it. There's an issue far more important than mine right now and I make sure I don't treat him any differently.

"You'll . . . need to go to your father's funeral, so—"

Andrew swings around at the waist, his eyes full of resolve.

"No, I won't be going to the funeral."

He slips a clean shirt on down over his abs.

"But Andrew . . . you have to." My eyebrows deepen heavily within my forehead. "You'll never forgive yourself if you don't go to your own father's funeral."

I see his jaw moving as if he's gritting his teeth. He looks away from me and sits on the end of the bed, bending over and wedging his bare feet down inside his low black running shoes, not bothering to untie them so they'll loosen.

He stands up.

I can only stand here in the center of the room, unbelieving. I feel like I should know something to say that will make him change his mind about the funeral, but my heart tells me that this is one argument I'm not going to win.

"I've got something I've gotta do," he says, shoving his car keys down inside his shorts pocket. "I'll be back in a little while, all right?"

Before I can answer, he steps up to me and cradles both sides of my head within his hands and leans in, touching his forehead to mine. I just look into his eyes, seeing so much pain and conflict and indecision among a storm of other things that I can't even begin to put a name to.

"Will you be all right?" he asks softly with his face inches from my own.

I lean away and look at him and nod.

"I'll be all right," I say.

But it's *all* that I can bring myself to say. I'm as conflicted and indecisive as he seems to be. But I'm also hurting. I feel like something is happening between us, but it's pulling us further apart than together like this whole trip had been doing. And it scares me.

I understand the logic. My walls are back up. But it scares me unlike anything ever has before.

He leaves me standing here as I watch him slip out of the room.

This is the first time since he came back for me in that bus station that he's left me. We have been together, practically inseparable, this whole time and now...since he walked out that door, I feel like I'm never going to see him again.

# Andrew

# TWENTY-EIGHT

*S*tartin' early, aren't yah?" the bartender says as he slides a shot across the bar top and into my hand.

"If you're open and serving already, then it's not too early."

It's already three o'clock in the afternoon. I left Camryn alone early this morning, well before eight. Kind of odd that we've been on this trip together all this time and neither of us ever thought to, or wanted to, bring up anything about swapping phone numbers. I guess it didn't matter much since she and I were always together. I'm sure by now she's long past wondering if I'm ever coming back, maybe wishing she had my number so she can find out if I'm all right—the glass on the cell is broken, but it still works. I'm starting to wish that it didn't though because Asher and my mom have tried calling dozens of times already.

I intend to go back to the hotel, but I've decided that it'll only be to get Aidan's guitar from the room and to leave a plane ticket for Camryn on my bed. The room is paid up for two more days, so she'll be all right. I'll leave her money for a cab ride to the airport, too. It's the least I can do. I'm the one that talked her into this shit with me. I'll be the one making sure her way home is paid in full and that it's not a bus this time.

It ends *today*.

I never should've let it go this far, but I was delusional and blinded by my painfully forbidden feelings for her. But I think she'll be all right; we didn't sleep together and no one said those three damning words that would definitely make things more complicated, so yeah...I think she'll be just fine.

After all, she never gave in to me. I basically laid the option out on the table for her: *If you were to let me fuck you, you would have to let me own you.* If that wasn't a blatant invitation then I don't know what is. Not very romantic, but it is what it is.

I pay for my shot and leave the bar. I just needed something to take the edge off. Though, for it really to do any good at taking *this* kind of edge off I would've had to drink the whole damn bottle. I slide my hands down inside my pockets and walk the length of Bourbon Street and Canal Street and eventually down streets I don't even recall the names of as I go past the signs. I walk forever, everywhere, much like on mine and Camryn's sporadic road trip with no direction or purpose. I just go.

I think I'm not trying to waste time so that the night falls and I can slip in and out quietly while she sleeps, but I'm wasting time hoping I'll change my mind. I don't want to leave her, but I know I have to.

I end up at Woldenberg Riverfront Park, sitting along the bank of the Mississippi and watching the ships and the ferry as it travels back and forth to and from Algiers. The night falls. And for the longest time my only company is a statue of Malcolm Woldenberg, until two girls, obviously tourists judging by the I Love NOLA t-shirts, walks up.

The blonde one smiles coyly at me while the brown-haired one goes in for the kill.

"Partying anywhere tonight?" She cocks her head to one side looking down at me. "I'm Leah and this is Amy."

The blonde, 'Amy', smiles at me in a way that I know all I'd have to do is ask her to fuck me and she would.

I nod, trying to be polite, but don't offer my own name.

"So? Partying tonight, or not?" the brown-haired one asks, sitting down next to me on the concrete.

I've already forgotten their names.

"No, actually I'm not," I say and leave it at that.

The blonde sits down on the other side, drawing her knees up so that her shorts hike way up her bare thighs.

*Camryn looks better in shorts like that.*

I just shake my head and look back out at the Mississippi.

"You should come with us," the brown-haired girl says. "There's a lot of action going on over at d.b.a tonight; you look bored as hell."

I glance over at her. She's pretty hot, just like the blonde, but I find myself completely turned off the more she talks. All I can think about is Camryn. The girl has wounded my soul. It'll never be the same.

I scan the brown-haired girl's legs and then watch how her lips move when she says, "We'd really like you to join us; it'll be fun."

I *could*... if I'm leaving and intend never to see Camryn again, maybe I *should* leave with these two, get a room somewhere else and fuck them both. I'm pretty sure at the rate things are going that they would do each other in front of me. Been there, done that a few times and it never really gets old.

"I don't know," I say. "I was waiting for someone."

I have no idea what I'm saying, or why I'm saying it.

The brown-haired girl leans over and puts her hand on my thigh.

"We'd be better company," she says in a sultry sort of whisper with all of the obvious overtones of a girl who has had way too many one-night stands.

I move her hand off me and stand up, thrusting my hands back inside my pockets and leave. Any other time I might be on it, but not today.

Yeah, my soul is probably wounded beyond repair. I've got to get out of this city.

As I walk away from the two girls without saying a word, I hear their voices fluttering on the air behind me. I don't give a shit what they're saying, or how rejected they feel. In an hour they'll be riding some other guy's cock and will forget they ever spoke to me.

It's after midnight now. I already stopped at an internet café and purchased Camryn's plane ticket to North Carolina online and afterwards stopped at an ATM and withdrew more than enough cash to pay her cab ride to the airport and one home from the airport in North Carolina.

On my way into the front lobby of our hotel, I ask the front desk clerk for an envelope, a piece of paper and something to write with and then I sit down on a couch in the lobby and write Camryn a note:

Camryn,

I'm sorry I left like I did, but I know I couldn't say goodbye face-to-face. I hope you'll remember me, but if forgetting me is easier then I can live with that, too.

Never hold back, Camryn Bennett; be sure to do what you want in life, say what you feel and never be afraid to be yourself. Fuck what everybody else thinks. You're living for you, not them.

The code below is what you'll need to give to the airport to get on your plane home. All you'll need is your I.D. The plane leaves tomorrow morning. The cash is for your cab.

Thank you for best two weeks of my life and for being there for me when I needed you the most.

—Andrew Parrish
KYYBPR

I read the note over five times before I'm satisfied with it and finally fold it and place it with the cash into the envelope.

I make my way to the elevator. One last hurdle is slipping out without Camryn knowing about it. I hope she's still asleep. Please just let her be asleep. I can do this if I don't have to see her, but if she sees me . . . No. I have to be able to do this either way.

And I will.

I step out of the elevator on our floor and make my way through one long, brightly-lit stretch of hallway past several rooms. Seeing our rooms out ahead makes my stomach swim nervously. I walk past quietly; worried that my shoes shuffling across the floor might be enough to let her know I'm out here. There's a DO NOT DIS-TURB sign hanging on her doorknob and I don't know why but seeing it causes my stomach to twist up in knots. Maybe because the only time I've ever hung one of those on a hotel door was when I was inside getting laid. The thought of Camryn being fucked by some other guy . . .

I grind my teeth together and walk past. How insanely pathetic was that? She's not even mine and I just got raped by a crazy-jealous reaction.

The sooner I get out of New Orleans, the better.

I slide my card-key in my door and slip inside the room. It looks exactly the way I left it: clothes strewn near my bags and Aidan's guitar propped against the wall underneath the mounted light fixture.

I move through the room, gathering up everything and have an *oh-yeah* moment when I realize I probably would've left my chargers in the wall if I hadn't seen them at the right angle when I passed. I unplug them and shove them along with my clothes down into my bag. Lastly, I hurry into the bathroom to get my toothbrush from the sink.

Camryn is standing in the doorway when I walk back out.

# Camryn

# TWENTY-NINE

*A*ndrew? Are you all right?" I look across at him, crossing my arms as the room door clicks closed softly behind me.

I've been so worried about him...worried because I was afraid he'd left without saying goodbye, but more worried because of the state of mind he was in when he left. Because his father just died.

I catch my breath quietly and he walks past me towards his bags sitting on the end of the bed.

Why won't he look at me?

I glance at the bags again and realize instantly what he's doing. I let my arms fall back to my sides and I walk closer to him.

"Please talk to me," I say gently. "Andrew, you scared the shit out of me—" He shoves his toothbrush into his duffle bag, keeping his back to me. "—if you need to go to the funeral, that's good. I can go back home. Maybe we can talk—"

Andrew whirls around.

"This isn't about the funeral or my father, Camryn," he says and his words hurt me without knowing the meaning behind them first.

"Then what is it?"

He turns away from me again, pretending to rummage through one of his bags though I know it's just a distraction. I see an envelope sticking out of his back pocket. RYN is written across the front; the first half of what I'm guessing is *my* name is covered by the fabric of his pocket.

I reach out and take it.

Andrew turns around again and his face falls.

"Camryn..." he breathes a sad breath and looks briefly down at the floor.

"What is this?" I ask looking down at my name.

Already I'm pulling out the top flap from inside the envelope with my finger.

Andrew doesn't answer; he just stands there waiting for me to read the contents of the note because he knows I'm going to anyway.

He wants me to.

I see the cash and leave it in the envelope without touching it and I set it aside on the foot of the bed. All I care about is the note in my hands that already is crushing my heart and I haven't even read it yet. I look up at him and down at the note a few times before finally unfolding it.

My hands are shaking.

Why are my hands shaking?

And as I read, a hot lump wedges itself in the center of my throat. My eyes are burning with anger and hurt and tears.

"Babe, you knew this trip had to end sometime."

"Don't call me babe," I snap, gripping the note tightly within my fingertips now down at my side. "If you're leaving, you no longer have that right."

"Fair enough."

I glare back up at him, my face full of pain and questions and confusion. Why am I so mad, so hurt? Andrew is right: it had to end sometime, but why am I letting it affect me like this?

Tears begin to stream from my eyes. I can't hold them back, but I'll be damned if I let myself bawl like a baby. I just look at him, my face tight and consumed by pain and ire. My hands are clenched at my sides, the top half of Andrew's note crushed in my fist.

"If you were leaving like this because of your father, because you needed time alone, and the number on the bottom of this note was *yours* instead of a ticket confirmation, then I could understand." I raise the crushed note up in front of me and let it fall back at my side. "But to leave because of me and pretend that nothing between us ever happened ... Andrew, that hurts. It fucking hurts."

I see his jaw twitch.

"Who the hell said I could ever pretend that it never happened?" he rips the words out, clearly stung by mine. He drops the duffle bag handle and moves away from the bed toward me. "I'll *never* be able to forget *any* of this, Camryn! That's why I couldn't *face* you!" He slashes the air between us with his hands.

I step backward and away from him. I can't deal with this. My heart hurts too much. And I'm pissed off that I can't make myself stop crying. I look down at the note in my hand and then back up at him and finally I walk around him to the bed and drop it down beside the envelope and the money.

"Fine. Go ahead and leave. But I'll pay my own way home."

I wipe my eyes and walk to the door.

"Still afraid," he calls out behind me.

I whirl around. "You don't know *shit!*" And I push open the door, dropping his extra key on the floor and go back into my room.

I pace. And pace. And pace. I want to hit a wall or tear something up, but I settle with finally bawling like a baby.

Andrew storms inside my room, letting the door smack the

wall on his way in. He grabs me by my upper arms, digging his fingers into my muscles.

"Why are you still afraid?!" Tears lace his eyes: furious, painful tears. He shakes me. "SAY WHAT YOU FEEL!"

His thunderous voice makes my body go rigid for a moment, but I shove his hands off me. I'm so confused. I know what I want to say. I don't want him to go, but—

"Camryn!" His face is full of wrath and desperation. "Say whatever it is that you feel! I don't care how dangerous or stupid or hurtful or hilarious—TELL ME HOW YOU *FEEL*!" His voice sears through me.

He doesn't stop:

"Be honest with me. Be honest with *yourself*!" His hands wave outward toward me in gesture. "CAMR—"

"I *want* you, goddammit!" I scream at him. "The thought of you leaving and never seeing you again *tears-me-up-inside*!" My throat burns like fire. "I can't fucking *breathe* without you!"

"SAY IT! Son-of-a-*bitch*," he says, exasperated, "just *say it*!"

"I want you to *own* me!" I can hardly stand on my own anymore. Sobs rock my entire body. My eyes sting and my heart hurts like it never has before.

Andrew grabs me, twisting my wrists together behind my back with one of his hands. He pulls my back harshly into his chest. "Say it again, Camryn," he demands, the heat of his breath bathing the side of my neck, sending chills throughout my limbs. I feel his teeth graze the flesh just below my ear. "Fucking say it, baby." His hand tightens painfully around my wrists.

"I *belong* to you, Andrew Parrish...I want you to *own* me..."

He coils the fingers from his other hand tightly within my hair, pulling my neck back and exposing my throat to him. He bites my chin and then down along my neck. I feel his cock pressing into me from behind through the barrier of our clothes.

*"Please..."* I whisper, *"don't let me go..."*

With my back still pressed into his hard body and my wrists in his hand, he slips his fingers behind my shorts and panties and tears them off. He forces me around toward the bed where my knees are pressed against the mattress and he lifts my arms above my head, slipping off my tank-top.

I don't look behind me when I sense him kicking off his shoes and removing his clothes. I'll only move when he allows it.

His rock-hard abs press firmly into my back. I feel his warm arms slip around my naked waist; one hand moving up to fully squeeze one breast, the other sliding down in between my legs. My neck falls back against his chest when he slips a finger between my throbbing lips below and teases me with it. I gasp, tilting my neck back so that I can reach his mouth. His tongue snakes out to touch mine; the fleshy warm wetness of it drives me insane. He crushes his lips against mine and kisses me ravenously, to the point that neither of us can breathe. And then he forces me forward onto the bed. My hands burrow into the sheets, my fingers curling into the fabric until he presses all of his weight on my back and my arms can't hold my body up anymore. He grabs my wrists again and pulls them around behind me, pressing himself against me.

"Goddammit, please fuck me, Andrew...*please*," I beg, my voice shuddering with my breath. I say what I feel this time without his prompt.

And it feels *so* right.

Andrew leans fully over me; I feel his hardness forceful and persistent. I want him inside of me so bad, but he's keeping it from me on purpose, making me feel like any moment he's going to shove it in me, but he never does.

Shivers attack my body again when I feel the tip of his tongue trace a path along the back of my neck. One side of my face is pressed against the mattress, the hard weight of his body on top of me forbidding me to move. I bite my lip when the sting of his teeth clamps down on my back, enough to cause pain, but not breaking the skin. And after he bites me he kisses and licks each spot to ease the tender pain.

As if my weight is nothing to him, Andrew flips my body over with one hand onto my back and slides me up to the center of the bed. He crawls in between my legs, bumping them apart with his knees so that I'm completely exposed to him. He presses the palms of his hands on the under-part of my thighs, forcing my legs to stay open.

His green orbs flash on me once and then he looks down at me spread open before him. He probes me teasingly, sliding the length of one finger between my lips and then around the edges of my clit. I gasp and shudder, feeling my insides squirm with every touch. He looks up at me again under dangerous hooded eyes and slides his fingers inside so deep. I move my hand down to join his and he lets me touch myself for a moment before refusing me any more. He fingers me furiously now, touching every possible spot sensitive to touch and I start to writhe gently, my head pressing back into the pillow. And as if he knows I'm going to come soon, he pulls his hand away to keep me from it.

He crawls his way on top of me, kissing and licking and biting my skin from my thighs all the way up to my throat and he holds my arms above my head so that I can't grasp him. His wolfish eyes study my mouth and then find my eyes and he says, "I'm going to fuck you so hard...God, you have *no* fucking idea." His words cut a path of pleasure from my ear all the way down into the throbbing wetness between my legs. He bites my tongue and then kisses me violently and we breathe heavily into each other's mouths, moaning against each other's lips.

His right hand moves down without breaking the kiss and he takes his cock into his hand and finds me, just barely entering me so that it drives me mad. I thrust my hips toward him, trying to force it deeper, kissing him harder and finally getting one hand around the back of his head. I grip his hair in my hand so hard that I feel like I'm pulling it out. He doesn't care. Neither do I. He enjoys the pain as much as I do.

And then very slowly, so that I can feel every painfully searing sensation shiver through my body, he slides himself inside of me. My neck arches back on the pillow, my lips part open. I gasp and moan and whimper. My eyes are tingling so much that they're heavy and I can barely pry my lids apart. His cock feels like it's swelling inside of me and my thighs are trembling against his body.

He fucks me slowly at first, forcing my eyes open to see his. He takes my bottom lip between his teeth and pulls back and then traces the full length of it with the tip of his tongue.

I crush my mouth against his, pushing against him with my hips and forcing him deeper.

My legs are shaking now. I can't control them. He starts to fuck me harder and I can't maintain the kiss anymore. My neck arches away from the pillow again, my back starts to lift, pushing my breasts toward him where he licks my nipples hungrily. I wrap my arms and legs around his body, digging my fingernails into his back, feeling his sweat bead underneath them. I break the skin. It just makes him fuck me harder.

"*Come with me,*" he whispers hotly into my ear and kisses me again.

Seconds later, I do. My body trembles and quivers as I feel myself constrict around him. "*Don't pull out,*" I whisper while we come together. And he doesn't. A deep, shuddering moan moves through his chest and I feel the warmth of him releasing inside of me. I tighten my legs around his waist until I can't anymore and slowly let my legs give way. He doesn't stop pushing himself inside of me until his body begins to relax.

He lies next to me; his face on my heart, my leg draped over his waist. And we lie like this for a while, curled into one another, letting our breathing steady and our bodies calm. But twenty minutes later, we're at it again. And before the night is over and we've fallen fast asleep in each other's arms, he's had me in more ways than I've ever been had.

The next morning, as the sun beams in through the curtains, he shows me that he's not always rough and aggressive by waking me up with sweet kisses. He kisses each of my ribs and massages my back and my thighs before making love to me softly.

I could die in this bed with him right now, wrapped in his arms and I would never know that I had died.

———

Andrew squeezes me against him within his arms and kisses my jawline.

"You can't go anywhere now," I whisper.

"I never wanted to."

I turn around to lie facing him, tangling my naked legs around his. He touches his forehead to mine.

"But you were going to," I say softly.

He nods. "Yeah, I was going to because…" his thoughts trail.

"Why?" I ask. "Because I was too afraid of the obvious?"

I know that must be why. I think. I hope…

Andrew's gaze strays downward. I lift my hand and brush the length of his eyebrow beneath my fingertip and then the bridge of his nose. I lean forward just a little and kiss his lips softly.

"Andrew? *Is* that why?"

My heart tells me that it's not.

His eyes begin to smile and he pulls me closer, wrapping me up tighter in his arms and kissing me hard.

"Are you *sure* you want this?" he asks, as though he doesn't believe I could ever want him in this way, which is utterly absurd to me.

I struggle to find the meaning behind his thought process, and I come up short.

"Why wouldn't I?" I say. "Andrew, I *meant* what I said: I can't breathe without you. Last night, after you had been gone all day, I sat down on the edge of this bed and was literally breathless. I thought you had already left and I started thinking about how I didn't even have your phone number and that I would never be able to find you—"

He touches my lips with his finger, calming me. "I'm here now and I'm not going anywhere."

I smile longingly and lay my head against his chest. His chin rests upon my head. I listen to his heart beating and the sound of his breath as it comes out through his nose in an even, quiet motion above me. We lie like this for hours, hardly saying a word. I realize this is exactly where I've wanted to be since I spoke to him on that bus that day.

I've broken every rule… Every. Single. One.

# Andrew

# THIRTY

The heart always wins out over the mind. The heart, although reckless and suicidal and a masochist all on its own, always gets its way. The mind may be what's best, but I don't give a shit what my mind is telling me anymore. Right now, I just want to live in the moment.

"Get up, baby," I say, patting Camryn on the ass.

She fell asleep in my arms again after we woke up together earlier this morning. I think maybe I did too at some point, but all I've thought about since last night is her and if I was ever asleep at all I'll never know.

She moans in protest and rolls over to face me, her body tangled in the white sheet, her blonde hair a matted mess, but still sexy as hell.

"Oh come on, baby," she says and my heart thumps hard a few times hearing her call me that, "let's sleep all day."

I throw on my t-shirt and step into my shorts and sit on the bed beside her, grounding one arm on the other side of her body.

I lean over and press my lips against her forehead.

"I want to do everything with you," I say, smiling so big that I realize how awkward it feels, but I don't care. "We can go everywhere, do whatever idea falls into our laps."

I've never been this happy before. I didn't know happiness like this existed.

Camryn smiles so sweetly up at me, her blue eyes glistening still with that just-woke-up innocence. It's like she's studying me, trying to figure me out, but enjoying the process.

She reaches out both of her arms.

"I'm afraid you'll have to carry me around everywhere," she says.

I reach out and take her arms into my hands and she lifts to sit upright on the bed.

"Well, I have no problem with that," I laugh. "I will totally fucking carry you around—it'll get a reaction out of people, but so what—But why do I need to carry you?"

She kisses me on the nose.

"Because I don't think I can walk."

Realization teases my smile into a dark grin.

She starts to get up from the bed, letting her legs fall over the side and I see the discomfort in her face.

"Oh shit, baby, I am *so* sorry." I really am sorry, but I can't stop smiling.

Neither can she, really.

"I'm not saying this to stroke that sexual ego of yours," she says, "but I have *never* been fucked like *that* before."

I laugh out loud, throwing my head back once.

"The shit that comes out of your mouth!" I say.

"Hey," she points up at me, "that's all *your* fault. You've turned me into a foul-mouthed, perverted nymphomaniac that will apparently be walking funny for a day or two." She nods her head once to underline these facts.

Carefully, I lift her into my arms, both legs over one arm instead of making her straddle me in her 'condition'.

"Sorry babe, but you were already kind of foul-mouthed when I met you," I say, grinning down at her looking up at me with a puffed-out upper lip. "Perverted? Maybe. But that was already in you, I just helped bring it out. Now *nymphomaniac?* That would mean you want to do it all the time, even if you're walking funny for a couple of days."

Her eyes grow wider and wider. "No, I am definitely out of commission, at least until tomorrow morning."

I kiss her forehead and carry her into the bathroom.

"Sounds good," I say, trading jokes for a softer expression. "I wouldn't let you anyway. Today, Camryn Bennett, you will be pampered. And first on the agenda is a long, hot bath."

"With bubbles?" she asks with a Bambi-eyed pouty face.

I smile down at her. "Yes, with bubbles."

I run the bath water while she sits on the counter where I put her, naked to boot.

"Bubbles might be a problem, babe," I say, squeezing what's left of the shampoo in the trial-sized bottle the hotel provides.

"You know what?" she says, swinging her feet back and forth with her hands propped on the edge of the counter. "I'm out of just about everything—my toothpaste tube is flat and I could use some body wash, or somethin'." She reaches down and feels her bare legs. "I practically have scales." She makes a face.

Twisting the inside of my mouth between my teeth I say, "I'll go to the store." Letting the tub fill up behind me I turn to her and check out the stuff she has lying on the counter. Then I go back into the room and come back with a tiny hotel pencil and a palm-sized square notepad. "What do you need?"

While she's thinking about it I write down what she already mentioned.

"Toothpaste, body wash—" I look up at her, "that's just liquid soap, right?"

"Well, not really," she says and I'm trying not to check out her boobs. "It's not hand soap, it's—well, you'll figure it out."

I jot down: not liquid hand soap

I look back up at her. "OK, what else can you think of?"

She purses her lips contemplatively. "Shampoo and conditioner, I prefer L'Oréal; it's in a pink bottle, but it doesn't matter really, just none of that shampoo+conditioner stuff—left the bottles I recently bought in the last motel. Oh! Also, get me a small bottle of Baby Oil."

I raise a very interested brow. "Baby Oil? You have something in mind?"

"No!" She hits me gently on the arm with the back of her fingers, but all I notice is how her boob jiggled when she did it. "Definitely not! I just like to use it in the shower."

I jot down: large bottle of baby oil (just in case)

"And maybe some snacks and a six-pack of water or non-lemon tea—something besides soda—and, oh!" She points her finger upwards. "Some beef jerky!"

I grin and jot that down, too.

"That's it?"

"Yeah, I can't think of anything else yet."

"Well, if you do," I say, pulling my phone from the leg pocket of my cargo shorts, "call me and let me know—what's your number?"

She smiles and happily tells me while I call her from my phone. Her voice mail picks up and I say: *Hey, babe, it's me. I'll be back in a bit; right now I'm a bit preoccupied staring at this incredibly hot blonde sitting naked on a counter.*

Camryn grins and blushes and pulls me between her suspended legs and kisses me hard.

"Oh shit! The water!" she says, noticing the tub close to overflowing.

I turn the water off quickly.

I set the phone and my grocery list on the counter and lift her into my arms.

"Andrew, I'm not crippled." But she's not exactly arguing with me, either.

I help her into the tub and she leans back into the warmth of it, letting her hair fall around her shoulders and into the water, too.

"I'll be back in a few," I say as I go to leave.

"You promise this time?"

That stops me in my tracks. I turn back to look across at her and this time she's not joking. It makes me feel bad that she even has to ask, not because it offends me, but because I had to give her any reason to ask in the first place.

I look at her very seriously.

"Yes, I promise, babe. You're kind of stuck with me, y'know that, right?"

She smiles sweetly, though it's laced with mischief. "Damn the things I get myself into."

I wink at her and leave.

# Camryn

Sex always changes everything. It's like you're living in a bubble where everything is safe and flirty and often predictable. An attraction to the right kind of person can last forever when that intimate mystery is left intact, but the moment you sleep with someone, safe, flirty and predictable often become their opposites. Will the attraction die out now? Will we still want each other as much as we did before we had sex? Are either of us secretly thinking that we made a huge mistake and should've left things the way they were? No. Yes. And no. I know this because I feel it. It's not overconfidence or the delusional dreams of a young, inexperienced woman with insecurity issues. It's a blatant fact: Andrew Parrish and I were meant to meet on that bus in Kansas.

Coincidence is just the conformist term for fate.

I soak in the bath for a while, but decide to get out before I start pruning. I am sore down there, but I'm perfectly capable of walking. I just think it's sweet the way he feels the need to take care of me.

I slip on my gray pair of cotton shorts I bought on the road and a black tank-top. I make up the bed and straighten the room a little before grabbing my phone to check my messages: same random stuff from Natalie. Still nothing from my mom. I always leave my phone on vibrate. I can't stand to hear a phone ring. It doesn't matter if I could have any kind of ring tone I wanted; a ringing phone is like nails down a chalkboard to me. I head over to the window and pull the curtains open wide to let the bright sun flood the room and I lean on the windowsill, gazing down at New Orleans. I'll never forget this place.

I think about Andrew and his father briefly, but shut it out of my mind. I'll give him a few more days before I try talking to him about it again. He'll hurt for a while, but I don't want him unintentionally using me as a barrier. He has to deal with it sometime.

I set my phone down on the windowsill and scroll through my music. It's been a while since I've listened to any of my stuff; surprisingly, I've not missed it much. Andrew's classic rock has more than just grown on me; he's made me kind of love it.

*Barton Hollow* by The Civil Wars. I stop on that one—my favorite for the past two months—and turn the speaker on, letting the music filter into the room with that folky-country style that is my guilty pleasure. I'm not much of a country music girl, but this band is an exception. I sing along with John and Joy, letting myself loose since I'm in the privacy of my room and I sing as loud as I can. I dance a little standing in front of the window. And when Joy's solo begins, I sing along with her like I always do, trying to work my untrained voice to sound as velvety as hers does. I could never sound like her, but it makes me feel good to sing along.

My lips snap shut and my dancing body freezes when I notice Andrew leaning against the wall by the door, watching me. Grinning, of course.

I melt under the blush of my face.

He walks the rest of the way into the room now that he's been caught and sets two plastic bags down on the TV stand.

"For someone oh-so-sore," he mocks, his dimples deepening, "you sure were workin' those hips."

Still blushing, I try to distract from my little performance as much as possible by making my way over to the bags. "Yeah, well you shouldn't be sneaking up on me like that."

"I wasn't sneaking," he says, "just enjoying myself—you really do have a sweet voice."

I blush harder, turning my back to him and rummaging through one bag.

"Thanks, baby, but I think you're kinda biased." I look back just long enough to playfully smirk at him.

"No, I mean it," he says and he seems serious, "you aren't as bad as you think you are."

"Not as bad?" I turn around, holding a large bottle of Baby Oil. "What does that mean exactly, that you think I'm only a *little* bad?" I scoff at him and hold up the Baby Oil. "I said a small bottle."

"Well, they were out of small bottles."

"Uh huh." I smirk again, setting the bottle on the TV stand.

"Well, no I don't think you're bad at all," he says and I hear the bed squeak as he sits on the end of it.

I look at him through the mirror in front of me.

"Well you did good on the shampoo and conditioner," I say, plucking the bottles out and setting them next to the Baby Oil. "But the body wash, not so much."

"*What?*" He looks truly disappointed. "You said not liquid hand soap. That clearly says body wash across the front." He points at it as if to justify.

"I'm just kidding," I say, smiling gently at his reaction. "This is perfect."

He looks relieved, letting his hand drop to his side on the bed.

"You should perform. At least once. Just to see what it's like."

I do not like that light-bulb moment he seems to be having right now. Not one bit.

"Ummm, yeah...*no*." I shake my head at him through the mirror. "Kind of like eating bugs or becoming an astronaut for a day, that ain't gonna happen."

I reach inside the bag and pull out...*oh no he didn't*...

"Why not?" he asks. "It'll be an experience, something you never thought you'd do, but afterwards you'll feel exhilarated."

"What-the-*hell*-is-*this*?" I ask turning around, holding up a box of Vagisil in my fingers.

He looks incredibly uncomfortable. "It's...well, you know," he winces, "for your...girly parts." He nods uneasily towards my 'girly parts'.

My mouth falls open. "You think I smell? Have you seen me itching?" I'm trying not to laugh.

Andrew's eyes pop wide open. "What—*No!* I just thought it might help with the soreness." I've never seen him look so embarrassed, and at the same time, shocked. "Hey, it wasn't exactly a comfortable thing standing in that particular aisle reading the labels and being a guy." He starts gesturing with his hands. "I saw it was for that general area and I tossed it in the basket."

I set the Vagisil down and walk over to him. "Well, that stuff isn't exactly going to help with soreness due to..." I purse my lips, "...'excessive friction', but it's the thought that counts." I sit on his lap, straddling his waist and lean in to kiss him.

He wraps his arms around my back.

"So, I guess it's safe to assume we don't need separate rooms anymore," he says, smiling up at me.

With my hands locked around the back of his neck, I lean

in and kiss him again. "I started to go over there to get your stuff myself while you were gone until I realized I threw your extra key on the floor when I stormed out of there last night."

He slides his big hands down and grips my butt, pulling me closer. Then he kisses me in the hollow of my neck and stands up, taking me with him.

"I'll go get it now," he says, letting me slide carefully out of his grasp. "I figure it'll take me a couple of days to learn to play that song and to learn the lyrics—you seem to have it down."

*Uh oh...*

I narrow my eyes at him in a sidelong glare. "Learn it *why?*"

His dimples deepen again. "If I do recall, you gave up your freedom after winning it at that game of pool."

His expression is all but pure evil.

I shake my head slowly at first and then gradually harder as the realization of the situation starts to sink in.

"Your words were," he nods once, "and I quote: *I don't want that freedom unless it comes to eating bugs or hanging my ass out the car window*—sorry, babe, but you should learn when to keep your mouth shut."

"No... Andrew," I step away from him, crossing my arms, "you can't make me sing in front of people. That's just cruel."

"To you or the audience?"

He grins.

I stomp on his foot.

"I'm kidding! I'm *kidding*!" He laughs out loud.

"Well, you can't make me do it."

He cocks his head to one side, green eyes lit up with a little bit of everything that makes him irresistible. "No, I won't force you to do anything, but..." Oh great, now he's fake-pouting. But worse, it's working! "…I really, really, *really* wish that you would." He cups my elbows in his hands and draws me close.

I snarl at him and grit my teeth behind my tightly-closed lips.

One Mississippi. Two Mississippi. Three Mississippi.

I take a deep breath.

"Fine."

His face lights up.

"But just once!" I point one finger. "And if anyone laughs at me you better not leave me in jail!"

He grabs my face, squishing my cheeks in his hands and kisses my fish-lips.

# THIRTY-ONE

*M*inutes later, Andrew's coming back through the door with his bags and his brother's acoustic guitar.

He is really excited about this.

I'm utterly terrified and already kicking myself for agreeing to it. But I have to admit, there's also a tiny pang of excitement in me, too. I'm not totally afraid to be in front of a crowd—had no problem giving a speech on endangered wildlife in eleventh grade, or playing the part of Nurse Ratched in *One Flew Over the Cuckoo's Nest* on stage my senior year. But singing is different. My acting isn't all that bad. My singing, especially a duet with someone like Andrew who sings like a blues-rock god who melts panties, is another story.

"I thought you didn't want to hear my kind of music, anyway?"

Andrew sets his bags on the floor and goes to the bed with the guitar.

"Well, whatever that song was you were so cutely dancing and singing to, I will let slide—I was diggin' it."

"The Civil Wars—my flavor-of-the-month, I guess," I say, coming out of the bathroom with wet hair, drying the ends with a towel (decided to rewash it after Andrew came back with the goods). "The song is called *Barton Hollow*."

"Very modern-folksy," he says, strumming the guitar a few times. "I like it."

He adds, looking up at me: "Where's your phone?"

I walk over and get it from the windowsill, scroll the progress bar back to the beginning and hand it to him. He sets it beside him on the bed and hits play. I go back to drying my hair while he does his learn-by-ear thing, stopping and starting the music over again and again, curling his fingers around the neck of the guitar and testing the sound of the strings until he finds the right ones that match the music. In a matter of minutes, after a few out-of-tune chords, he starts to play the first riff easily.

And by nightfall he's pretty much got the whole song down pat, with the exception of one short riff he keeps mixing up with another. Wanting to learn it as quickly as possible, he ended up looking for the music online and once he found it that definitely sped the progress up.

The lyrics were easier.

"I think I've almost got it," he says sitting on the windowsill against a dark and cloudy, rainy background. It started raining around eight and has been ever since.

Every now and then I would join in and sing some with him, but I've been too nervous. I really don't know how I'm going to pull something crazy like this off if I'm nervous with only him in the room. So much for not being afraid in front of crowds. I predict an extreme case of stage fright, after all.

"Come on, babe," he says with a nod, his fingers draped over the guitar, "just because you already know all the words doesn't mean you shouldn't practice with me."

I plop down on the end of the bed.

"You promise you won't make any of your goofy faces at me, or grin, or smile, or—"

"I won't even breathe," he says, laughing. "I swear! Come on."

I sigh and get up from the bed, putting my half-eaten strip of beef jerky on the nightstand. Andrew positions the guitar on his thigh and takes a quick sip of bottled tea to get his mouth ready to sing.

"Don't worry about it," he says as I'm slowly walking over, "the guy has way more lines by himself to sing than the girl—she only has that one solo, the rest you'll be singing right along with me."

I shrug nervously. "True," I admit. "At least through most of the song your voice will help drown mine out."

He places the guitar pick in between his lips and reaches his hand out to me. "Baby, come here."

I walk over and take his hand and he pulls me between his legs, the guitar between us. Once I'm still and where he wants me, he takes the pick from his mouth. "I love your voice, all right? But even if I thought you couldn't sing I'd still want you to do this. What anyone else thinks doesn't matter."

My lips lift into an unsure, demure smile. "OK," I say, "I'll do it for you, but it's *only* for you; better remember that." I point sternly at him. "You're gonna owe me."

He shakes his head. "First of all, I don't want you doing it just for me, but since practicing is more important than arguing with you about it, I'll wait until *after* you sing at Old Point to ask you if you got anything out of it other than giving me my way."

"I think that's fair enough."

He nods once and positions himself again and then starts to put the pick against the chords.

"W-Wait…maybe if you stand up, too, I won't feel so sin-gled out."

Andrew laughs and stands up from the windowsill. "Damn, girl—all right, however you want to do it. If you decide you want to do it with a bag over your head, you can."

I look at him as if entertaining the stupid idea.

"No way, Camryn, no bags. Now let's *do* this."

We practice well into the night until we're forced to quit because apparently we were disturbing the hotel guests on either side of us. And just when I was really starting to get the hang of it and letting loose a lot more, not worried what Andrew might be thinking of my singing.

I think I was doing pretty well.

We go to bed earlier tonight since our practice got cut short and we lie curled up next to one another and just talk.

"I'm glad you got fed up with my shit," I say lying in the fold of his arm. "Otherwise, I might be back in North Carolina right now."

I feel his lips press into the side of my hair.

"I have to confess something," he says.

My ears perk up. "Oh?"

"Yeah," he says, looking up at the ceiling where lights from the moving city outside move in strange patterns every now and then. "Back in Wellington, Kansas, in that first motel we got, when you were in the bathroom the next morning and I gave you two minutes to get ready…" He pauses and I feel his head move slightly as if looking down at me.

I draw my head away from his arm so I can look up at him.

"Yeah, I remember; what did you do?"

He smiles nervously.

"I sort of took a picture of your driver's license with my phone."

I blink back the mild stun.

"What for?" I rise up a little higher so I can look at him without risking my eyes getting stuck in the top of my head like that.

"Are you mad?"

I let out a spat of air. "I guess it depends on what you planned to do with the rather *personal* information."

He looks away, but I catch the blush on his face even in the darkness of the room.

"Well, it definitely wasn't so I could find you later and cut you up into little pieces or anything."

My mouth falls open. "Well *that's* a comfort!" I laugh.

"Seriously, though, why'd you take it?"

He looks back at the ceiling again, seeming lost in thought.

"I just wanted to make sure I knew how to find you again," he confesses, "you know…just in case we did decide to go our separate ways."

My eyes smile at him, but my mouth doesn't. I'm not mad that he took the photo for that reason—I kind of want to kiss him for it—but I'm not sure I like the whole 'just in case' part, either. It makes me feel more than I already did that he planned to leave at some point, no matter what.

"Andrew?"

"Yeah, babe?"

"Is there anything else you're not telling me?"

He pauses. "No. Why do you ask?"

I look at the ceiling, too.

"I don't know, I've just always sort of felt this strange…reluctance from you."

"*Reluctance?*" he says, surprised. "Was I reluctant to talk you into going on this road trip with me? Or reluctant to go down on you?"

"No, I guess not."

"Camryn, the only thing I've ever been reluctant about is wondering if it was right that we be together."

I lift up from the bed and turn fully at the waist to see him. The shadow across his face makes his eyes fiercer. He's shirtless and lies with one arm bent behind his head.

"You think we're not right?"

This conversation is starting to make my stomach fall in on itself.

He reaches out the hand not propped behind his head and takes my wrist gently. "No, babe, I...I think we *are* right in every way...and that's why I thin—that's why I *thought* it was better we didn't get involved."

"But that doesn't make any sense."

He pulls me down to him and I lie on the top of my hands on his chest.

"I just wasn't sure if we should go through with it," he says, combing his fingers through the hair beside my ears. "But, babe, you weren't exactly sure of anything, either."

I lie back down beside him. He's got me on that one.

The only thing I still don't quite understand is what were *his* reasons for being so careful to get involved, exactly? He knows why I left home and all about Ian's death. I have a laundry list of valid reasons stuck to the fridge by a banana magnet for all to see. Andrew's reasons are still hidden in a shoebox somewhere labeled Christmas Cards.

And I think it's more than just his dad.

He moves his arm out from underneath my head and climbs on top of me, a leg on each side, his body propped up by his muscular arms.

"I'm glad you can't sleep to music," he says, apparently recalling the first thing I ever said to him and then he leans in and kisses me.

I lift my arms and cradle his beautiful face in my hands, pulling him down to kiss me again. "And I'm glad that Idaho is famous for potatoes."

His eyebrows scrunch up in his forehead.

I just smile and pull him toward my lips again. He kisses me deeply, tangling his tongue with mine. And then he starts to kiss his way down toward my stomach. He traces a circle around my bellybutton with the tip of his tongue and curls his fingers behind the elastic of my panties.

"I don't think I can…" I say softly, gazing down at him.

He licks my stomach and then kisses my fingers as my hands move to his face and then into his hair.

"No sex," he says, "and I promise I'll lick you carefully." He slides my panties off and I lift my ass a little to make it easier for him.

He kisses my inner thigh. And then the other.

"I'll keep my tongue really wet so it doesn't sting," he says gently and kisses my inner thighs again, getting closer to my warmth.

I gasp a little when his fingers touch me very carefully and spread my lips apart.

"Damn, baby, you really are swollen." His comment is heartfelt and not at all teasing.

It does sting slightly, but my God I want this so bad…

I feel his breath hot between my legs. "I'll be very gentle," he says and my breath catches when his very wet tongue licks me once slowly, his fingers still holding me apart but without putting any pressure on the area.

My body melts into the sheets as he licks me over and over, putting just enough pressure on me that I feel no pain, but complete and uninhibited ecstasy.

————

We've been practicing *Barton Hollow* for two days, mostly in our room at the Holiday Inn, but we walked out by the Mississippi river at the end of Canal Street and did some practicing there, too. I think Andrew came up with the idea to sneakily try to get me more comfortable singing in public. There weren't many people out there at the time, but I was still nervous as hell. Most just walked past without stopping to check us out (we weren't in full performance-mode and often stopped and started over at different parts of the song, so it wasn't really much to listen to), but one or two here and there lingered as they walked past. A woman smiled at me. But I don't know if it was a pity smile because I'm horrible, or if she happened to like my voice.

I guess it could go either way.

By day three, Andrew is sure that we both have it down and is set on heading to Old Point soon to perform.

Me, not so much. I need another week or month or year or two.

"You're gonna do fine," he says while tying his boots. "Actually, you're gonna do *great*. By the end of the song, I'll have to beat the guys off you."

"Oh shut up," I say, slipping on a black open shoulder top with cute chain straps. I'm definitely not wearing the strapless one on a night like this. "I saw the way the girls were lookin' at you that night—I think having you up there with me is the only thing I've got going for me because everyone will be too preoccupied with you to notice my screw-ups."

"Baby, you know the song better than I do," he says. "Stop

being so negative." His black t-shirt tumbles down over his abs. He's wearing a black and silver belt, but only tucks the shirt in a little around the buckle, letting the rest hang freely around the top of his chiseled hips. Dark jeans, the front of his tousled hair spiked up a bit—*What was he saying?*

"The only thing you really need to try to remember," he goes on as he applies a layer of deodorant, "is not to sing every line in the song—got an opportunity not to sing as much but you still sing my parts, too." He raises a brow looking over at me. "Not that I mind, I just figured it would make you more comfortable having to sing less."

"I know, I'm just so used to singing along to the *whole* song—kind of hard to get the hang of not singing certain parts."

He nods.

I slip my feet down into my new heels and go to check myself out in the tall mirror over the TV stand.

"You are so damn sexy," Andrew says coming up behind me.

He slips his hands on my waist and kisses my neck, then slaps me on the butt of my tight *almost*-skinny-jeans and I yelp a little because it stings.

"And as always, babe, I love the braids." He reaches up and slides the two braids lying over each shoulder down the length of his thumbs and then kisses me playfully on the cheek.

I recoil and push him away teasingly. "You'll mess up my makeup."

He walks away smiling and grabs his wallet from the nightstand and slips it into his back pocket.

"Well, I guess this is it," he says.

He moves to the center of the room and extends one hand far out to me, placing his other arm horizontally across his back, and bows, grinning. The tips of my fingers inch their way across his and then he encloses my hand and pulls me along with him toward the door.

"What about the guitar?"

We stop just before he opens the door and he looks at me thankfully.

"Yeah, that might help," he says, taking the guitar up by its neck. "If Eddie isn't there, we might've been shit out of luck with no guitar to play with."

"Oh, well then I shouldn't have said anything."

He shakes his head and pulls me with him out the door.

# THIRTY-TWO

*T*his time we take the Chevelle. Andrew took one look at my shoes and knew I wouldn't make it all the way into Algiers wearing these babies and he wasn't about to carry me *and* the guitar. We take the freeway instead of the ferry and make our way across the Mississippi and are there by nightfall. Walking the rest of the way to Old Point like we did the first time would've been better, because right now as we drive closer, I know we'll be there in no time.

I'm starting to feel sick to my stomach.

We park along Olivier Street and get out. My feet are cemented to the road.

Andrew comes around to my side and pulls me into his arms, gently squishing me.

"I won't make you do this," he says, having a change of heart. I'm pretty sure I look like I'm about to lose the late lunch we had not long ago.

Pulling me away from his chest, he takes my face into his hands and gazes into my eyes. "I mean it, baby, all joking aside—I don't want you to do it if you absolutely don't want to, not even for me."

I nod nervously and inhale a deep breath; my face still cupped within his hands.

"No, I can do this," I say, still nodding, trying to pull my courage together. "I *want* to do it."

He brushes my cheeks under the pads of his thumbs. "Are you *sure?*"

"Yes."

He smiles in at me with those green eyes, which I'm starting to believe are bewitching me in some way, and then takes my hand. He plucks the guitar out of the back seat and we walk into Old Point together.

"Parrish!" Carla says from behind the bar. She raises her hand and waves us towards her.

Still hand in hand, Andrew weaves us through the thick crowd and over to her. The TV behind her head is playing commercials; the light from it casts a white glow around her.

"Hey Carla," Andrew says, leaning over the bar to hug her, "is Eddie here tonight?"

She puts her hands on her hips and smiles over at me.

"He sure is," she says, "he's around here somewhere. Hi Camryn, good to see you again."

I smile back at her. "You too."

Andrew sits on a barstool and motions for me to take the one next to him. I hop up and sit here nervously. All I can think about is how many people there are in this place. My eyes scan the room uneasily, over the tops of moving heads and through people standing up now that the band has started playing again. As the music picks up, Andrew and Carla are practically shouting at each other over the bar:

"Got any room for us tonight?" Andrew asks.

Carla leans in further toward him. "*Us?*" she says, glancing at me once. "Oh wow, are you *both* going to sing?" She looks excited.

My heart just jumped ship and fell into my knees.

I swallow down a nervous knot looking between them, but then another one just forms in its place.

Carla tilts her head and her already huge smile warms. "Oh honey, you'll do great—no need to be nervous; everybody here will love you." She reaches somewhere behind the bar and pulls up a shot glass. A man sits at the bar on the other side of me, obviously a regular since he doesn't have to tell her what he wants and Carla is already pouring him a drink.

She keeps her attention mostly on me and Andrew, though.

"I've been tryin' to tell her," Andrew says, "but this is her first time, so I have to cut her some slack."

"The first and *last* time," I correct him.

Carla grins secretly over at Andrew and then says to me, "Well, I'm not the violent type, but if you have any problems with anyone out there, just come get me and I'll throw them out the side door just like you see it done in the movies." She winks at me and then turns back to Andrew.

"There's Eddie now," she says, nodding in the direction of the stage.

Eddie is walking through the crowd, wearing the same sort of thing I saw him in the first time I met him: button-up white shirt, black slacks, shiny black shoes and a deep, wrinkly smile.

"Ga, dere come Parrish!" Eddie says gripping Andrew's hand and pulling him into a hug. Then he looks at me. "Galee! You look like dem lad'es in dem magazines, you do!" And he hugs me, too. He smells like cheap whiskey and cigarettes but I can only feel comforted by it for some reason.

Andrew is beaming.

"Camryn's going to sing with me tonight," Andrew says proudly.

Eddie's eyes get real big, like bright white balls of excitement fixed within the dark brown backdrop of his skin. It should make me more nervous like when Carla found out, but Eddie's presence is actually helping to ease my mind some. Maybe I should shackle him to my wrist while I sing.

"Oh sha," Eddie says, grinning in at me, "ah bet you sing as preddy as you are."

I blush hard.

"Well get'own up dere!" He points at the stage. "When dem's done playin' dis song 'ere!"

Andrew takes my hand and pulls me to his side. I feel like Eddie is like another father to Andrew and Andrew is happy that he seems to like me so much.

Eddie walks beside the stage and holds up three fingers at us. "Teree more minutes!"

"Oh my God, I am so frickin' nervous!"

Yep, Eddie should've stayed nearby.

Andrew's hand tightens around mine. He leans in to my ear. "Just remember: all these people here are just having a good time; no one's here to judge you—this ain't American Idol."

I take a deep, relaxing breath.

We listen to the band finish up their last song and then the music stops, followed by the usual sound of instruments being moved or tuned or just knocked against something the wrong way. A wave of chattering voices becomes louder without the music to drown it out, rolling through the space like an amplified, irregular humming. A thick layer of cigarette smoke makes the air feel stuffy, mixed with all of the bodies packed into the area.

When Andrew starts to pull me toward the stage my hands start shaking and I look down, realizing my nails are digging into the skin around his knuckles.

He smiles gently and I walk up with him.

"Do I look OK?" I whisper to him.

If I get through this without having an anxiety attack I'll be surprised.

"Baby, you look perfect."

He kisses my forehead and then sets his guitar next to the drum set so he can position the microphone.

"We're going to share the mic," he says. "Just don't head-butt me."

I narrow my eyes at him. "That's not funny."

"I'm not trying to be funny," he laughs softly, "I'm serious."

Several people in the crowd are already looking up at us, but most everybody else is doing their own thing. I can't do anything but stand here and that in itself is making me more nervous. At least Andrew is able to preoccupy himself with his guitar. I'm just twirling my thoughts around in my head.

"Are you ready?" he asks beside me.

"No, but let's get it over with."

We look at each other and he quietly mouths: "One. Two. Three—"

We sing together:

"*Ooooh…oooh…oooh…oooh!*" A one-second pause. "*Ooooh …oooh…oooh…oooh!*"

Guitar.

Dozens of heads turn all at the same time and the wave of conversations ceases like turning off a faucet.

While Andrew plays the first riff and he's gearing up to sing the first verse, I'm so terrified inside that I feel like I can't move anything but my eyes. But the more he plays the more my body can't help but move in time with the music.

Just about everyone in the place are already swaying and bobbing their heads to the sound.

Andrew starts to sing the first verse.

And then briefly together again: "*Ooooh…*"

Then comes the chorus and we both sing the words and I know
I'm going to have to hit a high note in—

*I did it!*

Andrew smiles deeply at me as he merges right into the next
verse, always strumming the guitar without missing a chord as if
he's known how to play this song forever.

The audience is really getting into it. They're nodding to one
another, the kind of nod that says: *They're really good*, and I feel my
face just light up as I start to sing my part with Andrew again and
with gradual confidence. I'm moving my body more naturally to
the music now and I think I've almost completely shed the fear, but
my solo…*oh my God, my solo is next…*

Andrew locks eyes with me as if to use his gaze as a means to
concentrate and stay calm and he strums the guitar.

He stops right in time with the music and taps the edge of the
wood before my first line, strums the guitar and stops again, tapping the wood after my second and so on until I hit my last note and
Andrew starts to play fully again while he says in a whisper to me:
"*Flawless*," and then he starts to sing again. He's grinning so wide.
So am I. We press our faces close as we sing our hearts out into the
mic during the faster interlude.

"*Woooh…ooooh…ooooh!*"

The guitar slows and we sing the last chorus together softly and
he kisses me on the mouth after we both say: "*…soul…*" And the
song ends.

The audience erupts into claps and cheers. I even hear one guy say: "Encore!" from somewhere in the back.

Andrew pulls me close and kisses me again, pressing his lips hard against mine in front of everyone.

"Holy shit, baby, you did awesome!" His eyes are bright, his entire face lit up by them.

"I can't believe I did it!" I'm practically screaming at him because the voices all around us are so loud.

I've got chill bumps from head to toe.

"Want to do it again?" he asks.

I swallow.

"No, I'm not ready! But I'm glad I did once!"

"I'm so proud of you!"

A few older men walk up with beers clutched in their hands. The one with the beard says, "You've gotta dance with me!" He holds his arms up at his sides and does an embarrassing little jig.

My face flushes and I catch Andrew's grinning eyes.

"But there's no music!" I say to the man.

"The hell there ain't!" He points at someone across the room and a few seconds later the jukebox kicks on next to the vending and gaming machine.

I'm so excited that I just got through singing that song on stage that it, along with how bad I'd feel if I told this guy no, makes dancing with him mandatory.

I glance back once more at Andrew and he winks at me.

The bearded man takes my hand, holds it high above my head and I instinctively twirl around. I dance with him through two songs before Andrew 'saves me' by smoothly cutting in and pressing my body as close to his as it will go and moves his hips around with me on them. His hands are on my waist. We dance and chat with people and even play a game of darts with Carla before finally leaving the bar after midnight.

On the car ride back, Andrew looks over at me and says, "So, how do you feel?" His lips ease into a knowing grin.

"You were right," I say. "I feel ... I don't know, different, but in a good way—I never thought I would do something like that."

"Well, I'm glad you did." He smiles warmly.

I unhook my seatbelt and move over next to him. He drapes his arm around me.

"So, what about tomorrow night?"

"Huh?"

"Do you want to sing tomorrow night?"

"No, I don't think I could—"

"Ok, that's fine," he says, rubbing my arm. "One time is more than I expected, so I'm not going to hound you about it."

"No," I say, lifting away and turning at the waist to see him. "You know what? I *do*. I want to do it again."

His chin draws back in a surprised motion.

"Really?"

"Yes, really." I smile with teeth at him.

He does the same.

"All right then," he says, hitting the steering wheel softly, "we'll play tomorrow night."

Andrew takes me back to the hotel and we have sex in the shower before going to bed.

We stay in New Orleans for two more weeks, playing at Old Point and then making our way to several other bars and clubs all around the city. A month ago, singing and performing live at clubs was probably so far down on the list of things I could ever see

myself doing that it would seem ridiculous, but there I was singing my heart out to *Barton Hollow* and a few other songs where I
could mostly shadow Andrew and not be the center of attention.
But everybody loved us. So many people stopped us after each performance and shook our hands and asked if we could sing this or
that song, to which all of them Andrew declined. I'm still too nervous with this stuff to be able to play by request. And to my dumb-
founded surprise, I was even asked for an autograph and a photo
with random people more than a couple of times. They must've just
been really drunk. That's what I made myself believe because anything else would just be weird.

By the end of those two weeks, Andrew had a new favorite band to add to his list. He loves The Civil Wars as much as I
do. And last night, our last night in New Orleans, we lay in bed
together and sang along to *Poison & Wine* coming from the phone
beside the bed...and...I think we told each other things through
those lyrics that we've been wanting to say...

I think we did...

I cried myself quietly to sleep in his arms.

I died and went to heaven. Yeah...I think I've finally died.

# Andrew

# THIRTY-THREE

*You need to do it, just to make sure," Marsters said sitting in his clichéd black rolling chair in his clichéd office wearing a clichéd coat.*

*"There's no need," I said, sitting on the other side. "What more is there to say? What more is there to find?"*

*"But you—"*

*"No, you know what?—Fuck you." I stood up, pushing the chair back across the floor and into a plant behind me. "I won't put myself through that shit."*

*I left, slamming his office door behind me so hard the glass shuddered in the frame.*

"Andrew! Baby, wake up," I hear Camryn's voice. My eyes pop open. I'm still on the passenger's side of the car. I wonder how long I've been asleep.

I lift up and crack my neck to both sides and run a hand over my face.

"Are you OK?"

It's night. I look over to see Camryn's concerned gaze fixed on me until her eyes are forced to look at the road out ahead.

"Yeah," I say, nodding, "I'm fine. I guess I was having a nightmare, but I don't even remember what it was about," I lie again.

"You punched the dashboard," she says, chuckling a little. "Your fist just shot out of nowhere; it scared the shit out of me."

"I'm sorry, baby." I lean over smiling and kiss her on the cheek. "How long have you been driving?"

She glances at the glowing numbers on the clock.

"I don't know, a couple of hours maybe."

I look up at the next highway sign to see if she did what I said to do and stayed on 90.

"Pull over up there." I nod to indicate a flat clearing alongside the highway.

She eases off the road and onto broken asphalt, putting the car in park. I start to get out, but she takes my arm and stops me.

"Wait... Andrew."

I look over at her. She turns the engine off and slips out of her seatbelt.

"I'm going to drive for a while and let you get some sleep."

"I know," she says looking over at me somberly.

"What's wrong?"

She drapes the fingers of both hands over the steering wheel and leans back against the seat.

"I'm not so sure about Texas anymore."

"Why not?"

I scoot over next to her.

Finally, she looks at me.

"Because what *then*?" she asks. "It feels like the last stop. You live there. What is there left to do?"

I know where she's coming from and I've been sharing these fears secretly with her for a while now.

"What's left is whatever we want to do," I say.

I turn around on the seat and reach out, taking her chin within my fingertips. "Look at me."

She does. I see a longing in her eyes, something scared and tortured. I know this because I'm feeling the same thing.

I swallow and then lean in and kiss her carefully.

"We'll figure it out when we get there, OK?"

She nods reluctantly. I try to force a smile, but it's hard to do when I know I can't give her any of the answers she's looking for. I can't give her the ones I *want* to give her.

Camryn moves across the seat and into the passenger's side while I get out and walk around the car. Two cars pass by, blinding us with their high-beams. I shut the door and sit there for a moment. Camryn's gazing out her side window, her thoughts undoubtedly in the same frame as most of mine are: lost and uncertain and maybe even afraid. I've never felt a connection to anyone like I have with her and it's killing me slowly. Reaching out to turn the key, I pause with my fingers pressing around the brass. I sigh heavily. "We'll take the long route," I say softly, not looking at her, and then the engine roars back to life.

I feel it when she turns her head to look at me.

I glance over. "If you want to."

A tiny smile gives her face life again. She nods.

I press the power on the CD player and the CD switches itself over. Bad Company starts playing through the speakers. Remembering our agreement, I go to change the music to something else, but Camryn says, "No, leave it," and her small smile grows even warmer.

I wonder if she remembers that first night we met on the bus, when I asked her to name any song by Bad Company. She had said

*Ready For Love.* And then I said: *"Are* you?" I didn't know why I said it then, but I'm realizing now that it wasn't so wrong, after all. Odd how that's the song playing right now.

We drive through much of the bottom half of the state of Louisiana and then we stay on 82 all the way into Texas. Camryn is all smiles this morning—despite being in Texas—and seeing her like this only makes me smile. We've been driving with the windows rolled down and she's had her bare feet hanging out for the past hour; all I've seen through her side mirror when I try to glimpse the traffic are her cute painted toenails.

"It's not a road trip unless you dangle your feet out the window driving down the highway!" she yells over the music and the wind rushing through the car. Her hair is pulled into one braid this time, but the wind keeps pushing the stray strands all around her face.

"You're right," I say, pressing on the gas, "and on a *true* road trip you also have to fuck with a truck driver."

Her hair slaps her across the face again when she turns her head.

"Huh?"

I grin. "Yep." I tap my fingers on the steering wheel to the music. "It's mandatory. Didn't you know—you have to do one of three things: one—" I hold up one finger. "You have to moon one."

Her blue eyes grow big in her head.

"Two: we have to drive next to one while you pretend to be touching yourself."

Her eyes get even bigger and her mouth falls open.

"Or three: simply pump your arm—" I raise my arm up and down with my fist in the air, "to get him to blow his horn."

Relief washes over her.

"All right," she says and a mysterious smile curves the corners of her lips, "the next one we see, I'll consummate this road trip by fucking with a truck driver." She says it indisputably.

Ten minutes later, our victim—well, 'lucky bastard' is more like it; it is Camryn, after all—comes into view out ahead. We're on a long stretch of straight highway tearing through a flat, treeless landscape on each side. We gain on the semi and keep a steady sixty-five-mile per hour pace behind him. Camryn, wearing those skimpy-as-hell white cotton shorts that I love so much, unfolds her legs from the seat and drops her feet onto the floorboard. She's grinning wickedly and it's kind of turning me on.

"Are you ready?" I ask, turning the music down a little.

Camryn nods and I look out my rearview and side mirrors first and then out ahead at the oncoming lane to make sure no vehicles are coming in either direction.

As I pull out from behind the semi and move over into the oncoming lane, Camryn slides her right hand down inside the front of her shorts.

I have an instant hard-on.

I thought she'd do the safe horn-pulling thing for sure!

I grin darkly over at her with all kinds of perverted thoughts swimming around in my head and she grins right back at me. I press the gas a little harder and gradually speed up until we're level with the truck driver's window.

*Oh my fucking God…*

Camryn's hand moves gently, but visibly underneath the thin fabric of her shorts; the index finger and thumb of her left hand is wedged behind the elastic, pulling it down enough to see her bare stomach. She leans her head back against the seat and slides down a little further. I'm almost too distracted to keep my eyes on the road. She bites her bottom lip and moves her fingers more furiously underneath her shorts. I'm starting to think she's not pretending at all. I'm so hard right now my dick can cut diamonds.

The semi is keeping pace, too. Distracted by Camryn, I didn't notice when my foot was slowly releasing on the gas and when the speedometer started to drop a couple of notches, so did the semi's speed.

A howling, gruff voice shouts from the semi's window: "Holy *hot-damn*! Gonna' give me a fuckin' heart attack, baby! Whoo-*hoo*!" He pulls on his loud horn excitedly.

Feeling a pang of possession, I drop from sixty-five to forty-five and fall back behind the truck. Just in time, too, as a van is coming up in the opposite lane.

I look over at Camryn knowing I must have crazy eyes. She pulls her hand from her shorts and just smiles at me.

"I didn't expect that!"

"That's exactly why I did it," she says, propping her feet back on the car door and blocking the side mirror with her toes.

"Were you really...*actually* touching yourself?"

Forty-five miles per hour has dropped to forty now. My heart is humming against my ribcage.

"Yeah, I did," she says, "but I wasn't doing it for the truck driver."

Her grin deepens as she pulls away a few strands of hair that have blown between her lips. I can't help but watch her lips, studying them, wanting to bite and kiss them.

"Well, not that I'm complaining," I say, trying to pay attention to the road and not get us killed, "but now I have a...bit of a problem."

Camryn's gaze falls on my lap and then she looks up at me again, cocking her head to one side with a look of mischief and seduction. Then she moves across the seat toward me and grabs a handful between my legs. Now my heart is *banging* against my ribcage. I'm white-knuckling the steering wheel with both hands. She kisses my neck and then my jawline and moves her lips to the shell of my ear. Goosebumps rape me.

She starts to unzip my shorts.

"You've helped me with my 'problems'," she whispers into my ear and then bites my neck again. "It's only fair that I return the favor."

She looks up at me.

I just nod stupidly because I can't think with the head on my shoulders long enough to form a sentence right now.

I press my back further against the seat as she takes the length of me into her hand and lowers her head between my stomach and the steering wheel. My body lurches a little when I feel her tongue snake out to lick it. *Oh my fucking God… Oh my fucking God… I don't know how I'm going to drive…*

When she slides me into the back of her throat I shudder, my head falls back some, still trying to keep my eyes on the road, and my mouth falls open. I'm only white-knuckling the wheel now with my left hand; as she sucks me harder and faster, my right hand has slid away from the wheel and is gripping the back of her head, her blond hair wedged within my clinging fingers.

Forty miles per hour has become fifty.

By sixty, my legs are shaking and I can't see straight. I grip the wheel with both hands again, trying to maintain some kind of control over *something*, especially the damn car, and I let out a gasp and moan as I come.

———

I managed not to kill us on the highway after Camryn's toe-curling head-job. We're in Galveston by morning and she's still passed out across the seat with her legs hanging partially on the floorboard. I don't bother to wake her yet. I drive slowly past my mom's house first, noting that her car isn't in the driveway so that means she's working at the bank today. To kill time, I drive the long way to my apartment, passing down 53rd. Camryn didn't get much sleep last night, but I guess the car moving slower than usual is enough to wake her anyway. She starts stirring before I pull into my complex at Park at Cedar Lawn.

She raises her beautiful blond head from the seat and when I see her face, a ripple of laughter bursts lightly through my lips.

She cocks her already crazy-just-woke-up head to one side and grumbles, "What's so funny?"

"Oh, babe, I tried to keep you from falling asleep like that."

She leans up, pressing her face into the rearview mirror and rolls her eyes once she sees the three long striped indentions stretching across one cheek all the way to her ear. She probes the indentions in the mirror.

"Wow, that kind of hurts," she says.

"You're still beautiful even with stripes." I laugh and she can't help but smile.

"Well, we're here." I finally say and pull into a parking space and shut off the engine, dropping my hands beside me.

The car is uncomfortably quiet. Even though neither one of us has ever actually said that our trip will end in Texas, or that things between us are going to change, it's like both of us can feel it.

The only difference is . . . I'm the only one who knows why.

Camryn sits perfectly quiet and still on her side, her hands folded loosely within her lap.

"Let's go inside," I say to stir the silence.

She forces a smile over at me and then opens her door.

"Wow, this place looks more like a campus dorm than an apartment complex." She shoulders her bag and purse, looking out at the historical building and giant oak trees sprawled across the landscaping.

"It was a U.S. Marine Hospital in the 1930's," I say, lifting my bags from the trunk.

Camryn grabs Aidan's guitar from the backseat.

We make our way down one curvy chalk-white sidewalk and come to my one-bedroom on the bottom floor. I fumble my key in the door and open it into the large living room area. The smell of un-lived-in space hits me as soon as we step inside; nothing funky, just vacant.

I drop my bags on the floor.

Camryn stands there at first, checking out the place.

"Set your stuff wherever you want, babe."

I move over to the couch and pluck my jeans from it hanging sloppily over the back and then grab a pair of boxers and a t-shirt from the chair and matching ottoman.

"This is a really nice apartment," she says, gazing around.

Finally she sets her stuff on the floor and props Aidan's guitar against the back of the couch.

"Not much the bachelor pad," I say heading into the dining room, "but I like it here and I wanted to be closer to the beach."

"No roommates?" she asks following in behind me.

I shake my head and step into the kitchen and pop the fridge open; the various bottles and jars in the side-door jangle against one another. "Not anymore. My friend Heath lived with me for about three months when I first moved in, but he ended up moving to Dallas with his fiancée."

Shutting the fridge door, I pull out a two-liter bottle of Ginger Ale. "Want a drink?" I hold it up to show her.

She smiles sweetly and says, "Thanks, but I'm not thirsty right now—what'd you buy it for: hangover, stomach bug?"

I smirk at her and take a swig from the bottle itself. She doesn't cringe like I halfway expected her to.

"Yeah, you got me," I admit, twisting the cap back on.

"If you want to get a shower," I say as I leave the kitchen and point down the hall, "bathroom's just right there; I'm going to give my mom a call so she doesn't worry and pick up some around here before I get one myself. My plant is probably dead."

Camryn looks slightly surprised. "You have a plant?"

I smile. "Yeah, her name's Georgia."

Her brow rises a little higher.

I laugh lightly and kiss her softly on the lips.

While Camryn is in the shower I work my way through every visible inch of my apartment in search of anything incriminating: disgusting, crusty socks (found one at the foot of my bed), unopened condom wrappers (have a box full on my nightstand—I stuff them in the very bottom of the trash), *opened* condom wrappers (two in the wastebasket in my room), more dirty clothes and one porn magazine (Shit! That's on the back of the toilet—undoubtedly she's already seen it).

Then I wash the few dirty dishes that I left in the sink before I left out and sit down in the living room to give my mom a call.

# Camryn

# THIRTY-FOUR

*W*hen I see the porn mag on the back of the toilet as casually placed as one on motorcycles might be, I can't help but laugh to myself. I wonder briefly if there are any guys in the world that *don't* look at pornography and then realize what a stupid question that is. I can't say anything; I've looked at my fair share of porn on the internet.

I take a long, hot shower and dry off with the beach towel Andrew gave me and then get dressed.

I don't like it here. In his apartment. In Texas.

Any other time and in some other circumstance, it would be different, but what I said to him the other night when we pulled over on the side of the road still holds true. This place, everything about it feels like *the end*. The magic of our time together on the road has all but literally evaporated with last week's rain. Not our feelings for each other ... no, those are so strong that thinking about the end at all is metaphorically bringing me to my knees. How we feel about each other is ... well, it's all that we have left. The open road is gone. The spontaneous stops and sometimes not knowing where we are but not giving a damn, is gone. The motels and the little things like beef jerky and Baby Oil and bubble bath, they're all gone. The soundtrack of our time together, our short life together, has faded away as the last song on the album ends. All I can hear anymore is the smooth vibration of silence coming from the speakers. I feel like all I want to do is reach out and start it over again, but my hand won't move to press the button.

And I can't understand why.

I wipe the tear from my face and push my emotions down into my lungs and hold them there, taking a deep breath before I open the bathroom door.

I hear Andrew talking on the phone when I move through the dining room:

"Don't fuck with me right now, Aidan. I don't need this shit. Yeah, so what? Who are you to tell me what to do with my life? *What?* Give me a fucking break, bro; funerals aren't mandatory. I personally would rather never go to another one again unless it's my own. I don't know why people have funerals anyway; just going to see someone you care about lying completely fucking lifeless in a goddamn box. I'd rather the last time I see someone it be of them alive. Don't give me that line of shit, Aidan! You know it's bullshit!"

I don't want to keep standing around the corner like I'm eavesdropping, but it doesn't exactly feel appropriate to walk in there on him yet, either.

I do it anyway. He's getting way too irate and I just want to calm him down. The second he sees me, he drops the angry tone with Aidan and raises his back from the couch.

"Look, I gotta go," he says. "Yes, I've already called Mom. Yes. Yeah, all right, I hear yah. Later."

He shuts the phone off and drops it on the oak coffee table next to his propped bare foot.

I sit down next to him on the split cushion.

"Sorry about that," he says, patting my thigh and then rubbing his palm across it.

"I'll never hear the end of it from him."

I move over and sit on his lap and he pulls me against his chest as if I'm what he needs to calm down. I drape my arms around his neck, interlocking my fingers around his shoulder. Leaning in, I kiss the side of his mouth.

"Camryn." He gazes into my eyes. "Look, I don't want this to be the end, either," he says, as though he had been reading my mind while in the bathroom moments ago.

Suddenly, he lifts me up and makes me sit upright on his lap facing him with my legs on either side, my knees bent into the couch. He takes each of my hands into his and looks right at me with gravity and intensity in his eyes.

"What if we…" he looks away, contemplating his words deeply, though I wish I knew if it was because he wanted to say them right, or maybe not at all.

"What if we *what?*" I try to prompt him. I don't want him to back out, no matter what it is; I want him to say it. I feel some revived sense of hope again and I can't bear to let it slip away. "Andrew?"

His intense green eyes lock on mine as my voice snaps him back into the moment.

"What if we go away together?" he says and my heart starts pounding faster. "I don't want to be here. And I'm not saying that because of my father or my brother—none of that has anything to do with how I feel. Right now. Here with you. How I've felt all this time, since the day I saw you sitting alone on that bus in Kansas." He squeezes my hands tighter. "I know you lost your partner in crime, but...I want *you* to be *mine*. Maybe *we* should travel the world together, Camryn...I know I can't replace your ex—"

Tears stream from my eyes.

He takes it the wrong way. His hands slip from mine and suddenly he can't look at me anymore. I reach out and cup his face in my palms, forcing his tortured gaze.

"Andrew..." I shake my head, tears rolling down my cheeks, "...it was always you," I whisper harshly. "Even with Ian, I felt something was missing. I told you, that night in the field; I told you that..." My voice trails. I smile and say, "You *are* my partner in crime. I've known that for a long time."

I kiss his lips.

"I can't think of anything in this world I'd rather do than to see it with you. We belong on the road. Together. It's where I *want* to be."

His eyes are watering, but he lets his bright smile push the tears away before they fall. And then he crushes his mouth against mine, both of us cupping each other's faces in our hands. His kiss steals my breath away, but I just kiss him deeper, drinking down as much of his own breath as I can. And without breaking the kiss his hands fall away from my face and he wraps them tight around my body, lifting me with him into a stand.

"You have to meet my mom today," he says, scanning my face, peering deeply into my eyes.

I sniffle back the rest of my tears and nod. "I would love to meet your mom."

"Great," he says, guiding me to slip away from his waist and stand on my own. "I'll get a shower and we'll go do some stuff around town for a while and head over to see her after she's off work."

"OK," I say, never letting the smile fade from my face.

I couldn't let it fade even if I tried.

He looks at me for a long moment like he doesn't want to pry himself away long enough even to shower, his smiling eyes as radiant as I saw them that night after our performance at Old Point. His face reads all sorts of things that one who is overwhelmingly happy might want to say, but he says nothing.

He doesn't need to.

Andrew finally leaves the room to shower and I go to check my phone messages. Mom finally called. She left a voice mail telling me all about her cruise of the Bahamas that ended up lasting eight days. It really sounds like she's into this guy, Roger. I might actually have to swing by home long enough to check him out and do my own douchebag inspection of his personality just in case my mom has been blinded by something he has that overshadows the warning signs: more money than my dad, a body sexier than Andrew's—well, that's not likely—or a really big...not sure exactly how I would find something like that out unless I asked Mom directly. That's not gonna happen.

My dad called, too. Said he's going to Greece in a month on a business trip and asked if I want to go along with him. I'd love to, but sorry, Dad, if I go to Greece anytime in the next year or so, it'll be with Andrew. I've always been Daddy's Girl, but you have to grow up sometime and now...now I'm Andrew's Girl.

I shake the dreamy thoughts from my brain and go back to checking messages. Natalie finally called instead of biting her tongue and sending a text message. I know by now she's beyond going stir crazy wanting to know what I've been doing and who I'm with. I think maybe I've made her squirm long enough.

Hmmm...I could just give her a morsel.

A devious grin spreads across my face. A morsel might be worse torture, but it's better than nothing at all.

When Andrew comes out of the shower, walking through the den with a damp towel around the back of his neck, I call him into the living room. He stands there, shirtless: the sexiest fucking thing I have ever seen in my life, with water dripping down his tanned abs. I want to lick it all off, but I refrain for Natalie's sake.

"Baby, come here," I say, curling my finger at him, "I want to send Natalie a picture of us. She's been on my back since New Orleans about you, but I still haven't told her anything, not even your name. She left me a voice mail." I start punching letters on my phone.

He laughs, drying the back of his hair with the towel. "What did she say?"

"She's about to explode, basically. I want to mess with her head."

Andrew's dimples deepen. "Hell yeah, I'm game." He plops down on the couch and pulls me down with him.

I snap a couple of shots of us together: one with us just looking straight into the camera, one with him kissing me fully on the cheek and one with him eyeing the camera seductively with his tongue snaking out of the side of his mouth and licking my face.

"That one's *perfect*," I say excitedly about the third one. "She's going to freak out. Prepare yourself; Texas might see Hurricane Natalie blow through here once she gets this pic."

Andrew laughs and leaves me on the couch with my phone.

"I'll be ready in a few more minutes," he says as he slips out of the living room.

I load the photo into a message and type in:
Here we are, Nat, in Galveston, Texas :-)
And then I hit send. I hear Andrew moving around in the

apartment. I start to get up to spy on him when in less than one minute after sending the photo, Natalie texts me back:

OMFG! R U sleeping with Kellan Lutz?!?!!!!?

I burst into laughter. Andrew comes back around the corner, unfortunately with a shirt on this time and he's tucking the front behind his belt. And he's already replaced the shorts with a pair of jeans.

"What, did she reply already?" He seems faintly amused.

"Yeah," I say with laughter in my voice, "I knew it wouldn't take long."

More messages start popping up in fast succession as if a machine is on the other end:

Cam, OMFG, he is fucking RAWR! What the hell???

Call me. Like NOW!!!!!!!!!!!!

CAMNRYN MARYBETH BENNETT! U better call me!!

I'm dring over here!!!

I mean DRING

GRRR!!!!!!

DAMN AUTO-CORRECT! I fucking hate this phone.

DYING, not dring!!

I can't stop grinning. Andrew comes around behind me and snatches the phone from my fingers.

He laughs scrolling through her mumbo-jumbo.

"Typo much?" he says. "Who the hell is Kellan Lutz?—is he ugly?" He looks at me with a twinge of fear in his eyes.

*No . . . ummm, definitely not ugly.*

"It's just an actor," I try to explain. "And no, he's not. Don't put too much thought into it; Natalie always, I mean *always* compares *everyone* to someone famous, usually with a serious over-exaggeration." I take the phone from him while he's halfway preoccupied by my explanation and set it on the couch. "She and I went to school with Shay Mitchell and Hayden Panettiere, Megan Fox was prom queen, Chris Hemsworth was prom king." I make a clicking noise with my tongue. "And then there was Natalie's worst enemy, a cheerleader who tried to steal Damon away from her in tenth grade; Natalie said she was the slutty version of Nina Dobrev—none of these people really looked like them, not really anyway. Natalie is just...odd."

Andrew shakes his head, smiling. "Well, she's definitely a character, I'll give her that."

Still hearing my phone buzzing against the couch cushion, I ignore it and step up to Andrew, wrapping my arms around his waist.

"Are you sure you want to do this with me?"

He gazes into my eyes, placing his hands on my cheeks. "I've never been more sure of anything in my life, Camryn."

Then he starts to pace.

"I always felt this...this..." his eyes are intense, concentrating, "...this *hole*...I mean it wasn't an empty hole, there was always something in it, but it was never right. It never fit. I went to college for a short time, until I sat back one day and said to myself: Andrew, what the fuck are you doing here? And it clicked in my head that I wasn't there because it's what *I* wanted, I was there because it's what people expected, even people I don't know, society. It's what people *do*. They grow up, go to college, get a job and do the same shit every day for the rest of their lives until they grow old and die—just like you explained that night you told me about yours and your ex's plans." He swings his right hand out as if slapping the air. "Most people never see anything outside where they grew up." He's pacing harder, stopping only every now and then when he wants to put emphasis on an important word or meaning. He hardly looks right at me; he seems to be saying all of these things to himself more, as though a river of answers he's been looking for all his life are finally flooding his mind and he's trying to take them all in at once. "I was never really happy doing anything…"

Finally, he looks right at me.

"And then I met you…and it was like something just went off in my head, or it woke up, I-I don't know, but…" He stands in front of me again. I want to cry, but I don't. "…but I knew that whatever it was, it was right. It fit. *You* fit."

I go up a little on my toes and kiss his lips. There are so many things that I want to say, but I'm overwhelmed by all of them and can't choose.

"I guess I need to ask you the same question," he says. "Are you *sure* you want to do this?"

My eyes smile warmly up at him.

"Andrew, it's not even a question," I say. "Yes!"

Andrew smiles so brightly at me that his devilishly sexy green eyes glisten.

"So then it's official," he says, "we'll leave here tomorrow. I've got money in the bank to get us by for a while."

I nod and smile and say, "I've not really earned the money I have in the bank and I've always used it sparingly because of that, but for this, I'll use every dime of it and when it runs out—"

"*Before* our money gets close to running out," he interrupts, "we'll work on the road, just like you mentioned before. We can play at clubs and bars and at farmer's markets." He laughs out loud at the idea, but is quite serious. "And we can even work in bars and restaurants cooking and washing dishes and doing the server thing and…I don't know, but we'll figure it out."

It all sounds like a crazy dream gone rampant, but neither of us cares. We're living in the moment.

"Yeah, *before* it runs out is definitely a better plan," I say, blushing. "I don't want to end up a panhandler or sleeping behind dumpsters or standing on street corners with Will Work for Food signs."

Andrew laughs and squeezes my shoulders in his hands.

"No, we'll never get to that point. We'll always work, but not in one place for too long and never doing the same thing over and over."

I look into his eyes for a moment and then wrap my arms around his neck, kissing him passionately.

Then he grabs his keys.

"Come on," he says tilting his head back and holding his hand out to me. I take it. "First things first: I've got to check on my car. She must be missing me!"

Porn magazines *and* a car revered as a woman!

I just shake my head laughing under my breath as he pulls me toward the door. I snatch my purse from the floor nearby and we head out.

# THIRTY-FIVE

*O*ur first stop is where Andrew left his vintage 1969 Camaro and I see my first real stereotypical Texan when we pull into the garage where Andrew apparently *used* to work.

"Y'know I fired yer ass, right?" a tall man wearing a cowboy hat and black cowboy boots says walking outside to meet us. He had been standing in the open bay talking to another man who actually looks more like a mechanic.

He shakes Andrew's hand and pulls him into a man-hug, patting his back.

"Yeah, I know," Andrew says, patting his, "but I had to do what I had to do."

Andrew turns to me.

"Billy, this is my girlfriend, Camryn. Camryn, this is my ex-boss, Billy Frank."

My heart leapt when he called me his girlfriend. Hearing him say that definitely had more of an effect on me than I imagined it could.

Billy reaches out an oil-stained, rugged hand and without hesitation, I shake it. "Nice to meet you." I smile.

He smiles back; his teeth are crooked and yellowed probably from too many years addicted to coffee and cigarettes.

"Well ain't she a beaut," Billy says grinning over at Andrew. "I'da skipped out on m'job too for a girl like that." He playfully punches Andrew on the arm. He turns back to me. "Has he been treatin' ya right? Boy's got a mouth on him that'll slap yer momma backwards."

I laugh lightly and say, "Yeah, he does have a mouth, but he treats me wonderfully."

Andrew's eyes smile at me from the side.

"Well, if'n he ever gives ya any trouble, ya know where ta' find me. Ain't nobody 'round here that can put him in his place like I can." He grins over at Andrew.

"Thanks, I'll remember that."

We leave Billy Frank and walk through the bay and then exit a side door that leads out into a fenced area where cars are kept. I know immediately which one is his even though I've never seen it before except camouflaged in the tree bark of Andrew's tattoo. It's the nicest one on the lot. Dark gray with two black racing stripes down the center of the hood. It looks a lot like his dad's vintage Chevelle. We weave our way through a maze of cars and he opens the driver's side door after checking out the body from front to back on each side first.

"If she hadn't needed some work when I decided not to take a plane to Wyoming," he says as he runs his fingers along the door frame, "I would've driven her instead of taking that bus."

"Well, not to think badly of your girl here," I say, smiling and patting the hood, "but I'm glad she wasn't up to drive you herself."

Andrew looks at me, his face lit up the same way I see it more and more every day.

"I'm glad she wasn't, either," he says.

For a brief moment, I think about where either of us would

be right now if that had happened, if we never met. But brief is long enough because thoughts like that wrench my stomach. I can't imagine never having known him. And I never want to.

"So, are we going to be driving this one instead of the Chevelle?"

Andrew chews on the inside of his mouth, thinking it over. He stands at the open door with one palm lying flat against the roof. He pats it once gently and looks at me.

"What do you think? What do you want to do, babe?"

It's my turn to chew the inside of my mouth in contemplation. I hadn't really considered that the option would be mine to decide. I step up closer to the car and peer inside, checking out the leather bucket seats and ... well, that's really the only thing that I check.

"Honestly?" I ask, crossing my arms.

He nods.

I look back at the Camaro again, mulling it over.

"I kind of like the Chevelle," I say. "I love this car—it's badass— but I think I'm just more acquainted with the other one." To make my case more solid I point at the seats. "And how would I lay my head on your lap, or sleep in the front with seats like that."

Andrew smiles gently and rubs the roof of the car as if to assure her that it's nothing personal. He pats it one more time and then shuts the door.

"Then we'll take the Chevelle," he says. "I'll just drive her home later and park her."

———

Andrew takes me out to eat and to a few random places he likes to go on Galveston Island. And then after rush hour traffic, he gets a call from his mom.

"I'm nervous," I say on the passenger's side as we head toward her house.

He wrinkles his eyebrows, looking over at me and says, "Don't be; my mom will love you." He looks back at the road. "She's not one of those stuck up bitches who thinks no one is good for her son."

"That's definitely a relief."

"Even if she was," he says, grinning over at me once, "she'd still love you."

I fold my hands together within my lap and smile. Doesn't matter; he can talk her up all he wants about how sweet she is and it won't do a thing for the nervous feeling in my stomach.

"Are you going to tell her?" I ask.

He glances over. "What, about leaving?"

"Yeah."

He nods. "I'll tell her, otherwise she'll worry herself over me straight into therapy."

"What do you think she'll say?"

Andrew chuckles. "Babe, I'm twenty-five. I haven't lived at home since nineteen. She'll be all right."

"Well, I just mean...you know...the nature of why you're leaving and exactly what we plan to do." I look away and back toward the windshield. "It's not like packing up and moving to a different city; even my mom could handle that kind of news. But if I told her I planned to travel all over to *wherever* and that I was doing it with a guy I met on a bus, she'd probably be a little freaked."

"Probably?" Andrew asks. "As in *if* you tell her?"

I look right at him. "No, I'm definitely going to tell her. Same as you, I think she should know...but, Andrew, you know what I mean."

"Yeah, I do, babe," he says and flips on his left blinker and turns at the stop sign. "And you're right; it's not exactly normal." Then he grins across at me and instantly it provokes a smile on my face. "But isn't that one reason why we're doing it? Because it's not normal?"

"Yes, it is."

"Of course, the biggest reason is because of the company," he adds.

I blush.

Two more blocks of cozy, suburban-style houses and white sidewalks with kids buzzing by on bicycles and we pull into the driveway of his mom's house. It's a one-level with a pretty flower garden that wraps around the front side and two puffy green bushes on both sides of the sidewalk leading up to the front door. The Chevelle purrs into the drive behind a white four-door family car parked inside the wide-open garage. I look at myself real quick in the rearview mirror to make sure there are no boogers on my nose or any lettuce in my teeth leftover from the chicken sandwich I had earlier and Andrew comes around and opens my door for me.

"Oh, I see how it is," I play with him. "You only open my car door when your mother might be watching."

He reaches for my hand and bows dramatically. "I will open the door for you from now on if you like that kind of thing, Milady...however..." I place my hand in his, grinning hugely at his display, "...I did not take you for the type."

"Oh, is that so?" I say in a horrible English accent and I raise my chin higher. "And just what type did you take me for, Mr. Parrish?"

He shuts the door and loops his arm through mine, keeping his back refined and his chin raised.

"I took you for the kind who didn't give a shit as long as it would open when you wanted out."

I chuckle.

"Well, you were right," I say and press against his shoulder as he walks me to the door inside the garage.

The door opens into the kitchen to the smell of pot roast. I'm thinking: She had time to cook a pot roast? But then I see the Slow Cooker on the counter. Andrew walks me around the bar and into the den area just as a pretty sandy-haired woman comes around the corner from a hallway.

"I'm so glad you're home," she says, taking him into a big hug, practically squeezing him with her little body. Andrew must be at least three full inches taller than she is. But I see where he got his green eyes and dimples from.

She smiles over at me with all the welcome in the world and to my surprise, takes me into a hug, too. I go all-in, pressing my arms vertically against her back.

"You must be Camryn," she says. "I feel like I know you already."

That strikes me as odd. I didn't know she knew I existed until today. I glance covertly at Andrew and his lips pull into a secretive smile. I guess he had plenty of opportunities to talk about me while we were on the road, especially before we started sharing a room, but what surprises me the most is why he would have said much about me at all.

"It's nice to meet you, Miss—" My eyes grow wide as I look to Andrew for the information that I'm going to kick him in the shin for not giving me sooner. My lips tighten in aggravation at him, but he just keeps smiling.

"Call me Marna," she says, letting her hands fall downward to grasp a hold of mine. She raises my hands up within hers, looking me over all the while with that glittering smile of hers.

"Have you two eaten?" she asks, looking at Andrew and then back at me.

"Yeah, Mom, we had something earlier."

"Oh, but you should eat. I made a pot roast and green bean casserole." She only lets go of one of my hands, the other she keeps grasped gently in hers and I follow her into the living room where a giant television is mounted over the fireplace. "Have a seat and I'll fix you a plate."

"Mom, she's not hungry, trust me."

Andrew comes in behind us.

My head is kind of whirling already. She knows about me, apparently enough to make her feel like she knows me. She's so kind and all-smiles as if she actually loves me already. Not to mention, she held my hand and not Andrew's to escort me through her house. Am I missing something here, or is she just the sweetest person with the most charming personality on the planet? Well, whatever the case, my feelings about her are mutual.

She looks at me and tilts her head to one side, waiting for me to speak up. I wince a little because I don't want to hurt her feelings and I say, "I really appreciate the offer, but I don't think I could eat anything else just yet."

Her smile softens. "Well how about something to drink?"

"That would be great; do you have tea?"

"Of course," she says. "Sweet, un-sweet, lemon, peach, raspberry?"

"Just sweet will be great, thanks."

I sit down on the center cushion of her burgundy-colored sofa.

"Honey, what would you like?"

"Same as Camryn."

Andrew sits down next to me and before she leaves to go back into the kitchen, she looks at us both for a moment, smiling with some kind of quiet thought. And then she slips around the corner.

I turn to Andrew swiftly and whisper, "What did you tell her about me?"

Andrew grins. "Nothing really," he says, trying to look casual but it's not working. "Just that I met this really sweet, unimaginably sexy girl that has a dirty mouth and a tiny birthmark on her inner left thigh."

I smack him on the leg. His grin just gets bigger.

"No, babe," he says, being serious now, "I just told her that I met you on the bus and we've been together since." He rubs his hand across my thigh reassuringly.

"She seems to like me a little too much for that to be all you said to her."

Andrew shrugs lightly and then his mom comes back into the room with two glasses of tea. She sets them down in front of us on the coffee table. They have little yellow sunflowers imprinted on the side.

"Thanks," I say and then take a sip, setting the glass back down gently. I scan the coffee table for a coaster to put it on, but there isn't one.

She sits down on the matching chair across from us.

"Andrew tells me you're from North Carolina?"

*Uh huh . . . that's all he told her, my butt!* I can just hear him grinning inside; it's as loud anything audible. He knows I can't glare at him, or smack him, or do anything I normally would do, really. I just smile like he's not sitting right next to me.

"Yes," I answer. "I was born in New Bern, but have lived in Raleigh most of my life." I take another sip.

Marna crosses her legs and folds her ring-decorated hands within her lap. Her jewelry is simple, with two small rings on each hand and a pair of little gold stud earrings and a matching necklace draped in the folds of her button-up white blouse.

"My oldest sister lived in Raleigh for sixteen years before she moved back to Texas—it's a beautiful state."

I just nod and smile. I'm guessing that was just the icebreaker topic because there's a bout of awkward silence hanging in the air now and I notice her glancing at Andrew a lot. And he isn't saying anything. I'm getting a strange feeling from the silence, as if I'm the only one in the room who doesn't know what thoughts are passing between everyone else.

"So, Camryn," Marna says, letting her eyes stray from Andrew, "what were you traveling for when you met Andrew?"

Oh great; I didn't expect that. I don't want to lie, but the truth isn't exactly something you just casually talk about over tea with someone you just met.

Andrew takes a big gulp of tea and sets the glass down.

"She was kind of in the same boat as me," he answers for me and his answer shocks me into silence. "I was taking the long road and Camryn was taking the road to nowhere and it just so happens that they led to the same place."

Marna's eyes light up with curiosity. She tilts her chin to one side, glances at me first and then back at Andrew and then looks at both of us. There's something warming, but very mysterious in her face and not the confused skepticism I expected.

"Well, Camryn, I want you to know that I'm very glad that the two of you met. It seems your company has helped Andrew through some hard times."

Her bright smile fades a little after her comment and I notice Andrew from the corner of my eye looking at her cautiously. I'm assuming she has said enough, or maybe he's worried she's going to say something that'll embarrass him in front of me.

Feeling slightly uncomfortable being the only one here without all of the obvious information, I force a slim smile for his mother's sake.

"Well, we've helped *each other* a lot, to be honest," I say, smiling more now because what I'm saying is so true.

Marna gently pats her thighs once with the palms of her hands, smiles happily and stands up.

"I need to make a quick call," she says with the flourish of her hand. "I completely forgot to tell Asher about that motorcycle he's trying to buy from Mr. Sanders. I better call him before I forget again; excuse me for a few minutes."

Her eyes secretly skirt Andrew just before she leaves the room. I saw it, surely neither one of them thinks I don't know that there's something else going on that I'm obviously not supposed to know about. I can't tell if she secretly dislikes me and has been putting on a show in front of me so as not to make Andrew uncomfortable, or if it's something entirely different. It's driving me crazy, and I'm not as relaxed as I quickly came to be upon first meeting her.

And sure enough, a few seconds after she slips out of the room, Andrew stands up.

"What's going on?" I ask lightly.

He looks down at me and I get the feeling he knows I'm not going to ignore this forever. He's fully aware that I've been more observational than he wanted me to be.

His eyes scan my face, but he doesn't smile, he just looks upon me as one might a person they're about to say goodbye to. Then he leans over and kisses me. "Nothing's going on, babe," he says, now deciding to be the smiling, playful Andrew I know so well, but I'm not buying it.

I know he's lying and there's no way I'm going to drop this. I will for now while we're here, but afterwards, that's another story.

"I'll be back in a second," he says and follows the path his mom took.

# Andrew

# THIRTY-SIX

*I* probably shouldn't have brought Camryn here because she's smart and I knew she would pick up on the tiniest fluctuation in the conversation. Mom didn't exactly make it difficult for Camryn, either. But this is an important meeting between them and I did what I had to do.

I walk through the den and down the hallway to my mom's bedroom. She's standing there waiting for me. She's in tears.

"Mom, don't do this, please." I take her into a hug, cupping the back of her head in my hand.

She sniffles and chokes and tries to stop crying.

"Andrew, will you please just go to the appointment and—"

"Mom, no. Listen." I carefully pull her away from my chest and I look at her, my hands secured to her shoulders. "It's been too long. I waited too long and you know it. I admit I should've gone eight months ago, but I didn't and now it's too late."

"You don't know that." Tears stream down her face.

I soften my expression, but I know she won't listen to me no matter how convincing I sound.

"It's gotten worse," I say. "Look, all I want is for you to know her. She is very important to me. You're *both* very important to me and I think you should know each other—"

My mom pushes her hand into my view and shakes it at me. "I can't talk about this," she chokes out, "I just can't. I'll do whatever you want me to do, and son, I already love her. I can tell she's a wonderful girl. I can tell she's so very different from any girl you've ever been involved with. And she's important to me not only because she's important to you, but because of everything she has given you."

"Thank you," I say and try not to cry myself.

My hands fall away from her shoulders.

I reach into my back pocket and pull out a folded envelope and I put it into my mother's reluctant hand. I kiss her forehead.

She refuses to look down at it. To her, it's a finality. To me, it says all of the things I won't be able to say.

My mother nods and more tears pour from her eyes. She sets the envelope on her tall dresser and grabs a tissue from a box next to her bed. Dabbing the tears from her cheeks and sniffling back the rest, she tries to gain her composure again before going back into the living room with Camryn.

"Why don't you just tell her, Andrew?" she says turning back to look at me in front of the bedroom door. "You should let her know so the two of you can do the things you've always wanted to do before—"

"I can't," I say and my own words rip a hole through my chest. "I want everything to happen how it normally would and not be forced to happen sooner because of something else."

She doesn't like my answer, but she understands it.

We walk back out together and she's smiling as much as she can for Camryn's sake when we enter the living room again.

Camryn keeps her smile, too, but it's plain in her face that she knows my mother has been crying.

Mom walks over to Camryn and instinctively Camryn stands up.

"I'm sorry I have to cut this visit short," my mom says, taking Camryn into a hug, "but I received some unfortunate news about a family member while I was on the phone with Asher. I hope you'll understand."

"Of course," Camryn says, her expression hardened by worry. She glances at me briefly. "I'm sorry to hear that. I hope you'll be OK."

My mom nods and pushes a smile through her teary eyes. "Thank you, honey. Have Andrew bring you back anytime; you're always welcome here."

"Thank you," Camryn says softly and takes it upon herself to hug my mom again.

———

"Andrew, what was that all about?" she asks before I even get my car door shut.

I sigh and turn the key in the ignition. "It's just sibling rivalry stuff," I say, trying not to look at her next to me. I start the car and put the gear in reverse. "Mom gets upset when Aidan and I are fighting."

"You're lying."

I am and I'll continue to.

I look over at her briefly and back the car out onto the street.

"She just didn't want to drag you into it," I begin and the rest of the lie just starts to fall into place. "But it has everything to do with my father's funeral. Notice she didn't bring it up in front of you. Taking me into the back room to talk about it was her way of sparing you."

She still doesn't believe me, but I can tell she's starting to.

"So, then what was this news about a family member?"

"There wasn't any," I say. "She just wanted to talk to me and I told her about the argument I had with Aidan on the phone before we left my apartment and it upset her."

Camryn sighs and faces her window.

"My mom really likes you."

She looks over. At first I get the feeling she wants to further the conversation about Aidan, but she drops it.

"Well she's a very sweet woman," Camryn says. "Maybe you and *Aidan* (she puts emphasis on his name as if she still doesn't fully believe my lie) should try to get along better so you two don't upset her so much."

Although misplaced, it's still not bad advice.

"Baby, look, I'm sorry; maybe I should've waited to bring you to meet her."

"It's OK," she says and scoots over to sit next to me. "I'm glad you did. It made me feel…special."

I think she believes me now, or maybe she's just trying to push her gut feeling into the back of her mind because she realizes I'm not going to crack the truth anytime soon.

I slip my arm around her.

"Well you *are* special."

She lays her head on my chest. "You didn't tell her about leaving tomorrow."

"I know, but I will. I might call her later tonight and fill her in." I squeeze her gently. "Now that she's met you and definitely loves you, I think she won't be as worried about me doing something so *ab*normal."

Camryn slips her hand in between my thighs and smiles up at me. "Yeah, now I just have to tell *my* mom." She lifts up suddenly like a thought just dawned on her. "I could just wait to tell her when we drive through North Carolina and drop in so you can meet her."

That beautiful blue-eyed smile of hers is beaming.

I smile back and nod. "You want to take someone like me home to meet your mom? What if she takes one look at my tats and steals you away from me?" I joke.

"No way," she says, laughing lightly. "If anything, she'll be enamored by you."

"Uh oh, gonna get me some cougar action!"

Her eyes bug out of her head and I throw my head back and laugh.

"Baby, I'm kidding!"

She snarls at me and takes a deep, aggravated breath, but she's not hiding the humor from her face very well, either.

"Hey, have you ever…you know…?"

She can't say it out loud and I think it's hilarious.

"Been with an older woman?" I say, smirking.

This topic is clearly uncomfortable for her, but she's the one that asked and so I'm at complete liberty to torture her with it as much as possible.

"Yeah, I have."

Her head snaps around and her eyes are even wider than before. "You have *not*!"

I laugh while at the same time saying, "Yes, I have."

"How old was she? Or…*they*?" Her head turns at an angle, but her eyes never move.

The plural version looks like dangerous territory all of a sudden, but I do want to be completely honest with her. Well, about this sort of thing, anyway…

I put my hand on her leg. "A couple of times. One was only about thirty-eight which to me is not much different from twenty-eight. But I also slept with a woman who was around forty-three."

Camryn's face is hot from blushing, but she's not jealous or pissed off in any way. Though I think she might be a little... worried.

"What do you like better?" she asks very cautiously.

I try not to grin.

"Baby, it's not about age," I admit. "I mean, I'm not into grannies or anything and I think any woman, no matter how old she is, who keeps herself lookin' hot is totally fuckable."

"Oh my *God*!" Camryn laughs. "Talk about the dirty mouth on *me*!"

She shakes off the stun of my words and then says, "You didn't answer my question."

"Technically I did," I mess with her some more. "You asked what I like better and there's really not a solid answer to your question, just a generality."

I know exactly what her question really meant and I'm sure she knows as much. But I never pass up an opportunity to make her squirm.

She narrows her eyes at me.

I laugh and finally give in.

"Baby, you are the best sex I have ever had," I say and she purses her lips as if to say: Yeah, right, you're just saying that because you're currently biased. "And I *mean* that, Camryn. I'm not just filling your head with shit because you're sitting in front of me and because I cherish my nutsack."

She smiles and rolls her eyes, but believes my words now. I pull her closer to me again and she's happy to lay her head back on my chest.

"You're the best sex I've ever had because I got something out of you I've never gotten out of a girl before."

She tilts her head upward to look at me, waiting to hear what exactly that might be.

I smile back down at her and say, "I de-virginized your innocence, made you more comfortable with yourself sexually. And that is so hot to me."

Camryn leans up and kisses my jawline.

"You just like me for that head-job on the highway."

I look upward and grin. "Well, I did really, really, *really* love that, but no, babe, that's not what I like you for."

I think she finally feels validated again. She nuzzles her head against my chest and grabs me tight with her right arm across my stomach.

We ride the rest of the way back to my apartment without saying anything. I sense that her silence is less grim than my own. But I don't want her to worry or to be brokenhearted. Not right now. Not ever. It's inevitable, but I want to hold it back for as long as I can.

We spend four hours watching movies in the living room, both of us sprawled out across the couch. I hold her in my arms and kiss her when she's trying to pay attention to an important scene and I stick my tongue in her ear just to make her scream about how gross it is. She's so cute when she's 'grossed out', so it's her own damn fault that I enjoy doing it so much. We throw popcorn into each other's mouths and take score. She won, six to my four, before we gave up and actually started eating the popcorn instead of playing with it. And I introduced her to my plant, Georgia, who didn't die while I was gone. Camryn told me about a mix-breed dog she adopted from an animal shelter that she named BeeBop, and I told her how sorry I felt for that dog to have been given such a fucked up name. Coincidently, BeeBop died of congestive heart failure just like my dog and best friend, Maximus. I showed her pictures of him and she happened to have one of BeeBop with her, too. It was so ugly, it was cute.

We talk for hours and hours until she crawls onto my lap on the couch, straddling me. She lays her body against mine and says so softly that it makes my insides shiver, "Let's go to bed..."

I stand up with her legs still wrapped around my waist, her ass propped within my hands and I carry her to the bedroom. I slip out of my clothes, all of them, and lie down in the center of the bed. I was rock-hard before I brought her in here. And I watch her as she slowly undresses in front of me, stripping not only her clothes but her usual shy demeanor. She crawls on top of me from the foot of the bed and positions herself on my lap so that I feel myself pressing in between her warm lips below. She never takes her eyes off mine as she leans her body over to bring her mouth closer to mine, kissing my chest and circling my nipples with the tip of her tongue. I keep the heat of her thighs underneath my hands until she kisses me and I reach up and fill them with her breasts.

"You feel so good," I whisper against her mouth just before she steals my breath with her kiss.

I press gently into her below and she presses back a little harder, teasing me and making me want to shove myself deep inside of her. But right now, she's the one in control and I'll gladly let her have it.

She breaks the kiss and then she kisses one side of my neck and then the other, always moving her hips so slowly that it makes me want her that much more.

"Let me get you wet first," I whisper up at her, my hands locked around her little hips. She's already wet, but that's beside the point. "Crawl up here, baby," I say, lifting my chin to indicate my face.

She licks my lips first and then when she starts to move up, I push myself down a little further upon the bed to give her room.

I waste no time when her thighs press down around my head and I start to lick her furiously, sucking on her clit so hard that she begins to grind her hips against my face, her fingers clutched around the top of the headboard. She's so fucking wet. When she starts to moan and whimper, I stop. And she knows why. She knows I want her to get off with me.

She crawls back down over the length of my body and sits on my lap, rubbing herself across my cock before reaching down and taking it into her hand.

When she slides herself down over me slowly, we both gasp and shudder.

After a night of making love, she passes out in my arms and I hold her there, never wanting to let her go. I cry quietly into the softness of her hair until eventually I fall asleep, too.

# Camryn

# THIRTY-SEVEN

*A*ndrew?" I say, rolling over onto his side of the bed. Waking myself up further, I lift my head slowly to see that he isn't there.

I smell bacon.

I think about the night we had and can't wipe the obvious smile off my face. I untangle myself from the sheets and get out of bed and slip on my panties and t-shirt.

Andrew is standing at the stove when I walk into the kitchen.

"Baby, why are you up so early?"

I walk over to the fridge and open it, searching for anything to wet my mouth. I need to brush my teeth, but if he's cooking breakfast I don't want to make it taste funky mixed with toothpaste.

"Thought I'd bring you breakfast in bed."

It took him a few seconds longer to answer than I feel like it should have and his voice sounded off. I look up from the fridge and over at him. He's just standing there, staring into the grease.

"Baby, are you all right?"

I let the fridge door close without getting anything from it.

He barely lifts his head to glance at me.

"Andrew?"

My heart is beating faster and faster, though I'm not sure why.

I move over next to him and put my hand on his arm. He lifts his gaze from the grease and looks at me slowly.

"Andrew..."

In a sort of cruel slow motion, Andrew's legs give way and his body crashes against the white tile floor, the spatula he had in his hand hits the floor with him, splattering hot grease. I reach out to grab him but I can't keep him on his feet. Everything is still moving in slow motion: my scream, my hands as they grab at his shoulders, his head as it bounces against the tile. But then when his body begins to shake and convulse uncontrollably, slow motion becomes fast and terrifying.

"ANDREW! OH MY GOD, *ANDREW*!"

I want to help him up but his body won't stop shaking. I see the whites of his eyes and his jaw clenched in a horrific display. His limbs have locked up stiffly.

I scream out again, tears barreling from my eyes. "Somebody help me!" And then I snap into my senses and run for the nearest phone. His cell phone is on the nearby counter. I dial 911 and in the two seconds it takes for them to answer, I'm turning the fire off from the stove.

"Please! He's having a seizure! *Please*, someone help me!"

"Ma'am, the first thing you need to do is calm down. Is he still seizing?"

"Yes!"

I watch in horror as Andrew's body shakes against the floor. I'm so scared I feel like throwing up.

"Ma'am, I want you to move anything nearby that could hurt him. Is he wearing glasses? Is his head in danger of hitting furniture or any other objects?"

"No! B-But he hit his head when he fell!"

"OK, now find something to put under his head, a pillow, something to protect it from hitting anything else."

I look around the kitchen first but see nothing and then I run frantically into the living room and grab a small couch pillow and bring it back. I set the phone down long enough to slide the pillow underneath his jerking head.

*Oh no...oh my God, what's happening to him?!*

I put the phone back to my ear.

"OK, I put the pillow under his head!"

"All right ma'am," the 911 operator says calmly, "how long has he been seizing? Does he have a known condition that causes seizures?"

"I-I d-don't know, about...maybe two minutes, three at the most. And no, I've never seen him do this before. He's never told me about any..." It starts to dawn on me: he never told me. All sorts of things start attacking my mind, only causing me to lose my calm again. "Please send an ambulance! Please! Hurry!" I'm choking on my own tears.

Andrew's body stops jerking.

Before the 911 operator has a chance to respond, I say, "He's stopped! W-What do I do?"

"OK, ma'am I need you to help roll him over onto his side— we're going to send an ambulance. What is your address?"

While I'm rolling him onto his side, I freeze with her question.

*I don't...I don't fucking know! Goddammit!*

"I-I don't know the—" I shoot up from the floor and rush over to the counter where a stack of mail has been sitting and I find the address on the top piece and read it off to her.

"An ambulance is on its way. Would you like to stay on the phone with me until it arrives?"

I'm not sure what she said, or if she ever really said anything at all and I'm just imagining it, but I don't respond. I can't tear my eyes away from Andrew, lying unconscious on the kitchen floor.

"He's unconscious! Oh my God, why isn't he waking up?!" My free hand lingers on my lips.

"It's not uncommon," she says and I finally snap back into her voice. "Would you like me to remain with you until the ambulance gets there?"

"...Yes, please don't hang up. *Please*."

"OK, I'm right here," she says and her voice is my only comfort. I can't breathe. I can't think straight. I can't speak. All I can do is watch him. I'm even too scared to sit on the floor next to him for fear of him seizing again and me being in the way.

Minutes later I hear sirens blaring up the street.

"I think they're here," I say into the phone distantly.

I still can't look at anything but Andrew.

*Why is this happening?*

There's a knock at the door and finally I get up and run over to it to let the EMTs in. I don't even remember dropping Andrew's phone on the floor with the 911 operator still on the other end. The next thing I know, Andrew is being lifted onto a stretcher and strapped down.

"What is his name?" a voice asks and I'm sure it's one of the EMTs, but I can't see his face. All I see is Andrew's as he's being wheeled out the door.

"Andrew Parrish," I answer quietly.

I vaguely hear the name of the hospital the EMT tells me they are taking him. And when they leave, I just stand there, staring at the door where I last saw him. It takes me several long minutes to get my head together and the first thing I do is grab his cell phone and search for his mother's number. I hear her start to cry on the other end when I tell her what happened and I think she dropped her phone.

"Ms. Parrish?" I feel the tears stinging the back of my eyes. "Ms. Parrish?" But she's gone.

Finally, I throw on some clothes—I have no idea what I'm even wearing—and grab Andrew's car keys and my purse and rush out the door. I drive the Chevelle around for a few minutes until I realize I don't know where I'm going or where I'm at. I find a gas station and stop to ask for directions to the hospital and they give them to me, but I still barely find my way there without getting lost. I can't think straight.

I slam the car door and run into the emergency room with my purse sloppily over my shoulder. I could drop it and not know the difference. The nurse at the desk types on her keyboard for information and then points me in the right direction where I end up in a waiting room area. And I'm all alone.

I think an hour has gone by, but I could be wrong. One hour. Five minutes. A week. It doesn't make any difference; it would all feel the same to me. My chest hurts, I've cried so much. I've paced the floor so hard that I've started counting the specks in the carpet on my way back and forth.

Another hour.

This waiting room is so incredibly insipid with brown walls and brown seats lined neatly in two rows down the center of the room. A clock high on the wall above the door ticks around and around and even though it's too faint for me to hear, my mind believes that I can hear it. There's a coffee pot and a sink nearby. A man—I think—just walked in through a side door and fills a small Styrofoam cup and then walks back out.

Another hour.

My head hurts. My lips are chapped and broken. I keep licking them, only making it worse. I haven't seen a nurse walk by in
a while and I'm starting to wish I would've stopped the last one I
saw before she slipped down the long, sterile fluorescent lit hallway
outside the waiting area.

What's taking so long? What's going *on*?

I hit my forehead in the palm of my hand and just as I go to
reach for Andrew's phone in my purse, I hear a familiar voice:

"Camryn?"

I turn swiftly at the waist.

Andrew's younger brother, Asher, is walking into the room.

I want to be relieved that someone has finally come to talk to me,
to lift this deep sense of painful nothingness, but I can't be relieved
because I only expect him to tell me something horrible about
Andrew. Asher wasn't even in Texas as far I know and if he's here
suddenly then that must mean he took the first flight out of wherever
he was and people only do that when something bad has happened.

"Asher?" I say, tears straining my voice.

I don't even hesitate and I run over into his arms. He hugs me
tightly.

"Please tell me what's going on?" I say, tears streaming from
my eyes all over again. "Is Andrew all right?"

Asher takes my hand and leads me to a seat and I sit next to
him, squeezing my purse in my lap just to have something to hold
onto.

Asher looks so much like Andrew it hurts my heart.

He smiles gently at me.

"He's fine right now," he says and that small sentence is enough to fill my entire body with a surge of energy. "But he probably won't stay that way."

And just as quickly, that hopeful energy drains right back out of me, taking other parts of me with it: my heart, my soul, that tiny bit of hope that I had maintained all this time since this happened. *What is Asher saying . . . what is he trying to tell me?*

My chest shudders with tears.

"What do you mean?" I barely get the words out.

He takes a calm breath.

"About eight months ago," he says carefully, "my brother found out he has a brain tumor—"

My heart is gone. My breath is gone.

My purse falls onto the floor, spilling everything with it, but I can't move to pick it up. I can't move . . . anything.

I feel Asher's hand take up mine.

"Because of our father's condition Andrew refused to get further tests. He was supposed to go back to see Dr. Marsters that same week, but he wouldn't go. Our mom and our brother, Aidan, tried everything to get him to go. As far as I know, he agreed at one point, but he never went through with it because our father's condition worsened."

"No . . ." I shake my head over and over again, not wanting to believe the things he's telling me, "no . . ." I just want to force his words out of my head.

"It's why Andrew and Aidan have been at each other's throats," Asher goes on. "Aidan just wanted him to do what he needed to do, and Andrew, as stubborn as he is, fought Aidan at every turn."

I look toward the wall and say, "It's why he never wanted to see his father in the hospital . . ." The realization numbs me further.

"Yeah," Asher says quietly, "it's also why he wouldn't go to the funeral."

I look right at Asher now, my eyes boring into his, my fingers dancing on my lips. "He's afraid. He's afraid the same thing is going to happen to him, that his tumor is inoperable."

"Yes."

I shoot up from the seat, a tube of lipstick cracks underneath my shoe.

"But what if it's not as bad?" I say frantically. "He's in the hospital now; they can do what they need to do." I start to march toward the exit. "I'll *make* him get the tests. I'll *force* him! He'll listen to me!"

Asher grabs my arm. I turn around.

"From what they can tell right now, his chances are very small, Camryn."

I'm going to throw up. My cheeks feel like there are thousands of tiny pins prickling them as more tears push their way to the surface. My hands are shaking, too. My whole fucking body is shaking!

Asher adds softly, "He let it go too long."

Both of my hands come up and cover my face and I sob into them, my body trembling uncontrollably. I feel Asher's arms wrap tightly around me.

"He wants to see you."

His words cause me to look up.

"They've already got him in a room; I'll take you to him. Just wait here for a few more minutes until my mom leaves his room and I'll walk you back."

I don't say anything. I just stand here, wordless... dying inside, the worst pain I have ever felt.

Asher looks at me once more to be confident that I heard him clearly and then he says carefully, "I'll be back shortly for you. Just wait here."

Asher leaves and to keep from collapsing I grab the nearest chair and sit down. I can't even see straight, the tears are burning my eyes, rushing down my cheeks. My chest feels like someone literally reached inside of it and ripped out my heart.

I don't know if I'll be able to see him without going completely out of my mind.

Why did he do this?!

*Why* is this happening?!

Before I go completely fucking crazy and start breaking shit or hitting something and hurting myself, I crawl on my hands and knees to my purse on the floor. I didn't even notice that Asher had picked everything up and put it back inside for me and then set my purse on the chair. I dig for my phone and call Natalie.

"Hello?"

"Natalie, I-I need you to do something for me."

"Cam…are you *crying?*"

"Natalie, please listen to me."

"OK, yes, I'm here. What's wrong?"

"You're my best friend," I say, "and I need you to come to Galveston. As soon as possible. Will you come? I need you. *Please.*"

"Oh my God, Camryn, what the hell is going on? What happened? Are you all right?"

"Nothing happened to me, but I need you here. I need someone and you're all I have. My mom won't un—Natalie, please!"

"A-All right," she says with deep worry in her voice. "I'm on the first flight out. I'll be there. Just keep your phone on you."

I drop my hand to my side, my phone crushed in my fist and I stare at the wall for what seems like forever until Asher's voice pulls me out of myself. I look up at him. He walks toward me and reaches out for my hand, knowing I'm going to need it. My legs feel fragile, like I'm walking on prosthetics and I don't have full use of them. Asher holds my hand so tight. We step out into the brightly-lit hallway and head toward an elevator.

"I have to calm myself," I say out loud, but more to me than Asher. I pull my hand from his and wipe my face and run my fingers through my hair, over the top of my head. "I can't see him in hysterics. That's the last thing he needs right now is to be trying to calm me down."

Asher doesn't say anything. I don't look at him. I see our reflections in the elevator door, warped and discolored. I notice the number on the elevator moving up two floors and then the elevator stops. The door opens. I just stand there at first afraid to walk out, but then I take a very deep breath and wipe my eyes again.

We walk to the middle of the hall to a room with a large wooden door that has been left cracked open. Asher pushes the door open the rest of the way, but I look down at the floor and at the invisible line that separates me in the hallway from Andrew inside the room and I'm so scared to walk over it. I feel like once I do I will see that all of this is real and there really is no turning back. I squeeze my eyes shut and force back a new rush of tears, breathing deeply with my fists clenched around my purse.

And then I open my eyes when Andrew's mom steps out.

Her soft face is exhausted by emotion, just as I know mine must be. Her hair is tangled. Her eyelids are enflamed. But she manages to smile lovingly at me, placing her gentle fingers on my shoulder.

"I'm glad you're here, Camryn."

And then she walks away from the room hand in hand with Asher.

I watch them for a brief moment as they slip farther down the hall, but their figures appear blurred into their surroundings.

I look into the room from the doorway and see the end of the bed where I know Andrew is lying.

I step inside.

"Baby, come here," Andrew says when he sees me.

At first, I'm frozen here in this spot, but when I look into his eyes, those unforgettable green eyes that have such a hold on me, I drop my purse on the floor and rush over to his bed.

# THIRTY-EIGHT

*I* practically fall over his body and into his arms. He holds me so tight, though not as tight as I want him to. I want him to crush me to death and never let me go, to take me with him. But he's still weak. I can tell that what he's going through is quickly draining him.

Andrew holds my face in his hands and he pushes my hair away from my eyes and he kisses away the tears that I tried so hard to keep hidden for his sake, so he wouldn't have to waste any of his strength on me. But the heart has a mind of its own and it always gets what it wants, especially when it's dying.

"I'm so sorry," he says in a painful, desperate voice; my face still framed by his hands. "I couldn't tell you, Camryn...I didn't want our time together to be anything but what it was."

Tears pour from my eyes, dripping over his fingers and down his wrists.

"I hope you're not—"

"No, Andrew..." I choke back a few tears, "...I understand why; you don't have to explain. I'm glad you didn't tell me..."

He seems surprised, but happy about it. He pulls my face toward him and kisses my lips.

"You're right," I say. "If you would've told me then our time together would've been dark and...I-I don't know, but it would've been *different* and I can't bear the thought of different—but Andrew, I wish you would've told me for one reason alone: I would've done anything, *anything* to get you to a hospital sooner." My voice begins to rise as the sad truth of my words hurts me to say them. "You could've—"

Andrew shakes his head. "Baby, it was already too late."

"Don't say that! It's not too late *now*! You're still here, there's still a chance."

He smiles gently and his hands finally fall away from my cheeks, resting at his sides on the white knit hospital blanket that covers him. An IV snakes from the top of his hand and to a machine.

"I'm being realistic, Camryn. They've already told me that my chances don't look good."

"But there's *still* a chance," I argue, forcing back more tears and wishing I controlled their off switch. "Small is better than no chance at all."

"If I let them operate on me."

I feel like I was just slapped in the face.

"What do you mean, *if*?"

His eyes stray from mine.

I reach out and take his chin vigorously in my hand, turning him back to face me. "There's no 'if', Andrew—you can't be serious."

Andrew reaches out for me and moves himself to one side of the bed. He guides me to lie down next to him and as I curl my body into his lying on his side, he lays one arm over me and pulls me close.

"If I had never met you," he says, peering into my eyes just inches from his, "I never would have gone through with it. If you weren't here with me right now, I wouldn't do it. I would think it was a waste of money and time and would only put my family through a false sense of hope, dragging out the inevitable."

"But you're going to let them do the surgery," I say suspiciously, though it's more like a question.

He brushes my cheek with the pad of his thumb.

"I will do *anything* for you, Camryn Bennett. I don't care what it is, I don't care…anything you ever ask me to do and I would do it. No exceptions."

Sobs rattle my chest.

Before I have a chance to say anything else, Andrew moves his hand across my cheek, pushing back my hair. He looks deeply into my eyes. "I'll do it."

I crush my mouth over his and we kiss feverishly.

"I can't lose you," I say. "We have the open road ahead of us. You're my partner in crime." I force a smile through my tears.

He kisses my forehead.

We lie together for a little while and talk about the surgery and the tests that still need to be done and I tell him that I won't leave his side. I'll stay here with him for as long as it takes. And we go on and on about the places we want to see and he starts picking songs out of the air that he wants me to learn so we can sing them together on the road. I've never been so willing to sing with him as I am right now. I would try to belt out Celine Dion or an opera singer—I don't care. I would do it. I would most certainly send everyone screaming for the exits, but I would do it. A nurse comes in to check on him at one point and Andrew gains back some of his playful personality and he messes with her head, telling her she could join us if she wanted in a little 'two on one' action.

The nurse just smiled, rolling her eyes and went about her busi-

ness. It made her feel good about herself and that's all he was aim-
ing for.

For a time, as I lie in this bed with Andrew, it feels like it did
when we were on the road. We don't think about sickness or death,
and we don't cry. We just talk and laugh and every now and then
he tries to touch me in all the right places. I giggle and push his
hands away because I feel like I'm doing something wrong. That he
should be resting.

Eventually, I give in and let him. Because he's persistent. And,
of course, he's irresistible. I let him finger me underneath the blanket and then I do the same for him with my hand.

After another hour, I get up from the bed.

"Babe, what's wrong?"

"Nothing is wrong," I say smiling warmly and then I take off
my pants and my shirt.

He's grinning from ear to ear. I knew that the perverted gears
in his head would start churning before anything else.

"As much as I would love to have sex with you in a hospital
room," I say as I crawl back into the bed with him, "It's not gonna
happen; you need all your strength for your surgery." I would totally
have sex with him in this bed, but right now, it's not about sex.

He looks at me curiously as I lie back down next to him wearing only my panties and bra and I curl my body against his like
before. All he's wearing underneath the knit blanket are a pair of
thin blue hospital pants. I press my chest firmly against his and tangle my legs around his. Our bodies are perfectly aligned, our ribs
touching.

"What are you doing?" he asks, growing more curious and
impatient, but loving every second of it.

I move my free arm down and trace his tattoo of Eurydice with my fingers. He watches carefully. And when my index finger finds Eurydice's elbow where the ink stops, I move it along my skin to pick up where his left off.

"I want to be your Eurydice, if you'll let me."

His face lights up and his dimples deepen.

"I want to get the other half," I go on, touching his lips with my fingers now. "I want to get Orpheus on my ribs and reunite them."

He's overwhelmed. I can see it in his glistening eyes.

"Oh, baby, you don't have to do that; it hurts like hell on the ribs."

"But I want it and I don't care how much it hurts."

His eyes begin to water as he looks at me and then his mouth covers mine and our tongues dance with one another for a long, loving moment.

"I would love that," he whispers onto my lips.

I kiss him softly and whisper back, "After your surgery, when you're well enough then we'll go."

He nods. "Yeah, Gus will definitely need me there to make sure the placement of your tattoo lines up with mine—he laughed at me when I went in to get this on my ribs."

I smile. "He did, huh?"

"Yeah." He chuckles. "He accused me of being a hopeless romantic and threatened to tell my friends. I told him he sounded like my father and to shut the fuck up. Gus is a good guy and one helluva tattoo artist."

"I can see that."

Andrew spears his fingers through my hair, constantly brushing it back over the top of my head. And as he watches me, scanning my face, I wonder what's going through his mind. His beautiful smile has vanished and he looks more intent and careful.

"Camryn, I want you to be prepared."

"Don't start that—"

"No, baby, you have to do this for me," he says with worry in his gaze. "You can't let yourself believe one hundred percent that I'm going to live through this. You can't do that."

"Andrew please. Just stop."

He puts four fingers on my lips, hushing me. I'm already crying again. He's trying to be as gentle with the truth as he possibly can be, holding back his own tears and his own emotions even better than I can my own. *He's* the one who might die and I'm the one with no strength. It pisses me off, but I can't do anything but cry and be pissed at myself.

"Just promise me that you'll continue to tell yourself that I might die."

"I can't make myself say something like that!"

He squeezes me tighter.

"Promise me."

I grit my teeth, feeling my jaw grind harshly behind my cheeks. My nose and my eyes sting and burn.

Finally I say, "…I promise," and it wrenches my heart.

"But you have to promise *me* that you'll pull through this," I say, pressing my head underneath his chin again. "I can't be without you, Andrew. You have to know that I can't."

"I know, baby…I know."

Silence.

"Will you sing to me?" he asks.

"What do you want me to sing?"

"*Dust in the Wind*," he answers.

"No. I won't sing that song. Don't *ever* ask me that again. Ever."

His arms tighten around me.

"Then sing anything," he whispers, "I just want to hear your voice."

And so I start to sing *Poison & Wine*, the same song that we sang together back in New Orleans when we lay in each other's arms that night. He sings along with me a few verses, but I can tell just how weak he really is inside because he can barely hold a note.

We fall asleep in each other's arms.

———

"Got some tests to run," I hear a voice say above the bed.

I open my eyes to see the ménage à trois nurse standing at the side of the bed.

Andrew stirs awake, too.

It's late afternoon and I can tell by the view from the window that it'll be getting dark soon.

"You should probably get dressed," the nurse says with a knowing smile.

She probably thinks Andrew and I got it on in here at some point considering I'm half-naked.

I crawl out of the bed and slip on my clothes while the nurse checks Andrew's stats and apparently gets him ready to leave the room with her. There's a wheelchair near the foot of the bed.

"What kind of tests?" Andrew asks weakly.

The weakness in his voice causes me to look up. He doesn't look good. He looks...disoriented.

"Andrew?" I go back over to the bed.

Carefully, he raises one hand to ward me off. "No, baby, I'm all right; just a little dizzy. Trying to wake up."

The nurse turns to me and even though they are trained to

appear relaxed and not show the true measure of concern in their faces, I can see it in her eyes. She knows something's not right.

She forces a smile and goes around to help him sit up, moving his IV out of the way.

"He'll be gone for an hour or two, maybe more, while they run more tests," she says. "You should go grab a bite to eat, stretch your legs and come back in a little while."

"But I-I don't want to leave him."

"Do what she says," Andrew mumbles and the more I hear him try to talk, the more fearful I become. "I want you to go eat." He manages to turn his head to see me this time and he points a stern finger. "But no steak," he demands playfully. "You still owe me a steak dinner, remember? When I get out of here, that's the first thing we're doing."

He gets the smile out of me that he was shooting for, although it's weak.

"OK," I agree, nodding reluctantly. "I'll be back in a few hours and I'll be waiting for you."

I move back over and kiss him softly. He looks deeply into my eyes when I pull away. All I can see is pain in his eyes. Pain and exhaustion. But he tries to be strong and a tiny smile tugs one corner of his mouth. He gets into the wheelchair and looks back at me once before the nurse wheels him out of the room.

My breath catches.

I feel like I want to scream out to him that I love him, but I don't say it. I love him with all my heart, but deep down I feel that if I say it, if I finally admit it out loud, that everything will come crashing down. Maybe if I keep it within me, just never say the words, then our story will never be over. Saying those three words can be a beginning, but for me and Andrew, I fear it will be the end.

# THIRTY-NINE

*I* wouldn't be able to eat if my own life depended on it. I only told Andrew that I would to satisfy him. Instead, I venture outside and sit in the front of the hospital for a while. I just don't want to leave the premises while he's inside. It took everything in me to let that nurse wheel him away from me.

I get a text message from Natalie:

Just landed. Taking a cab. Be there soon. Love you.

When I see the cab pull up to the front of the hospital, it takes me a second to go to my feet. It's been a while since I've seen her; since we had our Damon issue.

But none of that matters to me anymore. It hasn't for a while. Best friends, no matter what they do or how much they hurt you, it only hurts as much as it does because they *are* your best friend. And none of us are perfect. Mistakes were made for best friends to forgive; it's what makes being a best friend official. In a way like Andrew, I can't imagine not having Natalie in my life. And right now I need her more than any time I have ever needed her.

She runs across the concrete when she sees me, her chocolate-colored long hair blowing freely behind her.

"Oh my God, I've missed you so much, Cam!" She practically squeezes me to death.

All it took was for her to be here and I'm taking advantage of her hug and sobbing into her chest. I just couldn't keep the tears contained. I've never cried as much in my life as I have in the past twenty-four hours.

"Oh, Cam, what is going on?" I feel her fingers comb through my hair as I cry softly into her shirt. "Let's go sit down."

Natalie walks me to a stone bench sitting underneath an oak tree and we sit together.

I tell her everything. From why I left North Carolina to meeting Andrew on the bus in Kansas and all the way up to this point, sitting with her on this bench. She cried and smiled and laughed with me as I told her about my time with Andrew and I've rarely seen her this serious about anything before. Only when my brother Cole got sent to prison and after my parents divorced. And after Ian's death. Natalie may be a crazy, outspoken, party-girl that usually doesn't know when to shut up, but she knows there's a time and place for everything and in a time like this, all she gives me is her heart.

"I just can't believe you're going through this after what you went through with Ian. It's like some cruel fucking joke that fate is playing on you."

It does feel like that in a way, but with Andrew, it feels much worse than some cruel joke.

"Girl," she says, laying her hand on my leg, "think about it: what are the chances that everything that happened the way it did, were just coincidence?" She shakes her head at me. "I'm sorry, Cam, but that's just *too* much coincidence—you two were *meant* to be together. It's like some wicked fucking fairytale love story that you just can't make up, y'know?"

I don't say anything; I just contemplate it. Normally, I would comment on her dramatic usage of words, but this time I can't. I just don't have it in me.

She forces my gaze. "Seriously, do you think you would be put through all this only to watch him die?"

Her using that word stings, but I hold it down.

"I don't know." I look out at the trees on the lawn, but I don't really see them. All I see is Andrew's face.

"He's going to be OK." Natalie cups my face in her hands and stares into my eyes. "He'll get through this, you just have to tell death to piss off, that *you* got this one, y'know?"

She surprises me sometimes. Right now is one of those times.

I smile gently and she wipes the tears from my cheeks.

"Let's go find a Starbucks."

Natalie stands up with her giant black leather purse dangling from one arm and reaches out her hand to me.

I'm reluctant.

"I...Natalie, I really want to stay here."

"No, you need to get away from this bad energy for a while— hospitals suck the hope out of everything—come back when he's back in his room and then you can introduce me to that sexy piece of Kellan that I'm oh-so-fucking jealous of you for." She smiles a huge, toothy smile.

She always gets me to smile, too.

I take her hand.

"All right," I give in.

We take the Chevelle to the nearest Starbucks. Natalie drooled all over the car all the way here.

"Jesus, Cam, you really hit the jackpot with this one." She sits across from me sipping her iced latte. "Guys that perfect are rare."

"Well, he's not perfect," I say, sloshing my straw around in my cup. "He's got a dirty mouth, he's stubborn, he forces me to do shit I don't want to do and he always gets his way."

Natalie grins and sucks on her straw.

Then she points at me briefly. "See, like I said: perfect." She laughs and then she rolls her brown eyes. "And *pu-lease*—makes you do shit you don't wanna do, *my ass*. Something tells me you love it when he tells you what to do." She slaps her hand upon the table and her eyes bug out. "Ooooh, he's rough in bed, isn't he? *Isn't* he?!" She can hardly contain herself.

I did tell her that we had sex, but I didn't exactly give her the juicy details.

My eyes stray downward at the table.

She slaps the table again and a guy sitting behind her looks over at us.

"Oh my God, he *is*!"

"Yes, he is!" I hiss, trying not to laugh. "Now will you be quiet?!"

"Come on, you have to give me an itsy-bitsy detail." She presses her thumb and index finger together to show just how itsy-bitsy and she squints one eye.

Ah, what the hell? I shrug and lean across the table and look to both sides of me to see if anyone seems to be listening.

"The first time," I start to say and her head looks frozen in time, eyes bugged out, mouth parted, "he practically forced himself on me…you know what I mean…of course I *wanted* him to, you know."

She nods like a bobblehead, but doesn't speak because she wants me to continue.

"I can tell he is naturally dominant and wasn't just doing it because I told him it's what I like. I can also tell that he was still being careful, not to go too far because he wanted to be sure if it was OK."

"Did he ever take it any further?"

"No, but I know he will."

Natalie smiles.

"You're a freaky little sexual deviant," she says and I blush so hard I can't look up for a moment. "Sounds like he's exactly what you needed in *every* aspect. He brought shit out of you that Ian and Christian couldn't." She looks upward as if at the heavens and says quickly, "You know I love you, Ian," and kisses two fingers and pushes them toward the sky. She looks back at me quickly.

"Well, that's not why I love him."

Natalie's mouth snaps shut. So does mine. I think all of the air was just sucked right out of the room. I didn't even realize what I was saying.

Why did I have to say that out loud?

"You're in love with him?" she asks, though she doesn't seem so surprised.

I don't say anything. I just swallow down any other words I had been prepared to say.

"If you *weren't* in love with him after everything you've been through with him, I'd think you were the one with the brain tumor."

Even though I hate that she used those two cruel and horrific words, I know she didn't mean anything by it.

But regardless of her lighthearted banter and her way with so easily making me forget that things aren't so great right now, I've already exhausted my ability to play along with her anymore. I'm grateful for her helping me to lift my mind of the depression and fear for Andrew, even if only for a few minutes with her talking about sex and being like we used to be.

I can't anymore.

I just want to get back to the hospital and be with him.

Natalie and I head back after sundown and we walk together through the front doors and hitch a ride on the elevator.

"I hope he's already done," I say nervously, staring at that blurred reflection on the elevator door again.

I feel Natalie's hand slip around mine. I look over at her to see her smiling gently at me.

The elevator opens up and we head down the hallway.

Asher and Marna are walking towards us in the opposite direction.

The look on their faces causes my heart to fall into the pit of my stomach. I squeeze Natalie's hand so tight I'm probably crushing it.

When Asher and Marna stand face to face with us, tears slip relentlessly down her cheeks. She grabs me into a hug and shudders out the words:

"Andrew fell into a coma...they don't think he's going to make it."

I step back away from her.

Every little sound, from the air filtering through the vents in the ceiling to the people shuffling past us in the hallway, it's all shut out in an instant. I feel Natalie's hand go for mine, but I absently push it away and stumble back further, my hands pressed over my heart. I can't breathe...I can't breathe. I see Asher's eyes, glistening with tears as he looks at me, but I look away. I look away because he has Andrew's eyes and I can't bear it.

Marna reaches into her purse and pulls out an envelope. She steps up to me carefully and takes both of my hands, putting the envelope into them.

"Andrew wanted me to give this to you if anything happened to him." She folds my fingers over the envelope with her own fingers. I don't look down at it; I just look at her, tears drenching my face.

I can't breathe...

"I'm sorry," Marna says, her voice trembling, "I have to go." She pats my hands motherly. "You're always welcome in my home and in my family. Please know that."

She nearly falls and Asher wraps his arm around her waist and walks her away down the hall.

I just stand here in the center. A few nurses walk by, but go around me. I feel the wind brush my face lightly when they walk past. It takes me an eternity to gather the courage to look down at the envelope in my hands. I'm shaking. My fingers fumble the flap on the envelope.

"Let me help you," I hear Natalie say and I'm too outside of myself to protest.

She slips the envelope from my fingers carefully and opens it for me, slowly unfolding the letter inside.

"Would you like me to read it for you?"

I look at her, my lips quivering uncontrollably and I shake my head as I finally understand her question. "No...let me..."

She hands me the letter and I unfold it the rest of the way, my tears falling onto the paper as I read:

Dear Camryn,

    I never wanted it to be this way. I wanted to tell you these things myself, but I was afraid. I was afraid that if I told you out loud that I loved you, that what we had together would die with me. The truth is that I knew in Kansas that you were the one. I've loved you since that day when I first looked up into your eyes as you glared down at me from over the top of that bus seat. Maybe I didn't know it then, but I knew something had happened to me in that moment and I could never let you go.

I have never lived the way I lived during my short time with you. For the first time in my life, I've felt whole, alive, free. You were the missing piece of my soul, the breath in my lungs, the blood in my veins. I think that if past lives are real then we have been lovers in every single one of them. I've known you for a short time, but I feel like I've known you forever.

I want you to know that even in death I'll *always* remember you. I'll always love you. I wish that things could've turned out differently. I thought of you many nights on the road. I stared up at the ceiling in the motels and pictured what our life might be like together if I had lived. I even got all mushy and thought of you in a wedding dress and even with a mini me in your belly. You know, I always heard that sex is great when you're pregnant. ;-)

But I'm sorry that I had to leave you, Camryn. I'm so sorry... I wish the story of Orpheus and Eurydice was real because then you could come to the Underworld and sing me back into your life. I wouldn't look back. I wouldn't fuck it up like Orpheus did.

I'm so sorry, baby...

I want you to promise me that you'll stay strong and beautiful and sweet and caring. I want you to be happy and find someone who will love you as much as I did. I want you to get married and have babies and live your life. Just remember to always be yourself and don't be afraid to speak your mind or to dream out loud.

I hope you'll never forget me.

One more thing: don't feel bad for not telling me that you loved me. You didn't need to say it. I knew all along that you did.

Love Always,
Andrew Parrish

I fall to my knees in the center of the hall, Andrew's letter clutched in my fingertips.

And that's the last thing I remember about that day.

*Two months later . . .*

# FORTY

The sun is shining and there's not a cloud in the sky. I even hear birds chirping. I guess it's kind of perfect for a day like this. The heel of my shoe presses against a soft patch of grass. I'm dressed in a cute white and yellow sundress that falls just above my knees. My hair is braided around to one side, how Andrew always insisted I wear it. My hands are folded together down in front of me as I stare down at the gravestone that reads: PARRISH in big chiseled letters across the back. It was hard to come here, but it has been a long time coming.

I keep my eyes down, staring absently at the mound of clay-like dirt that still seems fresh after two months since the burial. Not even the rain pounding on it over and over again seems to help flatten it any. I glance out at all of the other graves, most of them already covered by grass and I can't feel sad, only comforted as though these people here, although long gone to all of us, have each other's company.

A pair of hands slip around my waist from behind.

"Thank you for coming here with me, babe," Andrew says into my ear and then kisses my cheek.

I take his hand and pull him around to my side and we look down one last time at his father's grave together.

We leave Wyoming later that night, but we go by plane. Our plans to travel around the world have only been put on hold. After Andrew's coma and surgery, he began to recover within three weeks. The doctors were as surprised as the rest of us, but he still has needed time to recover fully and so I've been with him ever since, living in Galveston. He goes to physical therapy once a week, but already it seems as if he doesn't need it.

Andrew insisted that we get up off our asses and get on the road like we planned—he's suffering from that elated second-chance-at-life feeling which makes him more eager than ever to do just about everything. Hell, he enjoys washing dishes and doing laundry. But his mom, Marna, and I have strictly forbidden him to do too much, or to over-exert himself. Andrew doesn't like it, but he knows better than to stand up to both of us at once.

We will, quite literally, kick his ass.

But Andrew and I still plan to travel the world and keep our promise not to stay grounded to the monotony of life. None of that has changed and I know that it never will.

Natalie went back to North Carolina and we talk every single day. She's dating Blake now, the guy Damon attacked that night on the roof. It makes me smile to know they are together. When I talk to them on Skype, I can just tell they were made for each other. At least for right now; with Natalie, one never knows what'll happen. Damon, on the other hand, ended up getting busted for drug possession. It's his second offense and he's probably going to be spending a year in prison this time. Maybe he'll learn from his mistakes, but I doubt that.

My brother, Cole, however, I think Andrew was right about him. Andrew and I took a plane to North Carolina to visit my mom and while there we went with her to see Cole in prison. He seems different, sincerely remorseful. I could see it in his eyes. He and Andrew hit it off really well. I think maybe my brother *will* be like the big brother I used to know once he gets out. And with Andrew's help, I have forgiven Cole for what he did. I'll always hurt for that family he destroyed when he killed that man in the wreck, but I've realized that forgiveness cures a lot of things.

My mom is still dating Roger. In fact, they're getting married in the Bahamas in February. I'm so happy for her. I did manage to meet Roger and run him through my douchebag inspection and am happy to say that he passed with honors. Mom is rarely home anymore; he's always sweeping her off to somewhere.

And she deserves every bit of it.

Andrew's mom and brothers welcomed me into the family with open arms. Asher and I are really close. And regardless of how standoffish I always thought Aidan was, I love him to death. He was never really a jerk to Andrew. Honestly, Andrew deserved it. Aidan and his wife, Michelle, talk to me and about me as if I'm *Andrew's* wife. It always makes me blush. More importantly, Andrew and Aidan have been getting along. Before Aidan and Michelle went back to Chicago after a quick visit last week, I just beamed watching them mess with each other and wrestle in the living room. They almost broke the television, but me and Michelle just sat back and laughed and let them show each other up with their alpha male testosterone.

And today . . . well, today is going to be a little different than Andrew is used to.

I walk into the living room where he's kicked back on the couch watching *Prometheus*.

He reaches out for me as I walk toward him.

"No," I say, shaking my head, "I need you to get up."

"What's up, babe?" He lifts from the couch and reaches up to scratch his head. His hair has started growing back, but he's still not used to how it feels, especially around the scar where he had the surgery.

He drops his legs onto the floor to sit upright fully and I step in between them, running my hands over his head. He kisses one of my wrists and then the other.

"Come with me." I nod my head back, take his fingers into my hand and he follows me to the bedroom.

As always, when I take him into the bedroom he automatically thinks it's sexual and his sexy green eyes light up like a boy.

"I just want you to lay down with me for a little while," I say, taking off all of my clothes.

He seems a little confused, but it's so cute.

"OK," he says, smiling. "You want me naked, too? I'll definitely get naked. What the hell am I asking for?" He starts to strip.

He lies down next to me and we face each other, pulling our bodies close and tangling our legs. He wraps his arms around me and then his fingers trail across my tattoo of Orpheus that I got two weeks ago. It's perfect, lined up with Andrew's flawlessly. When we lie next to each other like this, the two pieces become one.

"Are you OK, baby?" Andrew gazes at me curiously, his fingertips brushing softly across my ribs.

I smile and kiss his mouth.

Then I pull away just a little and take his hand, sliding it to my tattoo, toward the area that extends over onto my belly.

"I love my tattoo, baby," I whisper into the small space between our faces, "but I think in about seven and a half more months, Orpheus might be a little bit stretched out."

Andrew blinks confusedly and it takes him a few seconds to understand what I'm saying.

His head draws back in a slightly stunned motion and then after a pause, he lifts up.

"I'm due in May."

His eyes grow wide first; he's stunned and wordless, but then he manages to say, "You're pregnant?" His hand immediately goes to my stomach.

His reaction makes me smile even bigger.

His dimples deepen as he looks down at me and the next thing I know his tongue is in my mouth. His kiss steals my breath away and he lifts me into his arms in the center of the bed.

"Marry me," he says and now I'm the one stunned wordless. "I was going to ask you tomorrow night when we went out, but I can't wait now. Marry me."

I start to cry and he wraps me in his arms again and kisses me some more.

When he finally pulls away and looks into my eyes again, I answer: "Yes, I'll marry you, Andrew Parrish."

"I love you *so* fucking much," he says, kissing me again. He grabs my face. "Now let's have pregnant sex."

What can I say? That's Andrew and I wouldn't want him to be any other way.

## BONUS MATERIAL: SPOILER ALERT!

Dear Reader,

THE EDGE OF NEVER ended for so many people on a heart-wrenching emotional note and I admit that when I wrote it, I was just as affected as everyone else. I felt that if I added anything else that not only would it be far too long of a story, but any addition might diminish that experience that many felt. I definitely didn't want to do that. However, after the book was published, I got a swarm of emails and comments from people all over the world asking me for one thing: *Will you please write the hospital scene from Andrew's point of view?*

How could I say no?

So, I got to work right away on it and finished it in a day. But then I sat on it. For a long time. I intended to post it on my blog and let everyone read it from there, but at that time, I was still hoping that a publisher would take interest in my book. I started envisioning that scene being in the book itself, not as part of the story, but as a little something

# BONUS MATERIAL

special inserted in the back for all of those who asked me to write it.

And then my dream came true and a publisher did take interest, and now you all get to read that special "extra" chapter from Andrew. Readers can finally get into his head and know what he was thinking when he was lying in that hospital bed with Camryn curled up next to him. And you get to see what happened when he and Camryn parted ways as the nurse wheeled him out of the room.

I also want to take this opportunity to thank all of the fans out there who have made Camryn and Andrew's story what it is—for supporting it and spreading the word so relentlessly that the book became a *New York Times* bestseller! Without all of you, none of that would have been possible. A huge thanks to my Super Agent, Jane Dystel, who rescued me from some truly troubled times, and my foreign rights agent, Lauren Abramo, who rocked those foreign deals every day it seemed. And of course to Grand Central Publishing/Forever Romance and my editor Megha Parekh, who loved THE EDGE OF NEVER and believed in it enough to give it a home at Forever Romance.

So here is the bonus scene from Andrew's point of view in the hospital. And I'd love to hear from you, tell me what you think about it by commenting on my Facebook page.

# WARNING: SPOILER ALERT!

(Facebook.com/J.A.Redmerski), Twitter (@JRedmerski),
Goodreads or at my website www.jessicaredmerski.com!
Thanks again and enjoy!

J. A. Redmerski

# BONUS MATERIAL

## THE HOSPITAL SCENE FROM
## ANDREW'S POINT OF VIEW

I really thought that I had more time. It's been less than a year since Marsters dropped the load in my lap, pretty much telling me that I was going to end up like my father. Well technically he didn't say that, but that's what I got out of the few words he did say. I know I was just being an ass; Dr. Marsters—and my family—tried to get me to go back, do more tests, find out how serious it was, but what more could he tell me that I didn't already know? There was no hope for my dad. He had all the tests. He went to all of his appointments. He took the medication they gave him and had treatments. For a while. Until he realized he was going to die anyway and refused to prolong the inevitable. Emptying out his bank accounts to everyone but his family. But I'm his son and I assumed stuff like this was hereditary. That's why I never went back to Marsters myself. Because like my father, I didn't want to drag it out. It wasn't until six months after I was diagnosed that I finally broke down and did some research on it. I found out that brain tumors typically aren't hereditary at all, only about five percent. I read something about rare syndromes. I don't have any syndromes and neither did my

# WARNING: SPOILER ALERT!

dad. But by then the headaches had gotten worse. Much worse. And then I started having seizures. Scared the shit outta me.

By this time, I knew it was too late. I didn't want to face Marsters, looking for some magic solution that I knew he wouldn't be able to give me. Because I waited too long.

But enough of that.

All that matters right now is Camryn. I'm an asshole for putting her through this, especially after...goddammit, what was I thinking?! Her last boyfriend died and here I am doing it to her all over again.

I guess I'm nothing short of selfish. Because I love her and because I knew from the moment she spoke to me on that bus back in Kansas that she was the one.

But fate is cruel, and if Fate were standing in front of me right now I'd kick him in the fucking nuts.

I just hope Camryn can forgive me....

The door to my hospital room opens and then I see her for the first time since last night when I made love to her. She just looks at me for a moment, her face full of heartbreak, torture—damn, it's killing me. And then she comes toward me, falling into my arms. I hold her so tight. I never want to let her go.

God...I never want to let her go....

I hold her cheeks in my hands and push her hair away from her eyes and kiss away the tears streaming down her face. I choke back my own tears, knowing that seeing them will only make Camryn feel worse.

# BONUS MATERIAL

"I'm so sorry," I say in a painful, desperate voice. "I couldn't tell you, Camryn...I didn't want our time together to be anything but what it was."

More tears pour from her eyes.

"I hope you're not—" I start to say.

"No, Andrew...I understand why. You don't have to explain. I'm glad you didn't tell me...."

Now I feel even guiltier. I deserve to be slapped! *Please baby, just slap me! Scream at me! Do something other than tell me it's all OK....*

I pull her face gently toward me and kiss her lips.

"You're right," she says. "If you would've told me then our time together would've been dark and...I-I don't know, but it would've been *different* and I can't bear the thought of different— but Andrew, I wish you would've told me for one reason alone: I would've done anything, *anything* to get you to a hospital sooner." Her voice begins to strain. "You could've—"

I shake my head. "Baby, it was already too late."

"Don't say that! It's not too late *now*! You're still here, there's still a chance."

I smile gently and my hands finally fall away from her cheeks, resting at my sides on the white knit hospital blanket that covers me. An annoying IV snakes from the top of my hand.

"I'm being realistic, Camryn; they've already told me that my chances don't look good."

"But there's *still* a chance," she argues, painfully. "Small is better than no chance at all."

# WARNING: SPOILER ALERT!

"If I let them operate on me."

She looks like she was just slapped in the face.

"What do you mean, *if*?"

I look away.

She reaches out and grabs my chin, forcing me to face her. "There's no 'if', Andrew—you can't be serious."

I move to one side of the bed and then reach out for her, guiding her to lie down next to me. I pull her close.

"If I had never met you," I say, peering into her eyes, "I never would've gone through with it. If you weren't here with me right now, I wouldn't do it. I would think it was a waste of money and time and would only put my family through a false sense of hope, dragging out the inevitable."

"But you're going to let them do the surgery," she says suspiciously.

I brush her cheek with the pad of my thumb.

"I will do *anything* for you, Camryn Bennett. I don't care what it is, I don't care...anything you ever ask me to do and I will do it. No exceptions."

Sobs rattle her chest.

I move my hand across her cheek, push back her hair, and look deeply into her eyes, "I'll do it."

She crushes her mouth over mine and we kiss feverishly.

"I can't lose you," she says. "We have the open road ahead of us. You're my partner in crime." She tries hard to smile through her tears.

I kiss her forehead.

We lie together for a long time and talk about the surgery and

# BONUS MATERIAL

the tests that still need to be done. She tells me that she won't leave my side and that she'll stay here with me for as long as it takes. And we go on and on about the places we want to see, and I start picking songs that I want her to learn so we can sing them together on the road. Of course, she's really stuck on The Civil Wars, and I don't mind one bit.

"You've got to learn *Tip of My Tongue*, Andrew," she says with such excitement in her eyes. "It's such a fun song and I can just see us performing it. I've already got it all figured out in my head!"

I can't bear to say anything negative or foreboding and risk that smile draining from her face right now. I feel in my heart that we'll never get to that point, that I'll be dead and gone before I ever get to perform with her again.

But I keep the smile on my face. I won't let her see the defeat in my heart.

"We could be like a cover band or something," she adds, beaming. There's a little blush in her face, too, as though the suggestion embarrasses her in some way.

I think on it for a second and say with a nod, "That's not a bad idea. I've played at a lot of bars and clubs from here to Louisiana. I know the owners. Hell, we could even go to Chicago and play at Aidan's bar."

Her face lights up and she nestles her head next to mine. I kiss her hair softly.

"Then that's what we're going to do," she says. "You and me, on the road doing what we love. It's not exactly backpacking, but it's..." she pauses, pondering the meaning of it all and then she says with enthusiasm, "It's an upgrade."

# WARNING: SPOILER ALERT!

I laugh lightly and run my fingertip down over her temple and the side of her cheek. It hurts my heart to hear her say these things, to be so strong in letting herself believe that any of it will ever happen. It hurts so damn bad that I'm not going to get to be here with her. It wouldn't matter to me how our lives turned out as long as we were together.

For a time as we lie in this bed together it feels like it did when we were on the road. We don't talk about sickness or death. We just talk and laugh and I go all pervert-mode on her, slipping my fingers here and there, teasing her. She giggles and pushes my hand away, but eventually she gives in and lets me do what I want to her. And she returns the favor.

And then we just lie here together, sometimes looking into each other's eyes, sometimes looking right through each other as if we're both immersed in deep, heartbreaking thoughts.

Camryn gets up from the bed.

"Babe, what's wrong?"

"Nothing is wrong," she says smiling warmly.

She slips off her pants and shirt.

I'm grinning like a little kid. I've never done it in a hospital bed before.

"As much as I would love to have sex with you in a hospital room," she says while crawling back into the bed with me, "it's not gonna happen; you need all your strength for your surgery."

I gaze up at her curiously as she lies back down next to me wearing only her panties and bra. She presses her chest firmly

# BONUS MATERIAL

against mine, tangling her legs around mine. Our bodies are perfectly aligned, our ribs touching.

"What are you doing?" I ask with a curious smile.

She moves her free arm down and traces my tattoo of Eurydice with her fingers. I watch her intently, loving her movements, her touch, her warmth. Her index finger finds Eurydice's elbow where the ink stops and then she moves it along her own skin to pick up where mine left off.

"I want to be your Eurydice, if you'll let me."

My heart stops for a second, and my breath quietly catches. The girl just caressed my very soul with her lips. I want to cry, but what comes out is a huge fucking grin.

"I want to get the other half," she goes on, touching my lips with her fingers now. "I want to get Orpheus on my ribs and reunite them."

It still takes a moment before I can speak.

"Oh, baby, you don't have to do that; it hurts like hell on the ribs."

"But I want it and I don't care how much it hurts."

I feel my eyes finally start to water and I lean in and enclose my mouth around hers.

"I would love that," I whisper onto her lips.

She kisses me softly and whispers back, "After your surgery, when you're well enough then we'll go."

I nod. "Yeah, Gus will definitely need me there to make sure the placement of your tattoo lines up with mine—he laughed at me when I went in to get this on my ribs."

# WARNING: SPOILER ALERT!

She smiles. "He did, huh?"

"Yeah," I chuckle. "He accused me of being a hopeless romantic and threatened to tell my friends. I told him he sounded like my father and to shut the fuck up. Gus is a good guy and one helluva tattoo artist."

"I can see that."

I spear my fingers through her hair, constantly brushing it back over the top of her head. But then cold, hard, cruel reality slips back in between us and wakes me up. I had almost let myself become completely delusional.

"Camryn, I want you to be prepared."

"Don't start that—"

"No, baby, you have to do this for me," I say. "You can't let yourself believe one hundred percent that I'm going to live through this. You can't do that."

"Andrew please. Just stop."

I place my fingers on her lips, hushing her. She's crying again. It hurts me to see her cry, but this is something that needs to be said.

"Just promise me that you'll continue to tell yourself that I might die."

"I can't make myself say something like that!"

I squeeze her tighter.

"Promise me."

She grits her teeth.

Finally she gives in and forces herself to say, "...I promise."

It's only for my sake. I know she won't do it.

"But you have to promise *me* that you'll pull through this," she

# BONUS MATERIAL

adds, nestling her head underneath my chin again. "I can't be without you; Andrew, you have to know that I can't."

"I know, baby...I know."

Silence fills the space between us.

"Will you sing to me?" I ask.

"What do you want me to sing?"

"*Dust in the Wind*," I answer.

"No. I won't sing that song. Don't ever ask me that again. Ever."

My arms tighten around her.

"Then sing anything," I whisper. "I just want to hear your voice."

And so she starts to sing *Poison & Wine*, the same song that we sang together back in New Orleans when we lay in each other's arms that night. I sing along with her a few verses, but I'm weak. Weak with emotion. Weak with sickness and stress. Weak with a broken heart. Weak with inevitability.

We fall asleep in each other's arms.

———

"Got some tests to run," a voice says above the bed.

I stir awake the rest of the way to see one of the nurses standing at my side of the bed. I feel dizzy, strange. I feel a lot like I felt minutes before I passed out in my apartment. When I woke up in this bed, all I could remember was the smell of bacon. I could still smell bacon for hours afterwards. I kept asking the nurses if the cafeteria was nearby because the bacon was so strong.

# WARNING: SPOILER ALERT!

"You should probably get dressed," the nurse says with an assuming smile.

I guess she figures Camryn and I did a lot more in here than visit and sleep considering we're both half-naked.

Camryn gets out of the bed and gets dressed while the nurse checks my stats. There's a wheelchair near the foot of the bed.

"What kind of tests?" I ask weakly.

I feel a little disoriented. Shit. Please just let Camryn leave first before something else happens to me . . . .

"Andrew?" Camryn comes back over to the bed. She knows something is wrong.

I raise one hand to ward her off. "No, baby, I'm all right; just a little dizzy. Trying to wake up."

The nurse comes back around to help me sit up, moving the IV out of the way.

"He'll be gone for an hour or two, maybe more, while they run more tests," she says. "So you should grab a bite to eat, stretch your legs and come back in a little while."

"But I-I don't want to leave him."

"Do what she says," I demand, though in the kindest voice I can manage. "I want you to go eat." I turn my head to see her this time and point my finger at her. "But no steak," I say playfully. "You still owe me a steak dinner, remember? When I get out of here, that's the first thing we're doing."

I get the smile out of her that I was longing for, although it's not as bright as I had hoped.

# BONUS MATERIAL

"OK," she agrees, nodding with reluctance. "I'll be back in a few hours and I'll be waiting for you."

She rushes back over and kisses me softly and we share a wordless moment.

Finally, I get into the wheelchair and the nurse wheels me out of the room. I look back only once but then I tear my eyes away from her. Because I feel like this is the last time I'm going to see her. The bright white floor moves like running water beneath me as I'm pushed down the length of the hallway. Patterns in the shiny tile start to appear as I stare fixedly because I can't bring myself to raise my eyes. At first I think it's just lack of willpower, but I start to realize that it's something else. We turn right at the next corner. I hear voices coming toward us, but I never look up. I hear the wind brush my exposed back as the wheelchair seems to pick up speed. My head feels so heavy, like a block of concrete placed between my shoulders.

I hear Camryn's voice and I think I'm raising my head to see her, but really I haven't moved at all. It's not Camryn's voice. It's the nurse. She's saying something to me about how many fingers—

It's the last thing that I remember before everything goes black.

———

*Death. It's an odd thing. I never imagined it like this. Everything feels weightless. My body. My mind. The hand I continuously try to move in front of my face.*

# WARNING: SPOILER ALERT!

*I hear voices around me all of the time, but I can never make out what they're saying.*

*Am I really dead? I don't understand this at all. How long have I been here like this? And where the hell am I?*

*I feel like I've been sleeping forever. But what bothers me is how I'm even conscious of it.*

———

"Andrew? Please wake up...."

"Andrew...."

# ABOUT THE AUTHOR

J. A. Redmerski, *New York Times* and *USA Today* bestselling author, lives in North Little Rock, Arkansas with her three children and a Maltese.

You can connect with her online at:
JessicaRedmerski.com
Twitter, @JRedmerski
Facebook.com/J.A.Redmerski
Pinterest.com/ jredmerski